Copyright Burdizzo Books

Edited by Em Dehaney - Burdizzo E

All rights reserved. No part of this book may be reproduced in any form or by any means, except by inclusion of brief quotations in a review, without permission in writing from the publisher.

This book is a work of fiction. The characters and situations in this book are imaginary. No resemblance is intended between these characters and any persons, living or dead.

This book is sold subject to the condition that it shall not, by way of trade or otherwise, be lent, resold, hired out or otherwise circulated without the publisher's prior consent in any form or binding or cover other than that in which it is published and without similar condition including this condition being imposed on the subsequent purchaser

Published in Great Britain in 2019 by Matthew Cash/Em Dehaney Burdizzo Books Walsall, UK

WELCOME TO A TOWN CALLED HELL

Welcome TO A TOWN CALLED HELL

Foreword

It seems like a long time ago that I was invited to become a resident of a little town in Colorado called Hell by the local mayor Calum Chalmers.
Now, let me tell you a bit about Calum Chalmers.
Mayor Chalmers is a whisky-swilling, tobacco-chewing, rotten-egg-farting boar of a man, he looks like someone shoehorned a leprous hippopotamus, a walrus and a sweaty cheese sandwich into that there teleportation booth that Jeff Goldblum had in The Fly and he was the result. But beneath this hideous exterior beats the heart of a man who loves his town with a passion like no other man can ever love a town. He invited me to visit with the opportunity of taking up permanent residency, he invited a few of us to visit and most of us stayed, whether we wanted to or not.
This here is a record of the last days of Hell, I'd like to personally thank Mayoress Chalmers for taking this dictation via the Ouija5000 'helping us read the words the dead said' - one of Mayor Chalmers own inventions that he had patented just before the events that follow.
This is for Mayor Calum Chalmers, Hell will always be your town and I'm sure I can say on behalf of all of us residents who are now living in a different kind of Hell that we sincerely hope you'll be joining us soon.

    Matthew Cash

Hell
A
Turbulent History
by
Elliott Hoole

WELCOME TO A TOWN CALLED HELL

Local historian Elliott Hoole takes a look at some of the weirder events that have taken place in Hell.

The Founding of Hell.

On January 5 1859, prospector George A. Jackson made the first substantial gold discovery in Colorado. By 1867 the trail had led to a mountainous area surrounded by a fast flowing river (now known as the Styx.) Those who dared brave the torrents were rewarded, however the river claimed many lives. Before the town was formed, prospectors would merely set up camp before heading into the river, they didn't need to ask permission nor did they sign any logs to say they were heading out. In effect no one knew who was prospecting in the area. Camps were regularly found abandoned, whether it was through drowning in the dangerous waters or through something far more sinister. Prospectors tended not to look out for one another, territory was fiercely defended and it wasn't uncommon for people to go missing, therefore these incidents went largely unreported. To define territories lawless prospectors would string up bodies of those who wandered too close to their land, stories of brutal demises spread like wildfire as people tried to scare people away.

The Gruesome Death of Jimmy Trent.

Jimmy was a relatively young prospector being only seventeen when he started. His good manners and eagerness to help others gave him almost celebrity like status across Colorado, with the other prospectors treating him like a much loved son.
As mentioned before, competition was strong but Jimmy seemed immune to this. He walked the State sharing the most dangerous sites with the most dangerous of men, however, this freedom didn't provide him any riches.

On the March 1st 1869, whilst residing in Santa Fe, New Mexico, Jimmy declared his intention to pan for gold in what would eventually become the town of Hell. Townsfolk knew the dangers this river held. Stories of lawless gangs, brutal murders and torture led many to voice their concerns. Eventually it was decided that one of the Sheriff's deputies would accompany Jimmy during his travels. This unheard of gesture only highlights the standing this young man held.

There are no records detailing the exact route these men took, but we do know they were seen to set up camp on the river shores, on what is now known as Black Beach, around the March 15. Prospectors in the area confirmed that both men were seen wading into the waters, each tied to nearby trees, thus anchoring them to land.

On the March 29th 1869 two men rode in to Santa Fe, with them they carried the dismembered remains of the towns' Deputy, Henry MacDonald. The town was up in arms; fearful for what may have befallen Jimmy Trent (from all records I have come across no one seemed too bothered by the murder of the Deputy).

Local Sherriff John 'Wild Buck' Winters effectively turned a blind eye to the area for most of his career, the territory was deemed lawless. However, with his Deputy murdered and Jimmy Trent missing he was forced to round up a posse and head out to investigate. On arrival they came across what was described as a 'Hellish Nightmare'.

The camp was abandoned, blood still stained the dirt despite heavy rainfall. A bloody axe was quickly located and the scene of the Deputy's demise picked for clues. One of the had men noticed that the rope used to support the men wading into the river was pulled taut and stretched out into the river not far from the shore. The men gathered round, expecting the worst they pulled on the rope

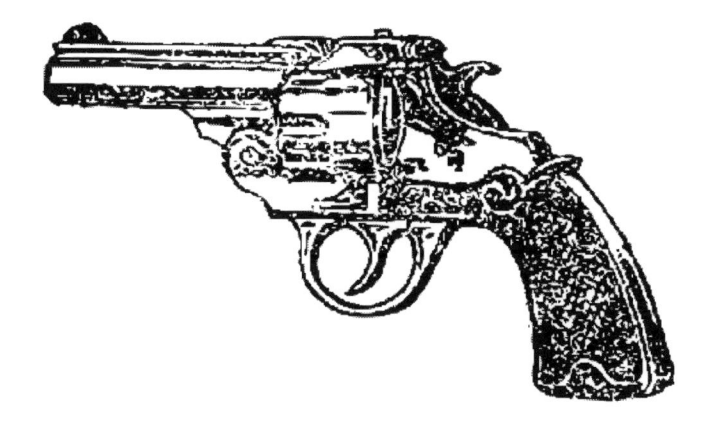

Suicide Solution
James Jobling

Dean Lancaster had barely made it through the school gates before he noticed that something wasn't quite right. Two stocky police deputies were standing at the front entrance, and Dean could see the parking lot to the side of the playground was crammed with hastily parked cars. And, abandoned lopsidedly in the midst of the disorder, was his very own beaten-to-hell Toyota, meaning Linda must be there.

Shit, don't tell me I'm running late, Dean thought as he rushed across the playground. He checked his watch to make sure that he was on time and realised that it had only just turned three o'clock. He had another fifteen minutes before the bell rang. And, even if he was late, would his tardiness require two behemoth cops with dour expressions awaiting his arrival?

Jogging nervously across to the two stone-faced deputies, Dean came to a breathless stop. One of them was holding a clipboard in his gloved hands. He stared at Dean through tinted sunglasses.

"What's happened?" Dean winced through a creasing stitch.

"Sir, do you have children who come to this school?" the deputy asked, glancing at his clipboard. A sobbing middle-aged mother squeezed past the policemen, cradling a girl of about the same age as Charlie in her arms. The police deputy cleared his throat, prompting Dean for an answer.

"Yes, my son, Charlie, Charlie Lancaster. He's six years old." Dean looked up into the grey heavens as a helicopter hovered above the school. It wasn't a police helicopter (at least Dean didn't think it was) because it was bright red with some kind of logo stencilled on its underbelly. It looked more like paparazzi. Dean turned back to the deputies. "Please tell me what's happened."

The deputy scanned the clipboard and scribbled something on it. "Unfortunately, an incident occurred here this afternoon."

"An incident?" Dean hissed. "What do you mean, an *incident*?"

"Sir, would you like to come with me?"

"No!" Dean bellowed. His voice echoed around the school playground. "I want to know what's going on! And I want to know right fucking now!"

Dean's thoughts became blurred with images from past news bulletins. Names such as Columbine and Sandy Hook tormented his disorientated brain. You hear about horrific shootings all the time - some lone nut-job wandering halls armed with his old man's service pistol and opening fire on students and teachers alike before eventually turning the gun on themselves. It had happened before. It would happen again – it was just a question of when.

Dean opened his mouth to apologize for using such foul language, but Linda called his name from the school hall. Jostling past the two policemen, Dean could see Charlie was riding her hip. Her flushed face was stained with snail-trails of mascara and her eyes were bloodshot from crying. Her hair had worked itself free of the ponytail and was hanging in lank rat-tails around her shoulders.

"Linda? Linda! What the hell's happened?"

Grabbing a hold of her hand, Dean reeled her towards him and wrapped his arms around her waist, hugging her tightly. This was strange. His wife was not known for showing such outright emotion. The deputy holding the clipboard stepped beside Linda and asked if they would vacate the premises now that she had given her statement. *Statement?* Linda agreed, and they walked towards the parked Toyota, hand-in-hand.

"Linda, what's happened?"

"Oh, Dean it was terrible."

"What was?"

"Miss Carter. She died in the assembly hall."

"Miss Carter?"

"Charlie's math teacher."

"What? You mean she had a heart attack or something?"

Linda shook her head. "No, she killed herself."

Dean stopped walking, his deadweight pulling his wife back. "*Killed* herself?"

Linda nodded. Fresh tears pooled up in her red-rimmed eyes.

"She shot herself, Daddy!" Charlie declared, looking at his father with wide, innocent eyes.

"*Shot* herself?" Dean glanced down at Charlie. "In front of *you*?"

"No. I was playing soccer, Dad. She did it in front of afternoon assembly, though."

"What? Why? How?"

"She had a gun, Daddy."

Dean looked nervously across to Linda.

"It's true, Dean."

"What kind of gun?"

"Does it matter?"

"Guess not. Do you know why she did it?"

"Nobody knows anything." She pulled the car keys from her handbag and used the fob to unlock the Toyota. Opening the backdoor, she hoisted Charlie into his seat and strapped his harness around his waist. "It's all very much Chinese whispers at the moment. The school rang the pharmacy, said that the children were safe but the headmaster wanted everybody to be collected."

"Did he mention the suicide?" Dean asked.

"No. I did manage to speak to Phil, though."

"Sheriff Marlowe?"

"Yes. He told me Miss Carter just walked into the assembly hall and asked the kids to quiet down before pulling a gun out from behind her back and shooting herself through the mouth."

"Shit. That's terrible. Should he be telling you stuff like that? I mean isn't it against protocol or something?"

Linda shrugged her shoulders. "Not like I'm going to go broadcasting it, though, is it?"

Dean nodded absently and pulled the passenger door opened, scrambling inside as Linda hopped behind the wheel. "Did she say anything?" Dean asked. "You know, give any indication as to why she shot herself?"

"According to Phil, she just walked into the hall and said something like 'Dark hours are coming. I wish you all the best. Don't have nightmares,' before pulling the trigger."

Dean shuddered as Linda reversed out of the school gates. When Linda reached for the gearstick, Dean noticed that the back of his wife's hand had broken out in a rash of gooseflesh. He closed his eyes and lolled his head against the cushioned headrest as they drove home.

Dark hours are coming, he thought. Don't have nightmares.

The Crash
Ryan J. Fleming

This cockpit was a serene place compared to Joe Thorne's Cessna. A captain for twelve years now, with a further seventeen years as a trainee and co-pilot under his belt, there was no place he would rather be. The instrument panel in front of him showed myriad black screens, all displaying unchanging green information. Various other dials and switches, all digital and mostly touchscreen, sat inert, waiting for the pre-landing protocols to kick in as they began their decent into Los Angeles. That wouldn't happen for another few hours. In the meantime, they sat in their default positions, many not displaying any sort of information at all. This allowed Thorne and his co-pilot, Chris Archer, to focus on the readouts that mattered. Not that any did right now. The aircraft was flying itself, with the autopilot keeping them steady and true, at 43,000 feet above sea level. It was punching the giant aircraft through the thin air at just over three quarters of the speed of sound, encountering little to no turbulence. Any that they did encounter proved no problem for the computer's lightning-fast reflexes, as it rode out the pockets of thinner or thicker air. Nobody on deck would ever know anything about it.

He loved this part of the flight, especially on this trans-American route. The skies up here, above the clouds, were a so clear and crisp. Not too far above them lay the unforgiving emptiness of space, and Thorne, craning his neck to look up through the windshield, stared wistfully at it. It was something that never grew old to him, despite his thousands of hours in the air.

"Anything?" came the tinny, radio-transmitted voice of Archer, obviously noticing him gazing upwards.

Thorne sat back in his seat and glanced over to the younger man in the number two seat.

"No, just a fleet of city-sized alien spacecraft entering the atmosphere."

His co-pilot's reply was equally deadpan. "Better get Jeff Goldblum to fire up his Macbook then."

Thorne chuckled and allowed the cockpit to return to silence, broken only by the rustling pages of Archer's old-fashioned logbook and the always-present but barely noticeable noise from the four massive engines outside.

Despite being a seasoned traveler, Jason was still awestruck whenever he flew. He understood the dynamics of flight well enough, so it wasn't like he was mystified as to how the plane stayed up in the air, and he wasn't scared of flying either. In fact, given his choice, he'd happily sit and watch airplane disaster movies for the whole eleven-hour flight. As it stood though, he was currently in a quandary. He'd already decided on another movie, as the last one had killed the boring night time portion of the flight, when everyone else was asleep and there was nothing to see out of the window, but now dawn was approaching and he wanted a film that he could dip in and out of whilst watching the sun break over the horizon.

Jason's journey had so far taken him from Warsaw to London, where he caught up with some old friends that were studying there. From there, he decided to hit Australia but stop off at home in LA first. He'd managed to sell three of his concepts whilst in London and one of the investors had shown a very healthy interest in the other two he had on his books. So much so, in fact, that he'd paid for Jason's flight to LA as an unofficial 'deposit'.

As a result, Jason now found himself sitting in business class on a UKAir Airbus A380, pondering his next movie choice.

He'd spent the first three hours wandering about the mammoth, double-decker airliner. He had marveled at the high levels of quality throughout, even in 'cattle class'. He'd even managed to 'accidentally' walk up into First Class and gaze in envious wonder at the opulent luxury, before he was gently and very politely ushered out.

Jason glanced out of the window at the black sky. The lights of the glowing cabin behind him, reflected in the glass, were all he could see, so he placed his hand over the glass and formed a cocoon, hoping to see more. He was sure he could just make out the slightest difference in shades between the black sky and the blacker ground but he wasn't certain.

Defeated, Jason slumped back in his seat and stared at the movie selection screen in front of him, aware that the creaking of his leather seat was the only other sound in the silent cabin, apart from the constant sub-audible rumble from the engines outside.

He glanced around at his fellow passengers. The aircraft was full, even up here in Business Class, and he noted that his expectations were not met. He thought Business Class would be full of suited men and women, busy the whole flight on their laptops, but that wasn't the case. Most other people were asleep, many with blankets drawn up over them and with eye masks on. They all seemed to have mastered the art of sleeping on a plane, Jason thought, as they had all adopted a similar position in their seats.

The only other person awake as far as he could tell was a twenty-something blonde woman on the row next to his, just across the aisle. Jason studied her for a moment. She was dressed casually in low slung blue jeans, with a studded belt hanging fashionably loose. She had been wearing Converse, the same as him, but had kicked them off, her bare feet occasionally toying with the metal bar at the base of the seat in front. She was slumped in her chair, much like he was, and was watching the screen in front of her, again, much like had been. He noticed she had bangles and bands and bits of tied-off ribbon all along her left arm. She wore a t-shirt over a long-sleeved top that covered her athletic-looking frame. There was a simple gold pendant hanging around her long neck, visible through her cascading, curly blond hair. She had a lip ring in on one side of her mouth, which was slightly open, showing beautiful white teeth that, every so often, a tantalizing tip of tongue would dart out and rub against. She had the cutest nose he'd ever seen and that sat under the brightest, most piercing blue eyes. Eyes that were full of life and fun and were looking straight at him.

Shit! Fuck! Crap! Jason thought to himself as he fidgeted and desperately scoured his mind for a plausible reason why he was drooling at this chick.

The woman frowned ever so slightly, the tiniest of creases appearing on her forehead.

"Are you okay?" she asked, her voice as sweet as her features.

"Ah... shit, sorry. I didn't mean to stare, It's just... I'm just bored!" he blurted out.

To his amazement and relief, she smiled gently at him. Then, using her eyes to motion towards his screen, she said, "Try channel 99. Hold it down for five seconds."

Now it was Jason's turn to frown. He turned to the screen and selected the main menu. Looking back at her, he asked, "Nine nine?"

She nodded once. "Yeah. I think you'll like it," she replied, smiling again and turning back to her screen.

Jason did as she said and was rewarded with a plan view diagram of the aircraft. Dotted around it in various places were interactive green dots. He suddenly figured out these were real-time cameras positioned on the aircraft and, by selecting one, he could see the plane from various angles. He realized he was smiling like a fool at this, as he had always been a plane nut. He quickly turned back to the woman and got her attention. She pulled an earbud out to hear him.

"How did you know that'd be my thing?" he asked.

She smiled again before answering. "I've noticed you throughout the flight. I figured you might like that screen. They don't advertise it but anyone can use it if they know how to find it."

Jason smiled in mock embarrassment. "Busted, huh?" He extended his hand across the aisle. "I'm Jason. Look, I owe you a drink for that."

She shook his hand. "Danielle. Let me finish my film and I'll take you up on that. Enjoy your nerdgasm," she nodded her head towards his screen, "and give me an hour. Deal?"

Jason shook her hand once, theatrically, and smiled as he replied. "Deal."

Three hours later, the cockpit was flooded with the brilliant blue skies of a crisp morning over middle America. They were roaring westwards over Minnesota. Thousands of feet below them, farmers and schoolchildren and bank staff and husbands and wives were all having breakfast or getting on buses or heading out onto the freeways. Up here, life was quiet and simple. The heavily-secured cockpit allowed them to be isolated from the cabins behind them, which were no doubt getting noisier as people started waking up and scurrying about. Captain Thorne still liked the solitude of the cockpit.

A gentle ping came through his headphones.

"Kansas City ATC, UA One Six Nine from London Heathrow to Los Angeles International," Archer said into the radio.

There was hardly any delay. "UA-169, Kansas City ATC. Good morning and go ahead," came the tinny reply.

"Kansas City ATC, UA-169, good morning to you too. Entering Kansas CTA. Flight level 43. Heading one three zero," Archer replied.

"UA-169, roger that. Maintain flight level and heading. Skies are clear and the weather is good for at least three hundred miles, over."

"Copy that, Kansas ATC, thanks for the report. 169 out," Archer said, finishing off his conversation by touching a button on his headphone and cutting the channel. He glanced sideways at Thorne and slid his left headphone back off his ear.

"Fancy some breakfast?"

Thorne nodded. "Something with lots of bacon. No eggs. A gallon of coffee."

Archer was already picking up the phone handset that would connect him with the forward galley. "No eggs, got it." he repeated.

There was a pause, presumably as someone in the galley pushed through the rush of breakfasts being prepared for the passengers to get to the cockpit phone, before Archer continued in a semi-flirtatious voice.

"Hell-o Jennifer. Could we order some grub for up here please?"

Another pause, a short one, then, "Captain Thorne will have a heavily-loaded bacon sandwich and a large mug of strong, black coffee. Yes, that's right, no sugars. I'll have the-- what? Oh, hang on..." Archer moved the handset away from his mouth and turned to Thorne. He was about to ask him something but Thorne cut him off.

"Brown sauce?"

Archer smiled slightly before speaking into the phone again. "Brown sauce please, hun. Yep. And I'll have cheese on toast twice, with Worcester Sauce on it and some tea. And don't scrimp on the sugar: I want the spoon to stand up in it. Thanks sweetheart, see you in a bit."

Archer replaced the phone in its cradle and faced forward. Thorne looked at him out of the corner of his eye for a bit.

"Diabetes or a slap round the face?" he said.

"Sorry?" Archer replied.

"I'm trying to figure out what you're going to get first."

Outside, in the far distance, the sea of clouds rose sharply into the stratosphere.

Danielle was good to her word. The plane had woken up. People were wandering about the cabin, getting drinks from the bar towards the front. The crew were wandering the aisles, makeup freshly applied, rictus grins plastered across their pretty faces, handing out drinks and repeating the same breakfast chant over and over again.

The guy in the aisle seat next to Jason, who had slept practically since leaving Heathrow, was now awake and had very kindly offered to switch seats with him, probably because he was fed up with Jason leaning across him to talk to Danielle. Then, when that got on his nerves, he offered to switch with Danielle. So now Jason and Danielle were sitting next to each other. Jason had resumed his spot by the window, occasionally peering out at the sea of brilliant white clouds below the impossibly blue sky above.

Danielle was a singer from just outside London and she'd been 'discovered' a few months back when one of her songs was used in some indie film. Now, the Hollywood music machine was fawning all over her and regularly flew her back and forth to sign bits of paper, record demos, meet people and suchlike. He had told her what he did for a living and she'd good-naturedly smiled and feigned interest. Nobody ever cared what his job was really about except for those it made rich.

After breakfast, Danielle asked if she could take a nap and would he mind? He, of course, said that would be fine and she dutifully curled up on her seat and rested her head against his shoulder. He felt a wonderful tingle rush through his body as he became aware of the weight and warmth of her head on his shoulder and her soft, warm hand resting on his arm. She seemed comfortable with him and he knew he really liked her. He sat back slowly, as not to disturb her, in his chair and smiled. He started making silent plans to himself about how he was going to show her around his home town and take her to some good live music bars. If she was up for it, of course, which he suspected she would be.

He stole one last glance at her, sleeping deeply already, and turned to look out of the window at the world rushing beneath them, hidden by those heavenly clouds.

The cloud bank they had flown into was starting to give Thorne some concern. Not only had the weather computer failed to give them any warning of it but neither Kansas nor Denver ATCs had mentioned it when they spoke a short while ago.

The view out of the cockpit windows was of nothing at all. Everything was a dull, grey, off-white. There was no sensation of movement whatsoever. In fact, if it weren't for the instruments telling him otherwise, the aircraft could be flying backwards.

He spoke to Archer, this time keeping his eyes aimed straight ahead. "Chris, get Denver on the horn and find out what they've discovered about this crap, would you?"

"Yeah," came Archer's short reply, as he radioed through to the ground. "Denver ATC, Denver ATC, UA-169. Over."

Thorne could hear the heavy interference in the crackled reply from Denver.

"UA-169, Denver ATC, go ahead."

"Denver, 169. Request weather check for our location, over."

There was a pause of roughly ten seconds as the Denver air traffic control guy pulled up the relevant information on his screen. Then came the reply.

"UA-169, Denver ATC. Weather for your location shows clear skies above with a cloud ceiling below of three thousand feet AGL, over."

Archer looked at Thorne, his eyebrows furrowed in mild puzzlement. He keyed the mic again, still looking at Thorne.

"Denver, 169, received. Request ground speed check and transponder ident check, over."

"Stand by, 169," came the reply.

Archer muted his mic briefly as he spoke to Thorne. "They better have us where we're meant to be. We've got mountains coming up."

Throne smiled slightly. "He's probably looking at the wrong flight. 183 is an hour in front of us, heading for San Francisco. Plus it's coming up for shift changeover for them, so he's probably knackered."

Archer didn't seem convinced. He opened his mic channel again as the guy from Denver came back on the air.

"UKAir flight 169, I show your over-the-ground speed as 641.35 miles per hour and I have you at 43,035 feet over Burlington, Colorado, over?"

Archer deepened his brow even further as he turned back to face forwards, this time studying his own bank of instruments. He eventually keyed the mic. "Uh, roger that, Denver. Uh, we're flying through some very dense cloud here right now. Are you sure you don't have that on your screen?"

The reply was instant. "Negative, 169, my screen shows clear from three thousand feet all the way up."

There was a pause, then the Denver guy spoke again. "169, is everything alright?"

Archer responded immediately. "Roger that, Denver ATC, everything's fine. All systems are green and we're sailing along just lovely. This cloud must be an anomaly, over."

"Copy that, 169. We got nothing on our scopes here. We show you clear all the way to the coast but if you're seeing it, you're seeing it. I'll make an advisory. Can you estimate size and depth? Over."

"Negative, Denver, we're in the thick of it. I'd say we entered the bank about fifteen minutes ago, if that helps?"

"A little. Any idea of the ceiling, 169?"

"Negative again, Denver. It looked bloody high though!" Archer replied, his humour returning indicating to Thorne that he was calming down a bit.

The Denver ATC guy chuckled into the mic from his end before replying. "Roger that, 169. I'll pass this on to NASA and the National Weather Service and see what they make of it. I need to ask again, are you okay out there?"

"We're absolutely fine, Denver, thanks for asking. I'm sure we'll be through it soon enough."

"Roger that, 169. Radio clear of weather when you see the sun again, if you don't mind." Denver said.

"Happy to, Denver, over."

"Thanks, 169. Denver out," came the reply as the connection was ended.

Archer turned to face Thorne, who had never taken his eyes off of the front windows. "Whaddaya think, Joe? Descend and find a way around or stick with it?"

Thorne didn't even have to weigh up the options. "We stick to our course. Corporate would have our bollocks for breakfast if we came in light."

Archer nodded slightly and settled back into his seat. He turned back to face Thorne and was opening his mouth to say something when the plane dropped, losing hundreds of feet in altitude in seconds before leveling out again. Alarms beeped and pinged throughout the cockpit, then fell silent, one by one, as automatic systems shut down response-required switches and buttons. The silence that came was replaced with the muffled shouts of terror from the cabin behind them.

Archer, who had enough training to always keep at least one hand on his armrest, had managed to stay in his chair as the aircraft plummeted. He calmly fastened his seatbelt and began running through a checklist, visually marking off things on screens in front of him. As he did, he spoke to Thorne.

"Wind shear?"

"More like dead air. Nothing this big lump can't handle," Thorne replied. The aircraft was still in autopilot but Thorne's instincts and experience told him not to have his hands too far from the manual controls, even though the aircraft was flying smooth again.

Thorne was glancing down at the autopilot overrides when a blur of motion from the very corner of his vision caught his attention. He snapped his head to the left, leaning across, his harness cutting into him as he did. He could see back to the huge port side wing, with its two massive Rolls-Royce Trent 980 engines slung underneath, their turbofans spinning at thousands of revolutions per minute, gulping in the rarefied air. Nothing else was visible, just the impenetrable wall of cloud. Every so often, the wing would vanish into this cloud, only to reappear seconds later.

Thorne continued to stare towards the wing.

"What've you got? It's not Will Smith and Harry Connick Jr. is it?" Archer asked.

Thorne heard him but didn't reply straight away. Instead, he continued to stare at the wing and engines. After half a minute, Thorne, turned back to face forward, his chest hurting where the straps of his flight harness had been digging into him.

"Captain?" Archer began. When he got no reply, he asked again. "Captain? Joe!"

The use of his first name snapped Thorne out of his daydream. "Uh, sorry, Chris. Zonked out there for a moment."

Archer smiled and replied, "Just how much coffee did you dri-"

He never got to finish his sentence. The huge Airbus suddenly rolled over forty-five degrees and began to fall out of the air. The cockpit was once more filled with alarms. This time, the computer voice was shouting at him in a stern male voice, loud enough to be heard over the alarms.

"Rapid descent. Rapid descent. Rapid descent," it repeated, over and over.

The whine from the engines outside was nearly matched by the screaming from the cabin behind them.

"Disengage autopilot," Thorne said in a loud but calm voice. Archer pressed some buttons and the entire airframe shuddered as the computer stopped doing the flying.

"You have the aircraft!" Archer shouted, his voice not as calm as Thorne's.

"I have the aircraft, roger. Adjust the flaps and reduce engines to fifty percent thrust," he ordered.

Archer pressed more buttons.

Thorne was pulling back on the control joystick down by his left thigh. He could feel the aircraft fighting him, even though it was only simulated by the computer based on readings taken from probes and sensors all over the skin of the giant machine. Thorne's face remained calm but inside he was beginning to get the first wave of adrenaline enter his system.

"Passing flight level four zero!" Archer called out, as the plane continued its downward trajectory.

"Chris, I want you to start going through your control surface failure checklist but first, get everybody back there in their seats. Get the cabin crew running the aisles. No exceptions. No politeness."

Archer grabbed the relevant folder with the checklist in it and put it on his lap. At the same time, he picked up the intercom phone with his left hand. Still holding the phone, he hit the button that would connect him to all galleys and crew stations. As soon as his light panel showed all the phones had been answered, he started speaking.

"Get everybody in their seats right now," he said, using his now free right hand to hit the 'seatbelt sign' activation button. "Get 'em seated and strapped in. No exceptions whatsoever. Get the toilets cleared. Use your keys if you have to. Everybody must be down and tied within sixty seconds. Am I understood?"

Archer heard a bevy of acknowledgments and slammed the handset back down. He immediately started on his checklists.

Thorne flicked his eyes from screen to screen, desperate to find the source of the problem, but nothing presented itself to him.

"Run a full systems diagnostic. I'll get Denver on the horn."

"Yes sir," Archer replied, all business now.

Thorne tapped the required parts of the screen in front of him and opened a frequency to Denver air traffic control.

"Denver ATC, Denver ATC, this is UKAir Flight 169, declaring an emergency. Repeat, declaring an emergency, do you copy? Over."

The radio remained silent.

"Denver ATC, Denver ATC, UKAir 169 declaring an emergency, over," he repeated.

Still the radio remained silent.

"Possible comms malfunction. Cancel that diagnostic and get on this instead. I'm not happy about flying over the Rockies with no radio, not with all the military traffic on the other side of the mountains zipping about."

"Yes, Captain. Do you want me to make the announcement to the passengers?" Archer replied.

Thorne allowed himself to relax slightly before he answered. "No, it's alright. I'll do it."

When the plane dropped a few hundred feet, it wasn't the sensation that woke him but the cacophony of noise it produced inside the cabin. Heavy plastic fittings rattled and banged. Overhead lockers popped open and shut. Gasps and shrieks soon drowned that out but they too dissipated quickly. The only noise he heard was the panicked whine of the four huge jet engines as they strained to return the plane to its altitude.

The jolt woke Danielle too. He knew this because she dug her nails into his arm. She looked up at him from her shoulder-pillow position, worry etched on her face. Those big blue eyes were wide with query. He was just about to tell her it was just a tiny bit of wind or plain old turbulence when the aircraft dropped again. This time, it seemed to bank over to the left too. Jason's internal gyroscope told his mind that he, and everything else, were now leaning over at a forty-five degree angle and falling.

He looked at Danielle, who was now struggling to sit upright.

A series of soft 'bong' noises chimed throughout the cabin and the air crew scurried along the aisles, snatching drinks cans and bottles and barking orders sternly but politely. As one such crew member got to Jason and Danielle, she didn't even slow down. She instead threw them both a quick glance and said, "Seatbelts on!" then carried along behind them, out of sight but still repeating that same phrase all along the huge plane's length.

Danielle was sitting now and, rather than putting her belt on, like Jason was doing, was instead putting her shoes on.

The plane dropped.

Again, there were screams and crashing and banging. This time, the lights flickered, adding to the fear. The engines were screaming now and Jason glanced out of the window to see nothing but fog and the occasional glimpse of wing.

Then the plane leveled out.

The jets calmed back down to their usual whine. The cabin settled down too, as the air crew came walking back up towards their stations.

Moments later, the captain came over the intercom, announced by a soft chiming jingle.

"Ladies and gentlemen, this is Captain Thorne. We apologize for that patch of rough weather we just encountered but we seem to be out of the worst of it now. Regular passengers on this route will tell you that it's just the warm air being pushed up by the Rocky Mountains. Due to rough weather in the Seattle area, we've had to divert slightly further south. Now don't worry; we're still on schedule. In fact, we've made up twenty minutes. Now, the good news is that we'll be over the Rockies in just a few minutes, so that should give you some spectacular views from either side of the aircraft. Apologies once again for the -."

"Captain!" another voice over the intercom shouted.

"Jesus Chri-" The Captain started before the intercom cut off.

"What the fuck was that?" Archer screamed hysterically.

"Fuck me! Strap in!" Thorne shouted, equally shocked and horrified by what he just saw.

He stabbed his finger at some panels on the touchscreen in front of him and slammed the engine thrust levers all the way forward. Immediately, the huge plane seemed to lurch forwards as the four enormous engines revved up to their maximum output.

"Jesus fuck, we need to-" Archer began before Thorne cut him off.

"Get Denver on the fucking horn. Get NORAD. Get anybody!"

Suddenly, the aircraft flipped over onto its side again. Now he was sitting directly above Archer. He had a split second to register this before a whole bank of green screens across the cockpit snapped to red, followed by a cacophony of alarms. The joystick was wrenched out of his hand. He grabbed it again and fought against it, getting nowhere. He glanced down at Archer once more. He was about to ask him for help when Archer turned his head to look up at him. Chris Archer, forty-five years old, experienced pilot and airman, ex-military pilot, was crying uncontrollably, his face a mask of terror. He looked genuinely terrified, which sent a wave of absolute fear through Thorne.

A massive, violent shudder and bang signaled something catastrophic. More alarms blared. Thorne's mind suddenly went into a calm state and he released the control stick, which caused the aircraft to angle even steeper towards the ground, and sat back in his chair like someone who'd just returned from a shopping trip and was relaxing for the first time that day.

Archer was wailing uncontrollably now, staring at Thorne as if he were the personification of pure evil. Thorne, in return, was smiling gently to himself as he stared serenely out of the cockpit windows.

Alarms wailed and pinged and bonged. Then, above all that, the computer voice kicked in with a sense of urgency.

"Terrain. Terrain. Pull up! Pull up!" it said, over and over and over, as the view outside the cockpit windows gave nothing away.

Jason looked at Danielle, who was staring past him out of the window. He followed her gaze and turned his head just in time to see the massive wing ripple violently up and down, as if it were being shaken by a huge child. The airframe started to shudder immensely and the panic inside the cabin started up again. He stared, transfixed, out of the small window as the nearest engine to him, huge, powerful and fixed to the wing by an impressive-looking strut, started vibrating wildly. Then it snapped off and seemed to fly alongside the plane for a moment, before dropping down out of sight.

The whole massive aircraft flipped over onto its side. Jason was now looking down at an approaching sea of clouds. Already the wing tip had disappeared into the fog.

He felt his internal organs all shifting to his right. He became aware of Danielle's weight. She wasn't strapped in.

He forced his now-heavy head to turn to face her. She was being slowly lifted out of her seat towards the overhead lockers as the plane fell from the sky. She floated him, her eyes wide in sheer terror. He reached out to grab her as the plane plummeted, its remaining engines screaming tortuously. She was reaching out to him, her long, slender fingers outstretched. He willed his arms to grow longer as he felt the tips of their fingers touch.

"This fucking bridge, it'll be the death of me..."

Carly smiled as the truck driver walked past her car and back to his tanker a few vehicles ahead. She'd felt like that every time she'd got stuck on this road for the first ten years of living here. Then, one day, she just decided to accept it. There were far more things to get stressed about, she decided.

Carly instead turned her attention back to the coffee cup she was nursing and the soft music coming from the stereo. The car vibrated gently as it sat idling on the two-lane suspension bridge that connected the pretty little town of Hell to the outside world.

Carly had considered taking the mountain pass road, the only other drivable route out of town, but it was as bad as this one. Worse really, if she was honest with herself, as it didn't afford her the chance to just sit in traffic and have a look about.

She took a gulp of her warm coffee, enjoying the vanilla extract she'd put in it this morning, and studied her surroundings. The cliffs in front of her that seemed to cuddle the other end of the bridge tightly were, as always, imposing and ominous. But she knew different. She knew that, on a warm summer's evening, when the setting sun was just right, they could be like a wall of blood red fire, a beautiful reminder from Mother Nature just who was the boss around here.

Either side of her, through the gaps in the motionless traffic, was nothing but white, as if God had forgotten to colour in the scenery today. That was something else that took her a while to get used to: the sheer white walls of mountain fog. It gave one the impression that the bridge was suspended miles about the Earth, rather than the hundred or so feet about the raging, angry River Styx below. As with everything in Hell though, once you saw it a few times, and had seen it at its best, that fear blew away like fine sand.

The trucker down the line sounded his horn, snapping her out of her daydream. He must be a new guy on this route, as everybody who's ever driven into and out of Hell more than once knows to just sit it out. The traffic frees itself up just as quickly as it grinds to a halt.

She stared at the brake light on the Expedition in front of her. The driver must be sitting with his foot on the pedal, rather than put it in 'park'. Another out-of-towner, most likely. However, that unblinking red glare captivated her for a moment. She drifted off to an hour previous, when she had driven towards the bridge by way of the east of town. She liked to vary her route as much as she could. She had seen a small fire, like a bonfire, in the woods as she'd trundled along in traffic. It took her the rest of the journey to figure out why that was odd and it was only now that she knew why. She grabbed her bag and fumbled around inside for her cell. Then she realized she'd put it in the trunk. Assuming, as always, this traffic was going nowhere for five minutes at least, she unclipped her belt and climbed out of her car. The cold mountain air, chilled further by the strong crosswind on the bridge, hit her like a slap to the face. She squinted and yanked her coat collar tight around her as she walked to the back of the car. She glanced into the car parked behind her. Bob McCormack sat there watching her fight the cold, a smile on his mustachioed, ruddy face. He raised his own coffee cup in a salute. She smiled back and made a 'Crazy, huh?' gesture towards him.

Opening the trunk of her car, she spotted her phone straight away. She grabbed it, shut the trunk and then heard the noise.

Screaming. Lots and lots of screaming. And it was growing rapidly, as if thousands of people were all joining some unholy choir and all singing the same note.

She turned to Bob's car to see if he could hear it. He wasn't looking at her though. He was looking out of the side window, his ever-present smile gone. For some reason, she couldn't take her eyes off him and she now watched him climb out of his car, slowly, constantly staring out into the wall of pure white, which was now starting to glow orange faintly.

That noise. It was getting so loud now. That screaming. What was it?

She looked at Bob again but he wasn't there. His car door was open.

Wait, there he was. He was running back towards town. Others were doing the same. Hell was half a mile away across the bridge.

A jet engine. That's what it sounds like, Carly thought as she turned to look out off the side of the bridge.

Just in time to see the biggest plane she'd ever seen in her life punch through that white curtain of cloud so violently it seemed to ripple it.

The plane was on its side, somehow fitting in along the canyon. The cockpit looked tiny surrounded by the rest of its immense bulk. She could see two minuscule figures in the warm, yellow cockpit as it rushed towards her.

It's missing an engine, was Carly's last thought as the plane hit the bridge.

The A380 was pitched over on its side and trailing fire from its starboard nacelle. The jagged metal stump that used to carry the number three engine was spewing burning aviation fuel that seemed to chase it through the canyon, illuminating the walls.

The control surfaces, useless at this angle, sprayed ice and rocks as the wing tip pointing up at the sky clipped outcroppings from the top of the canyon walls above.

The port wing, aimed directly downwards at the river below, bit into the water as the plane lost altitude laterally. This caused the whole aircraft to pitch vertically down. The nose cone of the plane, hollow and housing the radar and other avionics equipment, impacted the road deck of the bridge right where Carly was standing. For the briefest of moments, it seemed Carly was spared as the front of the airplane crumpled around the much stronger iron bridge.

Then the airframe impacted. Carly was instantly blown into orange and white chunks as tonnes of metal hit her at over six hundred miles per hour.

As the plane continued its journey through the bridge, it started to separate and fly apart. Fuel and gas lines ruptured and, combined with suddenly-severed electronics cables, massive explosions began.

The strong roadway now began to bend horizontally, something it was never designed to do. As the leading edge of the massive A380's enormous wings hit the cables supporting the roadway, they shredded, igniting the thousands of gallons of fuel stored within them.

By the time the huge tailplane reached the bridge, the fireball was already hundreds of feet across. It engulfed everything on the roadway, as well as anybody running along it.

The heat of the fireball, combined with the burning fuel and the bending roadway, caused the bridge to fail.

All at once, the cable snapped with a musical vibrato that would be terrifying to any engineer. The two towers that supported the roadway collapsed inwards and onto the deck and the roadway itself exploded outwards, sending chunks of concrete, metal and burning fuel rushing across the canyon.

All of this happened in less than three seconds.

Three seconds after that, the fireball was already losing its glow as the fuel ran out. Now, it became a black mushroom cloud, rising hundreds of feet into the air. The ear-splitting compressed air explosion was heard all over the town.

At the crash site, a mere fifteen seconds after impact, all that could be heard were loud splashes as chunks of rock, metal, concrete, people, cars, trucks and earth hit the uncaring and disinterested river below.

Nothing could live through that. Not even in Hell.

Rising: Part One
Christopher Law

There was a small rectangle of grey sky above James Trent's head, taunting him. He didn't have the energy left to cry or scream. Sleep would have been a welcome release, after days without food or proper rest he was exhausted, but he wasn't to be spared a second of suffering. The fear and dwindling hope of rescue that had kept him going, constantly searching for some way out, had run out and all he could do now was sit and wait. There could still be one to find, some turning he had missed, but the search would mean returning below. He couldn't do that, not knowing that escape would only give him a stay of execution.

The end was coming for everyone.

The patch of sky was framed by a drain. If he rose he could look out at the street, confirming for himself again what he'd known all along. There was a layer of undisturbed snow obstructing his view, even when he reached an arm out to sweep it away, but he could just make out the shattered remains of a gas station, thin plumes of smoke rising from the dying fire. The neighbouring buildings were also damaged or destroyed. The few cars he could see had been abandoned at angles in the street, doors hanging open. In the hours he'd spent screaming for help after finding the upper chamber he hadn't seen any sign of life, not even a bird crossing the sky.

A slow sound rose from the circular opening a short distance from where he sat, slumped against the wall. It was a belching groan and he knew what it meant before the smell of sulphur drifted up. It was too late to find a way out now.

The slime was down there, tired of waiting for him.

Hell was one of the first towns he passed through after taking to the road, almost twenty years before he found himself trapped there. Every few years since then he had returned, finding himself drawn here by some strange magnetism, preferring to get away from the beaten track when he crossed the mountains. Like much of the country it had become less welcoming over the past decade, particularly to drifters. James made his own way, working when he needed to, but he felt safer arriving after dark. He was hoping to rest for a few days and get away without anyone noticing.

His memory was good but he'd only used the camp site a few times before and finding the path down the cliffs in the dark was difficult. There was no moon and he didn't dare use his flashlight for more than a few seconds at a time for fear of being seen from the road or bridge – small town cops were always bored. Reaching the bottom of the ravine with only a few bruises, he couldn't be sure the site was even still there, the Styx as prone to flash-floods and sudden changes as any mountain river. Clambering over the rocks, the start of a long stretch of rapids below the town, he was glad to find it unchanged.

For most of its course the Styx ran fast, squeezed through a succession of narrow ravines and waterfalls. There were places where the walls widened and there was room for it to meander. Black Beach was a sandbar that had gathered in one of those stretches, a short distance upstream from the bridge. The canyon was wider there than anywhere else and the river curved and broke apart over the rocks before plunging into the rapids that started just past the bridge. An outcrop hid most of the beach from the bridge but from certain points it was visible, a far more impressive feat of engineering from below.

At the bridge end of Black Beach was a storm drain outlet, part of the overflow network carved into the rocks Hell sat on. It was overly large and complex for a town the size of Hell, built decades ago and a constant bone of contention with locals ever since. Never seriously needed, the interior of the drain was more like a cave, and a good place to shelter when it rained. Local teens had been coming here longer than James and there was the remains of a fire not far from the drain, the dirty sand littered with beer cans.

The weather was turning when he arrived so he went straight to the drain and set up his camp there, building a small fire in the mouth, using the driftwood stacked against one wall. The ground was dry and with no wind to drive the rain he started to feel snug, cooking field rations over the fire. He read while he ate and cleared his litter before unrolling his sleeping bag. James lived on the road but he wasn't a tramp or hobo. He kept himself clean and sober, shunning society except when he needed to. It was a good life, or at least the only one he'd ever been suited for.

His dreams were brutal that night, trawling through the vast cityscapes of his childhood. Giant rats and albino alligators crawled from the sewers, blood ran in the streets. He dreamed of his siblings, the brother they found with a needle still in his arm and the sister who did what she thought she had to – the trial had still been pending when James left, tired arguments about abuse and self-defence coming out to play. In his dreams they wanted him to share the misery, the way they'd spread it into his life until he cut all his ties.

There was a dusting of snow when he woke. It would be heavier on the cliff tops. The clouds were low and heavy, dark grey with streaks of black and it was sharply cold. It was early in the year for the first snow but the winters had been getting harsher as the summers grew hotter. He had planned to stop for a few days, get his energy back before leaving the mountains, maybe visit the thrift store in town. The promise of more snow and risk of getting trapped changed his mind.

He was washing in the river, stripped to the waist and shoeless, shivering at the icy water, when he heard the bass thrum. He dismissed it as a heavy truck crossing the bridge, making the metal vibrate and echoing strangely, and continued soaping his bald head, the little hair he had left easy to keep short. The thrum grew steadily louder, joined by screeching tyres and horns from the bridge. Drying his face he rose and looked towards the bridge. He thought about his childhood again, the time they had spent living near an airport. The memory seemed random until he recognised the roar of jet engines, distorted by the clouds and mountains.

He started running a second before the plane emerged, only a few hundred feet up. His backpack, boots and clothes were nearby, he had planned to leave as soon as he was washed. There was no time to grab them as he sprinted for the drain. Looking back he could see the massive bulk of the plane, tilted almost entirely on its side, bearing down on the bridge. People were running for their lives, others jumping over the side in the hope the fall wouldn't kill them.

The plane hit the bridge as James reached the drain, stumbling as he ran inside. He caught a glimpse of the bridge and plane crumbling around each other, the twisting wreckage consumed by a fireball as the fuel tanks caught. Impetus carried most of the plane on, tumbling upstream and tearing huge chunks from the cliffs, the shock enough to trigger several faults.

He didn't stop and continued further into the drain than he'd ever gone before. He came to a wire mesh fence, the gate loosely fastened with a padlock and chain. He pushed himself through the narrow gap, bare feet digging into soil that was much wetter here than by the mouth. The air was filled with the roar of the crash impact, the wreckage reaching Black Beach and the drain. The ground shook beneath his feet as he finally forced his way through the gate and fell into the inner drain.

Picking himself up, he started to run again when another explosion tore along the drain, lifting him from his feet and slamming him down, already unconscious.

It was pitch black when he woke. His ears were ringing and he hurt from head to toe. Thoughts slowly forming through the wire wool inside his brain as he fought the urge to slip back into sleep. The air was only just above freezing and the ground he was lying on was damp, slimy against the bare skin of his back. His left hand was lying in a small pool of water, only an inch deep but as slimy as the ground.

If I stay here, I'll freeze to death.

The thought of moving, of forcing his tired and aching limbs to work, was so unpleasant it almost seemed better to stay where he was and freeze. It wouldn't take much to let his thoughts drift and exhaustion take him again.

Eventually stubbornness forced him up, moving slowly and carefully. It was still completely black all around and he squashed the fear that something had happened to his sight as he checked himself for wounds and broken bones. He could remember what had happened. It made perfect sense that he couldn't see if the tunnel had collapsed.

He found nothing that seemed too serious, except a tender spot on the back of his head he could do nothing about. His small supply of painkillers was in his pack, with his matches and flashlight. Examination over, he turned to his surroundings on his hands and knees and feeling with his hands. It hurt less to move than he had expected.

Miniscule shafts of light must have been filtering in from somewhere above, just enough for James to be able to differentiate between up and down. There was a slight slope inside the drain and he followed it down, although he was certain what he would find. Less than twenty feet from where he'd woken, the tunnel was completely sealed with a plug of rock and dirt. The ceiling had come down and the cliff above with it. A tight enough seal had formed that the small trickle of water running down the drain, not usually enough to wet the soil in the mouth, had started to pool. A couple of inches had gathered, as icy as the puddle his hand had been in.

Regretting leaving his flashlight he tried digging in the dark, finding the edges of large rocks near the top and pulling. He broke two fingernails, one tearing into the quick, and brought a small cascade of dirt down on his face before abandoning the attempt. Even with better light, he suspected the task would have been impossible.

He walked back up the tunnel a short distance, stubbing his toes against loose rocks, and finding nowhere dry squatted down, arms wrapped around his legs. Starting to shiver, his thoughts turned bleak. No-one was going to come looking for him, even if they found his stuff by the river. They'd just be part of the jumble from the crash; he had no ID amongst his belongings to point to his presence. Eventually, someone would find his remains when they cleared the drain. It would be too late by then.

The alternative – wandering into the sewers half naked with no light – seemed no better than sitting here and waiting to die. Urban legends, gleefully related by his sister before she became a domestic abuse statistic, of people living in sewers came to his mind.

"Fuck!" he screamed. "Fuck! Fuck! Fuck!" His voice echoed back but there was no reply, just the ringing in his ears. "Fuck!"

The cold forced him to move again. It gnawed at his bones, half-merging with the hunger growing in his stomach. With one hand on the wall, still feeling stiff and weak, he got to his feet. He coughed, a bolt shooting through his head from his left eye, and started to move carefully forward, deeper into the sewer.

There were patches of slime on the wall, the first one he put his hand on making him shout with disgust. It was thicker and stickier than the water and it left a tingling sensation on his skin, like he'd held it too close to an open flame. For a short space he tried walking freely, hands out in front of him like he was playing Blind Man's Bluff. There was too much debris on the ground and after falling heavily twice he went back to the wall for support. His progress became painfully slow as he shuffled forward, touching the wall as lightly as he could and sweeping his feet forward so he didn't trip.

The slope appeared abruptly, his feet striking the bottom just before his outstretched hand found it. He stumbled and fell heavily against the sharp incline, scraping his chin on the concrete. The exhaustion and probable concussion swept over him again, tempting him with sliding down the slope and closing his eyes. His tongue was thick and dry, the presence of so much filthy water a cruel taunt.

He allowed himself a moment's rest, resting against the slope. When his legs started to slowly buckle, sleep happily creeping over him, he pushed himself up. Working up as much spit as he could to moisten his mouth, he felt out his surroundings. The concrete of the slope was smooth in places, where the original finish hadn't rotted away. The rest was pitted and crumbled under his fingertips, saturated by the water it had been intended to funnel down to the river.

There was no other way to go, except back. In the centre of the slope was a wide channel, and he used the edges to haul himself to the top. It wasn't far, no more than seven or eight feet, but the effort was enough to leave him drained as he crawled over the lip. He collapsed on his front beside the channel, one hand lying in the sluggish, slimy water. The air felt warmer, but tasted fouler. Despite his thirst the water running over his fingers wasn't tempting.

Sleep took him by surprise, just as he was summoning the willpower to lift his hand from the water.

There was a light in the dark when he woke, a faint beam coming from far away and a steady diffuse spot somewhere closer. They could have been as distant as the stars, but they were enough to spark fresh hope.

His initial attempt to scramble to his feet and run failed, as blood rushed to his head and he pitched forward. Moving more carefully he tried again, trying to call out as he did. The words caught in his throat, trapped by the sticky phlegm. He started to cough and had to stop until the blockage cleared. It felt solid and he heard it land with a soft splat. There was more to shift but he was able to shuffle forward as he coughed, stopping every few steps when the punch to his diaphragm was too hard.

"Hey!" his voice rasped, too weak to echo. He coughed and spat. "Hey! Somebody there?"

There was no reply except the drip and trickle of water. The beam and spot of light didn't move. He knew that the source had to be a flashlight, most likely lying on the ground. The hours he had spent in the dark felt like days.

Drawing closer he saw that the glowing spot was a patch of brick wall. It grew larger and more diffuse until he could make out the low, curved ceiling and narrow concrete walkways either side of the shallow channel. The beam itself was coming from a side corner, the first turning he had encountered.

"Hey," he called. "If anyone's there, I'm coming round the corner. I ain't dangerous."

He peered around the corner, and swore.

The man lying at the bottom of the ladder was clearly dead, arms and legs horribly twisted. He was wearing municipal overalls, torn to shreds by the fractured bones poking through his flesh. The fall hadn't taken his face, something more deliberate had done that. There was enough of the skull and jaw left to support the yellow hard-hat but everything soft was gone. A few strands of muscle and skin, filigree nerve endings clung to the bone in places around the edges but the whole had been torn away, eye sockets and cheekbones shattered in the process. There was a green residue around the wound, glistening in the light.

"Oh, Jesus," James said, one hand up to shield his eyes from the flashlight – one of the powerful kind as wide as a hand.

James crept forward and snatched the flashlight from near the dead man's hand, half-expecting the corpse to sit up and scream. If he hadn't been watching so closely, vaguely aware he might be close to delirium, he wouldn't have seen the large glob of green goo fall from the ladder shaft and onto the ruined face. It fizzed in the wound, turning to a pinkish foam that broke down quickly and trickled away. Tendrils of smoke rose, greasy and black as they disappeared into the shaft.

A few seconds later, whilst he was staring in disbelief, a second, larger drop fell. Unable to take his eyes from the corpse and the dissolving ruins of a face, James backed the short distance into the main passage. He stepped over the channel and pressed himself against the far wall before he felt safe enough to cast the beam of the flashlight along the tunnel.

To his left was the way he had come, the slope too far away for the beam to reach. To his right the tunnel ran a short distance further and came to an effective dead end – a half-dozen pipes, sharply angled and barely large enough to squeeze inside, emptied into the drain. The ladder was his only way out, unless he went back to the start and tried digging free with a torch to highlight the futility.

The choice was obvious but he spent a long time in the tunnel, back against the wall. At that distance he couldn't see the individual drops as they fell, just the occasional wisp of black smoke. He tried timing them and found no rhythm. The longest gap he counted was a minute, the shortest a couple of occasions when one drop fell immediately after another. There was one triple drop.

He noticed other things as his eyes grew used to the light. The walls were in a serious state, bulging in places and missing bricks in others. Moss and algae, other things that liked the dark, clung to every crevice and crack, steadily replacing the mortar. All of them had a sickly hue that grew stronger as they were exposed to the light. It wasn't as virulent as the goo falling on the corpse but it was close enough. Looking at the shallow trickle by his feet, only a few inches wide and deep, he could see green there as well, diluted to a sheen but strong enough to make him sick to think he almost drank some.

Fortified by adrenaline, he stepped over the channel and hurried along the short passage to the dead man and the ladder. Coming to a stop a few feet away he studied the drops again, observing how they fell rather than how frequently. There was no variance, each one falling exactly where the last had, hollowing out a little more flesh. Getting closer, so he could look up the shaft, he saw that the man's face had become a bowl, half-filled with liquidised flesh. Sooner or later the goo would eat deeply enough to sever the neck, letting whatever remained of the head to fall to the floor.

The shaft was narrow and it was impossible to guess how far up it went. No matter how he angled the flashlight he couldn't see to the top. He didn't think it could be far, unless it led straight to the surface. It was claustrophobic and daunting, the dripping acid just another added charm. The dead man must have fallen when he was first struck, his final position grim chance.

James had the advantage of knowing the goo was coming, and he was leaner than the dead man. The drops were falling to one side of the shaft, away from the rungs set directly into the wall. If he was careful, he thought he could squeeze by. Making the climb with the flashlight would be difficult, it was too large to grip at the same time as the rungs. He'd taken his belt off to sleep by the river and hadn't got round to putting it on again before the plane came down. Reluctantly he looked at the dead man again, and the tool belt around his waist.

It was harder than he expected to retrieve the belt. The dead man was over two hundred pounds, there was a lot of dead weight to move. Eventually he managed it, making the torso flop forward as he did. The pooled remains in the hollowed face splashed out, the fresh activity causing more smoke to rise. He was unable to avoid getting a waft of it in his nose – it stung and left the stench of burning rubber.

The corpse slumped further as James put the tool belt on and rid himself of what he didn't need, keeping the hammer and utility knife as well as the larger screwdrivers. He put the tongue through the flashlight handle and buckled tight. For a moment he thought about moving the corpse away from the acid drops, falling now on its broad back. It was beyond his capability, not with someone so big. He barely had the energy for the climb ahead as it was.

He rested for a moment, looking away from the bubbling wound starting to appear in the dead man's back. There was no way to block out the hiss and fizz of each drop, eating eagerly into the unbroken skin.

As soon as he could trust his legs, he started hauling himself up the ladder. It was slow work, made harder by having to press himself as close to the rungs as possible. The flashlight dragged the belt down and got stuck on the rungs, its light as much a hindrance as a help when it got in his eyes. His shoulders screamed with every reach and pull upwards, a crick developing in his neck from straining to see the acid drops over his shoulder. He only saw a couple, falling scant inches from his naked back, but his flesh cringed from them all.

The climb wasn't far, no more than fifteen or twenty feet, but it left him drained, only just able to step from the ladder and into the next level of sewers. The ladder shaft was in a small alcove in the wall, only connecting the two levels. Before examining his new surroundings he shone the light at the ceiling above the ladder, his stomach turning a slow, sickly flip.

A large patch of black mould covered the alcove roof, the first tendrils starting to spread down the walls. Towards the centre of the mass it grew thicker and twisted stalactites were forming. The longest was six or seven inches, the acid dripping from its tip. If it had been falling from just one or two more of the twists he wouldn't have made the climb unharmed. He couldn't help wondering which direction the dead man had been travelling, exactly where on the ladder he had been when he fell. If he had been alive long enough to feel the first drops landing on his face.

There was nothing he could do for the man now, and nothing to gain by hanging around. His body was screaming for rest and his headache was gathering strength. Not even the certainty that he'd never wake again lessened the urge, death almost seeming a fair price to pay to escape the ache and exhaustion. He still couldn't get himself to start moving for a moment, taking in his surroundings properly for the first time to keep his mind working.

He knew they must have been built around the same time but the tunnel he was in looked much older than the one below. It wasn't as high or as wide and the crumbling bricks lining the walls were the thin, anaemic yellow kind he always associated with the early twentieth century. Only a few still had any trace of the original glaze left and several were missing completely, replaced by straggling, diseased looking plants. There was no light to feed them, the gloom beyond the powerful flashlight beam was absolute. He didn't want to think about what they fed on instead.

There was only a walkway on one side, the remaining two thirds of the width given over to the water channel. Casting the beam down James saw that it was close to overflowing, the water sluggish and dark. The green sheen he had seen below was still present, almost iridescent in the occasional bubbles that rose to the surface.

The tunnel was curved and he could only see thirty feet in either direction before the angle blocked his view. There were no turnings or alcoves he could see, nothing to indicate which way he should go. From the angle of the walls he was somewhere on a circle, both directions leading to the same place.

Making the choice seemed impossible, too much for his throbbing head to comprehend. The urge to sleep rose up again. He might have succumbed if a particularly large bubble hadn't formed in the water by his feet. He watched it drift by for a few feet until it burst. It might have been a trick of his tired eyes or the harsh light but he was certain he saw little wisps of smoke rise from the burst bubble.

It was enough to make his mind up and he started to shuffle upstream, telling himself that if he followed the water it would only lead him back below. His thoughts were as sluggish as the water but he knew, wherever he went, it couldn't be there.

Hours passed. Scared of the batteries running out he spent most of it fumbling in the dark, feeling his way cautiously along the slimy walls. Every opening he found was small, barely wide enough to fit his shoulders. He began to imagine that the fabled maze below the streets of Hell was something far simpler, just a few tunnels and shafts emptying into the river. The town wasn't that large, and the complexity of the task had always seemed unlikely to him. He began to move a little faster, his tired body responding to whatever hope he could muster. Any moment now, just around the next gentle curve, he'd find a ladder leading up to the street.

As soon as his guiding hand felt the edge he knew that he had found something more than another pipe or alcove. The breeze was too strong. He turned on the flashlight and found himself looking across a tunnel. There were walkways on either side of a wide channel, a sluice-gate separating it from the side-passage he had followed so far. The gate was clogged with waste, slowing the flow of water to the main channel – it frothed and gurgled along, glistening green in the torchlight.

He almost didn't see the rat sitting on the opposite walkway, coming to a dead halt when he caught the glint of its eyes. It was a monster, the largest he had ever seen. Patches of its fur were missing, the exposed skin covered in sores. It glared at him, green pus dripping from one eye, and for a moment he thought it was going to leap the channel, make a run for his throat. Instead, it turned and fled downstream, moving quickly despite the wounds.

Heart racing, James peered carefully around the corner, looking both ways before daring to step out. The sewer ran straight as far as the beam reached in both directions with no turnings or doors that he could see. No ladders up or down. The stink of sulphur was stronger, tickling the back of his throat. He told himself it was just because the water was more agitated, that it wasn't any more toxic than he'd already been exposed to.

There was no option but to keep heading upstream, away from the slime and mutant rats. He kept the flashlight on for longer than he'd dared so far, skin crawling at the thought of how many similar monsters he might already have passed. He remembered the horror stories passed around campfires about street people lost to rats, ambushed in their sleep.

Acutely aware he was only wearing jeans, every pebble or cracked paving brick he trod on turning into the first ratty nibble, he moved faster and faster until he started to run. It was a jog at first but it released adrenaline, a big enough jolt to override his exhaustion and hunger. In a moment he was running faster than he had in years, so fast that he only just saw the side tunnel in time to dive along it when he saw a second rat, almost as large as the first, crawl from the water a few yards ahead.

He found himself in a patch of service tunnels, a narrow mini-maze that dead-ended in padlocked doors and doubled-back on itself until it finally spat him out into a different part of the sewer. The bricks here were larger, the curving ceiling dirty yellow and the lower walls dark green. It felt newer than where he'd fled, and the walkway was a metal catwalk set in the flow rather than brick.

The burst of energy over, he slumped down in the doorway sitting on the damp concrete floor of the service tunnel. His eyes slipped closed and his head slumped. He couldn't fight the exhaustion any longer.

He woke with a start, jumping up and casting the light around, looking for rats. There were none but the beam had grown noticeably dimmer. He turned it off, red shapes swirling across his vision in the dark, and back on. It brightened for a second, and dimmed again.

He was no less thirsty or hungry but the unplanned rest had restored his strength a little. His thoughts were clearer, enough to regret his earlier panic. There was some small hope it had led him closer to escape; if he was in a newer section, he had to be closer to freedom. The hours of battery life wasted as he slept was the problem. He started shuffling in the dark, the catwalk grid painful on his bare feet.

A few hundred yards later he was forced to turn the flashlight on again. The tunnel split into a Y, with his approach along the stalk. The feeder tunnels were equal size, walkways connected to his by a bridge across the channel at the intersection. The channel was five feet across, slow running. There were no rails on the walkways or bridge, all of them only just wide enough to walk on. He shone the light down them as long as he dared, seeing no difference between the gloom. Eventually he chose the left, switching the flashlight off once he crossed the bridge.

A hundred yards later he came to another junction, a crossroads this time. Two of them were narrow, little more than wide gutters. Along one of them he could see what looked like the narrow openings of soil pipes. Keeping the beam on he took the remaining tunnel, starting to hurry again when he caught his first glimpse of the room ahead.

It was a large square chamber, a cube of concrete in the surrounding brickwork. Three tunnels, including the one James came along, fed into the chamber. All he really saw, however, was the steel staircase set into the far wall, leading up to a sturdy iron door.

"Thank you, God," he said, stopping a second to be sure his eyes weren't lying.

He almost slipped crossing the channel, jumping the last bit to avoid falling in. Taking the stairs too fast he did trip, catching his shins painfully.

He was starting to climb again when the explosion rocked the chamber. It was something he felt more than heard, the stairs bucking underneath him and the air pressure changing painfully. He managed to keep his feet, until the second explosion hit.

The iron door was blown from its hinges and across the chamber as huge chunks of the ceiling and walls came free. The staircase twisted and snapped as it came away from the wall, James still clinging to the rail as he fell with it. He hit the floor heavily and only just had enough presence of mind to shield his head from the falling debris.

Several minutes passed before he felt safe enough to try moving, terrified he'd find himself pinned. A variety of new aches and pains flaring up, the deepest in his shoulder, he pushed the light layer of rubble from his chest and shone the light around. He had come close to being trapped, a sizeable chunk of the ceiling was embedded in the floor just inches from his feet and the frame of the stairs had bounced others away from him. Picking his way clear of the wreckage he felt lucky for the first time since this started.

The explosions, whatever they had been, had destroyed his way out. He could have climbed up to where the door had been but it was gone behind the sagging ceiling. Trickles of dirt and pebbles were still falling in places, none of it looked stable.

Head ringing, his sense of good luck gone, James sat on a rock and cast the dying light around. The tunnel leading downstream and one of the upstream branches were undamaged. The third was half-filled with rubble, enough to dam the flow. Eddies had formed on the near-side of the dam, the muck from the other branch flooding in and bouncing back.

At least his options were clear…

Th

BABY FOUND IN WOODS, TAKEN IN BY LOCAL FAMILY

Duffy family members were unavailable for comment today, on a story circulating Hell that the latest addition to their family is not all he seems. Rumour has it that the baby boy was found on the edge of woods out by Black Beach

He put the knife to the curve of my nose.

"Just a bit more... here."

A sliver of my flesh slid from the blade and fell away.

"That'll do." He placed the knife on the pitted surface of the workbench. "For now."

He pushed the chair away from me, tilted his head to avoid the dangling light bulb, and stood up. He dwarfed me. I wished I had a body too.

His name was Ephraim. I hardly knew him, but I knew I was in love. His eyes seemed as if they'd been steeped in alcohol until pink. His clothes were heavy cloth, dark colours, with a haze of sawdust spread out across his chest. A thick woolen hat clung to his skull, with tufts of hair sticking out of the many holes. His beard was as thick as a wire brush and grey as the clouds that were spitting out a steady blanket of snow outside of the cabin, yet my yearning for him was nothing to do with his outward appearance. After all, we looked nothing alike in any case, at least not yet. I was certainly older than him, of that I was sure, but then I was probably older than most people, if not all. I'd watched him for a few hours, ever since he had dug out my eyes. It was the way he handled the knife that had drawn me. It was nothing short of art. The pain of the blade as it stripped away my layers was nothing compared to the joy of being dragged into existence by his craftsmanship.

If only he had carved me a mouth from the same lump of bristlecone pine that still held my skull.

The room smelled of butchered tree-flesh. The walls were dark brown, varnished, made from more wood cut into planks. I wondered if they had felt as I did when they had been dissected and laid out, their corpses offering shelter in death. I wondered if they had thanked him for the chance to be a part of his life.

A whistling drew my eye. Ephraim was boiling water upon a stove, in a kettle blackened by soot. Chunks of tree-flesh burned in the cavity of the stove beneath, giving themselves up to his will. The steam was forming a cloud between the rafters of the one storey building. No, not one storey, one room. Ephraim's house was as modest as he was, or as I imagined him to be. Yes, he must certainly be modest, I decided. Modest yet pragmatic. A good cook. A good listener. A caring soul. Perfection.

I wondered how I had come to know what water was, or a stove, or had any thoughts at all. I had probably taken them from Ephraim when he had run his calloused fingers over me. Perhaps he had gifted me a little of the life that burned within his fragile flesh and bones. Whatever the truth was, it didn't matter. Such concerns were the least of my worries, not least because the bottom half of my face was still trapped in wood and cracked bark. I needed to be released.

Ephraim poured a little of the hot water into a battered metal cup, along with a spoonful of coffee – the desiccated and treated seeds of another plant. His life was connected to mine, to the work of plants, in so many ways. If anyone understood the sacrifices that the greener things made for the meat-bags, it would be him. We gave of ourselves with love. Perhaps I could find a way to ask him to do the same for me. It would only be fair.

He glanced towards me with the cup at his lips. I saw his watery eyes widen.

No, this will not do. I must be more modest, more reserved. I cannot lay my heart bare when I do not yet have a heart.

I turned my eyes away from him, and fixed them on the floor in the center of the room.

I heard the mug clatter to the floor. A flurry of footsteps rattled the floorboards. I looked up and the door to the cabin was now wide, letting in an army of snowflakes that threw themselves onto the warm wood in a kamikaze mission, melting within moments. There was no sign of Ephraim.

Don't leave me.

I knew he couldn't hear me, but that didn't stop my mind crying out for him, for his love.

Time passed.

I saw movement outside in the black-and-white shadows. A shaking hand rounded the door frame, followed by Ephraim's face. His lips trembled within his beard. He seemed afraid. I didn't want that, but I had no way to communicate with him except my eyes. I had to show that I was not aggressive.

I closed my eyes. When I opened them, he was gone.

More time passed. The heat from the cabin began to bleed out into the night. A puddle of dead snowflakes began to creep across the floor.

Finally he appeared again, this time brandishing a shovel in front of him.

"What are you?"

I couldn't answer him, at least not without a mouth, so I blinked. It was all I could do. His shoulders tensed at the action, but he did not run.

Such a brave soul.

He approached me cautiously, with the shovel held out before him.

"I've been good, always been good," he said to me, stopping when the blade of the shovel came to rest upon my roughly carved forehead. "I don't deserve this."

I blinked again and I felt a tear roll down my cheek.

Ephraim pressed a tongue to his lip, mouth wide, before scraping the edge of the shovel against my face. It hurt, but I did not blame him for the action. He couldn't understand me, not yet. He pulled the shovel back and lifted the blade to his eyes, staring at the tear that he had dragged from my face. He held the fingers of his other hand over the golden bead before gingerly pressing his fingertips to it. He rubbed it between his callouses, before sniffing it like a hound.

"Sap." He lowered the shovel. "I'm a patient man, so I'm gonna ask you again. What are you? You need to tell me, right now."

He couldn't see my predicament. Something hot flared in the front of wherever my mind was stored, before I managed to coax it back down. Perhaps it was difficult for Ephraim, difficult to think when your brain was meat and impulse. I frowned and blinked again.

"That's freaky as anything," he murmured. He leaned on the shovel, but did not approach, not yet. It was still progress of a sorts, so I thanked him with another blink.

"You understandin' me?" he asked. "Blink once for yes, twice for no."

I blinked.

"Blink twice, just so's I know you really understood."

I blinked twice.

"Holy Hell."

He leaned the shovel against the leg of the workbench, tugged the hat from his tangled hair and rubbed a scarred hand over his forehead. Despite the chill from the door – which was still open – he was sweating.

He pulled his chair up in front of me and sat down. We stayed like that for a while, just me and him, staring deep into each other's eyes. When he spoke, it was a question, the first of many.

"You some kind of ghost?"

Two blinks.

"Demon?"

Two blinks.

"Are you like... uh... some lumberjack what fell and then ended up inside a tree? Something like that?"

Two blinks. What could I say? I was me, nothing else.

Ephraim seemed to catch hold of my mood. He was a clever man, that's for sure. "Do you know what you are?"

Two blinks.

Ephraim leaned back in the chair, staring at me over those bristles of his.

"Do you need somethin' from me? Is that why you're here?"

Yes. Yes. A thousand times. One blink.

"What is it? What do you need?"

A pause. What could I do? I looked downwards, letting the wood of my forehead knot as I stared at the bark and raw tree that held my jaw, in potential at least.

"Sick of talkin'?" he asked.

My eyes shot up. Two blinks. *No. Please.*

"You like talkin'?"

Blink.

"You like me?"

Blink. A pause, long enough for emphasis and to let him know it was repetition, not denial. Blink.

"Can you move at all?" he asked, before adding for emphasis, "If you can, and if you come at me, then I will knock seven shades of shit outta you. I mean it."

How could I move? I was no spectre. I was alive.

"Did I piss you off?" he asked. "Sure looks like it."

So sensitive. I let the tension slip from my face, before looking down once more.

"You want me to make more of you?"

I pinned my eyes to him. Blink. Yes. Carve me with your knife. Hollow out my cheeks. Run your blade over my jaw. Free me with sharpened metal and art.

He got up and made his way over to the spilled coffee. After mopping it up as best he could with a dish rag, he made another cup, pushed the front door closed, and sat back down. He looked over to a wall mounted clock in the shape of a birdhouse. It looked broken – a bird's head was stuck in the perpetual action of pushing a door open to move around on its track – however the clock face still worked.

"It's late," he said. "Suppose I'd better get this done quick."

Ephraim worked deep into the night. He asked me whether what he was doing was hurting me in any way. It was *all* pain, every shave of his knife, but I didn't tell him that. It would have broken his heart, and he would have probably stopped. It was my agony alone to bear.

He spoke to me as he worked. He started off with mundane topics, areas that were impersonal, and safe. He told me that he carved models of miners for the tourists to buy in the local gift shop, with little wooden helmets and pickaxes clutched in their wooden hands. He also carved models of totem poles that were supposed to be sacred to the Shoshone who had once dwelled in the hills surrounding what was now called Hell. He had no real idea if they were or not, he just looked at old photos in history books and copied, and where he couldn't copy he made it up. Neither task provided him with much money, but he didn't need much, he just needed enough. He was able to buy wood for the winter, and ice for the summer, so he was set. He had no family, not any more. He didn't say why.

I could tell he was giving me his best work, despite the late hour. There were no rough strokes. Each was the right one for the time, direct, pure. The sun was rising by the time he finally sat back and nodded to himself.

"Beautiful."

He stretched his arms over his head, blinking away tears. Perhaps they were exhaustion, but I hoped they were tears of love.

"Thank you," I said.

He blinked a few more times. "I din't know if you'd be able to speak."

"Neither did I."

My wooden teeth clicked with every movement of my creaking lips.

He looked over at the clock, before shaking his head. "I know I'm tired, 'cos I'm checkin' out the time like it's important, when there's a wooden head talking to me."

He laughed, and I laughed with him.

I wanted to stay that way, right there, just us, laughing together for all of eternity, but fate cares little for those it puppets.

The floorboards began to shake. For a moment I thought it was my wooden brothers, coming back to celebrate my new life, but as the sound increased like rolling thunder, it took on a metallic edge.

Ephraim looked around himself as if the answer would present itself from the walls, before kicking his way off the chair and barreling over to the window. I could see little from where I was perched upon his workbench, but I felt the cracking in my soul like snapped branches before a predator. Something colossal roared over the lip of the canyon.

"What is it?" I asked.

Ephraim licked his lips. "A plane. Headin' for the town."

Another sound consumed all others, as a flare the color of maple leaves seared the hillside. Ephraim stood back, wringing his hands as he looked around the cabin.

"Wait," I said.

He ignored me. After another few minutes of aching silence, filled only by a distant cacophony, he finally seemed to reach a decision. He reached out for his jacket, thick fur and cloth, and also for a knapsack. He filled it with bottled water, bread and jerky, before slinging it over his shoulder. The last thing he took was a walking stick, carved from tree-flesh, of course. Me? He left me, right there on the workbench.

"Don't leave," I begged, but he was already half way out of the door.

Ephraim looked towards me as the snow tumbled behind him. "I'll close the door," he said, as if that would make anything better.

I didn't reply.

He returned later, when the world had become dark. His face was pale.

He dumped his knapsack by the stove. It was empty. His hands were stained red. He reached for a cloth, ran it under the tap, and began to clean himself.

"You left me," I said.

He paused, but he didn't look up. "I thought I mighta dreamed you." He carried on cleaning his hands. The water ran pink.

"I'm real," I said.

"Sure seems that way," he said. He ran his hands over the lip of the sink before wrapping them around it, as if he were fixing himself in place, or stopping himself from falling.

"You're upset," I said. It was important that I showed I understood him, so that he could understand me. It was the root of any relationship.

"Sure am," he mumbled. "Found four people in the woods, four or five. Maybe six. They were bits mostly, maybe cut up by the turbines, or maybe the trees did the work. Only one alive, a boy in his late teens. He was caught up in the branches."

"You saved him?" I asked.

I saw a shudder run through Ephraim's shoulders. "No," he said. "No. His guts were a lot further down than the rest of him was, all tangled on the snow. He asked me for some food and water. Said he was hungry. He looked more confused than in pain. I don't know a lot about death, what it feels like, but I reckon it was taking away his worries, cutting him back until he was a baby. Just cry, eat, and sleep. Or mebbe not. I fed him anyways. His guts still moved the food around, before they started going grey."

He took a deep breath. I could see he was trying to hold something in.

"Couldn't get all the way into town to help anyone else, if I even helped that kid. I heard somethin', a howlin' in the trees. Forgot to take my gun. Thirty odd years out here an' I forget a simple thing like that. I couldn't even find my way back easy. I got lost in my own woods, can you believe that? I shoulda slept last night. I shoulda slept."

I didn't reply.

"And then there's you," he said. "If that ain't a pointer that I'm not in my right mind, I don't know what is."

"I'm real," I said again.

"You know, you can keep tellin' me that, but it won't make it any easier to believe. Do you even know what you look like?"

I couldn't shake my head, as that was all I was, for now.

He stalked over to the bed, which was little more than a nest of tangled blankets on a wooden frame, and pulled a mirror down off a shelf above it. He thrust it out towards me. "Take a look."

I was even more beautiful than I had imagined. My eyes were almonds, stylized but true to themselves, fitting perfectly within the suggestion of an aquiline skull. They moved in a curious way, as if the wood of my face was remolding itself. When I looked left, it appeared as if that was how I had been carved. My mouth was full lipped, and when I opened my mouth I saw two rows of teeth over an impossibly dark throat, a throat that shouldn't have existed due to the shallow depth of wood that made up my short neck.

Ephraim put the mirror back in its place. "Still say you're real?"

He sat down on the bed and his whole body sagged. Each blink seemed to be slower than the last. A thought roused him for a second and he stomped over to the light switch, and flicked it off. I could still make out his stooped form in the fading sunlight, but probably not for long.

I considered my answer carefully, before replying. "More than ever. You made me real."

"If you're real, you got a name?" His voice slurred. He wasn't even looking at me anymore.

"Not yet," I said. I could feel the tension between us, bubbling over like soup. I wanted it gone, so I reached out again. "You can name me, if you want."

He gritted his teeth as he forced his boots off his feet. His socks were stained red, and as he removed them I saw his feet were covered in the remains of burst blisters. The dead skin hung like leaves from a tree.

"I'll call you Anna," he said, a stray smile slipping across his lips.

"Anna," I said, turning the word over on my wooden tongue. "Why?"

Ephraim waved his hand in my general direction. "I'm going to bed. When I wake up, I expect you'll be gone."

I tried to stay strong but my voice cracked like a dead branch. "Do you want me to go?"

He lay back, over the knotted covers, and closed his eyes. He pursed his lips to say something, but was asleep before he could say it.

The door rattled on it hinges. I saw Ephraim wave his hands in front of his face as he fought his way out of sleep. The light outside would probably have been described as grey but was closer to black. Snow covered most of the window panes and continued to fall in thick waves.

The knocking continued, and it was joined by a voice.

"Eph! Lemme in!"

Ephraim slid his ragged feet off the bed and staggered over towards the door. He paused for a second as if he were about plunge his head underwater, before unlocking and opening the door.

A thickly clothed shape with a rifle slung over its back bundled its way in, encrusted with snow. It turned and slammed the door shut before Ephraim could do anything about it. He stood there, watching dumb, as two coats, a scarf and a hat were discarded to reveal a middle-aged woman, thick around the waist, dressed in a sweater and waterproof trousers. Her face was covered in wealts. She cupped her hands around her eyes and squinted out of the window into the white.

"What time is it?" asked Ephraim, seemingly forgetting where the clock was.

"Before eight," replied the woman. "Can you hear 'em?"

Ephraim rubbed his eyes as he tried to swallow, listen, and reply all in one. "Don't know. Hear who?"

I had heard them, all night, calling to each other through the trees. The woods belonged to them now. The sound had shocked me at first, before I had realized what they meant for me and Ephraim. They meant that we could stay together, that we *had* to.

Unfortunately, I hadn't counted on *her* turning up.

"Wolves, too many to count," said the woman. "You musta been sleepin' like the dead not to hear 'em."

"Always been wolves, Cathy," said Ephraim. "They stay up over the ridge. No deer down here. Ain't nothin' to worry about."

"They was on my porch, Eph. They was scratchin' at my door."

"Bullshit," said Ephraim, though not emphatically enough to hide his doubt in his own voice.

Cathy flared. "I din't struggle a mile through that damn snow to play a prank on you." She softened as soon as the words had died in her mouth, and reached out a hand for his sleeve. "Sorry, but I mean it. They was after me."

Ephraim pulled his hand away from her as if she were a beetle. "Well, whaddya want me to do about it?"

Cathy's voice was a snowflake, fragile and melting. "Nothin'."

She pulled the rifle strap off her shoulder and propped the weapon against the door.

"Just wanted to warn you. Gotta stay safe. Why you so ornery?" She likes him. The realization hit me like the blade of an axe, right between the eyes. Bit the comfort right out of me.

"Not enough sleep," said Ephraim, before doing the math in his sluggish mind. "Or too much. I din't mean nothin' by it. That plane crash got me good. Went out to the woods..."

Ephraim looked down at his hands and rubbed the fingertips together.

"Doesn't matter."

"I been listenin' on the radio," said Cathy. "Terrible thing. Don't think anyone got out alive. Wonder why it happened."

"No point wonderin'. We don't know nothin' 'bout stuff like that, do we? Couple o' wild mountain folks like us? I ain't even seen a plane this way before, 'cept those private ones."

Cathy was about to reply when she spotted me upon the workbench. I kept my eyes straight ahead, blanking her. There was no way I was giving her my attention. All she was doing was getting Ephraim worked up.

"Oh," she said, like that single pitiful sound could sum me up. She was so damn petty. "You made that?"

That, like I was just a thing, a lump.

"Uh huh," said Ephraim. He looked at me with narrowed eyes, shoulders hunched. I saw it all that through my peripheral vision. I wasn't gonna look at him either. Not until she was gone.

She stepped forwards and put a hand on my face. She ran a finger over my eyeball. I felt her fingertip come to rest on my pupil. I took the pain, but not for her sake, for his. "You done well. Looks good. Arty."

I didn't let her late compliment dent my resolve to show her she wasn't welcome. She got no reaction from me.

Behind her, I saw Ephraim's expression loosen, and his shoulders fall. His voice was thick with relief. He was happy with me for not rising to her. I felt a swell of happiness at his approval. "Did it last night. No, the night before. Craziest thing though, I imagined I could hear her talkin'."

"Anna," said Cathy, her lips pressed together like she was afraid of losing them. I felt my soul jar. How could she know my name?

"I guess so," said Ephraim. "She always did like to talk."

"I know you miss her, Eph."

Ephraim looked at me with something else then, a devotion I had been craving, but another feeling was swelling from the deep and readying itself to wash my pitifully small delight away.

"I do miss her," he said. "Ever' day. The nights are the worst."

No. No please no. Was that all I was? Some memorial to a meat-bag, a memory of the short-lived cut from the flesh of a tree?

"Strange thing though, it didn't have her voice..."

I felt something writhing within me. I wasn't about to show it on my face but I let the feeling engulf me within. I reveled in the despair, embracing it because at least it was *mine*, and if he wasn't going to give me his soul, then I would find another reason to live on.

Beneath me, the bench shivered.

Cathy looked about herself, at the floor that was slick with melted snow, at the walls and beams and ceiling.

"You feel that?" she asked Ephraim.

"I did. Mebbe it was some tremor from down the mountain. That plane hit the bridge, after all. Could be some more of it broke off." Ephraim had his eyes on me, but I didn't care. I told myself I didn't care, at any rate.

"I knew I should have stayed with my folks down south this winter. Things go wrong out here, damn hard to fix." Cathy wrapped her arms around herself. "Damnit, now I have to pee." She bit her lip and looked towards the front door.

"Out-house is only a few feet away," said Ephraim.

"Don't matter if there are wolves between me and it."

"Right, right." Ephraim pressed his palms onto the window ledge and peered out over the snow, before cupping his ear and pressing it to the glass. "I can't see nothin' against the snow. Unless they're white wolves, I'd say you're fine."

Cathy still seemed unconvinced, but eventually her feeble body made up her mind for her. She wrapped herself back up like an onion. After pausing for a moment on the threshold, she pushed her way back out into the blistering white.

Ephraim and I were left alone.

"You don't love me," I said.

Ephraim sucked in his breath. "Damnit." Softer then. "Damnit, damnit, damnit."

"You'd rather have anyone but me, wouldn't you? Even her, that awkward fleshy thing. It's the skin, isn't it?" I said, throwing the word out of my mouth with my tongue. "It's not my fault I don't have skin."

"You ain't real," he whispered.

"Stop saying that!"

He pressed his hands to his head.

"Don't ignore me," I said. I deserved more than this, more than him, and it was time he knew that. It was time to accept that he was *lucky* I was here. I had forsaken oblivion to share his life. "I've shown you nothing but devotion."

He screwed up his shoulders and held his hands out to me. "What are you talking about? None o' this makes any damn sense! You ain't even here! You ain't Anna."

"No, I'm not. You gave me that name. I don't even know who she is."

"She was..." Ephraim shook his head. "No, I ain't tellin' you. She's gone."

"I'm here," I said. "I'm here and I love you." It was the first time I had said it, and from the look on his face it was no more than a splash of seawater on a cliff face.

Ephraim looked down at his feet, as if they contained an answer. "It's fine, jus' fine. Just in my head. Stop listening. Nothing's gonna happen. Nothing's gonna happen to Cath."

"You get rid of her," I said. "Or I will."

"An' how you gonna do that?" he asked. "Ain't nothin' but a wooden head on a table."

He had no idea of my potential, as was often the case in a troubled relationship. "Are you willing to bet her life on my staying like this? Don't you think I'm capable of change? Do you know how fragile a skull is compared to wood?"

That struck the mark. He looked up at me, a wounded beast surveying a master it didn't understand. It felt curious to think of him in such primitive ways, but love was like that. It wasn't driven by the mind, but something else. Anything could love, but understanding it was a different matter.

The blast of cold air surprised both of us. Cathy stomped in, awkward and heavy.

Ephraim cast one last look towards me, like a child would to an adult he knew was watching his every move, before placing his hands on Cathy's shoulders.

"Get out, now. Go home."

Cathy's hangdog face was still smothered in scarves, but her eyes showed water.

"What'd I do?"

"Nothin'," said Ephraim. "I ain't gonna try and make somethin' up, 'cos I'm no good at stories, and I ain't gonna protect my skin at the expense o' yours. I'm hearing things, bad things."

She took a step, but it was towards him, not away. Flesh was loyal, and stupid. "Eph?"

"Like in films," he said. "Just like films. A voice, clearly speakin'. One voice. It wants me to kill you."

That made Cathy start.

"I would never do that, never, but I'd rather you ran and told the cops than risk doin' anythin' to you."

He still didn't understand me, but if the result was the same, if she *left*, then I was willing to let the lie wear the truth's clothes.

Cathy stumbled over a few words, trying to find her way, and eventually, inevitably, the flesh chose poorly. "Somethin's obviously gone wrong in you, maybe 'cos of the plane crash, maybe 'cos it's ten years since she's gone, or maybe it's nothin' to do with that at all. Whatever it is, I ain't leavin'."

Ephraim mewed like a cat with a broken spine. "Cath, please..."

Enough. Now it was my turn. "Too late," I said. "Too late. She's made her choice."

Ephraim pounded his fists against his cheeks. "Shut up! I ain't listenin' to you."

Cathy stood as still as I had ever seen her do in the small time I'd known her, before she teased the scarf away from her face. Her eyes were moons.

"Ephraim, it spoke. That thing spoke. I heard it."

Ephraim blinked, looking first towards her, and then towards me. His breath caught in his throat. Finally he realized, finally he accepted me. He knew I was real.

"Dear God."

"Too late!" I screamed. It was time to show him what I could do.

I laid down roots. That's what trees do. They were strong roots, thick with sap. They spilled out of my roughly cut neck and snaked around the workbench, working their way into the fibres of its planks. The workbench's legs shifted and jerked before falling under my command and surged forwards. As the bench rattled across the floor towards the two meat-bags, I threw out yet more roots, digging them into the planks of the walls. This place was mine now.

Ephraim was clever, I'll give him that. He didn't bother trying to fight me but instead went straight for the door. He even got it open a little before I forced the frame to erupt with green shoots to block his path. His body was strong but cumbersome, and I was quick. His legs kicked at branches, snapping many, but twice the number took their place. One of them grew through his arm, first cutting his skin as a sapling, before swelling to adulthood and tearing his muscle apart. He screamed, and for a moment my resolve failed, but his eyes went to Cathy, not me, so I knew that he still had more of the lesson to learn. I opened up the planks at his feet and let his ankles slip into the gap, before closing them again. There was a snap. Bones certainly were brittle. It wasn't the way I'd hoped it would be, but least I knew he wouldn't go anywhere now.

Cathy had backed against the wall, wedging herself between the stove and a book case, as if that would save her. I tapped the legs of the workbench on the floor near her, and smiled as she jerked. She was giving out a low moan, like a drunk waking up to a world that had forgotten about their existence. Ephraim was yelling at her to go, but by the time the message had sunk in it was too late for her. She ran to a window and tried to open it, but my roots had already sealed them all. She tried to pick up Ephraim's axe, but I had already bound it to the wall, and as she watched I warped the shaft and forced the metal head to clatter to the ground. Everything here was mine, and so was Ephraim, my foolish meat. Cathy's love was nothing compared to it, a fact she proved when she tried to push past him. He screamed as she stretched his broken arm against the branch that had pinned him like a butterfly. Well, I couldn't have that, could I?

He was mine to love, and mine alone to hurt.

I sent a root snaking out of the wall and wrapped it around her neck, while threading more past her boots and up her trousers. Her flesh was warm, and soft. Perhaps I could see the attraction after all. I decided to try her on.

I pulled her head from her shoulders as swiftly as I could. There was some bone in the middle of the neck, but it offered little more resistance than the meat. Her blood splashed across the floor, but if Ephraim minded the mess then he didn't say so. He was quiet now, apart from his breathing, which was quick and stifled with tears. Even when she was dead – or at the very least dying within seconds – he couldn't take his eyes off her. All of this was so unfair.

I crawled my workbench forwards and used the roots to lift my head from the table, before placing it as best I could on the ragged remains of Cathy's neck. After plunging more roots down into the flesh and knotting them around the bones I was able to move her arms and legs, after a fashion. It certainly wasn't as easy to co-ordinate a body as the humans made it look. She was leaking patches of red onto her clothes, where the roots pierced the skin. It was all very untidy.

Eventually I managed to work out how to use the hands. All it took were a few more carefully placed roots, down to the digits. I used the fingers to peel off the clothes, until Cathy's body, my body, was naked. It was rather stained now, but the blood had to stop soon. Her heart had, at any rate.

I stood before Ephraim. "Is this what you wanted?"

He wasn't looking at what was left of Cathy now, or me. He wasn't looking at anything.

"Answer me," I said. I reached forwards and placed Cathy's hand around his jaw. The fingertips left stamps of blood on his cheek.

He licked his lips. He tasted her blood, either on purpose or by accident. "What do you want?" He didn't sound scared anymore, so that was at least something.

"I want you," I said. "You made me who I am."

"I don't unnerstand," he said.

"What?"

"None of it, none of it makes any sense. Wood shouldn't speak. It can't grow faster than I can move." He looked at his arm in a daze, at the branch that skewered it. A thick trail of blood was creeping its way downwards from the wound, across the bark.

I blinked. "And why not?"

"Because that's not how it is."

"Well, it is now, and it is here. And you're staying with me."

"I don't love you."

I didn't let him know how deeply he'd cut me. I couldn't. "Seawater can grind down any cliff face, it just takes time."

He raised his free arm and pushed at Cathy's chest. My head rocked on her shoulders. He groaned with pain. "I'll never love you."

"Never is a long time," I said. "Longer to you than it is to me."

He laughed, and it soon turned into a cry. "I can't stay here forever, not like this. I'll die."

"I know," I said. "But you'll love me before then."

I started to bring it in, all of it. I moved the planked of the walls, the floor, and the roof. I discarded the junk and metal into the snow and dragged the wood inwards. It was all we needed. Branches sprouted, grew, and wrapped themselves within each other, just as Ephraim and I would eventually, spiritually if not physically. The sunlight disappeared as we entombed ourselves within a new tree. It soared upwards, our new home, forever sealed against the world.

"This town really is Hell," he said from within the freezing darkness. "I thought it was just a name."

"This isn't Hell," I said, leaning forwards until my wooden lips touched his. A splinter of my flesh pierced his skin, the first of many. "This is Heaven."

We talked and talked, and the wolves came by to listen to us as we bargained and wept and screamed into the night, in our chattering tree.

Feast for the Flies
Shawnee Luke

WELCOME TO A TOWN CALLED HELL

A derelict house sat on the edge of town, not even two miles from the crash site. The house on Barker Road had no nearby neighbours, which was probably a good thing. What was once tan siding was falling apart and aluminium foil covered the windows. The yard was cluttered with used car parts, beer bottles and other trash. And guarding it all was a red and white pit bull. Her only shelter from the elements was the hollowed-out Datsun she was tethered to. A dusting of snow and ash covered the layer of ice in her water dish and the remains of her kibble. She barked constantly into the smoky sky, having no other respite from the cold or her own fear.

The dog's latest kill lay just under the car; a young snowshoe hare who had the misfortune of wandering within her reach. For two days the creature's broken corpse had been the dog's favourite toy. When she wasn't chewing it, she was laying on it. Despite the cold weather, flies had found it and the rabbit's dirty white fur writhed with the maggots crawling underneath.

The interior of the home was just as cluttered and dark as the yard. It was a small house, with a single bedroom and bathroom off of the main room, where the line between tile and carpet was all that separated the kitchen from the living room. The plane crash had knocked out power to the house, as well as other houses in the outlying areas of the town. For now, a variety of candles along the counters and dining room table provided the only source of light.

Molly Dalton was in her early thirties, but looked older. Her mahogany hair had once hung down to her waist. Now it was thin and brittle. Her nose had been broken enough times that it was permanently crooked and she was missing a few of her teeth. Even her dark brown eyes had become dull and bloodshot. She stood at the stove, browning ground beef in a cast iron skillet.

She paused long enough to open the kitchen window and yell "Shut up!" into the yard. The dog stopped barking for a few seconds before continuing again.

At that moment, the lights flickered on and the old model refrigerator sputtered to life. Not long after, the door opened and a man stepped in, immediately shrugging off his coat as the door slammed behind him.

"You got the generator working," Molly said, glancing away from the stove just long enough to acknowledge him. "I didn't think you had enough oil."

Travis Dalton didn't acknowledge her at all. Instead, he muttered something about all of the goddamned lights being on while walking from room to room. Once he'd turned off the bedroom and living room light, he made his way toward the refrigerator. When he finally spoke to her, it was to lean in briefly and growl, "Don't ever yell at Scarlett again, got it?"

Without breaking from her task, she muttered back. "I hate that dog. All she ever does is bark, crap and kill things."

He retrieved a beer from the refrigerator and dug into his pocket for a bottle opener.

"That's a lot more than you ever do. And she's a lot better to look at." He stepped forward to lean into her personal space as if he were being intimate. When she tried to move away, he moved his arms to either side of her, trapping her between his body and the stove. "I mean, look at you. Who knew the homecoming queen would turn into some dried out old tweaker? Nasty!"

"Yeah?" Goosebumps were rising on the back of her neck and she was already bracing, but she couldn't stop herself from taunting him back. "What about you, Prince Charming? Thought you were supposed to be some big name actor by now."

The man that Molly had married twelve years earlier was a handsome, ginger twenty year-old who had big dreams of film school and running off to Hollywood. But the man leaning against her bore no resemblance to that memory. Some men looked sexy bald. Travis was not one of them. His face, his ears and especially his hairless head always seemed red and puffy. Years of drunkenness had left him with a distinct beer belly. But the worst of it was the constant odour on his breath and skin – as if stale beer wept from his pores. The only part of him that was still attractive was his pale blue eyes.

"This is ten years of being married to you, baby," he whispered in her ear. Then, with one sudden movement, he slammed his fist down on the handle of the skillet. Molly cried out as the metal slammed against her chest, sending sizzling meat and grease splattering up the front of her blouse and into her face. The hot pan clanged against her legs and then her bare feet on its way to the ground.

He was laughing as he pushed himself away, forcing her against the stove in the process. "You should be more careful."

Some of the grease had made its way through Molly's shirt, where the cotton and underwire bra trapped it against her skin. Her first instinct was to run to the bathroom and wash it off, but she knew that would only provoke him to do more. If there was one thing Travis loved, it was making her run. For now she stood with her arms to at her side and her face turned away from him while she bit back a sob.

When he didn't get the reaction he was waiting for, Travis scoffed and headed toward the bedroom. "You should clean that up."

Once he was out of her sight, she lowered herself to the floor and began using a rag to scoop the meat back into the pan. A pair of flies had come in from outside and were making passes around her and the surrounding mess. Annoyed, she swatted one away only to have it return again. One of them disappeared from her vision, but she could hear it so close that she wondered if it was in her hair. Eventually, she ignored it as it settled onto the grease dripping down the front of the stove.

She had gotten most of the larger chunks off of the floor when the dog began to bark and whine. Moments later, the door opened once again. Scott Parsons was a scrawny and greasy-looking man, a good ten years younger than Travis. Around Hell, Travis and Molly had become the couple to be avoided – he being the angry drunk and she being the woman stupid enough to stay with him. But somehow, Travis had found at least one person who liked him. Molly couldn't remember when or where it was that Travis had picked Scotty up, but now the younger man was his constant companion. Molly wasn't sure where he slept, but it seemed that his waking moments were always spent at their house.

As usual, he entered without knocking. Then, seeing the mess in the kitchen, asked "Holy shit! What happened?"

She tossed the frying pan into the sink before turning on the faucet. The water that came out had a foul smell as it sizzled against the skillet. And she couldn't be sure, but there seemed to be a strange, almost green tinge to it. Immediately, she shut the faucet off and responded. "What always happens around here, Scotty. Why do you even bother asking anymore?"

"Sorry," he muttered while quickly averting his gaze.

Molly sighed and stepped away from the sink. "I'm guessing it's pretty ugly out there."

"Oh yeah. It took out the bridge and Duffy's gas station. It's a mess. The cops are too busy to give a shit about anything else right now." He paused and called to the bedroom. "Hey Travis, do you think Risky's is gonna be open tonight?"

Travis emerged from the bedroom, pulling on a cleaner jacket. "It better be. I need a drink. We can get something to eat on the way. I'm starving." He winked at Molly and then continued. "Hey Scotty? What do you say to a woman with two black eyes?"

"What's that?"

"Nothing you haven't already told her twice already!"

Travis laughed hard at his own joke and Scotty smirked. Then the pair were out of the door.

Molly waited until she heard the sound of an old truck

driving away before she walked into the bathroom and flicked on the light. Once her shirt and bra were off, she could see that the skin underneath was bright red and she had the beginnings of a blister in the cleft between her breasts. As she stared at herself in the mirror, a fly flew in from the kitchen and landed on the surface; positioning itself just over her counterpart's right iris. In the crappy lighting, it looked like a jagged hole through her eye. The image enthralled her for a few seconds before she leaned forward, scaring the insect away.

She opened the medicine cabinet and searched through a collection of prescription pill bottles. At first, she considered just taking something for the pain, but decided against it. She didn't want to be stoned. Not while she had the mess in the kitchen to clean up. It took opening a few bottles before she finally shook a few pills into her hand and turned on the tap. Once again, that foul smell filled the room.

"Dammit!" she hissed to herself before turning it off and swallowing the pills dry.

She wandered into the bedroom and began digging through piles of clothes to find something clean. A blue hoodie lay half on Travis' side of the bed, with the other half on the adjoining nightstand. As she scooped the hoodie up, she heard something thump against the floor.

Shit! It was one of Travis guns. In fact, it was his favourite gun; a single-action revolver. He'd spent a month's worth of grocery money on that gun and she knew what would happen if he even suspected she had moved it. And Travis did check to see that his toys had not been messed with. The dime she

saw on the floor beside it could be just a dime, much like all of the other random crap around the house. Or it could have been sitting on top or beside the gun so he could see if the weapon had been disturbed. Her husband delighted in these games, because they gave him an excuse to 'correct' her.
The thought made Molly shake, not just with fear but rage. It didn't help that the flies were on her again. Apparently not satisfied with their feast in the kitchen sink, they were back to circling around her hair and getting so close to her ear that it felt like they might climb inside. Swatting them away seemed only to intensify their harassment. And suddenly Scotty's words came back to her.

The cops are too busy to give a shit about anything else right now.

Scotty was right. Every first responder in Hell was tied up with the plane crash. A lot of people had died. Would anyone care if one drunk asshole went missing right now? She didn't have to live like this anymore. This could end.
Molly picked up the revolver and tucked it into the waistband of her jeans. Then she pulled on the hoodie. The metal was cold against her skin and it occurred to her that she'd never actually fired a weapon before. But she'd seen Travis do it enough times. It couldn't be that difficult. And after tonight, she wouldn't be afraid of him ever again. The feeling left her with a euphoria that overrode any doubts.

From outside, Scarlett began a new flurry of deep-chested barks. Had she been barking the whole time or had she taken a break? Molly couldn't tell. Somewhere along the way, she'd managed to tune it out. *When he's dead, I'll shoot that stupid dog, too,* she thought. The thought startled her. Sure, she hated the dog but she had never been hurt by her, or any other animal, before. But suddenly that thought seemed so appealing, along with the feel of the gun against her skin.

Molly put on her shoes and stepped outside. Scarlett paused from her barking to whine and tug on the end of her lead, calming only when her mistress got closer and rested a hand on her head. As the dog licked her hand, Molly spoke to her.

"Your life sucks worse than mine. I'm doing you a favour." She untied the rope from the dog's neck and stepped away. Then she cocked the gun and fired it into the air. The spooked dog ran down Barker Road, howling in panic along the way.

"Trust me, honey. Wherever you're off to, it's a hell of a lot better than here." She watched until the dog disappeared from view before stepping back into the house.

After turning off the lights, she sat at the dining room table facing the door. And then she waited in the candle-lit kitchen. With the barking dog gone, she was left to a silence broken only by the crappy refrigerator and the flies. Travis' favourite weapon had been fired and his dog was gone. There was no turning back now.

It was hours later that she heard the pick-up pull into the front yard.

"It's time," Molly whispered to herself as she stood and rested a hand on the butt of the revolver.

The engine shut off. A door slammed and she could hear him out there, with his voice barely audible to start with. Then she heard him whistle and call the dog. Within a minute, she heard a loud "Fuck!" before he raced into the house, slamming the door behind him.
"Where the hell is my dog?"

Unlike most other drunks, Travis didn't stagger or slur his speech. Were it not for the smell, one might pass him on the street without noticing that he was wasted. He could even drive convincingly. Instead of being a falling down drunk, Travis was an angry drunk. And right now, he was in a rage.
For the first time ever during one of these episodes, Molly wasn't afraid. She merely shrugged. "You mean she isn't out there? Wonder how that happened."

The confusion in his voice made her smile for a second before she heard the other door slam. *Dammit. Scotty is still with him.* Before she could decide how she planned to deal with Scotty, the door opened again and the younger man, who actually was falling down drunk, stumbled in behind him and planted himself on the love seat. Immediately, he slumped until his head nearly touched his knees and it looked as if he might throw up on the floor.

"Why couldn't you drop him off on your way home? Why does he always have to be here?" Molly's hand was still under the hem of her hoodie and gripping the revolver. The methamphetamine she'd popped earlier was rushing through her bloodstream. Already, her heart had begun to race and her skin suddenly itched everywhere. And there was an odd noise. A distant but high-pitched humming that gnawed at her senses. She couldn't tell if she was hearing it with her ears or in her mind. While she was used to being spun, it normally didn't last so long. And the mixture of sensations was worse than normal. Scotty's presence was an agitation she didn't need.

"She didn't untie the rope by herself. What did you do to my dog, you psycho bitch?" Travis grabbed a picture frame off of an end table and threw it at Molly. It bounced off of her breast and then shattered on the floor.

Molly didn't flinch but instead forced herself to smile. "I guess she is in a better place now."

His hands were clenched at his sides and it seemed like he tried to calm himself. "If you don't tell me what you did with her, I'm going to kill you."

Somewhere nearby, the fly began buzzing again. Only now, it seemed so much louder. While Molly couldn't see the source of the sound, she could have sworn it was right beside her ear again. Or maybe it actually had climbed in and the buzzing was in her head now. She couldn't be sure. And then, somewhere in that buzzing, she thought she heard words.

It's time. Do it.

And she wanted to. But first.

"God dammit, Scotty, go home!"

The man on the couch made a half-assed attempt to lift himself up. He was nearly standing before Travis crossed the room again and pushed him back into the seat. Then Travis turned on her.

"This is my goddamned house. I pay the bills. Scotty isn't gonna be the one leaving tonight, Baby."

Forget Scotty. Do it.

"Yeah, whose bills are you paying?" Molly could feel a cold sweat collecting under her arms. "One of those girls down at Risky's? I bet she appreciates it."
"God! Shut up and tell me where my damned dog is!" he roared.
"I mean, it's not like you have anything else to offer," she continued. "That thing in your pants hasn't worked in years. I doubt you can even see it anymore."
"Either you shut your mouth, or I'll shut it for you." Travis' teeth were clenched and his voice went back to that barely-tempered rage. She could see that his face had turned an ugly red and the veins in his neck were bulging. Their episodes were not usually so close together, but he was as ready to go as she was. The only thing between them was a few feet and the dining room table.

Do it! The buzzing said.

"Go ahead." Molly purred. "Do it, Big Man."
Travis stepped forward and grabbed the edge of the table. But before he could tip it over, or whatever he meant to do with it,

the gun was in her hands and pointed inches from his head. His eyes widened and he froze when she cocked it.

Then he smirked and leaned in until the barrel of the gun was inches from his face. "You like messing with my shit, Molly? When we're done, I'm going to take that gun out of your hand and beat you to death with it."
"No, baby. You won't." Molly whispered back, though she could no longer hear her own voice.

The flies spoke louder. *Do it. Do it now!*

And with that she squeezed the trigger, sending a jolt of pain up both arms and pushing her backward. The bullet entered Travis' right eye. The surrounding socket exploded as blood and skull showered the kitchen behind him. He remained standing for what seemed like too long, staring at her in disbelief out of his remaining eye. Then he fell backward onto the ground, pulling the flimsy table and all of its contents down with him. His body landed with his arms splayed at his sides and his legs crossed at the ankles.

The noise in her head reached a crescendo. There, the flies delighted in the carnage they had created. She was vaguely aware that Scotty was on his feet and stumbling away to vomit in the nearby bathroom. He was yelling, she thought, though his voice sounded muffled.
"Jesus, Molly! What did you do?" When she finally looked at him, he had his cell phone in his hand and was smashing a finger against the glass.

Despite the meth pumping through her veins, she was curiously numb. Even the fear had gone. "Come on, Scotty. The phones haven't worked all day. Anyway, I think he's a little beyond help. You've got part of his brain on your jeans."

To his credit, he didn't vomit again despite making a dry heave sound. But he did keep trying to dial his phone.

"You crazy bitch! They are going to put you away until you rot! You know that, right?"
Molly pulled the hammer back once more and pointed the gun in his direction.

"Hey! Look! The crazy bitch you're threatening has a gun! Fuck, I always knew you were a stupid kid."

The smell of urine reached her nostrils, though she couldn't tell if it was from the living man or the dead one. Scotty's bottom lip quivered. He was whispering and his mouth was moving as if he were talking, but she couldn't hear any words. The flies in her head were all consuming and they egged her on.

"Until I rot? I've been rotting for years now! Do you honestly think that prison is going to be worse than how I've been living? I have no family. No friends. Just an asshole husband who gets off on beating the hell out of me."

Kill him.

"I know. I know, Molly. Please put the gun down!" He was backing away from her and whimpering. She could see that his face was covered in either snot or tears, maybe both. It was hard for her to tell. But the sight gave her an odd sense of pleasure and she found herself wondering what it would be like to send a bullet into that pathetic face. Maybe she'd put one into his knee first just to hear him cry. The flies loved the violence, and they demanded more of it.

"Why shouldn't I kill you? Hmm? You just told me you're going to run to the police. And besides, how many times did you look the other way? Or laugh at his stupid jokes? Look at you!"

She waved the gun, aiming it down his body and delighting in the way his hands moved to block its path. "Do you even have anyone besides us, Scotty? Who the hell is going to miss you?"

His only response was to lean himself against the wall, as far away from her as he could get, while sobbing "I'm so sorry. I'm sorry."

"You should have left when I told you to, Scotty."

Do it! Kill him!

She aimed the gun at his head and squeezed the trigger. There was an audible click and the cylinder rotated. At the same time, Scotty screamed out and held his hands to his face. But the shot didn't come. And with that empty click, the noises in her head subsided. Once again, it was just her and the young drunk she hadn't planned on killing.

"Get out of here. Now!"

But he didn't move right away. He was still cowering against the door and staring at Travis' body. By then, a puddle of blood had pooled around the linoleum around the dead man's head. And there was so much of it.

She cocked the gun again. "One chamber was empty. Do you want to bet on the next one?"

"Okay, okay. Jesus," Scotty sobbed as he ran out of the house, flinging the door open along the way. Any warmth left in the home seemed to be sucked out as a cold breeze blew in a flurry of snow. As she stood and tried to resist those voices in her head that craved more blood, she could hear him just outside, screaming into the night.

The buzzing voices were clearly disappointed that they hadn't gotten a second kill, but eventually they quieted to a dull hum.

Once she was back inside and alone with the corpse of her husband, Molly took a step over him and kneeled down to stare into his ruined face. "Hey, baby. What do you tell a man with a big, fucking hole in his head?" she asked him.

Molly wasn't expecting a response. But then his torso jerked violently. With his arms spread to his side, his back arched upward off the floor before falling backward. She nearly slipped in the blood in her attempt to scramble away. As she watched, a few more tremors shook his body. Then, tremors became twitches. She wasn't sure how long she watched. But, finally, Travis seemed to realize that he was dead and lay still.

When she was convinced that he was done moving, she turned and ran toward the bathroom to heave bile into the sink. Then she was in the medicine cabinet again, digging around for anything to calm the pounding of her heart.

She was popping a handful of pills into her mouth when she heard it. From behind her, the corpse let out a loud moan. There was a distinctly liquid sound to it. She spun around. The corpse lay where she'd left it and it seemed that the dark puddle had ceased spreading.
"I'm losing my mind," she whispered to herself as she turned on the bathroom light. It came on and then quickly died, along with the refrigerator. Once again, the candles were her only source of light.

And the only sound came from the flies in the sink.

While hugging her arms against her chest, Molly stepped out of the bathroom and gingerly over the corpse. It was then that she noticed that his legs had uncrossed. Had that happened during the earlier tremors? She couldn't be sure. For another few seconds, she stared at him. But this time, he didn't move at all.
"When did you become such a monster?" she asked the dead man. "I loved you. I didn't care that we didn't make it to Los Angeles or that we were always broke. Hell, I didn't even care about the girls. And I know you loved me, too."
Of course, he didn't answer. And now she had a huge body to dispose of. She stood up to walk back toward the dining room table when something sharp cut into the arch of her left foot. She yelped and lifted her foot up to examine it. Imbedded in the pad was a shard of glass from the frame he'd thrown at her. In fact, there was glass all over the floor around her.

She limped into her bedroom. As much as she tried not to put any more weight on the foot, her hopping was clumsy and she ended up stepping down more than once. Then she settled on the edge of the bed and set the candle on the floor beside her. The glass was imbedded deep and she cried, despite herself, as she pulled it free. Blood coated her fingers and dribbled onto the drab carpet. A basket of laundry was on the floor not too far away. The lighting didn't allow her to see what she was grabbing, but she was pretty sure it was an oil rag.

From within the kitchen, she suddenly heard a chorus of flies. It was as if a nest of them had just been disturbed. Outside the wind rose and there was a sound of air rushing through the house. A cold gust circulated through the bedroom, blowing her hair back and snuffing the candle. Just as quickly, it was sucked away and she could hear the front door slam closed behind it.

"Shit!" she whispered to herself while wrapping the rag tightly around her foot. The fabric was rough and seemed to rub against the wound. As the meth-enhanced adrenaline rush began to dissipate, the pain intensified. Only now did it occur to her how damned cold it was. Even under her hoodie, she began to tremble.

More strange sounds came from the kitchen. This time it was thud and a series of wet slaps against the linoleum. Molly felt her breath seize in her chest. No vehicles had come into the driveway and she would know if someone else had entered the house. She scrambled to her feet, ignoring the pain long enough to search the drawer inside nightstand. After knocking over an ashtray and sending some coins to the floor, she found a lighter. It took a few clicks and a whispered "Shitshitshit!" before it finally lit. By then, the knocking sounds from the kitchen had grown quiet.

Once the candle was relit, she held it up to her chest and then nearly dropped it.

Travis – or at least his corpse, anyway – was standing. His arms were limp at his sides and he was slouched forward. His posture and the way he was framed by the doorway gave him the appearance of a marionette that was hanging on the end of its strings. The ruined side of his head was leaning against his shoulder, still leaking dark fluid down his arm. As the candle flickered, she could that he was staring at her with his remaining eye.

From somewhere behind him, the buzzing of the flies intensified.

Just as she was wondering what was holding him up, the thing that had been her husband took a step forward. The movement was disjointed, but unnerving in how quick it was. Molly pushed herself across the bed to get away, but she was now too aware of the fact that there was really nowhere for her to go. With her free hand, she drew the gun and fired. The kickback sent pain radiating up her arm. The force knocked her back and dropped the candle onto the bed. Despite opening a hole in Travis' midsection, the bullet did absolutely nothing to slow him down. In what seemed like a blur, there was now only the bed between them.

His slackened jaw moved, as if trying to speak. A gurgling could be heard somewhere in his chest. But no words came out. Dark bubbles formed at his lips, followed shortly after by a ribbon of blood that trailed down his chin. There were flies all around him. They were buzzing about the wound at his head and drifting around his shoulders. And there were so many of them. Where had they even come from?
The room slowly brightened. Though she could not take her gaze from the corpse, she could see out of the corner of her eye that the flame from the candle had caught onto the pile of comforters on the bed and was now beginning to grow.

Still holding the gun up, she tried to speak to it, begging as Scotty had not long before.

"Oh God, baby. I'm so sorry. This isn't how it was supposed to be." Then she cocked the gun and pulled the trigger, only to be met with an empty click. Followed by another. The gun was empty.
In the light of the flames, she thought she saw the corpse of her husband smile.

With nowhere to go, she dropped the gun and ran around the bed, hoping to get past it to the door before it caught her. She wasn't fast enough. Two big hands grabbed her and she felt herself being lifted into the air before she was slammed to the floor. The force took the wind out of her and she groaned, rolling over on her stomach.
Then the corpse was on its hands and knees, hovering over her with its mouth close to her neck. Its head brushed against her face, spreading red ichor across her skin before it sank its

teeth hard into the base of her neck. Then she screamed as she felt a chunk of her flesh being ripped away.

The thing that was her husband made a strange chortling sound as it ate its first bite. At the same time, the buzzing intensified, as if the corpse and the flies, now one in the same, were revelling in the same feast.

Smoke was beginning to fill her lungs and she coughed, each spasm sending more blood from the wound at her neck. Despite the flames nearby, she felt cold. Her eyes closed as she tried to prepare herself for the thing to bite her again.

The bite didn't come. Instead, she felt that huge weight fall away from her. When her eyes opened again, the corpse of Travis was beside her, but just out of reach. It stared at her out of one dead eye while twitching and struggling to rise. Vaguely she became aware of a set of cold hands closing around hers and pulling her up to her feet. Then someone whispered a single command into her ear.

"Come."

She obeyed, though she couldn't help but look back through the smoke, where Travis' corpse still writhed with what looked like a sword impaling him to the floor.

It wasn't until she stepped over the threshold of the bedroom and out of the smoke that she saw who her saviour was. Only now the young man leading her seemed different; calm and quiet rather than the whiny kid she had chased off earlier.

"Scotty?" she asked. She attempted to free herself from his grasp, but she was weak and he held on with a strength that seemed uncharacteristic of him. "Why did you come back? And... where the hell did you get a sword?"

The man simply stopped walking and turned to face her with an odd smile. It wasn't one of his usual goofy smiles or that uncomfortable look he sometimes got when Travis told off-colour jokes. There was an arrogance to this expression and something else. Pleasure ?

"Scotty? I have been called many names over the centuries. I am the Lord of Flies. The Lord of High House. There was a time that I was worshipped as a god. Did you know that the Caananites played drums to cover up the sound of the mothers wailing while the priests sacrificed their children to me?" His voice sounded different, too. It was as if there was a melodious hum weaving its way through his words.

Molly's vision was spinning. She made another attempt to get out of his grasp, but he was just too strong. In the bedroom, the corpse continued to writhe and thump. The flames from the bed had begun to uncoil and spread to the clothes on the floor on their way to the curtains. It moved rather slowly than she thought it would. "What the hell are you talking about? Scotty, stop playing around. We have to get out of here."

But the man she knew as Scotty only continued, smiling at her as he spoke in that eerily calm voice.

"I feast on disease and death, and tempt men with lust for power."

"Scotty, or whatever you want to call yourself. Please let just let me go."

He leaned with his face close enough to hers that she feared he might kiss her, and suddenly she realised that the odd hum in his voice sounded like flies. "You and your husband have entertained me well. But our time is now at an end. Goodbye, Molly."

His smile widened and he winked at her. His hand raised and she had a moment where she saw the glint of the blade before it was driven through her right eye and into her brain. Molly only had enough time to grunt before she fell to the floor dead.

The demon that once called himself Scotty stood in the living room of the burning house, savouring the destruction he had caused. Then he raised his arms and his body dissipated into a swarm of flies that collected on the new corpse.

A few minutes later, the corpse that was Molly rose to its feet as well. It entered the bedroom and pulled the blade out of her husband's back and threw it aside. Once the corpse of Travis was on its feet, the two of them stepped out of the house. Then, for the first time in years, the pair held hands and walked side by side toward Barker Road and the town beyond.

The Lovers: Part One
Edward Breen

WELCOME TO A TOWN CALLED HELL

Despite his muscles working to breaking point and lungs begging for air, he kept going. He could do it, he had to believe he could. The wall was just there. His salvation. All he had to do was get there. Although he was swimming through water, it felt like custard. Feet pointed, he kept pumping his legs. Fingers stretching forward a little farther with each stroke, rolling his shoulders to get that extra couple of inches.

His lungs were going to burst, he was sure of it, he was having to breathe every second stroke now, left, right, left, right. He saw the black painted line that signified three good strokes to the wall. He screamed inside his own head: One…you don't need another breath, two…just one more pull come on, three…

He hit the wall as expected with the tips of his fingers. His head shot straight up to find the clock. The red hand was ten seconds before the top. He did it, one hundred meters in under fifty seconds. A personal best! He couldn't wait to tell Maria. Alex punched the air. He looked around and the old woman who always swam in a hair net was looking at him like he was crazy. He waved and pulled himself out of the water on shaky arms.

The pool was pretty busy for a Tuesday. There was an aerobics class being led by an overweight instructor bounding around to The Final Countdown by Europe. The instructor had her back to the glass poolside wall that gave a fantastic view out across to the far bank of the River Styx. The river that cut the town of Hell off from the rest of the world. Alex slipped on his flip flops as he nodded in time to the music. But he was pretty sure the song didn't have an earth shattering whump in the middle of it. He turned just in time to see the aeroplane fly past by the glass wall. Alex's memory told him that it had happened in slow motion. He remembered seeing every little detail of the aircraft as it passed by. He remembers no sound after the initial whump and the final tooth loosening explosion that happened after. It felt like he was watching a movie or a newsreel played at the wrong speed. From where Alex stood he could see the bridge that crossed the river. Then he couldn't. The bridge had ceased to be. Alex didn't have time to see any more, however, as the enormous toughened glass wall exploded inward and he was thrown off his feet. Later he told himself that he heard the almost simultaneous second explosion. But it could have just been his head hitting the deck.

After a disaster like this, the expectation is screaming and shouting and sirens. But there was nothing. All he could hear was the wind blowing through the now open glass side of the building. The air was cold and snow was streaming in. Some flakes stuck and others melted as they got too near to the heat of the pool.

Bodies filled the pool, all of them face down in the water. He was sure he recognised the red swimsuit of Rebecca, one of the lifeguards. Alex's head was still ringing from the explosion and it took him a second to think about helping. He carefully got up off the floor, checking that he hadn't broken anything. He slid his foam soles through the debris, making sure not to pick up any glass. As his senses returned, he could see why his body had rejected the idea of entering the water before his brain had caught up. Aside from bodies there were little cubes of glass and long steel spikes. Everyone in the pool had at least one shard of metal through them and they were changing the water into something more like wine. They were all dead. He could do nothing for them.

Two screams wrenched him from his thoughts. The first was unmistakably male and the second female. He moved toward the sound of the first, still conscious of the glass on the floor. It had come from the men's changing rooms.

Getting up off the floor by using the wall as leverage, was Randy Lowenstein, the centre manager. Randy was an asshole, so Alex was glad to see the irregular wet patch on the front of his khaki shorts.

"Stop staring, homo," Randy said, his words fierce but his voice shaking.

Alex couldn't make fun of him, much as he wanted to. Not with all the corpses everywhere. They were in various state of undress some having just come from the showers, others changed for the gym and one guy who had just put his kid's right shoe on, the left was still in his lifeless fingers.

"What?" was all Alex could manage.

Randy's face twisted from fear to anger.

"I said stop looking at my crotch, bro," he said.

"Sorry," Alex said. "Are they dead?"

"Looks like it," Randy said.

Alex abruptly remembered the second scream. It had come from the gym on the mezzanine level above the pool.

"Come on," he said to Randy and took off at as much of a run as he could wearing flip flops and a towel.

The scene in the reception was the same. People who had minutes ago been going about their business appeared to have simply dropped down dead. Alex ran up the stairs toward the gym with Randy close behind. What they saw there was as bad as the rest. The safety switches on the machines had flipped on, so the people who had been using the treadmills were lying face down on static machines. There were people slumped over stationary bikes, ski machines and rowers. Some poor woman who had been bench pressing had her neck crushed under the bar, her head bent backward way too far.

The love of Alex's life was sitting in the corner hugging her legs and sobbing. Maria had gone one better than Randy in that she didn't have any wet patches on her trousers. But she was badly shaken.

"Oh my God Alex, you're okay," she said, getting up and hugging him.

"What's this? Happier about seeing this loser than you own boyfriend?" Randy said.

"I just didn't see you, of course I'm glad you're safe," Maria said, letting Alex go and running to hug Randy.

Alex felt a pang of jealousy. Of course Maria would never go out with him. Not when she had Randy Lowenstein.

"What's going on?" Maria asked.

They had no good answer. Alex told her about the plane crashing into the bridge and the glass wall imploding. They all agreed that it was beyond strange that everyone in the leisure centre had died. The bridge was far enough away not to destroy the centre. So why was everyone, apart from them, dead?

"The bridge?" Randy said. "You mean the only bridge out of this shitty town? Perfect."

A lot of the people who lived in Hell felt the same as Randy. The town itself was a left over from the gold rush and should have been abandoned along with the derelict mines years ago. The name Hell certainly allowed for a lot of jokes at the town's expense. Not that Alex thought Randy should be complaining. Randy's dad owned the leisure complex and the remoteness of Hell, along with a largely bored population meant that his family had done very well.

The three of them made their way through the gym, staying well clear of the bodies, and down the stairs to the pool. Even to Alex, who had witnessed the whole thing, it was an awesome sight. The glass wall had been longer than the Olympic standard pool. The building had been designed as a cube over eighty feet high. It resulted in an almost seven thousand square foot gaping hole in the wall. The wind whistled past the jagged remains.

Beyond the hole they could see what was left of the bridge. The plane had destroyed most of it and the rest was crumbling into the water below. Some had landed on Black Beach, a little spit of sand that lay beneath the structure where kids would go and drink. There was a sewer outlet there too, which was now completely blocked.

Snow was coming in at an alarming rate, but the residual heat of the pool seemed to be keeping it near the missing wall. It piled up just inside making a little mound of white. Despite the pool water obviously still being warm the air was now as cold as outside. Alex felt it keenly, he was only wearing a towel and damp swimming trunks.

"I heard two explosions," Randy said looking at Alex for an answer.

"All I saw was the plane," Alex said.

"Let's go to the office. We can check out the rest of the town from there," Randy said.

Alex told them he'd follow and went to the changing rooms to put on some clothes. All the people in the changing room looked like they were sleeping. He wondered if the explosion had knocked them out, like an EMP but for people. Kneeling beside a youngish man he recognised — Alex felt like he should pick someone he knew, so it wouldn't be so weird if they woke up and he was fully dressed — he checked for a pulse. The first clue was the coldness of the guy's skin. The second was the tone in his muscles; odd, thought Alex, rigor mortis can't have set in already, the crash only happened half an hour ago. Alex remembered from a TV programme that it was normally well into the second hour before that happened. The need to check for a pulse seemed redundant at this point, but he did anyway. Then taking his hand away he could have sworn there was a slight smell of rot in the air. Like a piece of chicken left a day too long in the fridge.

Satisfied the man was dead, Alex quickly got dressed and went to the office. It was a simple affair containing a steel framed desk with a computer on it. The room had been bolted on to the side of the leisure centre, another smaller cube protruding from the main one. This gave it a panoramic view of the town.

Randy was sitting on the chair with his head in his hands, Maria was standing next to him with a conciliatory hand on his shoulder. Alex didn't think Randy would be so worried about a glass wall. His father would have some insurance policy. He looked out at the town below and everything away from the crash site looked normal. In fact the snow made it look almost pretty. It covered the sloping roofs of the houses, the flat tops of the factories in the distance, the trees beyond that and the cars along the streets. Alex was marvelling at the beauty of it when a cloud of black smoke caught his attention. He knew where it was coming from. Duffy's gas station had blown up. It was just far enough away not to have destroyed the leisure complex, but the surrounding houses hadn't been so lucky.

Suddenly it hit Alex why Randy was so upset. His parents lived near there. Two houses away from the gas station. There's no way the building could have survived.

"Were they...?" Alex said.

"I don't know," said a deflated Randy. "They were going on vacation today."

"So maybe they'd left already," Maria said.

"I don't fucking know," Randy said not looking up from his hands.

Alex just stared at the fire and smoke. Emergency services had attended and their cars were still there, blocking the surrounding streets. Not that anyone would be coming from out of town anytime soon.

"I'm going to see if they're alright," Randy said, getting up off the chair.

Alex saw that he had changed into some clean trousers, but decided against mentioning it.

"We'll go with you," Maria piped up.

Alex said nothing, he just followed.

As they threaded their way through the gym, Alex couldn't help but think he could still sense that rotting smell from the changing rooms. Only it was stronger now.

"Does anyone else smell that?" he said.

"Real funny man," Randy said.

"Not that, I mean…something else."

"You okay?" Maria asked.

"Yeah it's just the smell. Can't you guys get it?"

"I read somewhere that when you hit your head sometimes you can see or smell things that aren't there," Maria said. "Maybe you should sit down?"

"I'm fine," Alex said. "Let's go."

They didn't notice the problem until they got to the entrance. The glass roofed walkway leading to the doors had been completely destroyed. In fact the entire entrance had been sealed shut by debris. There were rocks and pieces of glass and as far as Alex could see parts of a car mixed into the smouldering rubble that blocked their exit.

"The emergency door," Randy said.

The green signs with a picture of someone running toward an exit pointed toward a large metal double door built behind the reception desk on the opposite side of the foyer. Randy got there first and walked straight into them, arms out in front, pushing the locking bar toward the door. But the door didn't move. He tried again, shaking the bar and finally throwing himself, shoulder first, against the door. It didn't budge.

"What's the matter?" Maria asked.

"It won't open," Randy said, panting slightly. "Locked or something."

"That's impossible, you can't lock an emergency exit!" Maria said, her voice rising in panic. "The bar should open it from this side in case of a fire."

"You try it then," Randy shouted.

Maria tried. Then Alex tried. It was no good. It felt like a brick wall had been built right outside the door.

"Isn't there another exit?" Alex asked.

Randy shook his head. "There is supposed to be, but dad knows the safety guy and…"

"What are you saying?" Maria said.

"I'm saying we're stuck here," Randy shouted.

There was an awkward silence. Alex thought there was no point in taking sides.

"Can we at least eat something?" Maria said. "I'm starving."

The adrenaline seemed to put an edge on their hunger. They demolished the sandwiches Randy had retrieved from the fridge in the canteen, and the crisps they had filched from the display out front.

Alex felt a lot better after eating, he'd not really realised how hungry he was. Then he had a thought.

"Why don't we try escaping through the pool?" he said.

"Don't be an idiot, fucktard," Randy said "Unless you want to swim in the Styx then it's impossible."

"We should at least try," Maria said.

Alex felt himself blush at the support from Maria. Then he realised he shouldn't be blushing, which only made it worse. He started toward the pool to cover his embarrassment. The smell in the foyer wasn't at all as bad as the gym had been. Alex's spirits were rising with each step he took back toward the pool. They took a dive as soon as he emerged poolside.

The water had changed from azure to a dull reddish brown. The smell in the pool was worse, but different. Instead of rot, it was more like a sewer. As though everyone in the pool had simultaneously evacuated themselves and it was now fighting with the chlorine to become the dominant smell.

He tried to avoid looking into the water and walked around the shallow end on his way to the missing wall. When he got there he realised what Randy had meant. There was less than six inches between the edge of the building and the sheer drop into the Styx. The river below was a raging torrent, and Alex was sure that the fall, combined with the cold and the power of the river would mean death if they fell.

Randy looked smug when he and Maria caught up.

"What do you think now, supershit? You gonna fly across and get help?" Randy said.

"Leave him alone Randy." Maria said.

Alex took a step onto the narrow ledge. He couldn't back down. This was his chance to get out and save them both. His mind filled with fantasies of Maria jumping into his arms when he threw open the exit doors. The look on Randy's face would be spectacular as his girlfriend hugged Alex, thanking him for saving them.

Alex transferred his weight to the foot out on the ledge. He felt the snow compacting beneath his sneaker with its characteristic crunch. There was a little sideways slide and then his footing felt solid. A torrent of relief coursed through him as he shifted the rest of his weight and lifted his other foot ready to step out.

It happened faster than he could have imagined. First the outside foot seemed to have nothing underneath it, then his inside foot was dragged out by his body falling straight down. His hands shot up and grabbed hold of the aluminium window frame. Luckily, the toughened glass broke into dull cubes and not sharp shards. Otherwise his hands would have been sliced clean through. Instead they were merely lacerated and bruised. Not that he could feel that. His limbic system was on overdrive. Adrenaline was dulling the pain. His brain just screamed: hold on.

Randy and Maria dragged him up by his sleeves and put him on his back on the cold tiles.

"Oh my god, Alex. Are you alright?"

"Idiot," said Randy.

Alex said nothing, he just lay there shaking. Partly from the cold, partly from shock.

Maria made Randy go and get a first aid kit. Then she helped Alex so he could sit against the wall and he felt a little better. Probably because Maria was gently cradling his hands, whilst picking chunks of glass out of them.

Disinfected and cleaned, Alex realised he had done a lot less damage than he could have. His hands were bruised and cut but not half as bad as they felt. Randy bandaged them with alarming gentleness, citing his first aid training as the reason for doing it. Alex was sure it was some ploy to enamour himself with his girlfriend, who Randy probably realised was getting away from him.

"Thanks," Alex said, flexing his hands.

"Whatever, dick. I told you not to try it," Randy said.

There he is, thought Alex, the old Randy back in action.

"What about the phones?" Maria said, suddenly.

Alex stared blankly at her taking far too long to get up to speed.

"We could call them?" she said, looking at the others as if they had lost their minds.

Randy was first into the office. He threw himself into the chair and snatched the phone off the cradle. It made a digital beep and Randy pressed a button which was obviously the speed dial for his house. Then he held the phone up to his ear.

"It's dead," Randy said.

Alex watched the smile on Randy's face slowly die.

"Let me try," Maria said, grabbing the phone from Randy's hand.

She confirmed it with a solemn nod, like a doctor confirming her patient had passed.

"Cell phones!" Alex shouted.

They sprang into action again and ran to where their respective phones were stored. Alex's was in his bag in the locker room. He hadn't thought to put it back in his pants when he got dressed. Shock, he supposed. He switched it on and swiped his lock pattern across the screen. No signal.

Randy had followed him down and was around the other side of the lockers. Alex guessed he would be having the same luck. Maria was next door in the ladies.

WELCOME TO A TOWN CALLED HELL

Alex met Maria first. She came into the men's locker room to find them. She had gotten the same response from her phone. They went to find Randy who wasn't making a sound. They found him elbows deep in someone's kit bag.

"Hey, not cool." Alex said when he saw him.

"They're dead, man," Randy said. "They won't mind. Besides there might be a working cell phone here somewhere"

"I know but…still," Alex said.

It felt wrong to him, going through other people's stuff. Even if they were dead. He had to admit that Randy was right, though, they did need to find a working cell.

"Here have one of these," Randy said, throwing a shiny blue object to Alex.

"A protein bar? Are these yours?" Alex said.

"They weren't," Randy said, lobbing one to Maria, "but the way I see it if we don't keep our strength up we will die. And we won't be doing these people any good if we die too."

Alex didn't for a second think he was going to die of hunger. He knew someone would come and rescue them before that happened. The Army or the Marines or something. He was convinced it would only be a matter of time before they heard the thuka-thuka-thuka of helicopters flying over the snowy horizon. Still, the feeling of impending doom had given him an appetite and Randy was right about them keeping their strength up. He ate the bar promising himself that if the person wasn't actually dead — which the ever increasing smell in the locker room made seem unlikely — he would pay him back for it.

They found more cells, but none were working. They all had no signal.

No phones, no exit, no imminent rescue really does make an horrific situation simply boring. Despite the proliferation of quickly rotting corpses Alex was thinking that this was getting old, fast. At one point Maria advocated moving all the corpses into the pool. She reasoned that because it was the coldest room it would slow down their decomposition a little at least. Both of the others agreed with the idea. At least in principle. The trouble was nobody was willing to actually carry it out. Nobody wanted to put their hands on a dead person any more than they had to, especially their friends and work colleagues. In the end they rationalised that they would be saved long before it became an issue. All three of them pointedly ignoring the rising tide of stench.

After their evening meal of flapjacks and crisps, they had retreated to the office as it was the only place that didn't have any bodies in it.

"Are there any flash lights up here?" Alex said into the silence.

"Why? You afraid of the dark?" Randy said.

"Shut up Randy," Maria said.

Alex smiled to himself in the half light, keeping his back turned to Randy to conceal it.

"I was just thinking," Alex went on. "That we could use them to flag down one of the police cars on their way past. Or maybe someone in one of the houses."

Randy stood silent.

"Well?" Maria snapped. "Do you have any flashlights?"

"Alright, alright. In the desk. There should be a big one. I think they have some smaller ones down in reception."

"One should do it," Alex said.

So they waited. Then they waited some more. The daylight faded and the streetlights flickered on as the light level dropped. The ones in the distance came on first, then the ones in the centre of town, finally their faces were illuminated by the sodium glow of the closest lamp post.

"I think it's dark enough now." Maria said.

Alex nodded and started flashing out three short bursts of light then three long followed by another three short. He fervently hoped that whoever saw it didn't try to answer in Morse code. All he knew was SOS, but everyone knew that right?

"What the fuck are you doing?" Randy said as if in answer to Alex's unasked query. "Why don't you just leave it on and flash it around a bit."

Alex didn't answer, he just smiled to himself as Maria told Randy she needed him to put the centre lights on because she didn't know where the master switch was.

Sitting in the orange glow Alex tried flashing his light in all directions, but nobody answered. Either they didn't see or had their own problems.

Suddenly he heard voices.

At first, he thought it was Maria and Randy come back, but realised that it was all male voices that he heard, and that they were coming from outside. Then he saw them, three men walking down the street, they were obviously a rescue party of sorts. They stopped across the street, he could clearly make out their faces and almost what they were saying. It was something about 'devastation' but he wasn't quite sure. Wanting to get their attention he started banging on the window as hard as he could, shouting as loud as he could. But they just stood there, having their conversation. He tried flashing his light at them, but they didn't even blink. Then they strolled off down the road and out of Alex's memory.

That was the last any of them saw from the outside world.

The Soul Collector
EC Robinson

The headlights from Tommy Joe Flannery's four wheeler cut through the heavy falling snow late Wednesday evening as he did his rounds of the lake cabins. Since the plane crash had destroyed the bridge the night before, the patrons had been uneasy to say the least. The smell of burning flesh seemed to still be in the air. He was glad of the steampunk-looking goggles his grandkids had bought him and his trusty orange hunter scarf that he wrapped around his mouth. He had taken it upon himself to check on each of the occupied cabins surrounding the lake. Although it was his job to ensure the patrons of Solicitude Cabins were comfortable, he felt that going the extra mile and visiting everyday was definitely being appreciated. For whatever reason, this night felt different.

Shrieks and growls travelled across Lake Clifton, seemingly emanating from the mine entrance. The sounds unnerved everyone in the lodgings, everyone except Tommy Joe. He had seen and heard some strange things throughout his life here in Hell, not to mention on his hunting trips out in the wilderness of Colorado. He thought back and chuckled to himself when he remembered how his brother Billy had been convinced he had seen Bigfoot. They had all laughed at him - in fact, they never did quite let him live it down. Tommy Joe and the rest of the group had heard the strange noises that his brother had spoken of, but they did not see what he saw. Billy would swear up and down that he saw a huge hairy silhouette not quite briefly enough. For the rest of that hunting trip, he had nightmares that the Sasquatch was coming for him.

Nowadays nothing fazed him. To him, it was just the 'city-ites' over exaggerating, just like they do everything else. *"A bunch of pansy ass pussies!"* he would always say in the company of his friends. Unfortunately, these 'pansy ass pussies' were the ones who paid his bills nowadays, so he had to save that kind of talk for his trips with his old hunting buddies.

But tonight the lake had a strange green hue, which could clearly be seen through the thickening squall of snowfall. Bringing the 4x4 to a halt outside one of the cabins, he cut off the vehicle, dismounted and strode towards the water's edge, snow crunching underfoot. Through the flurry he spotted a lone skiff rocking gently as it drifted towards him, the gaping mouth of the mine almost framing the spectacle. A solitary figure, as still as a waxwork dummy, stood in the boat. Squinting, Tommy Joe strained his eyes to try and identify the skiff's occupant. Reaching in to his utility jacket pocket, he pulled out his flashlight, aiming it at the lake's new resident, the beam illuminating the water now bubbling around the belly of the boat.

The demon in its mellifluous form skimmed across the lake, just hovering below the water line, past the boat and with conscious velocity, it advanced towards the oblivious caretaker standing on the lakeside.

"Hey! You in the boat! Hey!" Tommy Joe called out, causing the figure to veer towards him. Tommy Joe gasped at the illuminated skull, the pale green and blue tinge emphasising the deep black sockets which fixed their gaze onto him. He froze not with fear, no, it was something else. He was mesmerized by the sight. Over the years he had seen many things, but this, this was something new; he had never seen anything quite like this.

Tommy Joe was spellbound by the Ferryman. It was Charon, servant of Hades, guide of souls to their eternal resting place. Tommy Joe was old enough to know the stories about paying the Ferryman, he remembered from being a young boy why taking the pennies from a dead person's eyes was not a good thing to do, even if you think the pennies are there for you to take and buy candy with.

The demon hung back a little, watching as his prey was overcome with the realisation of who was coming towards him. Finally, he took his opportunity, and with great speed glided up the bank.

Tommy Joe didn't know what hit him.

Eva twitched the net curtains at the kitchen window with soapy fingers when she heard the chugging of the four-wheeler engine as it cut off outside. The snow was falling thick and fast now, like the radioactive fallout from a nuclear explosion. It reminded her of a TV show she had watched called *Threads* as a kid and got completely freaked out by the thought of surviving a nuclear blast. Tommy Joe had made her watch it, so she would be prepared in case of another world war. She was traumatised by it, and seeing the snow like that made her shiver from the inside out.

"Pops is back," she announced to everyone and no one. Drying her hands, she stood by the door, her dishcloth resting on her shoulder, waiting for her father to walk in.

A colossal explosion broke her concentration. Her children, twin girls, came running through to the kitchen screaming, fearing there had been another plane crash. They were having a meltdown, sobbing and trying to catch their breath.

"I don't like it mommy!" cried Harriet. Henrietta clung onto her sister, sobbing.

"What in the hell is that?" hollered Henry from another room.

Henry was a bit of a jerk. He drank too much and spent way too much time helping other people when he should have really been at home helping his own family. This made him look like he was a 'good guy' to everyone else apart from the people who really needed him. He didn't get up and check what was going on; instead he sat on his ass watching a movie on DVD because the cable had been blown out by the plane crash. Caring only for his own comfort would be his last mistake.

Tommy Joe groaned as his eyes shot open. He was lying on the ground in the snow just in front of the four-wheeler. Somehow, he was outside the house he shared with his family. The demon now inside him, had taken full control over Tommy Joe. He didn't realise exactly how old this vessel was and it took a while for the demon to get the body to its feet.

Feeling stronger now, the possessed Tommy Joe kicked the door wide open. He stood in the frame, his shotgun aimed at his loser son-in-law in the chair. Snow swirled around him, goading him on with his demonic task. With only four more souls left on his quota, he was eager to begin his spree, then he could go back to the mine and wait for his promotion.

His eyes burned bright, black sputum bubbling from the corners of a contorted, maniacal grin. Thick drops dribbled down from his chin, swinging from his jowls. Tommy Joe's finger squeezed the trigger unleashing both barrels of the 10 gauge into Henry's face. The headless torso of his late son-in-law sat upright in the chair, blood, brain and skull splattered across the cracked brown leather, a smoking hole situated almost perfectly in the centre of the headrest.

Hearing the shots, Eva hurriedly ushered the twins up the stairs and in to their bedroom.

"Stay in the closet, close the door and keep quiet. Do not open the door. I don't know what's going on, but I need you to promise me you will stay here until I come and get you, okay? I love you."

She gave both girls a kiss on their foreheads, and gently touched their cheeks lovingly.

"We promise, Mom," said the girls, whispering in unison as they often did. They sniffled, but still tried to be brave.

Taking in a deep breath, Eva crept in to the lounge and shivered as the arctic breeze wafted around her, only then did she see that the door was wide open. Covering her mouth, she stifled a scream, her eyes filled with tears, her stomached cramped, she reached out to steady herself on the bookcase next to her. Then came the vomit.

She wiped her mouth with the back of her hand, fighting back tears. She knew there was nothing she could do for Henry (or what was left of him). Taking timid, shaky steps, she walked over to the open door, trying not to look at her late husband any more than she had to. Closing the door, she heard a creak from upstairs.

"Oh no," she exhaled as she whispered. Her thoughts went straight to her children.

BOOM! BOOM!

Eva bounded up the stairs. She didn't make it to the top.

Smirking at the small bloody corpses of the twin girls slumped against the wall of their closet before him, their blood dripping back onto them from the hanging clothes, Tommy Joe revelled in the scene he had created. He watched as the souls billowed up from the smoking gunshot wounds in their small chests. The blood seeped out and formed puddles that were inching towards where he stood, but the souls, those were going on his tally.

His head cocked to the side admiring his latest additions, his bright eyes now glowing. The demon twitched to the sounds of the thundering footsteps accompanied by Eva's primal screams as she scrambled up the steps to her children.

From the top of the staircase, Tommy Joe shot his daughter. Eva was flung backwards by the force of the blast. He had done enough, his goal achieved it was time to leave this fleshy host and return to the mine.

Tommy Joe woke up as the screams from a nearby cabin entered his consciousness, bringing him round. Staring up at the ceiling it took him a short while to recognise his surroundings. His head throbbed as he focused on the walls. He was home; this was his living room. The open door swinging in the wind and snow swirling around, dancing like little imps. He shivered, and lacking grace, he grappled himself upright.

"Shit!"

"Eva? Eva, where are you?"

As he wrestled his way to his feet, Tommy Joe saw the headless Henry slumped in the chair. Blood and brains shimmered as they slithered down the lifeless body, pooling in the seat. Tommy Joe slipped in a puddle of vomit as he started towards the kitchen.

At his feet lay the contorted corpse of his Eva.

"Oh no. No, no, no. Oh no, Eva, my Eva."

Scooping up the lifeless body of his beloved daughter in to his arms, cries rose up from the depths of his soul and tore through his heart like a blunt sword.

Tommy Joe gently laid down his daughter on the couch. He looked over at the bloody mess of his son-in-law, and then back to his daughter. *The twins!* Panic overtook him now and he bolted upstairs and in to the girls' room.

He couldn't cry anymore. For a while he stood as lifeless as the corpses of his granddaughters which lay before him. He knew what he had to do. He picked up each grandchild and took them downstairs to the lounge and placed them next to their mother.

The corpses of his family were now placed in the lounge, on the couches as if they were settling in for movie night. The leather on his favourite chair creaked and sighed beneath his weight as Tommy Joe sank into the cowhide. With the shotgun rested on his knees, he exhaled the saddest sigh even he had ever heard. Picking up the gun he placed the end of the barrel in his mouth. The cold metallic shank filled his mouth, the taste of oil a reminder of how well he had looked after the very weapon that had ended the lives of his family, and which would now end his own. A solitary tear slipped from the gathering in the corner of his eye and slowly crept down his face. He caught sight of his reflection in the blank screen of the TV, his gaunt shadowy features blankly staring back at him. Gathering himself briefly, he glanced around him at the scene he had created from the carnage. He couldn't stand the thought of being without his family.

Not being entirely sure of what had happened, he was certain of one thing, he wanted to be with his girls once more. He wanted to spend eternity with them in heaven, and he figured this was the only way. Tommy Joe inhaled one final breath before gently squeezing the trigger.

The back of his head exploded. Splashes of blood covered the knotted wood photo frame beside him and trickled down the snapshot of the family from much happier times. Shards of skull wedged in to the ceiling above him, globules of brain dangled from the ceiling. As if in slow motion, they splattered on to the rug below.

Standing at the mouth of the mine, the demon had done what it wanted with old man Tommy Joe. His already huge grin got slightly bigger and the glow in his eyes shone slightly brighter as he heard the shot echo across the lake. He waited for the small billow of smoke that was Tommy Joe's soul to glide towards him. It was time to gather with the others and welcome the end of days.

WELCOME TO A TOWN CALLED HELL

HORROR IN HELL MINES

Could one of Hell's founding families be cursed? The Railsback family, for whom Railsback Road is named, are dealing with another tragic death, this time in the mines. Mine foreman Mr P. O'Dowd reassured reporters that this was just a freak accident and nothing at all to worry about. Ther~~ have been numerous superstitions~~ ed to T~~he~~ ~~family~~ going ~~back to~~ five years ~~ago this is believed to be just another of the many unfortunate accidents befalling Hell's~~ founding f~~amilies~~

For the Love of A Father
Justin Zimmerman

Monday

Jacob Dawson shivered as he stepped outside the Hell Sports Gym and Recreation Centre. As he trudged through the snow toward his car, he pictured Rebecca Jenkins in the red bathing suit that hugged every curve of her body. When he first found out she was going to be a lifeguard he almost fainted. When he learned they would be working the same shift he felt like he was having a heart attack. On her first day of work she took a seat on the guard chair across from him and he struggled to take his eyes off her.

He swept the snow off the windshield of his beat up pile of a car and climbed inside. The engine sputtered and whined in the cold, but started. He began the drive home and the thoughts swimming through his mind changed. A vision of Rebecca summoning him transformed into a hulking man with long, brown and grey hair and a thick beard that matched the hair on his head.

He was thinking about his father.

Robert Dawson was a constant source of embarrassment for his son and the latest incident at the church made Jacob want to leave Hell forever. When Pastor John asked if any parishioner would like to address the congregation that Sunday, Jacob wasn't shocked when his father raised his hand. He remembered the pastor's eyes widening behind his thick glasses and knew the old man was pleased. Robert, thanks to his station as assistant manager of the grocery store, knew just about everyone in town and would often praise one of the customers or employees of the store in front of the church. He would praise a customer for helping someone reach an item on a tall shelf. He'd praise an employee for making a crying child smile. These proclamations were almost always short and met with polite applause and a round of 'bless his or her heart' from the pews.

In the past few weeks, Jacob noticed a change in his father while in church. Robert would sing louder than before, his deep voice drowning out those around him. At times he would tear up while singing and Jacob could hear him snort and sob the lyrics. When the pastor asked them to bow their heads and pray, Jacob would steal a glance at Robert and see a man in deep concentration, his brow furrowed and eyes pinched shut.

In Jacob's mind, his performance at St Jude's yesterday was a step beyond. Robert strode to the pulpit and offered a slight nod to the pastor before he began. He leaned on the lectern and Jacob wondered how it didn't break under the man's substantial weight. It started normal enough. He asked the others how they were feeling on another wonderful day in God's kingdom. He motioned toward his wife, Mary, and son and said that he thanks God every day for them. That was when the normalcy of the speech ended.

"Friends," he said as he stroked his beard. "There is a sickness here in Hell. It is the sickness of latency. It is the sickness of agnosticism. The sickness of atheism."

He scanned the room, eyes narrow, sweat beading his forehead.

"I see a lot of people here I didn't see last week. And I

don't see a lot of people I did."

The pastor, standing just behind Robert, grinned and nodded.

"I believe there is a reason my lovely wife, Mary, and I moved here some eighteen years ago. And I don't believe it was to manage the Piggly Wiggly."

Polite, somewhat apprehensive laughter permeated the crowd.

"No, friends. I believe my arrival in Hell was more spiritual, more divine, in nature. I believe our almighty wanted, nay needed, me to be here to spread His word to His flock. To bring as much of His flock back to the fold as possible."

The grin vanished from the pastor's face as his territory was infringed.

"Now, Pastor John is a fine man who does wonderful things here in the church."

This was met with a smattering of applause.

"But I see you in your day to day," he said as he pointed around the church. "I see you when you aren't in your Sunday best. I see what you bring home from my store."

"Thank you, Robert," Pastor John said as he moved toward the podium.

Robert turned and stared at the much smaller man. After what seemed to be an interminable amount of time, the pastor returned to his spot behind Robert.

"I see you with alcohol and tobacco. I see you purchase prophylactics and other products meant for fornication. I see men and women stand in front of the magazine racks with lust in their eyes as they stare at the near naked bodies on the covers."

A murmur started and became louder among the assembled worshippers. Robert held up his hand and spoke louder.

"Friends, there is a wickedness growing in Hell. I believe the founders of this town knew what they were doing when they gave their new home that name. They knew that one day this town, and the people who inhabit it, would be on the brink of eternal damnation. They knew it because they were holy enough to receive His word and they named the town Hell to serve as a warning."

Jacob didn't think that was true. He thought the name was because of the old mine they called the 'Mouth of Hell' and that the name was kept to attract tourists. The town was flooded with them every summer. They would come to hike and fish, but he thought most of them came to Hell as a joke. They would post pictures on Twitter and Facebook with captions like, "For everyone that told me to go to Hell, I took your advice," and, "Meet me in Hell." They would buy neon coloured t-shirts at the pop-up souvenir stands with clever sayings like, "I'm so bad I got kicked out of Hell," and, "I spent my summer in Hell."

He slumped in his seat as he looked around the church, wishing he could tunnel his way through the floor. He saw some shocked expressions, but he also saw some nodding heads.

"I am here to tell you, friends, we are on the brink. Soon, we will face the wrath of the Almighty God unless we change our hedonistic ways. Brothers and sisters, I hope and pray every day that it is not too late, but I am not sure my prayers will be answered."

Mary sat, listening to her husband, with a slight grin. She was a woman of few words and Jacob knew that, even if she disagreed with what he was saying, she would never speak against his father.

"The end is nigh," Robert said as he leaned back from the podium. "As the Good Book says, 'the present heavens and earth are reserved for fire, being kept for the day of judgement and destruction of ungodly men.' Repent, brothers and sisters. Repent."

Jacob remembered the heat emanating from his cheeks as his father walked, chest out and held tilted back, to where he and his mother were seated. The silence and stares from those around him made Jacob feel as though he was being crushed under the weight of a giant boulder.

The pastor stumbled back to the lectern and stammered his way through the beginning of his sermon. The rest of the morning's service felt like a blur.

After a silent drive home from church, Jacob told his parents he needed to go to his room to study even though he didn't have any homework and there were no exams at school to prepare for. Instead, he chatted with friends online and watched a horror movie on Netflix.

When it was time to join his parents for dinner, he ate in a hurry and excused himself to his room to continue studying.

As he walked up the stairs, his father called out his usual refrain.

"God loves you, son."

Yeah, Jacob thought. But what about you.

He couldn't remember his father ever saying a simple 'I love you' to him, his mother, or anyone. It was always prefaced with God, as if the man wasn't capable of love without help.

Jacob parked his car at the end of the driveway, knocked his snow caked boots against the side of the house, and stepped through the back door. He hoped that his father would be distracted by something and Jacob could make it upstairs without going through the usual rigmarole of questions about his day.

The house was quiet and dark. He climbed the stairs to the second floor and noticed his parents' bedroom door was open. On most days, the door stayed shut and it was rare for Jacob to ever see into, let alone set foot in, the master bedroom. He rapped his knuckles against the door and peeked in. His mother lay on the bed. Her eyes, half closed and distant, fixed on him and she managed a languid wave.

"Good night, Mom," he said as he left her room.

Once he was showered and changed, he went down stairs in search of food. He saw a light on in the living room and another in his father's den. As much as he didn't want to see or talk to him, Jacob knew he would hear about it tomorrow if he didn't tell his father he was home.

He crept down the hallway and became aware of a low murmuring coming from the den. At times the murmuring grew louder and he was able to decipher some of what the man was saying. He could make out 'canned goods' and 'no time.'

Jacob placed a hand against the wall and leaned forward to peer around the door. Inside, he saw his father pacing back and forth across the dirty, once white carpet of the den. He held a bible in one hand, a finger stuck inside marking a page. In his other hand was a pen which he used to scribble something on a yellow legal pad on his desk.

The thumping in his chest was so loud he feared his father might hear. He saw the man pace once again toward the fireplace and lay his head on the mantle. Jacob thought he could hear quiet sobs coming from him as he rested below the framed sword which hung above the fireplace.

Jacob always loved that sword with its shiny, black handle and the small crosses etched on the blade. As a boy he wanted nothing more than to remove it from its frame and play with it. He never understood the inscription below the sword. A pewter plate mounted to the stained wood frame read, "Should evil come upon us, the sword, or judgement, or pestilence, or famine, we will stand before this house and before You and cry to You in our distress, and You will hear and deliver us."

Robert lifted his head from the mantle with a high pitched gasp. He dropped to the floor, set the bible next to him, clasped his hands together, and prayed. He shook and swayed as he did and, while Jacob couldn't hear what he was saying, he knew better than to interrupt. He crept back down the hall, up the stairs, and retreated to his room.

Tuesday

The sound of boots stomping down the hall pulled Jacob from a deep and restful slumber. As he tried to blink the sleep from his eyes, his bedroom door flew open and his father burst into the room. Jacob reflexively grabbed his bed sheet and pulled it close.

"Son," his father said with wide, wild eyes. "A plane crashed. It took out the bridge. I need you to prepare the basement."

"What? A plane? Prepare? Prepare for what?"

"Just make room on the shelves. I'll be back as soon as I can. God loves you, son."

Robert hurried out of the room and Jacob collapsed back on his pillow. He let his father's words wash over him. Plane crash? Could it be true? He reached for his phone. There were no texts or emails which was not a surprise. He stayed up late messaging with friends online and assumed most of them were still sleeping.

He tapped open the internet browser to try to find information about the crash. A message appeared that read, 'Cannot connect to Internet.' He looked at the top left corner of the touchscreen and saw the words 'No Service.'

He got out of bed and went to his laptop. As he waited for the computer to start up, the possibility that what his father said was true began to gnaw at him. His heart beat faster in his chest and his legs shook as his need for information grew.

If it was true and a plane destroyed the bridge, everyone in town would be stuck. The bridge that spanned the River Styx was the only way into or out of Hell. The simple way of life he had known would be thrown into upheaval for the foreseeable future. The clean-up and construction would take months and the town might never recover from the loss of life. In a small town, every death is felt. If there were any residents on the bridge when the plane hit, the town would mourn them for a long time.

Please tell me Rebecca was not on the bridge, he thought.

Although there was no reason for her to be there, he couldn't stop his mind from going to the worst possible place. He checked his phone again only to find that it was still no more use than a brightly coloured brick.

The computer finished warming up and Jacob pounded the mouse to open the browser. Another message about no internet connection and he fought off the need to scream.

He bolted out of the room and ran down the stairs. He wanted to check the modem which was in the den.

He ran through the kitchen and then stopped. His mother sat at the kitchen table, a mug of coffee in front of her as she stared at the falling snow.

"Morning," he said.

When she didn't respond he tried his greeting again. Her head turned to him so slowly he lost patience and continued toward the den.

The lights on the front of the modem were lit with the exception of one, the light that indicated there was internet service. He turned the modem in his hands to check the cable connections when a dull, loud boom made him freeze in place. Was it another plane? Was it a terrorist attack?

He ran to the living room and saw, through the picture window, a large cloud of black smoke rising over the houses and into the grey sky above.

He stood rooted in place, watching the smoke, when an SUV burst into view. The black truck almost slid passed the driveway as the driver slammed on the brakes, righted course, and then gunned it up the slight incline toward the garage. He heard the door of the truck slam shut just moments before the back door of the house was ripped open.

"Son," his father yelled.

Jacob ambled into the kitchen and saw his father holding the door open with one leg while his arms clung to a large cardboard box.

"Hurry up, boy. Take this."

Jacob nearly crumbled under the weight of the box.

"What is this?"

"Take it downstairs and come back. There's more."

Jacob lugged the heavy box to the basement stairs and felt as though he would fall as he climbed down. When he reached the bottom, the box slipped from his grip and the sound of metal clanging together echoed throughout the unfinished basement. He flipped the light switch and rows of grey, metal shelves were illuminated. He never liked the basement. It made him feel as though his father was constructing a grocery store in their house. Shelf after shelf and row after row was stacked with canned foods, bottled water, batteries, and everything else one would need to survive the apocalypse.

He ripped open the box expecting to find more canned peaches and devilled ham. When he saw what was inside, his head jerked away from the box as though it contained poisonous snakes. It was filled with stacks of smaller boxes of bullets and shells.

"Jacob. Let's go, son."

He tore himself away from the box and went back upstairs. He saw a tower of four heavy looking boxes just inside the back door. Robert was removing his boots when he looked at his son.

"Let's hurry. There's a lot to do."

"What's happening? Did you find out anything about the crash?"

"No time for questions. Take these boxes downstairs. You'll arrange the items on the shelves later. When you're done, meet me in the den."

Jacob pulled the top one off the stack and headed for the basement. He was relieved that it was lighter than the last one. He set it next to the first box and ripped it open. He sighed when he saw it was just cans of soup.

After he finished moving the boxes, Jacob headed to the den. His father was kneeling in the middle of the floor.

Without opening his eyes, Robert said, "Pray with me, son."

Jacob knelt next to him and clasped his hands together. He thought more about Rebecca. She lived just two blocks over, but he had never been to her house.

"Amen," Robert said and then groaned as he stood up. "Get dressed. We have to go check on the neighbours."

For a moment, Jacob thought there might be something to this praying stuff. This could be just the excuse he needed to go to Rebecca's.

After they pulled on their boots and bundled up, Robert led the way and Jacob shut the back door behind them.

"What was that other sound I heard? It sounded like an explosion. Was there another plane?" Jacob asked as they marched down the driveway.

"Not another plane. I think it was probably one of the gas stations. Heard some people at the store talking about how Duffy's was on fire after the plane hit."

They went to the house next door and went up the front steps. Robert knocked on the door and an elderly woman wrapped in a blanket opened it. Frances McGovern peered at them through the thick lenses of her bifocals.

"Why hello, Robert. What can I do for you?"

"Oh no, Mrs McGovern. We're here to see if we can do anything for you."

"No, we're fine, dear. But my telephone doesn't seem to be working."

"Yes, ours as well. Would you and Bill like to come to our house? We have plenty of food and supplies."

"That's kind of you, but we're fine."

"I don't think you are, ma'am. I haven't seen you at church in quite a while."

The woman's eyes flew wide and her mouth opened, but she said nothing.

"I have been watching the signs for a long time, Frances. I believe we are experiencing the second coming."

"Dad," Jacob said.

Robert turned and glared his son into silence.

"It's only a plane crash, dear," Frances said. "It will be difficult to be cut off from the world for a bit, but we'll make out alright."

"I'm afraid you're quite wrong about that. You have let your faith lapse and you will be judged for it."

Jacob became aware that his mouth was hanging open as he listened to his father. The woman looked shocked as well as she moved back from the door and started to close it. Robert put his arm out to hold the door open.

"It's not too late for you or your husband," he said before stepping back.

She let out a huff and slammed the door.

"What was that?" Jacob said.

"Some people have a hard time with the truth, son," Robert said, heading back toward the sidewalk.

Jacob followed his father, staring at his back. He was dumbfounded. Robert was always kind to their neighbours in the past. He was as helpful and friendly as anyone could hope for. Now, even his walk was different. There was a purposefulness to his stride and his voice was deeper, more booming than before.

Around his father's broad shoulders, Jacob could see Eric O'Brien shovelling his driveway. Robert waved at the man and Eric stopped shovelling and waved back. O'Brien was about the same age as Robert and he and his wife, Doreen, were constant figures at the church.

"Robert, Jacob," the man said as they approached. "Hear about the crash? Awful news that is."

"Yes, Eric," Robert said. "I know all about it."

Eric placed his hand on Robert's shoulder and smiled.

"I wanted to thank you for what you said in church. I couldn't agree with you more. The number of people who have left the church troubles me."

Robert nodded.

"And I think we are beginning to pay for it."

Eric's smile vanished.

"What do you mean?"

"What's happened here today is only the beginning. The crash, the explosion are merely warning shots being fired by the Almighty. Judgment is coming."

Jacob felt he was going to be sick as he listened. What happened to his father? The man was always religious, but this was crazy.

"I think that's a little -"

"A little what?" Robert said. "Drastic? Brother, you've seen the signs as I have. You said it yourself. People are leaving the church. They have abandoned Him. He is a loving God, a merciful God, but He is also a vengeful God. What better place to display His wrath than a town called Hell?"

Eric stared at his neighbour wide eyed. Jacob thought he could relate to the man. That he must find all of this end of the world talk to be ridiculous. Then the man spoke again.

"So what do we do?"

Robert put his arm around the smaller man's shoulder.

"Join me, brother. Help me to warn others and tell them to come to my home. I have plenty of food. We can discuss what needs to be done to prepare for His coming. Then, we will pray together. God will hear us devote ourselves to Him and He will know to spare us."

"I will," said Eric.

He stuck his shovel in the snow, shook Robert's hand, and made his way across the street. Robert watched the man with a wide grin on his face like a proud father watching his child walk toward the stage on graduation day.

The rest of the day dragged on as they lumbered through the snow. Jacob stood on the sidewalk as Robert approached each door. If anyone answered, Robert would launch into his speech about the end of days. Sometimes the door would slam shut and Robert would walk back toward Jacob yelling over his shoulder about how the people in the house needed to repent before it was too late. Sometimes the door would stay open and there would be handshakes and hugs and even prayers before Robert would walk away from the house grinning like a fool.

They turned a corner and Jacob realized they were on Rebecca's street. The blue and white two story house was on the other side and Jacob stared at it as his father went door to door, proselytizing. There were more slammed doors, more hugs, and Jacob kept his eyes on the house, trying to decide which window looked into her bedroom. They had been walking through the snow for hours, but the minutes that passed before they reached her door seemed to last even longer.

There was no car in the driveway and no lights on in the house. Jacob wanted nothing more than to run to the house ahead of his father. He wanted to see if she was safe. He also wanted to warn her and her family about what his father was going to say.

His heart pounded as Robert kicked his way through the deep snow on the front walk. By the time his father reached the front door, Jacob felt like he would pass out. Robert rang the doorbell. When no one answered, he pounded on the door. The street was quiet and Jacob felt every one of those knocks like it was happening inside his skull.

He felt both relief and fear when Robert gave up and turned toward him. Relief because she wouldn't see his father and have to be face to face with an overzealous weirdo. Fear because he didn't know where she was or if she was safe. He stomped through the snow, cursing himself for never having the guts to talk to her, to tell her how he felt. He hoped the internet would be working when he got home. He became aware that his father was calling his name and turned around to see him stretching his back and looking up at the darkening grey sky.

"Well, son, I think we've done all we can for today. Let's head home. Folks will be coming over soon."

He sighed with relief as they headed for home. Robert put his arm around his son's shoulders and smiled.

"Dad, is it okay if I run ahead? I want to see if Mom is okay."

"She's fine, son."

"Yeah, but I just want to see."

Robert looked at him and sighed.

"Go on. I'll see you in a minute."

The snow crunched under his boots as he ran. He raced through the back door and pounded his boots together, knocking off snow and ice. He took the stairs two at a time and slammed his bedroom door shut behind him. Fumbling with his phone for a moment, he was able to gain control of his frozen fingers long enough to unlock the device.

Again, he saw the words, "No Service." He sat down at his computer and was not surprised when he couldn't get online. He threw himself face down on his bed and heard his father entering the house.

Jacob awoke, unsure of how long he slept. His stomach grumbled as he ambled out of his bedroom. Approaching the stairs he heard voices from the main floor of the house. The stairs creaked as he descended and, as he entered the kitchen, he could see people from the neighbourhood gathered in the living room. Bob and Nancy Peake sat on the couch next to Eric and Doreen O'Brien. Robert was in his recliner and Jacob's mother sat in a fold out chair in the corner of the room. In the loveseat was Carl Lancaster and his wife, Leslie.

He went to the fridge to find something to quiet his complaining stomach and tried to listen to the conversation. Having spent the day listening to Robert preach, he knew what it would be about.

"Most of the people in this town are blind," Robert said. "Blind to what is happening around them, what has been happening for years."

"Well, of course they are," a man that sounded like Eric O'Brien said. "Everybody nowadays just wants to be left alone. They want to get home from work, watch TV, play on the computer, and go to sleep. They don't want to change their ways to better serve God."

A murmur of agreement spread through the house.

Jacob scooped some leftover Mac n Cheese into a bowl and placed it in the microwave. He thought about how, not long ago, his father was one of those guys sitting on the couch watching TV and not thinking about God twenty-four seven. He liked that Robert much better than this one.

"We can't give up."

Jacob wasn't sure who was speaking, but thought that it may have been Carl.

"There has to be more people who would be willing to join us."

"We walked this entire neighbourhood just like the rest of you," possibly Doreen O'Brien said. "People just stared at us like we were nuts."

A chorus of voices echoed similar experiences and the voices grew louder with frustration until Robert spoke.

"They will listen. Just like that poor teacher at the elementary school. She knew what was coming. The war to end all wars. There will be more events, more things that can't be explained. Then, the latent will turn to God and we must forgive them their trespasses."

"Amen," a few people said.

The microwave dinged and Jacob took his bowl to his room and closed the door.

Wednesday

Jacob felt the side of his bed sag and opened his eyes to see his father sitting next to him.

"We have to talk, son," Robert said. "I know you lied to me yesterday."

Jacob blinked and shook his head.

"What? What are you talking about?"

"When you said you wanted to check on your mother. That was a lie."

Jacob looked into the accusing eyes of his father.

"I know it was not a big lie, but with judgement coming any sin must be avoided at all costs."

Jacob could only manage to shake his head some more.

"Remember, son, honour thy father and mother."

The bed rose as Robert stood. When he was out of the room, Jacob continued staring at the door where the man's large frame had been a moment before.

What is happening, he thought as he turned to face the wall and closed his eyes.

Sometime later Jacob untangled himself from his bedding and stood up. Peeking through the blinds, he saw wet, heavy looking snowflakes falling against a grey sky.

In the hall, he could hear frantic, excited voices.

"But I don't remember that from the Bible," someone said.

"Believe in me, brother," Robert said. "It is there."

"Well," a woman's voice said. "Why is it here now?"

"Don't you see?" asked Robert. "This is where the final battle will take place. A war between good and evil; heaven and hell; God and the devil."

"That's a lot to take from a rumour of a three-headed dog up in the woods."

"It's no rumour. It is happening and we must prepare."

"What do we do?"

"Go forth and gather as many believers as possible. Bring them here. Because we believe in Him, He will believe in us. Hurry, my brothers and sisters."

Chairs squeaked against the tile floor of the kitchen and Jacob could hear people standing and moving around the room. Robert asked for everyone to join hands and pray and, after a prayer was muttered that Jacob couldn't make out, a chorus of 'amens' sounded.

Once he heard the people in the kitchen leave, Jacob walked down the stairs. Robert was standing next to the table, gazing out the window. He was wearing a plush, red bathrobe and he stroked his beard while watching as the O'Briens, Peakes, and Lancasters fanned out across the neighbourhood.

"Good morning, son," Robert said without turning.

"What's going on?"

"One of the hounds of hell was spotted in the woods."

Jacob didn't know how to handle what he just heard.

"An unholy three-headed beast now roams God's earth," Robert continued then turned to face his son. "The day of reckoning will soon be at hand."

Jacob looked into his father's eyes and couldn't remember the last time he had seen him so excited.

"We have much to do, son. Many more of my people will be arriving before nightfall."

"Your people?"

"Yes, son. They will bring their families and we will pray and sing together so loud that the Almighty Himself will hear us."

As he spoke, Robert looked up at the ceiling and raised his arms out like he was forming a cross.

"Gather as many blankets as you can and bring them to the living room. We will also need more wood for the fire. Rush upstairs and prepare for the day, my son."

Jacob could only furrow his brow and stare at the man. He thought about telling him off, telling him that he was delusional, and asking what God would think knowing how much Robert was enjoying other people's misery. Instead, he turned and ran up the stairs.

When he heard his father leave the kitchen, Jacob crept to the door of the master bedroom. He turned the knob, trying to not make any noise and stepped inside.

His mother was still sleeping.

"Mom," he whispered as he approached the bed.

She didn't move. He stepped to the side of the bed and snapped his fingers next to her ear. She let out a slight groan, but her eyes remained shut. He looked at the nightstand and opened the drawer. It shook with the weight of its contents and the sound of pills and bottles could be heard. He pulled one of the bottles out of the drawer. Prozac. Another read Zoloft. There were others with names Jacob couldn't pronounce. The drawer was filled with full, half-full, and almost empty bottles of pills. He slid the drawer shut.

His mother stared at him, her eyes wider than he had seen them in a long time.

"Mom," he said with a start. "Mom, you have to get up. There's something going on with Dad."

She said nothing.

"Please. You have to talk to him. He's acting crazy like he thinks he's some holy man now or something."

Still, nothing.

Jacob felt his throat tighten and sting. He wanted to scream at her to stand up, to say something. He sighed, looked into her eyes again, then walked away.

He piled blankets on the couch in the living room. Robert was in the den. Jacob could hear him talking to himself. It might've been praying but Jacob didn't think so. The talking was interrupted by the sound of a pen scribbling on paper.

He pulled on his boots and coat and stepped out the back door. Large white flakes fell fast and heavy from the darkening sky as he trudged through the snow-covered backyard toward the woodpile. He gathered as many logs as he could carry and turned to the house.

He thought about Rebecca again. He imagined himself bursting through her front door and finding her family in trouble. He could picture himself as the hero. The kiss she gave him in his mind was so sweet, so tender that he closed his eyes as he crunched his way through the deep snow.

A far off, booming noise ripped him out of his daydream. His heart leapt to his throat as he scanned the sky above the trees looking for evidence of another explosion. Even with no perceivable, visible threat, he felt the need to be inside, away from the elements.

The door flew open and Robert stood in front of him, silhouetted by the light and warmth of the kitchen. Jacob hurried inside.

"Did you hear that?" he asked.

"I did," Robert said.

"What was it?"

"Another event. Another sign."

Robert moved to the window. He clasped his hands together.

"Dear Lord in Heaven, hallowed be thy name. Please guide our people back to us. Please spare them Your wrath. Please allow them to return to me, to this house which You have blessed. With all my heart, I love You. Amen."

Jacob felt melting snow drip down his hair and face and onto the floor. He knew he would have to mop it up later, but he couldn't bring himself to move. He glared at the man in front of him. Robert's hands were still clasped and his eyes still pinched shut. Jacob struggled to remember a time when he actually wanted his father to tell him he loved him. He tried to envision the man in the kitchen as being his father and failed. This was a stranger and Jacob wanted to be far away from him.

He hung up his wet coat on the rack near the backdoor and gathered the wood he had dropped. Robert remained in the kitchen. The praying was over but he stood motionless in front of the window, staring out into the snow.

He added the wood to the pile next to the fireplace in the den. He looked at the yellow pad of paper on the desk and saw a sketch of a cross with dimensions for height, length, and width. He sneaked through the kitchen. By the time he shut his bedroom door his mind was made up. He was going to leave.

He didn't know where he would go. The first stop would be Rebecca's, that was obvious. He then thought about two of his friends, David and Trent. Trent's house was closer, but in all the years he knew him, Trent had never invited him over. Maybe he wasn't welcome. He decided on David's, which would be a struggle in the storm but at least he would be away from his father.

He didn't think Robert would even notice he was gone.

A chorus of voices reciting the Lord's Prayer disturbed his vision and he felt his face flush as his anger surged. He stomped his way to the door with the intention of ripping it open and slamming it shut. He stopped when his hand touched the cool brass of the knob. Everyone would hear it of course. They might even stop mid-prayer. He thought that would only force a confrontation with Robert and he didn't want that. He wanted nothing to do with whoever that man was.

He threw himself on his bed. As he closed his eyes, he began plotting his escape.

He blinked his eyes as they adjusted to the soft light from the lamp on his nightstand.

"Jacob," a woman's voice said.

He turned and found himself face to face with Monica Price, David's mother.

"Your father sent me to get you. He wants you to join us downstairs."

The raven-haired woman turned to the door and stood, holding it open.

He grumbled as he stood. If she was here, David must be as well.

He followed her downstairs. A group of women were assembled in the kitchen, preparing food. He saw his mother sitting at the kitchen table, looking as though she, too, was pulled from her bed. Her eyes flickered as he went passed her and her head turned to follow him.

In the living room were the children. Kids as young as two and as old as seventeen sat, played, and talked all around him. He saw David standing near the entrance to the den.

"Hey," David said when he saw him.

"What're you doing here?"

"Didn't you hear? It's the apocalypse," David said and rolled his eyes.

"So, why are you here? What's wrong with your house?"

Jacob became aware of a tremble in his voice and hoped that David wouldn't notice that his hands were shaking.

"Beats the hell outta me. Mr O'Brien came over and talked to my parents for a while. Next thing I know, my parents are packing up some stuff and dragging me and my sister over here."

"Have you heard from Rebecca?" he asked.

"No. Why would I? Dude, are you still crushing on her? Think there are bigger things to worry about now."

David took a step toward the den.

"Listen."

Jacob moved to stand beside David, as his father preached to his flock.

"We will be safe here. Our Lord has blessed this house. I have envisioned the end of days, the destruction of ungodly men. The beast from hell in the woods was Satan's first strike. Now we hear talk of black winged creatures in the sky. God will answer him soon and it will be a powerful, vengeful blow."

His words were met with murmurs of agreement from the other men crowded into the den. Jacob didn't think he could stomach another syllable.

"Hey," he said to David. "You wanna get out of here? We could crash at your place."

"What are you talking about? You've heard what everyone is saying. We need to stay here and pray for forgiveness."

Jacob took a step back. He shook his head as if he was trying to clear water from his ears. David stared back at him with squinted, confused eyes. Jacob turned to walk away.

"Dude, where are you going? We're going to sing hymns soon."

Jacob hurried back to his room. He slammed the door figuring that Robert was too busy preaching to pay attention to him. He wanted to grab some clothes, stuff them into his backpack, and leave. He wondered if anyone would say anything. Thinking that they might, he made up his mind to wait until early morning before attempting his escape.

Thursday

The room was black when Jacob opened his eyes. He checked his useless phone and saw that it was just before 4:00am. He was careful to not make much noise as he pulled on his clothes.

The creak of his bedroom door seemed as subtle as a shotgun blast in the silence of the early morning. He was sure that every step he took on the stairs would wake Robert and he would be forced to create a story for why he was creeping down the stairs fully dressed with a backpack full of clothes.

He stood by the back door, pulling on his coat, and expecting to see Robert rushing down the stairs at him. When we was about to put on his boots, he looked through the kitchen toward the living room. There were people sleeping on the couch, on the floor, sitting in chairs. Through the window he could see the parking lot his snowy street had become. It was filled with pickup trucks and SUVs.

With his boots on, he slung the backpack over his shoulder and opened the door. He pulled it shut behind him and winced when it clicked. He sighed and took his first steps down the driveway.

A shadowy figure moved toward him. Jacob stopped where he was, eyes wide and heart jackhammering in his chest.

"Turn around, son," Carl Lancaster said. "Go on back in the house."

Carl stepped closer and Jacob could see he was cradling an automatic rifle in his arms.

"I pulled the early shift for the watch and your father asked me to be on the lookout for you. He heard you wanted to leave."

Jacob cursed David under his breath. He looked at the gun the man was carrying, but was sure that he wasn't in danger.

"Look, I know my father told you to keep me here, but I have to go. I have to check on my friend. I haven't heard from her since Monday and I'm worried something's wrong."

"It ain't my rodeo. I'm just a cowboy. So, please, go back in the house and get some rest."

Jacob felt his knees and hands tremble. Who was this man to give him an order? He needed to see Rebecca. He needed to get away from his father and this guy wasn't going to stop him.

He stared into Carl's eyes and took a step around him toward the street.

"Son," Carl said.

He took another step.

"Jacob."

Another step.

The gun was in his face so fast Jacob almost fell to the ground. He looked into the long, black barrel of the menacing piece of hardware.

"Don't make me do it, boy. I'm told to stop you by any means necessary," Carl said, pushing the gun even closer to Jacob's face. "It's for your own good, son."

Jacob tried to swallow, but his mouth was dry and he felt his throat catch. He turned back to the house. He could hear the crunching of snow every time Carl took a step and knew the gun was pointed at his back.

The back door opened and light from the kitchen poured out over the snowy landscape. A large figure stepped into the light, casting a long shadow over the backyard. Jacob didn't need to look up to know who it was.

"Thank you, Brother Carl," Robert said.

"He said he needed to go see some girl," said Carl.

Jacob stared at his boots, almost buried in the snow covered driveway.

"You have lust in your heart?" Robert asked as if the idea was somehow foreign to him. "Come inside, son. I need your help in the basement."

Robert held his backpack and helped him out of his coat. When his boots were off, Robert pointed toward the basement. Jacob, unable to meet the man's stare, walked down the stairs in silence.

Five men stood in the middle of the dimly lit basement. He recognized some of them, others he didn't know. One of them, Bob Peake, was holding onto a thick length of rope.

Jacob heard the sound of his father stepping onto the concrete floor. He turned to look at him, hoping to see some semblance of the man he once called dad.

"This is for you own good, son," Robert said as two of them stepped toward Jacob.

They grabbed him by the arms and began dragging him to the shelves. Jacob cried out.

"The devil is in your heart, Jacob," Robert said.

The other two men grabbed his legs and turned his back to the metal shelves.

"As your father, I must protect you in your time of need."

Jacob yelped in pain as the men dropped him on concrete while still holding onto his limbs.

"You are a heretic. A non-believer," Robert's voice grew louder.

The men held his legs to the floor and extended his arms to the side.

"But you are my son and I will not forsake you to a life of eternal damnation."

Bob used a folding knife to saw the rope in two. He moved to Jacob's left arm and wrapped the rope around his wrist. He pulled Jacob's arm back further and he called out in pain.

"I will help you, my son," Robert's voice grew quiet and he stepped across the room, closer to the men. "I will save your soul."

Bob tied the rope around one strut of the heavy, grey metal shelves and pulled tight. He moved to the other side and started the process again.

"Lord," Robert said, hands clasped and eyes closed. "Forgive my son as You have forgiven me and all of my children. He is weak and easily tempted by the wares of the devil."

Jacob screamed as Bob finished tying off his right arm.

"Spare him, O Lord. I, Your most humble servant, will deliver him into Your arms as a true believer. With all my heart I love You, God. Amen."

The men, satisfied with their work, stood and walked toward the steps. Robert looked down at his son. Jacob's chest heaved and throat burned. He choked back a sob and begged himself not to cry. He didn't want to give the man the satisfaction, the proof that he was weak.

Robert continued to stare and Jacob could swear he saw the corners of his mouth turn up in a slight grin before he turned and stomped his way up the stairs.

Hours passed and Jacob could hear movement above him. The day had begun and people were shuffling about the house in a flurry of activity. He drifted in and out of consciousness, but snapped to attention when he heard a creaking from the stairs.

Monica Price came down the stairs and Jacob was more than a little dismayed that she wasn't shocked to see him, tied up and in pain. She walked to one of the shelves near him and reached for canned peaches. When she had her item she turned to face him.

"Your father loves you a lot, y'know. You're very lucky. He's a great man and he's saving all of us."

Jacob hung his head. When he heard her go back up the stairs, he sighed and tried pulling at the ropes again. They were too tight and the shelf was too heavy to move. He felt tears well up and he allowed himself to sob.

More hours went by and on occasion someone would come to the basement. It was always a woman getting some ingredient from off the shelves. They were always silent until they had their item and were ready to return to the kitchen. Then, they would turn to him and tell him how Robert was doing God's work, how blessed he was, how blessed they all were.

Jacob wanted to scream and curse at them. Instead, he would lean his head back and listen until they walked away. Then, he would cry again and resist the urge to pray.

Friday

"Jacob," a voice said.

He heard the voice and, thinking he was dreaming, kept his eyes shut.

"Jacob," it said again and this time he knew it was real.

He opened his eyes and looked at the frail form of his mother. She was dressed in a white sweater and blue jeans and Jacob tried to remember the last time he had seen her not wearing a robe and pyjamas.

"It's okay. I'm here," she said.

Her green eyes were filled with tears and Jacob thought she seemed lucid for the first time in a long time.

"Oh, baby, I'm sorry."

The relief of seeing someone besides Robert or his followers washed away. He fought off tears and glared at her.

"I'm going to get you out of here, okay? You and I are going to leave tonight."

He continued glaring.

"I know you're upset. I know you probably hate me. I know I've been selfish. It's just that I've been so unhappy for so long. I've been so angry at your father. Angry at him for making us move here. Even angrier for making me stay."

Her tears ran down her cheeks as she spoke.

"It was easy to take the pills. It made life seem like a blur, like a dream. I know I've been a terrible mother, but I want to change that."

The sound of footsteps above made her pause. She looked to the ceiling. When she spoke again, she whispered.

"They don't know I'm down here. They think I'm still on the pills. I've been wandering around up there pretending, acting like I don't know what's going on."

She knelt down next to him.

"He's losing it. People are starting to talk behind his back and he's getting paranoid. People are doubting him. I don't know why anyone would believe him in the first place. I don't think he's ever read the bible all the way through. He's making mistakes and a lot of them are talking about leaving."

"How are we going to get passed his guards?" Jacob asked.

"I'll figure that out. For now, try to rest."

She walked to one of the shelves and returned with a plastic water bottle and snack crackers. She held the bottle for him and he gulped down the entire thing. She fed him the crackers and he almost bit her fingers trying to get them in his mouth.

"I'll be back tonight when they've gone to sleep."

She turned and went for the stairs.

"I love you, Jacob," she whispered and walked up.

Saturday

A loud chorus of excited voices woke Jacob. The burning pain in his shoulders had spread to his hands and he tried to move his fingers but couldn't. In the darkened basement, he strained to hear what was happening upstairs. There was yelling and he even thought he heard someone crying.

Robert's voice boomed louder than the rest but it wasn't possible to make out all of the words. It was clear he was upset, though. Then, his voice rang out like a thunder clap.

"I have spoken," he yelled.

There was a brief silence before another round of commotion. More feet shuffling through the kitchen, more excited voices.

The basement lights flicked on and there was loud stomping coming from the stairs. It was the same men who had tied Jacob up days before. They hurried to Jacob and began untying the knots from the shelf.

"Your father would like to see you, son," John O'Brien said.

The men closest to his arms tried to help Jacob to his feet, but his legs failed him and he slumped back to the floor. They each put one of his arms around their shoulders and dragged him up the stairs.

He blinked against the harsh lights of the kitchen. As he looked around, he could see the disaster the place had turned into. There were plates, both glass and paper, everywhere and empty cans of food overflowed from the garbage.

They dragged him to the living room and Jacob saw his father for the first time since he allowed the men to leave him trapped in the basement like an unwanted pet.

Robert was still dressed in the bathrobe. His hair was wild and matched the bushiness of his unkempt beard. His eyes were wide and, when he spoke, it was almost a growl.

"Leave him," he said.

"He can't stand," one of the men holding Jacob said. "His legs don't work."

As if they wanted to demonstrate they were telling the truth, they released him and he crashed to the floor.

"Bring him to my room," Robert said.

The men picked him up and dragged him toward the den. Blankets and a bed sheet lay in a crumpled heap on the small love seat in the corner. There was a stack of yellow legal pads and bibles on the desk. A six foot wooden cross with jagged corners leaned against the fireplace. Jacob noticed the sword was missing from above the mantle.

Robert turned to face him and Jacob saw the sword dangling from his left hand. He used the sword to point at the cross.

"There," he growled.

The men pulled Jacob to the cross and leaned him against it.

"Fetch the rope," Robert said to one of the men.

The man ran to the basement and, when he came back, used the rope to tie Jacob to the cross. Jacob wanted to fight back but all his strength had left him. He wanted to strike them but hours of being tied to the shelves had left him defenceless.

When he was tied to the cross, arms out to his side and legs strapped together, Robert pointed toward the door of the den with the sword and the men rushed out of the room. Then, he turned to Jacob.

"You are not my son. You have been plotting against me your entire life. All I tried to do was love you as a father should and teach you to be a man in the eyes of The Lord. I see the way you look at me, the contempt in your eyes. I see the way you are when we are in His house."

Robert strode around the room, leaning on the sword as though it were a cane.

"But now, I cannot allow your disobedience, your disbelief, to continue. You have broken one of His Ten Commandments. You have turned my wife against me."

With that, Robert lunged at Jacob. The man was nose to nose with him and Jacob could smell his foul breath and body odour.

Robert stepped back and said, "There is a man on the Styx offering to take people across the river. He is a demon from the Mouth of Hell. His price is your eternal soul. The battle between Heaven and Hell is happening right now and my own son refuses to believe it. I have prayed for you, night and day. I have begged God to help you, but still you will not believe. I have tried to be a kind and loving father and still you disavow Him."

Robert's voice was scratchy and he spoke with odd gesticulations Jacob had never seen him make before.

"Your sickness, your evil has infected those around you. Your wickedness has spread amongst my flock. Only the truly devout stand with me, with Him. You have left me no choice."

Robert stomped to the window and pulled open the blinds. The backyard was concealed by the darkness of winter until a spotlight was flicked on and Jacob could see the people who had been staying in his house, his neighbours, lined up in the backyard.

Men, women, and children stood hand in hand. They sang and Jacob strained to make out the lyrics to "Onward, Christian Soldiers."

When the first gunshot rang out, Jacob thought it was a mistake. He didn't have time to think about it as soon the flash of muzzle blasts lit up the backyard brighter than the spotlight. There were brief cries of pain and anguish and, just as soon as the gunfire started, there was silence.

Blood spread across the snow. Parents lay crumpled on top of their children. The eerie quiet that followed the singing and screaming and blasting of weapons caused Jacob's ears to ring. He laid his head back on the rough wood of the cross and closed his eyes.

"You have done this," Robert said through gritted teeth. "Your insolence caused this, caused them to wish to leave me."

Jacob felt the urge to scream at him, to tell him off one last time, but knew it wouldn't do any good. One look into the man's eyes and Jacob knew he was too far gone to care what he had to say.

"You even turned my wife against me."

Jacob's thoughts turned to his mother and he said the last words he would ever say to his father.

"Where is she?"

"Yes," Robert said. "Pretend that you care. Act like you have concern for someone other than yourself."

His father ran to the love seat and pulled off the blankets. Spread out across the cushions was the body of his mother. She looked like the crime scene photos Jacob had seen online. Long, jagged slashes covered her body. Her throat was concealed in dried, blackish red blood. Her eyes stared at the ceiling above Jacob's head, looking at nothing.

Jacob hung his head and, despite his best efforts, he sobbed. Robert stepped toward him.

"Let us pray," he said.

He recited the Lord's Prayer. When he finished, he held the sword to Jacob's side and slid the blade into his flesh.

Jacob exhaled as the sword entered his torso. The burning pain he felt was unlike any sensation he had ever felt before. He looked down to the wound and saw blood fountain around the sword and splash onto the carpet below.

Another gunshot rang out and Jacob, despite the pain, turned to the window. The men outside dropped one after the other. They held their guns to their heads and a fine red mist erupted from the side of their heads.

Robert ripped the blade from his son's side. Stepping back, he held the blade with two hands and placed it against his throat.

"God loves you, son," he said and dragged the sword across his flesh.

Blood poured from beneath his beard. A wide grin spread across his face and he dropped to his knees. He stared into Jacob's eyes as he fell to the floor.

Jacob felt his wound become cold. Soon, the cold spread throughout his body. His head leaned back on the cross and he closed his eyes.

Little Miss Colorado Dream Queen
Em Dehaney

When the plane hit, Frankie Mackenzie was passed out in a puddle of her own dirty underwear. Her phone vibrated a couple of times, inching its way along the length of the dusty bedside table before plopping onto the floor next to her head. It was only the following day, when the kitchen tap stopped dripping onto the stack of plates in the sink that Frankie opened one eye. Her brain fired into life with a headache like a steel toe-cap to the temple. Before opening the other eye, she ran through her post-binge checklist.

Am I dressed? Yes.

Am I in jail? No.

Am I at home? Yes.

Am I alone? This was a tricky one. Who knew what horrors might be lurking in her bed. Frankie peered over the top of the stained mattress.

Empty.

Snatching up her phone from the floor, the display showed two missed calls from work. She was about return the calls, but the phone was dead. Full battery. No signal. Frankie scrolled through her text messages, all sent between 9:22 and 9:25 the previous morning.

Where are you?

Get here now!!!

Are you OK?

You'd better get to work NOW if you are still alive.

Then, nothing.

Whatever shit her boss was trying to pull, Frankie wasn't going to fall for it. She stuck her phone in the back pocket of her jeans and padded through to the kitchen. With every step she became more hunched over, as if her head yearned to be back on the floor. Lifting the receiver of the touch-tone phone, she was relieved to find the landline was dead too. That meant she had some time to straighten up before she had to speak to her editor, Everett Roscoe. Whatever story he wanted her to cover, it was sure to be the result of some poor soul's misfortune. Frankie was the worst kind of hack journalist. No story off limits, no ambulance she wouldn't chase, no grieving family member out of bounds. That was why Roscoe hired her. And why he ignored her frequent three-day 'Russian holidays'. Why he never mentioned that she smelled of Smirnoff rather than Chanel. Why he never commented if she was wearing mismatched shoes. In turn, Frankie put up with Roscoe rubbing up a little too closely when he passed her in the office, leering down her top at the coffee machine and the sticking in an unwanted tongue each New Year's Eve when they kissed at midnight. He had goosed, groped, fingered and frottaged every woman that came to work for him, and branded them frigid when they objected. Frankie had cut his advances dead so many times, he called her Mack The Knife. She called him Roscoe The Sweaty Fat Fuck. Theirs was a relationship based on mutual understanding.

Whatever Roscoe wanted, she had better go and find out.

After a quick pit-sniff and a check for vomit stains down her top, she chucked on her ankle-length puffa jacket. Expecting to step out into the refreshing Colorado chill, she slammed the door and turned to find the world on fire.

Black smoke billowed from the direction of the town bridge. Snowflakes mingled with ash in the air, creating grey drifts against the kerb. Sirens wailed in the distance. Doors of nearby houses hung open and cars stood abandoned in the street, their insipid warning sounds dinging away to no-one. A figure appeared in one of the doorways and began to shuffle over. It was an old woman with two rollers in the front of her hair, dressed in a flowery housecoat of the kind Frankie's grandmother used to wear.

"You're not going over to help look for survivors?" The woman was close enough now for Frankie to see she was barefoot. One of her eyes was swollen and sagging slightly, causing her cheek to bulge.

"Survivors from what?" Frankie asked. "What happened?"

"They won't find anything but corpses, you mark my words. Even Saint Lawrence himself would have perished."

The woman decorated herself with the shape of the cross. Something seemed odd to Frankie, but her hungover brain was struggling to process what the woman was saying.

"Turn me over, I'm not done," she continued. Her good eye stared through Frankie as if she wasn't there.

"I don't understand."

"Saint Lawrence. Roasting in the fiery furnace on a spit of righteousness. That's what he said to the torturing sinners. Turn me over, I'm not done."

The woman smiled up to the heavens, ash drifting onto her face and settling on her eyelashes.

"O-kaay," said Frankie, backing away. "I must have missed that one at Sunday School. And you still haven't told me what survivors you're talking about?"

The woman's face dropped, and it hit Frankie why the way she crossed herself was so strange. She had done it upside down. The woman tutted and a shadow moved under her nose.

"From the plane crash, you silly girl."

An earwig crawled from the woman's nostril and onto her top lip. Seized by the urge to flee, Frankie stumbled backwards over her own feet.

"Dont'cha wanna know what happened? Nosy little girl like you, always in other people's business? I'll tell you all about it, come inside."

The woman sniffed, causing the earwig to shoot back up her nose. Frankie trotted away, mumbling about needing to be somewhere. Once she had rounded the corner and the creepy old bitch was out of sight, Frankie slowed down. Whatever had happened, Roscoe would tell her all about it and before giving her the most offensive angle for the subsequent story. Photos of dead children. Digging up dirt on the victim's private lives. Whatever scummy, lowlife, bottom-feeding piece of gutter-rag trash he wanted, she would write it.

Frankie had come to Colorado in the early Nineties, like many aspiring journalists, to investigate the infamous child murder in Boulder. Convinced she would be the one to break the case, she became frustrated at her lack of ability to find any new leads. So she slept with a couple of police officers to get some information. No big deal, she told herself. They were hot, and more than happy to spill details about the case over a post-fuck cigarette. Then she started stalking the parents, convinced they would slip up. She bugged the family car and even stole autopsy photos. Whatever it took to get justice for that poor little girl, found hog-tied and garrotted in her own basement. It was only when she cornered the victim's older brother outside his school that the Boulder Police Department got involved and she was slapped with a restraining order that meant jail if she came within one hundred yards of the Ramsey family.

She picked the town of Hell purely by virtue of its ridiculous name and applied for a job at The Hell Star, submitting a portfolio of her freelance work, all written under the name Frank E. Mackenzie. It still brought a smile to her lips when she remembered Roscoe's face as she walked into his office for the interview. A woman! A woman had written those stories with such cold detachment, even when reporting in grim detail the murder of an innocent child. He hired her on the spot, and she had been in Hell ever since. The little town had everything she needed, namely Hancock's liquor store, Risky's Bar and a couple of gas stations where she could pick up a pack of smokes.

The sign for Sandie's Gas came into view as the explosion knocked Frankie off her feet and into a snowdrift. A secondary blast wave sent a column of fire into the sky. The smell of gasoline mixed with the stench of cooking flesh and melting plastic. She ripped off her coat, screaming as it pulled away the skin on her back. The intense heat from the burning gas station made it hard for Frankie to open her eyes, but she rolled back into the snow with a hiss and assessed the scene of devastation in front of her. The flat roof of the gas station had been forced out at an acute angle and the glass from the windows was now strewn across the asphalt. It glittered in the flames, which were not only shooting up into the sky but also careering along the ground in waves. The sign for Sandie's Gas had been ripped off its post and was buried deep in the windscreen of a nearby car, now reading simply 'die'.

A mushroom cloud billowed upwards, raining down comets of fire. Lit from the flames below, the huge grey cloud looked flat and cartoonish. As Frankie stared, the plumes of smoke and ash began swirling with black creatures, a tangle of flailing limbs and pointed wings. She grabbed two handfuls of snow, closed her eyes and rubbed them with ice. Opening them again, this was no hallucination.

Black bodies were swarming out of a chasm that had opened up on the scorched asphalt. Several of the creatures had broken free from the smoke column and were diving and wheeling in the sky. They had female form with wings of taught black leather and slick, naked torsos. Their legs were covered with dark hair and one of them spun in mid-air revealing a long pinky-black tail with a vicious barb at the end. Frankie lay paralysed in the snow, hoping they didn't see her. More of the hideous harpies were pouring from the ground, chattering and screeching to each other over the roar of the burning gas pumps. Though their bodies were that of women, their faces showed them to be a mismatched troupe of chimeras. Some had hooked beaks for ripping flesh. Some had feathers, some had fur. Some had long ears protruding from the tops of their heads like raggedy hares. Some had faces like pigs with filth encrusted snouts. Bracing for an attack, Frankie was relieved when the monstrous pig-bat women soared up to join their friends in the clouds, and the whole flock moved away with hive-mind synchronisation. Frankie came to her senses and managed to slip her phone out of her back pocket in time to snap some fuzzy pictures of the creatures before they disappeared into the night.

Screw Roscoe and whatever reprehensible story he wanted. This was the story. Pig-rat harpies in the skies over Hell. Leaving her melted coat behind, Frankie packed some snow onto her blistered back and made a run for the newspaper office.

The Hell Star had been Frankie's second home for the last twenty years. She had seen reporters and office clerks come and go. She had made some friends, fucked a few of those friends, fucked over a few more of those friends, and watched everyone leave the rag for greener, and better paid, pastures. Only she and Roscoe always remained, the perpetual odd couple.

Frankie passed a few people on the way to The Hell Star, all with the same vacant look as Old Lady Earwig. At one point a mangy dog almost ran into her, barking twice before skittering off towards Easter Hill. By the time she arrived she was out of breath, viciously hung over and her back was a charred mess of pain. The office appeared dark from outside. Frankie's scalp tightened. She got the keys out of her pocket, but as she went to put them in the lock, the door swung open. Someone was here.

In the dark.

"Roscoe?"

Frankie flicked the lights to the main open-plan office. The ancient fluorescent tube lights pinged a few times but refused to fire up. She was always telling Roscoe to replace them and now they had finally given up. A dim light was coming from the cramped landfill at the back that Roscoe called his office.

"Roscoe? I know you're here. Forget the plane crash, I've got the story of the century right here on my phone. You won't believe it!"

She swiped a cigarette from a half smoked pack on her desk, lighting it with a shaking hand as she opened her top draw. A selection of miniatures lay there, twinkling up at her like precious jewels. Her pounding heart was calmed as soon as her fingers brushed the diamond glass of a tiny Absolut bottle. She drained it in one, and selected couple of Bombay Sapphires for luck.

"Listen Roscoe you mouth-breathing slob, I've got…"

Frankie's voice trailed off as she took in the scene before her, lit in silhouette from Roscoe's computer monitor. Her editor was reclined in his leather swivel chair, eyes closed, his face a picture of bliss. The top of a woman's head bobbed up and down in his crotch. Wet sucks and snuffles punctuated Roscoe's groans of pleasure. Only he could use a national tragedy as an excuse to get a blow job.

"Whoever that is down there, you can get off your knees now, honey," Frankie shouted at the shape between Roscoe's thighs. "No promotion for you to swallow tonight."

Roscoe spun his chair to face Frankie and the figure hunched over his thighs let out an ear-splitting screech. A pair of wings flapped under the desk. Roscoe stood, revealing a black cavern where his fat gut used to be. His intestines spooled out with a slick plop, and the smell of shit exploded as they hit the floor. Bile rose in Frankie's throat as the demon woman pounced on the innards, munching and slurping. Roscoe reached into the bloody ruin between his legs, plucked out a gristly lump of flesh and held it out to Frankie.

"This is what you want, isn't it Mack?" He jiggled the ragged collection of tubes and skin. "It's what you've always wanted."

Roscoe licked his lips with a black tongue and threw the mangled appendage at Frankie. She dodged out of the way as it skittered across the office carpet. The leathery creature under the desk stuck its ratty snout in the air, nostrils quivering and whiskers trembling. It flicked round to glare at Frankie, saggy mammaries swinging limply on its chest. Mangy feathers decorated its shoulders and neck. Greasy hair hung over its face, its elongated mouth tipped with two yellow teeth. They made eye contact and the thing hissed.

"That's it, girls," Roscoe said, with his hand pumping furiously in the hole where his dick used to be. "You two make friends. We can all have fun together."

The rat-harpy spread her wings and clambered onto the desk, claws scratching wood. Its tail whipped round, slicing Frankie across the face and waking her from her stupor. She felt the cool glass of the miniature bottles she was still holding, and in one smooth motion smashed them both onto the floor. Frankie dropped the lit cigarette from her lips as the creature jumped down from the desk.

"Suck my dick, Roscoe."

A whoosh of flames filled the doorway as Frankie ran from the office. Lying between her and the exit was Roscoe's discarded penis, now oozing green slime and inching its way along the carpet like a caterpillar. She booted it out of the way with an expertly aimed toe-punt and bounded out of the door. More of the pig-bird women were gathering in the sky above. Spotting the paper-boy's BMX propped up outside, Frankie jumped on the bike and pedalled home, flicking up grey slush from the wheels. Her legs and lungs were burning when she abandoned the bike on the street outside her apartment building with a clatter, struggling to get her keys out and dropping them in the snow. Scrabbling around in front of her door, she heard the approaching swarm of flying rat bitches chittering and howling. Finally slotting in the key and twisting, she fell into the dark hall and slammed the door, wheezing and puffing. She waited for the scratch of claws on wood. But it never came. Whatever those things were, they weren't after her. Frankie decided to pack a bag before they came back. It was time to get the fuck out of Hell.

Throwing a couple of t-shirts and a clean pair of underwear into a rucksack, Frankie headed for the liquor cupboard to get the only thing she really needed. Something about the dark kitchen was different yet strangely familiar. The tap was dripping again. The same green slime she had last seen seeping from Roscoe's mangled dick was now plopping in fat lumps into her sink. From the blackest corner of the kitchen, she heard a scratching sound. The rustling of polyester and lacy ruffles caked in grime. The shadow of long eyelashes brushing rosy cheeks. The smell of candy-apples in formaldehyde.

"Why did they kill me, Frankie?"

It was JonBenet Ramsey.

"Why won't anybody play with me?"

The tiny girl lifted a hand. Pink nail varnish glittered on the tips of her rotten fingers. Bare bone protruded from her knuckles as she curled her hand into a fist, held it under her chin and gave three little nods, a gesture that would have been cute when she was still alive. Miniature cowboy boots clicked on the linoleum, sequins flashing as she did a twirl, coming to a stop in front of Frankie. Her round, cherubic face was cratered and peeling. The perfect rosebud that was once her mouth, now blackened and dry, opened to reveal a mouthful of maggots instead of tiny tic-tac teeth. Frankie dropped the rucksack she was carrying with a smash and slumped to the floor. Now face to face, JonBenet gave a theatrical wink and held her hand out to Frankie.

"Will you be my friend?"

From somewhere outside Frankie heard a dull thump, followed by another and another and another. A ratty face slammed into the window. Scabrous wings flapped and scrabbled as more of the vile creatures piled themselves against the glass, now cracking under the strain.

Frankie looked into the blue eyes of the murdered girl, forever a broken china doll. She would never grow up, never get her period or kiss a boy and have her heart broken. She would never drink stolen whisky under the bleachers or stay out dancing 'til the sun came up.

"Sure JonBenet, I'll be your friend."

She took the tiny hand in her own as the window splintered inwards and the first filthy succubus forced its way in.

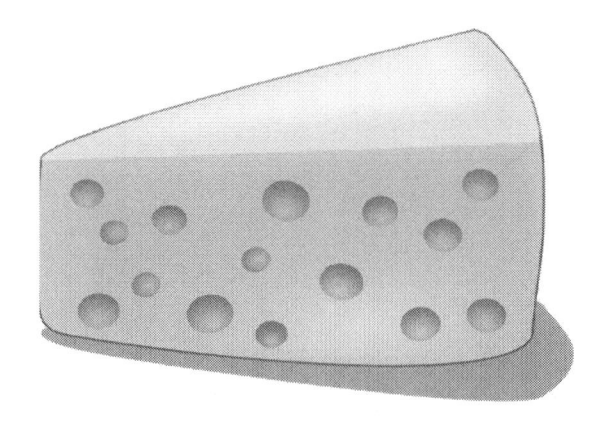

...AND HEEEEERE'S YOUR HOST!
David Court

"Ain't you that-"

As effortless and subconscious as a reflex action, Chuck's response was barked back.

"No."

The attendant leaned in closer, his pupils glinting dully beneath the peak of his 'Make Hell Great Again' cap. Chuck had noticed a display of them as he'd stepped into the gas station, a thick layer of overlaid stickers on each, one for each price drop.

The two of them stood in silence as Chuck awkwardly attempted to avoid eye contact. He could wander down Fifth Avenue in New York for a day and not be recognised, but here of all places, where he'd come for some peace and quiet, he'd potentially bumped into a *fan*.

Or possibly not – he could almost hear the cogs in the young man's brain grinding and whirring, and if the cap alone was an indicator of the boy's levels of wit, Chuck might be safe yet.

The attendant leant back in his chair and sneered, vein-like strands of neon pink bubble-gum clinging to his yellowing teeth.

"Naaah, you ain't him."

He said it as though he were trying to convince himself.

"Like I said," insisted Chuck, handing him the exact change for the gas.

The snow was continuing to fall as he walked back towards his car. As he left Duffy's gas station, he could see the attendant with his face pressed against the window staring intently at Chuck with a gormless expression. He was nodding at him as though the penny had dropped, as though the two of them were sharing some vast conspiratorial secret.

Chuck had come here to be left alone. The last thing he wanted was some idiot blabbing the news of his arrival.

As it turned out, thanks to nearly six hundred tonnes of aluminium travelling just shy of Mach 0.85, Chuck needn't have worried.

He'd missed a call from Dantzig, and – despite Chuck's better intentions to abandon his old life – he listened to it as he drove through the snow to the edge of town.

Lemuel always sounded ecstatically happy, but he only operated at a single level. He'd deliver a confirmation of voiceover work for a shitty local plumber with the same enthusiasm as he'd inform Chuck of a new twelve-episode cable gameshow.

Chuck had never seen Lemuel unhappy, which is one reason why he hadn't gone to visit him one last time before driving to Colorado.

"Chuck, Chuck. It's your friend Lemuel here, just wondering where you've gotten to. Sally says she hasn't seen you at the club for a while, and I was just wondering if everything was okay. I've got a little work for you – NBC have dropped *Foregone Conclusion*, but it's being rescued by a little cable channel. They want to commission thirteen hours of shows, and they're eager for you to host it."

Foregone Conclusion. It was another one of those shitty high-concept gameshows with idiot contestants, and rules too complicated for anybody without a degree in mathematics.

"Anyway, I'll leave you to your fun. Just give me a call if you're interested, and we'll discuss the finer points."

Chuck was quite definitely not interested in any of the *broader* points, let alone the finer ones. The tiny black tendrils that crept across his stomach wall were all that interested him presently.

He'd chosen his destination via the highly scientific method of throwing a dart at a map of North America, and the point (after one complete miss, and another in the depths of the North Pacific) had embedded firmly in Colorado. Scouring the pages of his road atlas, Chuck found a few appropriately sounding candidates. It turned out that Coloradans were quite fond of strange naming conventions.

There was *No Name* in Garfield County, but that was quickly usurped by both *Climax* in Lake County and *Last Chance* in Washington County. It was while Chuck was deciding to choose the preferable of the two – the one that would read best in the inevitable newspaper articles in the days to come – that he saw it.

A small tourist town nestling in the mountains, with the most perfect name.

Hell.

Chuck laughed upon reading it, failing to see how he could ever find anything more appropriate.

He'd booked the cabin under a pseudonym, opting, with his last reserves of cruel streak, to do so using the real name of his biggest showbiz rival, Dexter Hall. The talentless fuckwit had chosen it to replace his less-than-dynamic real name of Nigel Winthrop. Dexter had proven to be skilled at spending his entire career pipping Chuck to the punch, getting all the cushy jobs and leaving Chuck with the daytime and graveyard shift dregs. What Dexter *hadn't* proven so skilled at was hiding his fondness for underage girls, hence him having to vanish from both public life and the business, and *fast*.

When they found Chuck's body in a few weeks, it would only take a journalist armed with nothing more sophisticated than a search engine to join the dots and Dexter would find his name plastered all over the news again.

Shame Chuck wouldn't be around to see it.

The car's satnav chirped merrily to life as Chuck neared the cabin. It looked somewhat less impressive than it had on the website, but the view over the lake was beautiful, and it would more than suffice as Chuck's temporary tomb.

As Chuck stepped from the car and collected his meagre belongings, it suddenly dawned on him that it was likely the gas station attendant would be the last living soul he'd ever interact with.

Would they interview him? he thought as he lumbered through the snow in completely inappropriate and unseasonal footwear. *Oh yeah, I always knew it was Chuck Murray,* the boy would lie. *It was obvious it was him – he didn't even try and hide the fact.*

The key-card worked on the third try, the tiny red bulb flicking to bright green as the main door unlocked with a metallic click. He pushed his way inside and stamped the fine covering of snow from his stained leather brogues.

It was cosy in here, the radiators already warm. There was a small folder resting on the dresser in the hallway with a few details for his stay; a list of local landmarks, a map of the immediate area, and an emergency contact number.

He carried his luggage – a small satchel and single bulky leather holdall that noisily clinked and chinked with each step – into the kitchen. This room was as warm as the last, large bay windows giving an impressive view of the mountains that surrounded the town of Hell.

The holdall contained provisions for three days; some artisanal breads, a selection of expensive meats and cheeses which were placed into the fridge, and a selection of bottles of wine and whisky that were placed in drinking order on an empty shelf. The only thing left in it after that was a book that sat at the bag's bottom. He hadn't even bothered bringing a change of clothing, thinking it an unnecessary burden.

He placed the satchel down and removed the pistol from inside it with the reverence one would lift a holy relic, contemplating the cold weight of the Glock's metal in his hands.

"Have you fired a gun before?" the friendly man in Walmart back in Denver had asked.

"Yes," Chuck lied. Still, he only planned on firing this one just the once.

It's an odd turn of phrase in that a thing can never be riddled with anything *nice*. Consider it; Arthritis, bullets, mistakes, lies, corruption.

Cancer.

Chuck had, at first, put the twinges down to his liver protesting from his nightly drinking sprees, residual aches from a never-ending hangover. He'd been convincing himself of that for a *very* long time, before he'd begun coughing up blood in the mornings, dark black chunks with a corona of bright scarlet. He'd even tolerated that for a while, before each bout of regular-as-clockwork stomach cramps felt like a punch to the gut.

They'd prodded and poked him, attacking him with implements that at times looked more like tools of medieval torture than medical instruments. They spread jello over him and scanned him, and they stuck him in claustrophobia-inducing humming metal tubes.

It was those damned tubes that bothered Chuck the most – each visit felt like a fitting for a coffin.

It all culminated with a dourly delivered slide-show presentation; an atlas of corruption-boasting continents of malignance, an array of Rorschach blots where the monochrome images could only *ever* be interpreted one way.

"I'm very sorry," his doctor had begun, a statement declared without an iota of emotion.

He didn't sound that sorry at *all*.

Oh, there were treatments. From the cavalcade of options, there seemed to be a direct correlation between the amount of money he was willing to spend, and how long they could keep him alive.

He'd watched his mother die of cancer, a strong and independent woman reduced to a rasping and skeletal helpless stranger. Trying to keep her alive in those final weeks, in hindsight, was one of the worst decisions he'd ever made. Like they'd done with mom, the doctors had made it clear to Chuck that his own chances of recovery were also somewhere between non-existent and negligible. Like those grey and white hairs you keep dying black, you're only delaying the inevitable.

Chuck had no real remaining family to speak of, his dear wife departed several years before. The friends he had were fleeting, eager to spend their time and his money when he was famous, less keen to liaise when he was doing the voiceover for a cartoon penguin ("It's penguin-ing to look a lot like a Christmas sale!") for a little-seen fridge-freezer advert.

So, it was decided. Lovely scenery, fine wines and food and a good book.

And then out with a bang.

Settled in and having done some small reconnaissance of the property, Chuck was in the kitchen preparing himself an evening meal.

The Château Margaux Premier Grand Cru Classé was the first in the orderly queue, a 2009 vintage that had cost him as much as his first car. This was accompanied by doorstops of wonderful smelling bread, thick slabs of Black Forest ham, and wedges of Camembert and Gorgonzola so hefty that they could double as chocks for a light aircraft.

The fire in the lounge was fully ablaze, logs crackling and sparking. His book of choice, *The Sun Also Rises* by Ernest Hemingway, was on the chairside table, waiting for him.

Chuck carried the tray through to the lounge and, suddenly feeling light-headed from the warmth, thought it prudent to set it carefully down. As he dimmed the lights, letting the glow of the flames illuminate the cosy room unaided, he couldn't help but think that something was missing.

Music. He'd left his sleeve of CDs in the car.

Chuck stared at the window, watching the snow continue to fall. The wind was picking up as well, and blowing towards the house, giving the optical illusion of the house moving through a field of stars.

He couldn't read without background noise, and the television would be far too distracting. Begrudgingly, he stepped out into the hall, pulled on his coat and replaced his slippers with shoes, the leather now bitingly cold against his un-socked feet.

A dune of fine powdery snow had formed against the door, and, upon being opened, a small pile of it toppled into the house, quickly soaked up by the thick 'Welcome' doormat.

The snow was falling thicker than earlier. There was a thin frosting of the stuff on his car at the moment, but at this rate by next morning it'd be mostly covered. That said, he wasn't planning on driving it ever again.

As he stepped out into the biting winds, he realised how long it had been since he'd been out of the city. The only light out here was the radiance from the windows and open doorway of the house, a delicate circle of illumination surrounded by complete unbroken darkness.

The layer of snow against the car door dissipated to an icy mist as Chuck opened it, peering into the passenger foot-well for the small wallet of Compact Discs. It had somehow wedged itself under the passenger seat, and Chuck had to lean further into the vehicle to try and grab it. His hand brushed against the sticky carcasses and wrappers of long-lost boiled sweets and discarded drinking straws before he had hold of the thick fabric of the wallet, yanking it out in a single motion. With a sharp booming thud that caused Chuck to jolt and painfully bang his head on the car door-frame, the door to the house suddenly slammed shut.

Chuck staggered back, his heart racing as his free hand hurriedly patted the top of his head for any wounds or signs of bleeding. It was sore, but thankfully nothing worse.

"Fuck!"

An exclamation that was equal thirds of curse, nerves, and embarrassment. That damnable wind.

He pushed the car door closed and, pulling his coat tightly around himself, trudged back to the house.

Chuck made a mental note that if he was going to leave the house again, he'd close the door behind him. Even with a few more logs thrown on the fire, he was still shivering as he sat down to his food and wine. Despite the warmth of the house, it was clearly struggling to counteract mere moments of cold air having blown in.

Still, his bones were beginning to warm up now, with his armchair as close to the flames as to constitute a potential fire hazard.

Chuck relaxed, sinking into the soft aged red leather of the chair. John Coltrane's quartet were doing their best to drown out the howling winds outside, and all was temporarily well with the world.

Except for the tendrils of cancer spiralling through his gut and his impending death, but that was a matter for when the food and drink ran out.

Chuck raised the wine glass to his lips, closed his eyes to savour both the scent and the moment, before taking a sip of the Margaux. He winced and his throat tightened. He wasn't the best connoisseur of wine, admittedly, but it tasted *off*. Not wholly unpleasant, but not the great life-changing life experience that his sommelier, Albarossa, had promised him.

He placed the glass down, a slightly acidic aftertaste lingering uncomfortably long against his taste-buds, before turning his attention to the food.

The bread was already stale; he could see that without taking a single bite. Specks of powdery yellowing and green mould punctuated the aerated gaps in the loaf. He'd cut it less than half an hour ago. How could he have not noticed? The lighting in here was worse than in the kitchen.

At least the ham, Camembert and Gorgonzola were okay. The meat was a little chewier and drier than expected, but still quite delicious.

So, this wasn't quite as impressive as (one of the) last meals for the condemned as Chuck had hoped. The inedible bread and mediocre wine were more than a little disappointing. Still, one bad bottle from a batch of six wouldn't be too upsetting, and the rest of the bread would hopefully be much better.

So, with the repast of cheese and most of the meat finished, he relaxed back with his wine to the sounds of *avant-garde* jazz.

Chuck awoke with a start from a troubling dream to a room barely lit by the glowing of embers, orphaned flames close to death flickering impotently in the hearth. The dark imaginings of his sleep – of being a prisoner in darkness and mould - were dwindling also, leaving him as quickly as his awareness of his surroundings grew.

His arms flailed out to lift himself from the confines of the chair, colliding with the plate that he (only as he heard the earthenware cracking against the stone of the hearth) recalled resting on one of its thick leather arms.

I'd best not leave that there for long, he'd thought at the time. *It'll only get broken.*

In the dull light of the room, he got to his feet, peering into the darkness as he tried to recall the layout of the room. He recoiled as his slippered feet brushed against something that splashed onto his skin; cold, unexpected, and damp.

What the fuck was *that*?

He blindly staggered towards where he'd recalled the door being, breathing a sigh of relief as his fumbling hands touched the doorframe, then the wall, before tracing a path to the light switch. He turned the dimmer clockwise and the room lightened in gradients, revealing the grim scene.

The earthenware plate had landed face down and smashed into five similarly shaped segments, expensive crockery become child's jigsaw in one clumsy motion. The chunks of bread had been all that he'd left on it, and each had fallen to the carpeted floor.

But where each chunk of bread had fallen, it had splashed out into a small damp puddle stained deep green and black. All that remained of the bread itself were small sodden chunks of matter, and it had been one of these that he'd clumsily kicked his feet through.

The smell hit him as he leant in closer to one of the small pools – it smelt of something long since decayed, like bread left unattended in a larder for months and left to fester and sprout with mould.

This was insane. The bread was off, admittedly, but nowhere near as bad as this. How had it rotted so *quickly*?

He stared incredulously at one of the few remaining remnants of bread as it deteriorated in front of him, a thin layer of moss-green mould encompassing it and liquefying it, widening the pool it sat in. The scent – fresher now and suddenly stronger still – hit Chuck and he staggered to his feet, gagging. His stomach heaved and constricted, his ribs aching so much from each fresh convulsion that he yelped at each one, staggering to the doorway overwhelmed by nausea. He barely got as far as the hallway, suddenly doubled-up by the pain and stumbling forward onto his knees. His stomach - punished enough and long since tired of protesting - gave up its contents.

The cancer had given Chuck a life skill he'd never expected; that of getting used to the feeling of throwing up. This, though, felt different – it hurt and it seemed to last forever, as though he were vomiting up things he hadn't eaten since high school.

Eventually, there was nothing left to give. The nausea lingered, but felt more bearable now. As he staggered to his feet, he realised that he felt *exhausted*.

He looked down dejectedly at the garish heaped pools of bile and undigested food. He decided that he'd worry about it tomorrow and faltered towards the stairs.

He fell into the bedroom, and in turn onto the bed. A deep sleep followed, one that was thankfully dreamless.

For the second time in two days, Chuck woke suddenly. He'd awoken to a noise (an explosion?) and then it had felt as though the very ground beneath the house had briefly rippled. This was quickly followed by the sudden whip-crack of one of the bed's legs shearing into two halves, an act that caused that corner of the bed to slump to the floor. The noise of the explosion had passed now, and the final sound was from downstairs, the smashing and tinkling of a bottle smashing on a tiled floor.

Chuck sat up in his crooked bed, consciousness being forced on him quicker than he'd have liked. With awareness came the familiar twinges of pain that the comfort of sleep often hid, the back and stomach ache. And they, in turn, quickly reminded him of his illness. There were ever-present reminders of the cancer, and those three or four seconds upon waking were the only brief period of daily ignorance that he was ever granted.

Every step towards the window was greeted with a sharp stab of pain. Chuck opened the curtains to try and determine the source of the noise. Even through the condensation and the heavy snowfall he could make it out – a distant inverted pyramid of grey and black smoke on the horizon, belching out into the freezing air.

He was just preparing to summon the energy to deal with the mess he'd left last when he saw something else – between the house and his car, there were waist-high mounds of snow. They'd definitely not been there the previous evening when he'd fetched the CDs.

The windows up here were so misty, streaked with globules of water that he couldn't make out what the mounds were only their vague shapes.

Hoping that his mind had exaggerated quite how awful his pools of vomit were, he found himself disappointed as he descended the stairs. If anything, they were *worse* – congealed pools of matter, larger than he'd remembered, tendrilous traces of liquid expanding from each as a violent bloody Mandelbrot set. He stepped over them, trying not to gag at the smell. Opening the front door caused a fresh flurry of snow to spill inside, re-soaking the barely dried doormat.

From here in the doorway, Chuck could see that the mounds – of which there appeared to be five – were piles of flat rocks, stacked upon each other and now covered with a thick dusting of snow. They'd been *laid* here. There was also something decidedly un-rocklike on the top of each pile, each partially hidden by a white frosted covering.

Reluctantly, but equally baffled and intrigued, he put on his shoes and coat and trudged towards the nearest of the make-shift cairns.

Whoever did this must have done it while Chuck was asleep. He'd definitely have heard the click-clacking of stones being piled atop each other, and there were so many of them, it would have taken some time. Somebody was playing tricks on him. Pranks on the celebrity out-of-towner. Shit, Make Hell Great Again was probably sniggering about it with his gas station attendant pals right now, erupting with fresh laughter each time they considered the look on Chuck's face.

To hell with them.

He grabbed at the item from the top of the piled rocks, shaking the snow free from it.

It was a necklace of animal teeth; dozens of canines, incisors, molars, an assortment of species and an equally broad variety of states of decay, pristine white to aged, hairline-fractured yellow. They were all bound together by a thin twisted strand of cord threaded through tiny holes drilled in each. The twine was dark and damp, strands of meat and gristle wrapped around it. Repulsed, Chuck let it fall from his grip and the grisly charm vanished into the snow.

"This isn't funny!" he shouted aloud, his voice mostly lost to the wind. If there was nobody there, no shame. If there *was*, at least they knew he wasn't happy.

He could tell that the shapes on the top of the other cairns were varied, each bearing a different thing. However, Chuck's enthusiasm to get out of the cold and back into the house far outweighed any curiosity he might have had remaining. Let the idiots have their fun.

He slammed the door behind him, angrily throwing his coat onto the floor. He kicked his shoes from his feet, both of them scuffing the previously spotless magnolia-painted hallway wall. The smell from the vomit hit him yet again as he walked past it – it was filling the corridor now, and he couldn't put off cleaning it any longer.

The smashing glass he'd heard earlier was one of the shelved bottles meeting its maker – a 21-year-old Glenfiddich single malt that now lay in fragments on the tiled floor. The thick and pungent aroma of whisky that now filled the kitchen at least went some way to hide the smell of puke.

The detergent was easy enough to find (located amongst a cornucopia of cleaning products beneath the sink), as was a suitable bowl, but now Chuck found himself having problems with the faucets. An unimpressive spurt of water had initially emerged, followed by nothing else. Opening the faucet further just caused an awful bellowing and grinding noise from beneath the house, and Chuck was forced to switch it off. The small puddle of water that had been coughed into the bowl was tinged green. Chuck could see now that both the tap and sink were stained with rust, red spots and veins dotted across the dull metal surface. There had been water yesterday – he'd drank some. And he was positive that the faucets hadn't been in such a state then – Chuck wasn't the most observant soul on the planet, but even *he* would have noticed such deterioration.

He'd paid for quality accommodation in which to spend his final days, and this simply wasn't on.

There was no mobile signal inside or outside the house. He picked up the cabin's old-fashioned push-button telephone, which hung on the wall by the front door and dialled zero, in the vain hope that someone might answer. His mood worsened with each unanswered ring, and could feel that the staggering array of beta-blockers in his system were struggling to keep his blood pressure under control.

"You're through to Solicitude Cabins", said a friendly female voice.

"Hello," stammered Chuck. "I'm staying in one of your cabins and-"

"There's nobody to take your call at the moment, but if you'll leave a message after the bleep, we'll get back to you as soon as possible."

Fuck. An answering machine. He should have recognised it from the overly enthusiastic delivery.

Bleeeeep.

"Hello," he repeated. "I'm in one of your cabins and I've been having a few problems. This is Nigel Winthrop, and you've got my mobile number, so I'd appreciate somebody giving me a call. In case you can't find the number, it's –"

Chuck suddenly recognised the tell-tale sound of the phone being answered, a faint click followed by the faintest sound of crackling and white noise.

"Hello?" asked Chuck. "Is there anybody there?"

There *was* somebody there, the distorted sound of shallow breathing getting louder.

The silhouette of a figure suddenly emerged through the thickening snow, walking towards the house. Chuck found himself paralysed on the spot, unable to take the phone away from his ear as the figure drew closer.

It was an old man, wizened face and white moustache mostly hidden under warm winter clothing; a snow-spattered thick coat, thick orange woollen scarf, a Sherpa hat and what looked like some crazy goggles. He stared at the incredulous Chuck as he walked to where the necklace had been dropped, reaching into the snow and pulling it up from where it had fallen. The old man shook the snow from it, and, shaking his head in dismay, replaced it on the empty cairn.

He waved at Chuck, smiling. Without a care in the world, like a neighbour greeting a neighbour. Wordlessly, he turned on his heels and strolled calmly back into the snow.

The breathing on the phone abruptly stopped.

Chuck felt light-headed, his heart racing with panic. What was going on? Something felt very, *very* wrong. He'd pack his stuff, get back into the car, and get the hell out of Dodge.

Or, more appropriately, get his Dodge out of Hell.

He'd decide what to do on the way.

Holding onto the walls for support, he staggered into the kitchen, the bile rising in his throat. He needed to drink something, *anything*. The four remaining bottles on the shelf looked tempting, but then he remembered the milk.

It took him four attempts to open the refrigerator, all vestiges of strength and coordination failing him. The plastic bottle fell from his grip as soon as he grabbed it, spilling across the floor. The smell that filled the room was like nothing Chuck had ever smelt; acrid, sour, and bacterial. Curdled, discoloured lumps sat like islands in the pool, the liquid tracing itself along the gaps in the tiles, tributaries filling with the off-white foulness.

The ham, exposed to the air, deflated like a balloon in front of Chuck's eyes. Green mould burst through fresh cracks in the hardened rind.

The blocks of cheese had been reduced to nothing more than a light green, furry, writhing mass, pseudopod strands of which clung like vines to the inner fridge wall and shelves.

Chuck, half-blinded with stinging eyes and choking from the array of smells, lurched back into the hallway. He briefly experienced the sole of his slippered foot failing to gain traction as it slid on foul semi-viscous liquid, his head cracking noisily against a door frame, and then unconsciousness.

"He is in the ceiling."

Chuck stirred from his dreams, fragmented memories of nightly drinking in too many different hotel bars with too many different game show contestants. His thoughts were a churning chaos, semi-concussed and pained. His eyes opened to a scene from *Rosemary's Baby*, one that sanity told him couldn't be real.

Mia Farrow; nice girl, outspoken. She'd made a guest appearance on Chuck's show Stitch in Time back in the early seventies. Chuck had made a clumsy drunken attempt to seduce her, forgetting that she was married to Andre Previn. "I'm married," she'd insisted. "Happily married?" Chuck had countered.

Still, the view and the sound persisted.

"He is in the walls."

He was in the lounge, seated naked in the armchair, the leather clammy against his bare back. He couldn't move, his limbs drained of all strength.

Figures were in the room, chanting as one, an assortment of strangers, young and old. One voice stood out with the chanting, the distinctive rasping thirty-a-day tones of the woman from Solicitude Cabins.

"He is in the floors."

One by one, none of them making eye-contact, they approached him. Their actions were calm, rehearsed. The still snow-damp necklace of teeth was placed around his neck, the first of five adornments. Chuck tried to speak, a futile act that did nothing but spit out a strand of blood-flecked drool.

A band of moist leather was tied around his ankle, a bracelet of dried out fungi threaded like a daisy chain wrapped around a wrist. The other foot was lowered into an anklet of twigs that hung loosely, and the other wrist was wrapped in loops of thin strands of dried, dark meat.

"He is in the air."

The corners of the room were now darkened patches, Dalmatian spots of dark-green mildew erupting from each. The walls were similarly scarred, marbled patches criss-crossing each like the mould in his Gorgonzola. Pot plants in the windows were withered, petrified husks, skeletons of dried and cracked leaves and branches. If Chuck didn't know better, he'd have sworn the room had been long abandoned, a victim to decay and entropy.

There was somebody else here, now. He could feel their presence, see them out of the corner of an eye. Summoning what little strength he had left, he tilted his head – but the newcomer remained elusive, vanishing from his eye line with each movement.

A voice, ancient, ethereal, and unfamiliar, whispered Chuck's name into his ear.

The assembled crowd, satisfied now, echoed one last chant before filing out of the room, mutely, one by one.

"He is here with us now."

Chuck plummeted through feverish dreams; prize-laden conveyor belts travelling through vast underground caverns and spot-lit revolving platforms bearing ancient medieval siege engines. Each vision was sound-tracked with the familiar refrain of enthusiastic applause and excitable whooping. Whiteboards hurtled past him like signposts on a freeway, each of them bearing different words.

>Applause.

>Quiet.

>Laughter.

>*Wake up.*

Chuck opened a single eye, his right eyelid refusing to respond. It twitched, but would not budge. His head felt heavy, weighed down by something. A cry for help escaped him as a low guttural liquid moan, his throat filled with saliva.

He tilted his head to look down at himself, and whimpered at the sight. His arms, both resting on the chair, were bloated monstrosities – each was enlarged to twice the size, hands looking like poorly inflated rubber gloves. The skin on them was stretched taut, gossamer thin in places, cracked open into violent red grins in others. Chuck's single tattoo – his wife's name – was distorted, illegible.

What had happened to him?

The slightest of head movements provided more upset, panicked breathing joining the shallow sobs.

His chest was tightened across the bones of his sternum, the skin dried and cracked like parchment. His stomach was distended, the stretched skin a patchwork of red and purple, needle-thin black veins tracing a path across it like a spider's web.

He turned his eye to face the right hand side of his head, and his heart froze. It bulged out in obscene contours, his own right eye engulfed within the swollen mass, sphincter-tight. The diaphanous tumorous masses pulsed and throbbed, dark shapes swimming within each of them.

He had to get help somehow.

It felt as though he were trapped in an unyielding suit of armour – the biggest of his exertions simply resulted in the twitching of one of his bloated fingers.

Despite this, there was no pain. Despite the blasphemies wracking his corrupted form, he could feel none of it. All he could feel was the frenzied, panicked beating of his heart and the stinging of tears in his eyes.

As darkness fell across the house, he drifted into a fitful sleep.

"Hello, Chuck."

That voice again, loud as anything, reverberating inside his skull. He woke suddenly, his one functioning eye jerking open to early daylight.

The right side of his head had bloated even further, now visible in his periphery.

The room looked as though it had been abandoned for years – the dotted darkness in the room's corners had become bloated, spore-filled sacks of mould, the wallpaper now peeled and glistening with a thin layer of translucent slime.

He was still alone.

"This way," urged the voice, strangely familiar to him. It came from his right.

Chuck went to turn his head, but it wouldn't move.

"You won't be able to turn your head," came the voice again. "The tumours have covered most of your right-hand side, so you're stuck like that. And if you try, you'll just end up bursting one of them and I can't stop that hurting you. Just turn your eyes."

Chuck did as he was told, swivelling his single functioning eye to the source of the noise.

A face – or rather, the *beginnings* of a face – stared back. Vaguely human features had formed on the skin of one of the thicker tumours, two pitch-black spheres and a mouth resembling a slice taken with a knife. The slit slowly craned into an awkward smile, a black void beyond it. It bled as it moved.

Chuck gasped, and the tears began anew.

His heart began to beat like a poorly conducted military tattoo, damaged and arrhythmic, strained beyond reasonable limits. The saliva clogged in his throat, choking him. Now there was pain – pain like he'd never known.

Chuck was, in a method he'd never planned, dying.

A heartbeat was skipped, then three, then another.

"Stay with me, Chuck," the voice urged. "I'm going to try something."

A moment of crystal clarity for Chuck as all his senses were awakened, the foul smell of the room, the pain that wrapped around every inch of skin and coursed through the marrow of every bone. Then, as quickly as it had emerged, it was gone.

Chuck coughed out a mouthful of liquid, a pungent mixture of phlegm and blood. He gulped in huge mouthfuls of air, imagining he could feel his lungs re-inflate.

"You okay?" asked the voice.

"Who are you?" Chuck hissed through a red-raw throat.

"Some know me as Bubonis, others as Spate. In the Forbidden Tome of Paradoxae, the monks of Gehenna named me the Writhing Plague. I am the death of all things, and the life that springs from it. In the days before The Fall, I was the-"

It fell silent, a gristle brow furrowing over each of its blackened orbs.

"I'm sorry," it continued, its tone suddenly considerably less pompous. "But it's been a while. It wasn't the Writhing Plague, it was the *Thrashing* Plague."

"What's happening to me?" rasped Chuck.

"You, Chuck Murray, have been given the great honour of becoming my next host on this Earthly plane. Your flesh will become my flesh, your corruption and sickness my fuel and tether."

"Oh."

After all Chuck had seen since his eventful visit to Hell, he seemed beyond surprise now.

"You seem remarkably calm about all of this, to be honest."

Chuck coughed again, the last tricky clump of phlegm that had been blocking his throat now cleared.

"I'm dying of cancer. I'd come to this place to kill myself."

Muscle and matter shifted on the thing's face like Play-Doh, giving it a makeshift nose and ears. It looked concerned.

"I am drawn to those who reek of pestilence, those polluted of blood. My victims usually just don't *know* it. I forget how advanced you apes are, sometimes. Like I say, it's been a while."

There was an awkward silence in the air, hanging there with the malignance.

"I hope my acolytes didn't scare you too much. They do love their ceremonies, and they do sometimes go a bit over the top with all their summoning and binding rituals."

"Feeling tired."

"That'll happen. You get your rest. I'm not going anywhere, right?"

It was still daylight when Chuck opened his eye.

"It's tomorrow now, if that makes sense" whispered Bubonis. "You looked so peaceful sleeping, I didn't want to bother you."

There was an unusual noise coming from his stomach, the dull splashing of liquid.

"Don't look at it, Chuck. Look at me, or the room. Just don't look *down*."

Chuck looked down.

His arms and torso were dotted with large boils, clear yellowing spheres filled with a dark red liquid. Things writhed and thrashed within each of them, chittering night-black things, all claws and teeth.

"What the *fuck?*" Chuck yelled.

"I'm sorry, Chuck. You know what it's like. You want to go away for a while and all the kids insist on coming as well."

Chuck burst into tears, unable to do anything else than whimper in horror.

"Won't be long now, Chuck, won't be long."

Chuck looked to the ceiling, trying – and failing – to distract himself from the disturbing sights and noises. Sniffing back the tears, he tried to compose himself.

"Why here? Why *now?*"

"I'll be honest with you, Chuck, there's not long left for you apes. I could have sat it out, but I like this place. I've done some of my best work here, and I'll miss it. A couple of days for a bit of a wander, that'll do me."

"Best work?"

"Oh, absolutely. And I thought I'd pay the old place a visit in person, just one last time."

There was nothing Chuck could say to that.

"I know it'll only be small solace, but with what's coming up, you'll be best off out of it."

"Will it hurt? At the end, I mean?"

"I'll try my best for it not to. Least I can do, Chuck."

Chuck drifted in and out of delirium, little remaining of his frayed sanity. It was the sound of Bubonis speaking to him that roused him fully, brought him to his senses.

"The gang are back, Chuck. I think it's time."

The strangers were assembled at the far end of the room again, heads lowered. Chuck hadn't heard them arrive. They were chanting, a low hum that reverberated through the room.

"What'll happen to me?" asked Chuck, suddenly terrified and – after months of preparing for it – scared of his impending death.

"From one Hell to another, I guess," said Bubonis, pleased with his little joke.

That doesn't really seem very fair, thought Chuck.

"Don't fret," said the demon. "You will be properly rewarded for your sacrifice. All the pleasures of the body will be given unto you."

"Oh. That's nice."

"Thanks, Chuck. I'll see you on the other side. Try to remain as calm as you can. I'll make this quick."

Chuck closed his eye tightly. There was the feeling of something moving inside him, of weight shifting. All his senses briefly flared, before the blackness rose up to greet him.

Chuck Murray, come on down.

Bubonis teetered on his newly formed limbs, familiarising himself with his new physical form. Everything was different and new here, and it had been too long since his last trip to the mortal plane – gravity, air pressure, all something to get used to again.

He peeled the remnants of Chuck away from himself – mostly diaphanous now, man reduced to little more than the hollow membrane of a lanced boil. His coordination returning, he delicately placed it onto the floor. The sacs housing his young were still clinging to the mass, each fit to burst.

He stared down at his new form, a magnificent misshapen hulk of tumours and glistening polyps. Life-giving pus flowed through his atrophied veins, and all was good.

The acolytes were there, bowed. Only one dared to look up.

"We welcome your ascension, Baron of Corruption. The pathetic form of the tainted one is gone, replaced by your majestic presence."

Bubonis gave a single gesture, and the man suddenly clutched at his throat. Blood began to trickle from every orifice, crimson becoming a thick black tar. Skin tightened around bone, and he fell to his knees, screaming through a throat filled with liquid. Bones, decayed in seconds and brittle as parchment, slumped him to his back.

The other acolytes were standing now, staring in horror at their putrefying colleague, backing towards the window.

Bubonis kicked at the mossy clumps – all that remained of his tactless devotee now – scattering him across the room as a fine powdery mist.

"That was really *rude*," he said to himself. "I liked Chuck."

He glared at the acolytes.

"Begone. And make the most of what little time you have left."

He chuckled as they fell over each other in their rush to get out, each of them scrambling for safety.

Bubonis looked down at himself once more, flexing the fibrous lumpen muscles in his arms and admiring his rotten plague-ridden form; one previous owner.

"Ooh, it's really *roomy*."

Hell's Teeth
Dion Winton-Polak

Prologue: Scouts

(Monday night)

The pack was confused, frightened by the loss of its leader. They'd had purpose, but that purpose was gone, stripped from them by iron teeth. Without direction they would be lost, tearing each other apart, and so the female had seized control. She was of a lesser order than her mate but her glare was fierce, her jaws were mighty, and her will brooked no dispute. She would not turn back. The Call had been raised. Destiny awaited. And now, here in the far-land, a strange eye burned in the darkness among the trees, ringed by creatures that did not seem to belong. There were such smells! Seared flesh was prime among them, luring the scouts closer, but other tones teased at their senses. When all they'd known had been tossed into the air like jackrabbits, here was something that made sense; here was prey; vulnerable, sweet and blind.

Aoefa Schmidt lay flat on her back, wrapped snug in her bedding, and looked down at a sky full of wonder. She fancied she could feel the whole planet behind her careening its way round the solar system like a waltzer car at the county fair. She pulled a grimace of effort, straining against the imagined centrifugal force, and twined her fingers in the grass either side of her bed-roll. The grass was damp and shockingly cold but she held on tightly, relishing that sensation amid all the others. She flicked her gaze from star to star, bounding through the void in gleeful defiance of the awful distances involved. She was a superhero and such things meant little to her. Nine years old and she already understood that the world wasn't big enough. Her destiny was down there, beyond the clouds, beyond the stars—certainly beyond those stupid boys and their stupid fights.

Everywhere she went, every time she wanted to do something, it seemed the world was full of barriers. Things she wasn't allowed to do. Things she was too small for, or too big for, or too female to do. It made her mad. Rules were stupid! They were just things that grown-ups made up anyway, because they were so afraid all the time. And that was it, wasn't it? They were scared. We all live on a ball, screaming through a Space where Up and Down don't really mean anything at all, and there was nothing any of them could do about it. They were terrified, so they clung on any way they could think of; making rules for this and that so they felt like they had some kind of control. Augh! It was all so stupid. Aoefa let go of the grass in disgust and lifted her arms to the sky, ready to fall into it forever. She half imagined she was, till a shiver rippled through her body, as the cold night air rushed under her blankets.

She sneezed once, suddenly and with great force, and found herself sitting upright without really meaning to. She could smell the snow heading down from the mountains. She looked around the heavens and nodded her head as she saw the mountains being swallowed up by clouds. A stick cracked loudly and Aoefa caught the familiar wheeze of Mr Rourke's breathing as he came towards her. Aoefa smiled and turned to see the old man picking his way past the campfire, torch in hand. The sounds of tussling seemed to get more intense from the other side of the fire but Mr Rourke grinned and shook his head.

"Don't you pay 'em no mind, smidget. They just boys bein' boys."

He squatted down on his haunches next to her and produced a couple of skewers from nowhere with a practiced flourish.

"Want some marsh-mallers? I've kept a stash back for medicinal purposes, if yer feeling the need to warm yer innards."

She whisper-squealed her delight and snatched one of the skewers from his hand to inhale the sweet steam while it lasted. He laughed gently and patted her shoulder. A wolf's howl sang long and low in the distance, and the boys stopped scuffling to hear it. One boy started to howl in imitation but was immediately cut off by Mrs Carlsson, much to the other boys' delight. Their laughter hushed though when new howls replied, closer than comfort allowed. There were two of 'em by the sound of it, giving voice in weird harmony. Rourke's own grin vanished and he half stood, looking across at the scout leader. Mrs Carlsson's own eyes were narrowed and it seemed to Aoefa that she was counting, though the girl couldn't think why. The last echoes died away and Mrs Carlsson nodded firmly at Mr Rourke. At once he was up, gathering everybody closer to the fire, easing anxiety with soft words and warm chuckles. Meanwhile, Felicity darted out to haul the provisions up into the branches, tying the ropes off double time. Her face was easier to read, and Aoefa felt small once again.

When Mr Rourke told her where to sit and what to do, she obeyed without question, not through her own fear, but because she trusted him more than just about any grown-up. It upset her when her mother called him what she called him, and made those dark remarks about how he spent his free time. Mr Rourke was a good man. Conn Johnstone came over and sat down heavily next to her, knocking her torch from the log. She caught it within the instant and laid it over her knees instead. He was older than her but he kind of acted like a little brother. Worry was etched across his brow, so Aoefa decided to play nice. He might be a little on the quiet side but he was pleasant enough company, and he always took her corner when Hank and Auggie picked her out for their cruelties. She could be brave for him.

"Brett said wolves wouldn't come down this far," Conn quavered. "What are they doing coming off the mountains?"

Brett was Conn's brother, much older than him. He'd been in the army once, before he got burned. The smeared-shiny skin made him hard to look at but Conn worshipped him. Aoefa shrugged her shoulders and answered deadpan.

"I dunno. The weather's been pretty bad up that way. Maybe they just want to share our fire."

Conn looked aghast and swung his head around at the sentry flame.

"But Akela's just put more wood on! Won't it attract them?"

Akela was the role Mrs Carlsson played in the scout troop, their fierce leader. Mr Rourke was Baloo, their teacher. Aoefa rolled her eyes and butted Conn with her shoulder.

"Don't be silly, they'll be scared of the flames. Plus we'll be able to see them if they come too close. Anyway, wolves don't attack people unless they're really desperate and the people are all on their own and they can't fight back, or are sick or something. My dad said."

A foot scuffed leaf litter at the pair and Hank Lee stuck his torch-lit jowls into their personal space.

"We are all alone," he intoned in a spooky voice, before turning and cackling at his pal, Auggie. They moved off and found themselves a place in the circle, slapping each other's backs and laughing amongst themselves. Aoefa pulled a face and turned her attention back to Conn.

"Of course, there are other animals out here in the wild, but they're too stupid to be much of a threat."

She crossed her eyes and Conn grinned despite himself. It was like dawn breaking and Aoefa felt a twinge of pride. She looked around the camp to see what the scout leaders were getting up to. Akela was deep in conversation with Felicity, while Baloo loaded the rifle. He explained to the children that he didn't think he'd have to use it, because wolves and bears and such-like were basically timid creatures, but that a good blast in th' air was like to scare them off if they became too curious for comfort. She caught Dick Michaels' eye for a moment and blushed. Why was he looking at her? He shrugged and went back to reading his book, while her eyes lingered on his eyelashes and his beautiful brown fingers, with their perfect nails. She looked down at her own bitten-up monstrosities then hugged herself tight, to hide them from the world.

The air nipped at his nostrils something fierce, but Kevin Duffy sucked it in deep, relishing its crispness. The scent of pine was a velvet blue caress on his cheek and he turned in towards it with something akin to joy. The campfire nearly blistered his back but the sky and the mountains gave him true warmth. It wasn't something he could explain, even if anyone thought to ask. He didn't have the words. It was belonging, it was fitting in a way he never had. It was as if he saw it all through different eyes. There were times when the world of children, and school, and his family, and the gas station almost made sense to him – when enough repetition made the incomprehensible familiar – but it all moved too fast. The rules kept changing. His life was an ache of loneliness, though he was seldom alone. His size made him a shield rather than a target; sought after as an ally on the playground and on the sports field.

He was at best a temporarily useful lump and, when roused or feeling particularly wretched, an impersonal bully. It was only here in the wild that anything made sense – as though he'd burst through the clouds at the top of a plateau to find golden sunshine pouring over him. The fire burned, the stars shone, and he gloried in it all. A movement flickered in the periphery above him, and Kevin's muscles tensed, his whole being coming into focus on the darting shape. His hands dropped to his sides, landing on the thighs of the children to his left and right. Their outrage was a distant thing as he leapt upwards and clapped his hands together around his prize. He was caught entirely in the moment, and it was only with the shock of landing that he realised how far he'd let the mask slip. His shoulder hunched, at once defensive and intimidating, as he turned to face the outcry.

To Aoefa's left, an argument had broken out between Auggie and The Frog, which was a bit of a surprise to say the least. Auggie was a couple of years older than Aoefa but he wasn't much bigger than her in build. On the other hand, Kevin Duffy was fifteen years old and taller than everyone there except for Mr Rourke. If the size difference wasn't enough to make it weird, Auggie's shrieks of outrage made it so. He was normally so laid back, secure, self-satisfied. But there he was now, spitting in fury and swiping at Kevin while the brutish boy held him at arm's length. Aoefa wished she had more marsh-mallows.

"Get it away from me, you frog-faced fuck!" Auggie screamed, drawing gasps from the other children. Felicity was there now, trying to talk them down, reaching out but not quite touching either of them. They paid her no heed. The Frog's eyes were fixed on his victim, his teeth bared against the storm. Aoefa thought he looked sad, somehow. Lost, despite all his strength. And he was holding something away from Auggie in his other hand. What was it? All other eyes were fixed on Mrs Carlsson, who strode around the campfire like the wrath of God and poked The Frog in the chest. She wasn't much taller than Auggie, but her finger was iron and her fury could have buried Pompeii.

"What do you think you're doing, Kevin? Put that down this instant!"

"Yes ma'am. Sorry ma'am," he rumbled, and he bent down low as though to put something down, then stopped in confusion. He shook his head and stood up again. Auggie was incoherent with rage now but Akela's had cooled to an icy blast. She silenced him with a look and told him they'd be having words about his language later. Then she fixed The Frog in her gaze once more and demanded to know what he meant by disobeying her; to think very carefully before he answered. Kevin swung left and right like a toddler as he tried to formulate his thoughts, and now Aoefa could see that he had something small and furry clutched in his hand. He ruminated a little longer then, sighing, he swung his arm underhand. A creature arced out in a blur, drawing a scream from Felicity. Rather than falling though, it darted around drunkenly in mid-air before flying off into the night. It was a bat!

"It din't want to go on the floor, ma'am" Frog mumbled. "I'm sorry, m'm."

Their conversation took on a lower tone and, while some of the children tried to listen in, Aoefa's attention was drawn elsewhere. Dick Michaels turned another page of his battered book, Mr Rourke licked his lips and peered out beyond the halo of firelight, and the wolves— the wolves took up their howling once more in the distance. Aoefa shivered, suddenly wanting nothing more than to be back in her own bed, snuggled up with Toby-bear and listening to her parents argue. Conn's torch swung about trying to find the bat again, or any of its family, but his beam revealed nothing. She reached across and covered the torch with her hand. She shook her head solemnly and he sighed, flicking it off with his thumb. They huddled together against the cold and she wondered when they'd be allowed to go to sleep. Behind them, the fire crackled merrily, throwing dancing shadows up against the trees. A dusting of snow began to fall and it seemed to Aoefa, as her mind slowly drifted, that all the stars in heaven were falling.

Part One: Catastrophe

(Tuesday)

Philomena Carlsson woke to a bolt of pain searing its way through her forearm. She sucked frozen air sharply through her teeth then blistered the world with her hatred. She allowed herself a full minute of bile, pouring out every ugly thought, every violent impulse, every burning wave of sorrow and heartache in silent, shameful sobs, and then she got up and went out to begin breakfast preparations. The world had not been kind to Mena and the ravages of time were compounding this abuse. Her rheumatoid arthritis was just the latest lesson laid out to prove that life wasn't fair, nor apt to get any fairer in her last twenty-odd years of life. Still, she was Akela and that meant folk depended on her. Once she'd swept out the snow and reset the fire, she sat down and rubbed Doc Schuler's liniment up and down her arm; front and back, in small, firm circles. It hurt like a sonofabitch but so what? She rewrapped her arm in fresh linen, pulled it tighter with her teeth, then closed off the safety pin with the speed and ease of a triage nurse.

She tossed her old bandage on the fire and caught a lungful of smoke for her trouble. The smell of the stuff rankled and she coughed up a little. Might be that's what woke old Rourke up. Might be he was awake already, watching her through the tent flap. It wouldn't surprise her none. He always did relish seeing others work while he set back and rested.

"Ya having coffee, Rourke?" she asked quietly, never turning round. He didn't say anything for a second but she could practically hear him startle. He coughed a little to feign waking (Mena rolled her eyes), and then suddenly it turned into a real hacker, complete with his patented death rattle of phlegm. Mena waited patiently, poking at the fire with a stick until he dragged his skinny carcass out and finished wiping his eyes, then she turned to face the old goat at last.

"You done?"

"Yah... Yah," he gasped.

"Coffee?"

He nodded his head, gratefully. "Yah."

"Good, you can make me one while you're at it, y'old drama queen. And not so much cream in it this time, neither."

She stood up and started gathering the pots, pans, and trivets from her tent. Amos Rourke, Baloo to the kiddies, slumped back onto his pillow and (Mena assumed) took a moment to thank God he only had to spend time with her on the weekends. He stirred his stumps and started to make himself useful about the place. The coffee wasn't too bad neither, when it finally turned up. Mena made a face anyway to keep him on his toes. She cast occasional glances around the camp as she worked, seeing that everything was in order. Once the food was cooking she'd get Baggy to check on the kiddies and— she caught her rogue thought and dowsed the wicked smile before it could kindle on her face. Young Felicity never questioned why she'd become Bagheera instead of inheriting the title of Kaa when Caitlin Anders moved on to pastures new. Well, she'd never hear it from Mena's lips. Some jokes were best kept private. Baggy was a loving soul but she was wetter'n a fish's dick. She'd only take it to heart.

It looked like the tents had stood up pretty well to last night's snowfall at least. No collapses and no drifts. Seemed like Felicity was getting better at guiding the kiddies through the practical stuff: picking their spot, setting things up. Less'n old Rourke had taken a hand while Mena was gathering the wood, of course. The fat was starting to sizzle so she tossed in some sausages and got the next pan ready. Rourke set his cup down and went a little way from the tents to raise some steam. Mena cast her eyes elsewhere. No wolf tracks around, despite her slight misgivings. She huffed. Course not, fool. You couldn't always tell what a pack'd do, but it would always make sense when you thought about it afterwards. No sense in 'em coming this far off the mountain when there was still prey enough for them farther up. No dumb to be found in wolves. Not like in Men. Her eyes had wandered back.

"Rourke! You need me to come over there and teach you how to pee?"

Rourke turned away from the breeze, blushing furiously, and Mena allowed herself a small grin. A giggle came from the nearest tent and Akela became all business again. She tossed the bacon in, turned the sausages, then went to wake her junior assistant.

They decided to let the kiddies sleep in a little longer than usual that morning. Most of them were still spark out at half past eight. Of course, that was partly their own fault, whispering toothsome tales to each other long into the night for the pure pleasure of inflicting torment. The howling of the wolves had set a real edge to their fear too, and she reckoned some of 'em hadn't dropped off until near four a.m. On the whole it had been a good trip out, but 'worn down and crotchety' was getting to be the prevailing mood of the pack. They'd all be better for getting back home tomorrow afternoon and bein' coddled some by their parents. Aoefa was, as always, the exception to the rule. She'd hopped out of her tent right around the time Rourke had his little accident, and set to helping Akela with the breakfast things without any prompting.

She was a puzzle, that one. Couldn't find a more amenable child usually, and sharp as a tack too, yet every so often she'd come over all wilful and fierce; fightin' like a polecat and bitin' twice as hard. There was a pattern to Aoefa's behaviour, had to be, but she couldn't pin it down for the life of her. Her father had fought like stink to get her accepted into the pack, since the Girl Guides had disbanded, but Mena knew next to nothing of their home life. Yet. She'd come around to talking sooner or later. Right now the child was stirring the beans and watching the eggs like it was the most important job in the world. Mena watched her watching the breakfast and she ran over the plans for the day – making adjustments for the heavier snow fall that seemed to be coming – and all the while keeping half an ear our for what was happening in the rest of the camp. Bickering mainly. A little laughter. Exhortations. A lazy drone coming out of the clouds from a few miles off. Probably a charter plane on the morning run over the mountains. The birds were strangely silent.

By now Bagheera and Baloo had started rousting the young-uns from their beds and getting them ready for their morning exercises. Pyjama parade, it was called. Hardly army discipline but it got the blood pumping. Felicity thought it was cruel to make them do it in the snow, but then Felicity thought everything was cruel. They were allowed boots, weren't they? Aoefa hurried off to join them while Mena started serving up. Rourke had them all march around a little, then set them to running on the spot for a minute. Push-ups were omitted because that really would have been cruel, so jumping jacks were the final order of the morning. Mena paused to observe this last exercise in wry amusement as Felicity led, somehow managing to keep her loose-fitting trousers up without losing rhythm or pace. The oversized boots looked comical on the kiddies skinny legs but she felt a sense of pride in their struggle. Adversity was what would forge them into adults eventually, shaping them in body and in mind. They had all stood up to face their frozen destiny this morning when plenty of other children would have thrown tantrums, stayed in their beds, or cried off sick. They'd earned their breakfast all right.

Felicity hustled them off to get dressed before their food got too cold, while Rourke dove in quick to fill his plate. Ordinarily Mena would have slapped his hand away and cussed him out but she was...distracted somehow. The birds. There was no song and, now she came to really listen, no other sounds in the woods either. No natural sounds, anyway. Just the bustle of camp and that lone aeroplane drone getting louder and louder and then— cutting off. Just like that it was gone, and Mena's stomach clenched like a knife had just been stuck in. Something was terribly wrong. A scream cut through the camp, reverberating from the tents, the trees, and seemingly from the mountains themselves. Stunned faces appeared at the tent flaps and Mena snapped her mouth shut, but the sound continued. The screaming was all around her now. It hadn't just been her. The plane was going down and they could all see it now, dropping through the clouds. It was heading straight for town. Even as they watched, one of the engines detached, spinning out into the woodlands. How many souls were on board? How many more hung in the balance below that shrieking metal coffin?

And then there was fire, and destruction, and death.

The snow had begun to fall again, fat flakes spinning drunkenly in the breeze. Felicity and Rourke were doing their best to comfort the children. Good people, both of them. She let 'em do the job they did best. Philomena took a back seat and let Akela do hers. Her gaze tracked the route they would all have to take now: through the woodlands, past the long black lake and beyond it to town, where an inferno now blazed and sirens surely howled. Her eyes lingered on the flickering orange that warmed the clouds above Hell, but her mind was churning. Priority number one: she had to get the children home safe, and as quickly as possible. If they had a home left, of course. She figured they could make it in one push if they lightened the load - it wasn't like they'd be stopping for any of the planned activities now. The weather was against them though, and by the look of these clouds it'd get worse before it got any better. Leaving the tents behind would make for a faster journey, but if anything went wrong they'd be exposed overnight.

Slower then. Surer. Other considerations came to mind and she dealt with each in similarly short order. Had she been able to see into her own future, a young Philomena Carlsson would have marvelled at the calmness old Mena now exuded. It came from long years of practice and lessons learned hard. Mena pitied the girl, but never the woman she'd become. That woman had earned the trust placed in her. This was just another job to be done. She stood up on the log and whistled sharply to get everybody's attention, then she told them the plan. Within the hour they were fully packed and ready to go.

She had Rourke lead the way; his pace was easy enough for the scouts to match, and his ridiculous fluorescent hat was an ideal beacon to follow. At his heels were Aoefa and the Johnstone boy, Connor. Strung out behind them were Auggie Denholm, pulling the hand-truck together, and Hank Lee, who stuck close by Felicity. The crush that boy had on her was usually painful to behold, but right now he looked like nothing so much as a duckling cuddling up to its mother. Mena brought up the rear, chivvying Kevin Duffy along with brisk words and false optimism. The boy seemed haunted, eyes wide and nostrils flaring as he cast his gaze to and fro. There was no doubt about it, it was gonna be tough to hold everyone together until they got back to town. There was a queasy anticipation running through the pack like an electric charge, and sparks were apt to shoot off in unpredictable directions. Shock took people in different ways; some closed in on themselves, others went into flat denial. Duffy was exhibiting the first signs of hysterics, and that could be dangerous as hell in a small group.

Occasionally Mena thought she saw a flicker on the edge of her vision. Never anything concrete, never something commented upon by anyone else, but she started to feel like they were being followed. She started a marching song to draw the pack together, raise their spirits some. Their voices rose to answer her own, murmuring at first but growing stronger as their feet picked up the rhythm, and they began to eat up the distance. She had them tread in each other's snowy footprints to make the going easier and in this, as well as many other small ways, she brought some measure of normality back into the group. They stopped every half hour or so to rest and rehydrate, and Mena took these opportunities to share a few quiet words with the children, and with her colleagues. Her concerns began to centre around Hank Lee, who seemed little too eager to see the plane crash, and Kevin Duffy, who was deteriorating despite her best efforts.

As it turned out, both issues caused by the same thing. Hank had smuggled a wireless in amongst his belongings. He and Auggie had been sharing a set of earplugs to listen to music at night, but since the crash they were listening out for local news broadcasts. Auggie was festering under the new nick-name 'Scaredy-Bat' so he started using tid-bits of news as a weapon to jab Kevin with. Better that than his pen-knife, but he'd still gone too far. Told him that his parents had died. Told him it didn't matter, 'cause they weren't his real parents anyway. (Tch. Seemed that damned old story would never go away.) The smuggled radio was waved in his face as 'proof,' which pissed Hank off no end, and that was when the three-way fist-fight kicked off. This all came out in fits and starts of course, after Mena had dragged the three of them apart. To her chagrin there was nothing she could do about the audience, and the uproar at these revelations was immediate. Everybody began barking questions at the boys about what they had heard, about what was happening back in town, about their families and their friends.

Kevin and Auggie stayed sullenly silent but Hank puffed up visibly in the face of such attention. He tried to regale them with the facts as he remembered them but it soon became clear he was getting caught up in the dramatisation with bodies falling from the sky, and strange stories of murders and suicides.

In the end Rourke dropped the earphones into an empty tin cup as a make-shift speaker so they could all listen in to an actual broadcast. They huddled in a circle around the cup, chewing grimly on twists of jerky as the radio whispered its awful truths. Normal programming had been suspended to make way for rolling reports. Felicity wept hot tears of gratitude to hear her father's voice – ever gentle, ever caring – telling his listeners to stay home, to stay safe; and for those who could not, for those who had lost everything, he spoke of muster points, of food and medicine and comfort in the midst of disaster.

The pack were subdued, clinging to the crackling airwaves for details of their own homes and loved ones. They felt no cold, no damp, no breeze as they sat there; taking in the sobbing interviews, the medical advice, the panicked speculation and – finally – some confirmation. The plane had gone down at the South end of town, devastating the bridge and much of the surrounding area. Half of Montague Road seemed to have gone up in flames as burning wreckage set off the gas station and — choked cries blotted out the rest. Mena's heart cracked as realisation dawned. Kevin Duffy's family ran that station. She moved to comfort him, to offer him some small crumb of kindness in this darkest hour. He backed away, right into Connor Johnstone, who stumbled and fell. Kevin span around and, for a second, their eyes locked. In the moment it seemed to Mena that Kevin must have said something to the boy, bellowed it right into his face (though no sound passed his lips); such was the look of horror he displayed. Then Kevin was off, running as fast as his legs could carry him.

Pity fought with rising panic as Mena called after him, but soft words were never her strong suit. Rourke leapt to his feet, God bless him, and made to go after the boy – then Time turned to treacle. Grey shapes swept out from dark foliage between the trees, to the left and to the right; yellow eyes flashed, grizzled maws gaped in anticipation. And then the children began to scream.

Part Two: Torn

(Tuesday afternoon)

The attack came right out of the blue - snarling, savage, and swift. He din't count the wolves. He couldn't have. They was just there, leapin' into their midst, snappin' and sinking their jaws in. He tried to stop them but the first one knocked him straight down. Woulda ripped right into his face if he hadn't gotten his arm up in time. The snarls fair made him piss hisself but he barely felt the fangs. It all happened so quick. There were too many of 'em. They burst into the camp out of nowhere and two of 'em got ahold of little Aoefa from behind. They dragged her backwards. She was shrieking; everyone was. He grabbed his knife out an' stuck it in the neck of the wolf on his arm. He kept sticking it until it dropped, but the knife dropped with it, slippery with blood and snagged up on something inside. It seemed like Aoefa was reachin' out to him, like she was disappearing into darkness. He couldn't wrest his eyes from her. Hand floundering, he snatched up a stick, and suddenly he was moving again, throwing himself forward. He smacked it down over one of their snouts and the thing let go, yelping its pain. He thrust his hand out and grabbed hold of Aoefa's wrist, smashing the stick down on th'other wolf with an almighty crack. Was that how it happened? It let her go, anyways. He pulled her back, back behind him. There was a flash of light. A pistol had been shot – right into one of the other wolves. The din! The screams! The turmoil of flesh and fur. He pushed — had he pushed her? Backwards. Away. Behind. She must have run, or did she trip? Roll down the slope? But she din't — Whatever happened, she din't get far. The ravine opened right up and swallowed her down.

The wolves fled the gunfire, but it was too late for Aoefa. What was left was small, cold, and broken now. Rourke covered her face before anybody else could see it. The glimpse he'd had would haunt him the rest of his days. Aoefa had been a shining light, a brilliant child. The Scouts howled in pain and confusion, lost in the senselessness of it all. Old Baloo held on to them, soaked up their pain. He shed some tears of his own but swallowed what he could, choking it down to curdle in his guts with the rest of his grief. There weren't time for this, dammit. He had to be stronger than that. Weren't nuthin' much he could do for Aoefa now, but Kevin Duffy was out there, somewhere. Run off or snatched in all the chaos. An hour was all he could spare to gather up some big rocks; start building a cairn for Aoefa. Nuthin' fancy. Philomena'd see to it her body was brought back to Town later. He just needed ta keep critters from getting at the girl for now, while he went in search of some kind of redemption.

He knew Mena would understand. Knew she'd keep the others safe. He didn't expect her to fight him so damned hard, mind. Sure didn't expect the slap, though he'd earned it right enough. 'Tweren't like her to lose control like that in front of the children. Not at all. Seemed like maybe he didn't know her as well as he thought. Called him a damned fool and any number of things just about fit for a child's ear, and then she was huggin' him all a sudden and wishing him luck and telling him to get his skinny ass back to town sharp with young Kevin in tow. Strange times. Still, he knew what he was about. Grabbed the bare minimum and headed off, back into the foothills. A body could last mebbe five hours in the cold without shelter. He'd take the smallest tent and give himself six to get out there and find the boy. If he failed – well, he didn't rightly know if he could face coming back at all.

Most people had Frog Duffy pegged as a retard, leastways that's what the kids at school called him. So did his father, and his brother too. He knew it wasn't a nice word, just like he knew his name was Kevin and not Frog, but he tended to accept the names he was given. People seemed to understand the world so much better than Frog, so if they said he was a thing and he didn't know any better, then he must be that thing. It was his fifteenth birthday yesterday. Bagheera told him. She'd given him a cookie with a candle on it and he'd made a wish on it and his wish had come true. He didn't know for certain his father was dead but he had faith in God, and God had thrown an aeroplane at the gas station. Frog couldn't imagine for a second that He'd miss. He was free now. Free to join his own kind. Free to be wild.

He ran with joy in his heart, snatching at snowflakes with his teeth every now and then. He heard a name called once or twice but he paid it no heed. The name held no meaning for him now. It came from his old pack, the Man-pack. Weak and slow and blind. What did they know of the wild? Aoefa came close to it, but she thought of nature as loving and giving. She couldn't see how it took and tore for its needs. She didn't want to see. So The Frog had left them to live or to die. He didn't need them. He would run with the other pack. They called to him, drew him back into the foothills. He paused, panting, then raised his head to the clouds and howled his excitement. There was something invigorating about the notes as they echoed from the woodlands and the rising terrain. He drew life and love and warmth from them, as though the wolf-pack were responding. He raised his head once more and suckled from the sky.

The distant howl chilled Rourke but the strange double-throated reply a minute later raised his hackles in a way he'd never truly believed possible. He brushed his hand down them in consternation, then gripped the back of his neck as though to wrest back some measure of control from the animal fear that coursed through his veins. It was insane. Wolves usually hunted by night. They should be asleep some place, taking shelter and rest. Could they be so desperate for food? What was happening up in the mountains to bring them so close to man? Or what was happening down here? The ongoing snowfall made mock of his tracking skills but the wolf howls might yet offer some hope. If they was still hunting the Scouts they'd look to separate the group, pick off the easier targets. Alone in the wild, young Kevin would be too tempting to ignore. If he was quick, if he was careful, the superior senses of the wolves could lead Rourke right to the poor boy. He just had to hope he could get there in time to save him. He set off at a smooth lope.

It took Mena eight minutes of packing to discover that the ammunition box had been compromised by snow. Eight awful drawn out minutes that could mean the difference between Baloo bringing Kevin Duffy back alive and the pair of them being gnawed on 'til their bones spilt marrow. There was no way of knowing if the wet had gotten in before or after Rourke had grabbed his handfuls. No way of knowing if her heart were playing her for a fool when it hammered out her fears. What Goddam use was she? She'd fought like a lion, but Aoefa's eyes still haunted her. The trust in them. It was a miracle no-one else had died. The howls told her the wolves were active again, but farther back; higher up in the hills. She looked out and down, past the long black lake and over to the still-smoking town. Far enough, yet every step took the kiddies closer to safety. Relative safety anyway. But Felicity could guide them that far. Couldn't she? Mena hunched over her pack, paralyzed by indecision. Oh holy Mary, mother of grace, what was she going to do?

But she knew what she had to do, didn't she? She had to abandon them. Abandon them all and pray for their survival.

The echoes were leading him astray. Rourke hated himself for admitting it but the howls and yelps he listened out for were too widespread. They seemed to be coming from everywhere and nowhere now. The farther up the slopes he got, the harder the snow fell, reducing the world to a blur of black and white. An icy certainty began to creep upon him: he would die at the foot of this mountain. He thought of Philomena and her fierce hug. The children, wrapped up against the cold, but nuthin' to protect them from sorrow. Felicity, so capable, but easy prey to insecurity. He thought of his wife burning in Hell. That warmed his heart a little, at least. He may not survive the night but he knew he'd be Coming Home. He had faith in that at least, even if she'd taken everything else from him. Mena though… He wished he'd have been good enough for her. He wished—

A sharp snap pulled him from his reverie. He swung his head up, and round. There was movement and a flash of bright orange maybe sixty, sixty-five feet higher up than him, forty feet or so back. He only caught a glimpse but it was enough. He may have been half blinded by the snow but it seemed a divine light still guided him. He cried out for joy and glanced at his watch. There was time yet. He shouted up at where he'd seen Kevin; told him to stay right where he was. To sit tight; old Baloo was coming ta rescue him. The climb was pretty steep but it looked reasonably safe. Shouldn't have to use his hands too much, 'cept for a bit of extra grip now and then. Might have to work his way around a couple a tricky spots where bare rock spoke of shale sliding under the weight of snow. He figured his course for a few moments, adjusted the rifle on his back, drew in a few quick breaths to boost his adrenaline, then he started to climb.

At first he tried to keep his eyes fixed on the spot where he'd seen the boy, but he had to keep checking his footing, seeking the surest path. Seemed better to cotton a few landmarks and triangulate from there. His calf muscles burned, his fingertips froze, but slowly and surely he made the ascent. In the end he overshot by about five feet. Panic gripped his heart when he looked up and failed to recognise the landscape, but a slight noise from below came to him between breaths of wind. It sounded like crying but there was a strange echo to it. He looked down, past his legs, and 'steep' suddenly seemed vertiginous. How in heck did he think he was gonna get back down safely – let alone with a scared boy in tow? He started by reversing, trying to place his feet in the same positions he'd climbed up, but it seemed unnatural at this angle. He couldn't judge the distances properly. He tried to turn around, walk down it like any old hill. And that was when he slid.

  Breath exploded from him as he hit the rock shelf, but he thanked his lucky stars. There was a split in the side of the mountain, an ancient scar, invisible from below. A foot or two either side of it and his slide might have taken him a whole lot farther, but he stuck there at the base, dazed and panting. The weird cry came at him again and he realised with wonder that it came from the scar. He crawled up to the base of it and realised it was being used as a den. The animal scent was strong even through the frenzied flakes. The scar opened up into an entrance of some kind. He wouldn't have to crawl but neither could he stand altogether upright, if he wanted to go inside. He didn't want to, of course, but that was where the sounds were coming from. And they were unmistakeably human now; sobs punctuated with sniffs and occasional splutters. Rourke reached down and pulled his pencil torch out from the pocket of his cargo pants. The beam was too slender to be of very much use but it was strong, and that was something at least. He shone it into the entrance.

'All right now, Kevin. It's gonna be all right now. Baloo's here for ya. Gonna take ya back to camp. Come on, now.'

He moved the beam left and right, up and down, but twists in the tunnel walls defeated it every which way. The sniffling continued. There was no sound of movement, no sign he'd been heard. Rourke grimaced but there was nothing for it. He started to edge his way into the darkness. The first six or seven feet were the worst; narrow, low, awkward. Wouldn't have been a problem for a young'un like Duffy but old Rourke had to practically break his spine to wriggle through, and the rifle strap kept getting caught on the walls. Things gradually opened up after a bit though and, with a triumphant squeeze, Rourke made it into the den itself. He shone the torch low to the ground to avoid blinding the boy but what he saw on the edges of the beam as he moved it around made his heart skip beats. The boy was set down on his haunches, petting a couple of wolves. Parts of wolves anyway, either side of him. By the looks of 'em the kills were fairly fresh, though the pooling blood had been licked up. Some of it was on the chops of the two great wolves off to the rear of the cave. and some of it— Some of it was on the boy.

It didn't make sense. Why would they kill their own? What was Kevin doing in here with them, and where was the rest of the pack? The great wolves snarled furiously and the sound, magnified by the enclosing walls, practically flung Rourke back against the wall. But they didn't attack. Just lay there tense and growling, showing their hatred, flashing their fangs. Rourke raised his rifle, then lowered it, fearing the percussion in such a confined space. They looked at each other, wary, unmoving, for a minute or ten – time burned in the intensity of the moment – and then, moving sloth-slow, Rourke began to edge towards the boy, sliding his back along the wall. The snarling rose again as Rourke neared the kills, and the wolves belly-crawled a mite closer. They held him in their stares and promised him death if he came any closer. He could not hold their gaze but neither could he look away entirely; fixing his focus between their heads instead. Then he noticed something peculiar. There was no separation between their shoulders. It was as if they'd been moulded together as one creature. A name rang faintly in the back of his mind but there was something wrong. It didn't quite match. Meanwhile, his hand reached out at hip height, carefully tracing the wall towards the boy until he felt his warmth. He gripped his shoulder, pulled the unresisting boy closer, then hugged him tight.

    Metal clanked as the beast leapt forward, giving tumultuous voice to its rage. It was pulled up sharp some four inches away from Rourke's terrified face, and notes of agony wove through the frenzied cacophony. Rourke abandoned reason and raised his weapon, pulling the trigger in panic.

    The hammer fell with a sickeningly damp click.

Part 3 – The Pack

(Tuesday evening)

If she really thought about it, Felicity could have remembered plenty of times she'd been more scared but seeing Akela like that, frozen in place like she didn't know what to do, seemed to top the lot. Being a romantic at heart, Felicity fancied she knew what was in Mrs Carlsson's mind. Fancied she'd seen enough banter between the senior scout leaders to know why she'd be in this particular agony. She almost wanted Akela to run after Baloo; to rescue Kevin and to bring them both home safe, but it'd be the death of the rest of them. She loved the children dearly, but Felicity didn't have it in her to do this on her own. She hadn't picked up a weapon to defend the children when the wolves had attacked. She hadn't fought. She'd just stood there shrieking with the rest of the children. She placed her hand on Mrs Carlsson's shoulder and squeezed it gently. Come on, it said. We need you. And Mrs Carlsson let out a sigh that might have been a groan. That might have been a sob. She seemed to shake herself, then stood up, taking stock to see what was happening. Resolve came into her eyes and she was Akela once more.

"We're gonna get these kiddies home and we're gonna do it before nightfall. C'mon," Akela barked, "let's lighten the load a little."

It was Felicity who suggesting pitching the tent, rather than dumping it. It would keep the excess gear safe from the elements and Baloo and Kevin might be glad of it if they made it back this far. Akela nodded once, narrowed her eyes in approval, and then they got to work. They went through the kit and tossed in everything they figured they could do without for now. Hopefully they wouldn't need the last two tents but if they did get caught out they could all cram up inside. Conserve body temperature. Protect each other. Within a short time the Pack were ready to go on. No urging was required to get the Scouts moving at top speed. None of the children bickered, no-one begged leave to have a rest or go to the toilet. The snow seemed to be easing off at least. They practically ran the last thirty feet, and every one of them shed tears of relief as they left the shelter of the woods at the northern end of Lake Clifton.

The pale daylight was withering behind the clouds as evening approached, but the wolves on the wind seemed a little less threatening now their town glittered in view at the other end of the long black lake. Smoke rose from parts of it but it was home. All day long, the howls had trailed behind them, or were heard off to the side, though the creatures were rarely glimpsed. It was exhausting. They may not have regained the courage to attack again, but no-one held any misconceptions. These wolves had sent Aoefa Schmidt to her death. Kevin Duffy and Mr. Rourke were gone, too. They all may end up feeding the pack yet.

They needed to rest, desperately needed it, but Akela pushed them a third of the way down the western side of the lake before she let them collapse. Felicity did so with little grace and even less concern for appearances. Her lungs burned, her feet ached and they seemed so swollen she might never get her boots off without the aid of scissors. Auggie

Denholm flopped down a few feet away and Hank Lee bent down, offering her a drink of water from his flask. She took it gratefully, but was careful not to let him maintain eye contact. She'd never embarrass him with it of course, but she recognised a crush when she saw one. She knew only too well how intense, how innocent, and how painful those torches could be to carry. She took a long swig, then deliberately passed it on to Auggie – who seemed to be kissing the bottle neck rather than drinking from it – before it was returned to Hank. She turned her head so Hank could pretend she hadn't seen the taunt. Poor boy. She tried not to think ill of any of her wards, but Auggie Denholm really was a little shit at times. She let her breathing return to something like normal then stood herself up, brushed herself down, and moved on.

Felicity plodded over towards Dick Michaels and Connor Johnstone, who had tucked themselves right next to the lake in an area cleared for anglers. It could hardly be called a hiding place, but it made them feel safer. Akela stood nearby, breathing heavily. She didn't look right. She looked sick to her stomach. Grey. The two boys were crying, huddled up. Felicity folded them into her arms and made little shushing noises, stroking their backs in a soothing manner. As she did so, her attention got caught by something glimmering across the fog-bound water a little ways down to the south. She thought perhaps she saw some coloured lights. Were they on the other bank, or in the water? It seemed ludicrous to think anyone might be doing something as normal as fishing. They must have seen the plane go down. The fog roiled and the lights seemed to vanish, leaving Felicity wondering if they'd ever really been there at all. The black liquid lapped against the shore of the lake, beating a gentle rhythm to which stroking hand and lurching hearts at last began to synchronise.

Mena was worried. No, worried wasn't the word. She was furious. It had all come to mean much the same thing over the years as she found new ways to redirect the storm within. She'd learned long ago that the world could hurt her easy enough without the help of her own treacherous thoughts, but she could grasp some kinda control if she was strong enough, fling 'em straight back at the wounding world like a whip made of nettles. She stood there now, looking out at the lake, her mouth caught in a snarl as she chewed over their options. Run or fight. She could feel the wolves in the tree-line, still watching, keeping pace. They were quiet now. Rejoined. No more need to call. In terms of pure distance, they could make it home, weather be damned. But how much longer would the creatures wait? She looked around at her ragged troop. They were exhausted, all of them. Terrified. And now they had the lake to their backs, cutting them off. They'd been herded, harassed the whole way but there was something off about it all. The wolves seemed too intent. They weren't just trying to pick off the sick or the elderly to help tide the pack over. It was going to be wholesale slaughter. And what did Mena have to fight them with? Rourke had taken the rifle. That left her with a flare gun, an air-pistol, wishes 'n' pisses. She broke out the first two and got 'em loaded. Figured the rest'd come naturally.

It was crunch time. There was no way to hide it from the children. They all saw Akela break out the weapons and Felicity took a certain comfort in the knowledge that they wouldn't have to run any more. The children flung insane ideas between them; from setting up the other tents as barricades to breaking up the little jetty and using it as a raft. It was incredible – the disconnect between the fate that awaited them and this sense that somehow this was a game, a challenge that could be beaten if they could just figure it out. Felicity could have wept, so full was she of admiration and despair.

Auggie argued, because of course he knew best. It was tactics, wasn't it? He'd seen all the movies. You had to cover yourself in mud, he said. Hide your scent. Set your traps. You fight hand to hand if you need to. He brandished his pen-knife at this point, pitifully small. Dick Michaels reckoned he knew what he was talking about because he'd read about it in a book. He said you had to keep looking them in the eyes. Show no fear. Never turn your back, he said. Connor nodded along but all he could hear was the voice in his head. She said we'd be safe. She said they don't attack people unless they were really desperate, and the people were all on their own, she said. (But they were on their own, weren't they? No-one could help them.) Gone, she's just...gone. Aeofa's gone. (Was Brett gone too? His mom? His dad? They didn't get around too good these days.) Baloo's gone. The Frog's gone. (Gone mad, maybe.) Connor saw him run off, run like he'd been set free. Saw his lunatic expression and said nothing. Gone mad. Gone away, anyway. Away...

Well anyway, Hank was a gamer, hardcore. He'd faced these odds before and he'd kicked some serious butt! But what have we got to fight with? Sticks? Mud? A low splashing sounded across the water and Connor whirled, peered into the mist. Was that a lantern? His eyes strained to see through the fug. Some...shape was moving towards them, drifting slowly, slowly across the surface. Too big to be a log, too shallow to be a boat but— was that a mast? Or a man? The mists rolled together again and Connor felt his ears pop with a sharp stab.

"It's too late," Auggie croaked, pointing up towards the tree line. Silently, in scattered groups of three or four, the wolves began to emerge from the woods.

Akela handed the flare gun to Felicity, grim determination in her eyes. They counted thirteen wolves padding down towards them. They seemed to be in no hurry, as though they knew the race had been won. They could afford to jog the last few hundred metres, saving their strength for the final onslaught. Death was in the air, in the woods, across the water. It drew them down from the mountains like a silver stream, flowing with chill inevitability towards the lake. Felicity wondered if they would go on afterwards, into Hell itself. A shudder slipped down her spine and she breathed in heavily through her nose, snarling at herself to dispel such thoughts. The children were depending on them. She checked the cartridge was loaded, pocketed the other three. As the pack came down the slope, she stepped towards them and to the right, while Akela mirrored her movement. The children had ducked down by the jetty, out of sight, for all the good it would do them. There were curses and some frantic movements going on back there. Wood splintered, but she couldn't risk glancing round now. The wolves were getting too close.

Mena watched the movement of the pack as it approached, noting how they began to fan out in response to their defensive position. The stream became a semi-circle, became an em-shape, with the bitch queen of all dogs at the widow's peak. They nearly had it there and then, as she and Felicity both instinctively focused on the Alpha. Her peripheral vision caught a flicker as the leftmost members tried to outflank her, slinking along the shoreline, and the spell was broken. She turned swiftly and fired, screaming her rage and frustration at the beasts. The first halted in surprise and took a round in the throat. The second leapt over its carcass before it too went down under her bullets.

Felicity had shrieked, as much in surprise as anything else, but she lacked Mena's presence of mind. She was still half-fixed on the Alpha when the first attacker came at her. She kicked it solidly under the jaw but her flare gun was still swinging into position when she pulled the trigger.

Incandescence burst from the barrel but she knew right away it was going to miss. It flew between the third and fourth wolf, hitting nothing but snow. The creatures pulled away from the burning mass as it sizzled and spat its disgust. She back-pedalled a couple of steps, fumbling to get the next shell into the chamber as the flanking wolf shook its head and bared its teeth. It yipped in surprise as first one stone, then another struck it on the muzzle and the side of its head. Hank and Auggie were shouting their own defiance, and tossing rocks from the lip of the bank with surprising accuracy. The grey ducked low, flinching away from the next missile, but its eyes were fixed on the boys now. A growl built up into a snarl. Muscles bunched. Panic gripped Felicity but her body would not, could not react quickly enough. The wolf leapt straight past Felicity towards the suddenly screaming children.

The Alpha watched all this with apparent equanimity, then took a couple of deliberate steps forwards towards the jetty. It was a testing of boundaries. Mena realised the danger and tucked right a few steps to compensate. They were still being herded. The shape of the pack readjusted easily to once again encompass the group, and the Alpha grinned its satisfaction. Mena's eyes narrowed and she pointed her barrel right at the bitch, pouring all her scorn and hatred into a look that would wither a redwood. Her finger tightened but then her wrist was dragged to the side, gripped in the jaws of another flanker as it seized its moment. She spat out a curse and squeezed the trigger anyway, hoping at least to take out the Alpha. Paws hit her chest from another animal and the weight – such weight! – threw her backwards into the snow. There were snarls, there was hot breath, and then her throat was ripped from her with savage exultation.

The rifle clicked and, as it did, so memories began to unlock in Frog Duffy's mind.

Rourke swore, squeezed, and the rifle clicked again. Again. The gigantic wolf bent down and gnawed at the rusting trap around its feet, growling its warning the whole time. The boy smiled beatifically and tipped his head to one side. He stepped out in front of Rourke, utterly unafraid, and held out his hand; first to the left head, then to the right. All the while he made strange whining notes from the back of his throat and, to Rourke's ever-loving wonder, the wolves replied with similar noises. They touched their noses to the boy's cheeks, rubbed their heads against him, sniffed and licked at each other's faces, and then suddenly the three of them were wrestling in what looked increasingly like some kind of joyous reunion. Rourke thought once more of those ludicrous stories, of how the Duffy's boy really had been found in the woods. Of how wild children could be suckled by damn near any mammal. Of the abiding strangeness that these rare children were said to carry with them throughout their lives. The wolves raised their heads and howled their joy. Kevin Duffy echoed them and the crazy two-part harmony became three. Amos Rourke slid down the wall in something like shock, something like religious awe, and the elusive name fell into place. Cerberus. He barked half a laugh which turned into a coughing fit then felt around for his flask of brandy. Strictly medicinal, of course.

Hank screamed as the grey leapt towards him. He tried to stand, to fling himself to one side, but all he succeeded in doing was making himself the prime target. He realised his error even as he rose, but there was no time to change his mind. If the speed of the thing made him gasp, the weight of it took his breath away. The paws struck his shoulders simultaneously and he went down under it like he'd been hit by a truck. He thrust his hands forward, pushing his fingers deep into the thick, greasy fur of the creature's chest, desperately trying to push it back as the jaws slashed down towards his face. Once, twice, the fangs snapped mere inches from his eye, but Hank knew he couldn't hold it for long. Gun-fire blistered the air and Hank heard Felicity shriek. Her despair struck him harder than the wolf had, and his bowels turned to water. Arms weakened, mind staggered, he could hold it off no longer. Jaws sank into his neck and shoulder. Hot blood spattered the snow. And then the pair were struck from the side.

It seemed so unreal. Up until now it was like a movie – scary as shit, but still...just a movie. He just couldn't process it. And then the wolf had leapt at Hank and it was like the fucking thing had burst out of the screen, all teeth and snarl and fury. Auggie was screaming and Hank was screaming and the whole fucking world was screaming. His hand was a free agent, patting desperately in his pockets for his knife – but who was he kidding? Look at the size of the thing! He'd fooled around with his uncle's deerhounds but this was a whole other scale. The grown-ups couldn't help, he could see that. Connor and Dick? Hiding under the jetty, the little pricks. He hated them and he wished he was there with them at the same time. His fingers clasped around the knife's hilt, and he knew it was useless but he pulled it out anyway. His fingers felt fat and useless in the biting cold, and he fumbled trying to pull the blade out. Stupid fucking Swiss thing; he'd asked Santa for a KNIFE! There was a burst of gunfire, and then Bagheera shrieked. He just managed to get the blade out when the wolf's head snapped forward into his friend. He threw himself into it like a quarterback; speed, rage, and sheer adrenaline lending strength to his skinny frame. The impact knocked the grey to one side, and it let go its bite to snap at this new attacker. They rolled down the short incline, knife jammed between them, and Auggie felt something crack inside him. The wolf yelped oddly, on the in-breath, and then the two of them struck the freezing water.

Beneath the jetty, panic shot through Connor and he strained to pull another board free. At first they'd imagined using them as makeshift floats, but Dick had pointed out that wolves can swim. Connor was in such terror he would probably have tried anyway, but the mist on the lake seemed somehow to hold a greater terror within. The boatman – if boatman it was – would come to their rescue or not, but

Connor sensed that looking for him would be the direst mistake. Right now, they had planks they could swing, with ragged nails through them to give 'em some bite. Then the grey had leapt down at Hank, not five feet from them, and Connor and Dick had just stood there, looking on in nerveless horror until the waters closed over the combatants. Any second now they expected a surge of movement, for a wolf or a boy to burst up for air... But there was nothing. Up on top of the jetty, they could hear a low moaning. To the side, Hank gurgled and coughed, and bled out his last. Silence claimed the lake for a few shocking seconds, then they heard Felicity backing along the jetty, choking on desperate sobs. They looked at each other then - and Connor thought his heart would burst, he was so frightened - but he grasped his own plank and nodded to Dick Michaels. Together, they hauled themselves up onto the jetty.

    Felicity was pale as death, hand shaking like a palsied old woman. The wolves were advancing again and there was nowhere left to go. Three of the wolves were tearing into Akela; snarling constantly, but tolerating each other's presence. That still left seven to her swift count. Seven wolves and just three shells left. She could never get to Akela's gun. There was nothing she could do. In the distance, but closing fast, another pair or wolves raced side-by-side, late to the party but eager to join in the feast. Her knees weakened, nearly buckled, but the children who were now at her back helped stiffen her resolve. If they were going to go, there was one fucking wolf that was going to go with them! She pointed the flare gun straight at the Alpha's face and pulled the trigger. It's grin erupted, spewing gore and green smoke to the four winds, and the wolves jerked back from it in panic and confusion.

Cerberus raced towards the lake, free at last to reclaim his pack. His pack-brother was slow in following, but he would join them soon enough. There. That was his howl just now, rising from the tree-line. Nearing the scene of destruction, the chief of all wolves paused briefly to join his voice in chorus and announce his return. The triple-howl sounded and resounded across the wild, rooting all who heard it to the spot. The packs faced each other across the snow covered ground, each member scenting death. So close at hand. Nothing moved. Eyes were fixed. Hot breath hung in the frigid air like spectres come to witness the end. If such could be true, they were to be robbed for, one by one, the wolves turned and trotted away, called off by their Master's voice. This was not their great battle, these were not their prey. The pack ran towards the town, flowing together as one behind their Lord.

The boat rocked gently as cold fingers gripped cold timbers and four bodies heaved themselves aboard. They were all grey things now, bereft of the spark that had quickened them. Cargo, bound for a distant shore. The Ferryman held out his palm, gnarled fingers twitching for the traditional gratuity. The dead were slow to respond but

Charon had time. They always got the drift in the end. One by one, small items were passed to the Ferryman, who examined them all with professional care: a pocket-knife, bloodied and bent; a Walkman radio without headphones; a raggedy bear, poorly stuffed and sopping wet. Its amber eyes glinted, and the Ferryman sighed. If he squinted in this light they could almost look like two copper coins. And the last – a foul-smelling tube of liniment. By rights he should carve the eyes from their sockets to feed his black-feathered pets. They fluttered about him even now, cawing impatiently, but the Ferryman decided to they could wait. Cold eyes turned away from the shoreline, back across the water towards the town. The shrouded head tilted as though listening to a song or to a memory. It bowed then, in assent. Perhaps there could be mercy after all, here at the beginning of the end. He placed the items in the bow of the boat with exaggerated care, then he stood up straight once more and clasped both hands around the pole. Arms strained, timbers creaked, and the boat swung around, ready to follow the new trail set by the wolves. The dead found some peace in the gentle movements of the craft and they lay back, one by one. The Ferryman poled onward; his work had barely begun.

Through the mists, the lights of Hell glimmered like frozen tears.

NEW LEISURE CENTRE FOR HELL

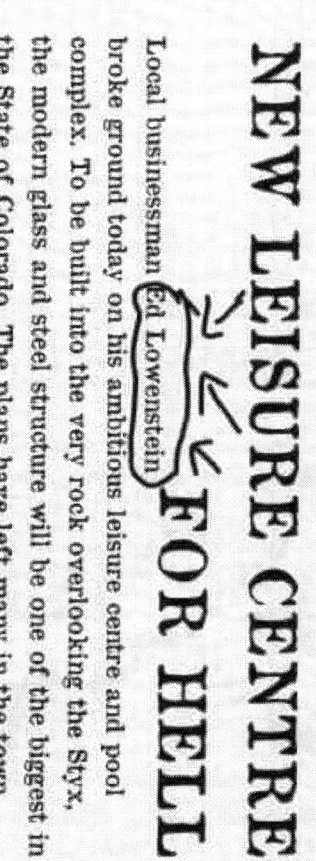

Local businessman Ed Lowenstein broke ground today on his ambitious leisure centre and pool complex. To be built into the very rock overlooking the Styx, the modern glass and steel structure will be one of the biggest in the State of Colorado. The plans have left many in the town wondering how a used car salesman raised the funds for such an ambitious project. Lowenstein claimed that he invested inheritance money from his grandmother on shares in GEnFoD Farm Feed in the eighties, however t̶h̶i̶s̶ ̶i̶s̶ ̶a̶ ̶p̶a̶c̶k̶ ̶o̶f̶ ̶l̶i̶e̶s̶. just

WELCOME TO A TOWN CALLED HELL

YOU CAN'T SAY YOU WEREN'T WARNED...
Ian Bird

WELCOME TO A TOWN CALLED HELL

"When the sky's on fire, that's usually a cue to stay home in bed, Cassandra..."

Hope's friend blinked. She did this the way that insects blink, which is to say extremely rarely and in a manner that makes your skin crawl.

"I'm talking about a client. An actual client with money. You know me, I'm just a girl who can't say *no*."

"Oh, what a terrible thing. A human client with money?"

Cassandra laughed. "Let's not be prejudiced: a government client with money."

They were sitting in the Pit Stop Diner and most everyone else around them seemed busy and on their way someplace else. The sky had literally fallen the day before, and the snows had become more bitter overnight, as if to mark the moment: it suddenly seemed unseemly to be idling and chatting away in a coffee shop at nine in the morning. Everyone wanted to be elsewhere.

But of course, the Airbus A380 had taken care of any such peregrinatory fantasies: no one was going anywhere for the time being.

"I don't know, Cass, I'm really not in the mood for work... I just want to go home and pull the covers over my head... Don't you?"

"One fucking airplane, Chicken Little. Meanwhile, I have a mortgage and twenty years on you.

Millennial hipster scum can hide from aircraft crashes under their artisanal comfort blankets, the rest of us have to go off and pay the rent."

"Rent? You just said that you had a mortgage…"

"Fuck you. Are you interested?"

"Can't have you finding some other millennial hipster scum. Can we get it done in a day?"

"If we start now and you do exactly what you're told at all times."

Cass led Hope out of the coffee shop and through the snow to her corporate headquarters across the other side of Main Street. Corporate headquarters was perhaps a bit of a grand title: under the Buy My Sole! shoe store was the sound-proofed basement she'd been running for the last fifteen years as the HQ of Underground Sound. That sound-proofing came not just from Cass's scrupulously assembled jigsaw of convoluted acoustic foam panelling, but by the impromptu baffling provided by the stacks of tape decks and other reel to reel unfathomables the engineer had collected and outgrown but refused to jettison. Gargantuan analogue machinery that had been obsolete for years cramped already-narrow corridors, giving the entire windowless labyrinth the orgone air of a fifties science fiction movie. A six-foot, sixteen track Ampex MM-1000 stood to attention like a Kubrick monolith up against one wall, a baffling array of knobs and meters that Hope was certain Cass played with when no one was watching. Cass never seemed to have any money, but Hope hoped that the junk in this place would one day be worth a fortune.

The basement office, studio and workshops seethed with life, crackling like static on your skin, but usually there was only ever Cassandra Murphy in residence. Cassandra wasn't just the founder and CEO of Underground Sound, she was also its single member of staff: everyone else came and went under a series of short term contracts. She wrote the contracts, she watched every penny, she knew the purpose of every single cog and fuse. It would have been easy to make fun of Cass for her obsessive focus; people said that she would treat a contractor like just another machine to tinker with and program, but Hope appreciated that while this was true, it was also a far happier comparison. After all, Cass loved these machines, these systems, and in that same way she loved her contractors as well. They were all, machines and people alike, complicated but knowable with predictable moving parts that she could assemble and manipulate to create something with a purpose. She had even built her own anechoic chamber in one of the rooms down here, expertise coming from friends and colleagues and contacts from years gone by – nothing was ever truly obsolescent to her. That chamber, its walls a strange beehive she had designed herself, was a testament to Cassandra's ethos: you had to be prepared to receive the signal, wherever it came from, and you had to be ready to act upon it. It was fun to take the mickey out of Cass, but you underestimated her at your peril.

Besides, Cass had pulled Hope's fat out of the fire before, on more than one occasion. Work for an actress in this tiny Colorado town, miles from anywhere, was hardly as forthcoming as the snow and the sleet, so voiceover work for one of Cassandra's projects could be the difference between eating and not eating that week. Hope had recorded adverts and cartoons here, even one or two radio plays that her friends had hired Cass to produce. She hadn't set out to be a voiceover artist when she had ordered those head shots, but Hope was wise enough to recognise when she was spending more time with this strange blonde mole woman than with her agent.

"What's the job, then?" Hope asked. "If it's a radio spot advertising a confidential welfare cheat hotline then I may have to report a conflict of interest."

Cassandra looked up from her laptop. Everyone was still staring obsessively at their smart phones and laptops, Hope had noticed back at the café, even in this cold new world amputated from internet and mobile phone signals. People were staring at their unresponsive screens just as Cassandra had wasted years in the seventies listening for voices amidst radio static, lazily hoping for word from beyond. Electronic Voice Phenomenon: it's not just for paranoids and nerds anymore.

"I finished agreeing the contract by email just before the bridge came down," Cass said, printing off text from her laptop. "The script came through just before the blackout.

Good timing. Means we can earn while they fix the fibre circuits."

"Attagirl. So, what is it?"

"Public safety announcement."

"Sexy. Condoms and high schoolers?"

"A little less hopeful than that..." She handed Hope the sheets of paper she had printed.

Hope hopped up onto her stool, pulled on her headphones and flicked through the script. "Jesus."

"Ready?"

"Yep." Hope looked through the soundproofed glass into the darkened studio, where Cassandra sat in shadows. Her face was barely illuminated by the light from her laptop, now plugged into her console and controlling everything. Cass pulled on her own headphones and plugged that cable into the laptop as well.

"And... go."

"This is the State of Colorado Department of Public Safety Emergency Broadcast. This is a recording. Please listen and follow all instructions and advice. This broadcast is not live. This broadcast will be repeated.

"This country has been attacked with nuclear weapons. Our communication systems have been severely disrupted, and at this time we do not have reliable information on the extent of the damage or the number of casualties. When information has been received and verified it will be broadcast on this frequency on the hour every hour. Remain tuned to this frequency, but switch your radios off in between broadcasts to conserve battery power."

Hope stopped speaking.

"What's up?" Cass asked.

"Christ, after everything that's happened the last couple of days, do we really need to do this now?"

"I did look for a job narrating a documentary about baby rabbits, but didn't have any luck."

"Five hundred people just died a couple of miles from here…"

"Probably more."

Behind the glass, her friend's face was electric blue highlights in a sea of black. Cass's eyes had a glossy neon sheen in the laptop glare, like the nictitating eyelids of a crocodile, reflecting the light all wrong.

That line from Job… why did Hope even know it?

His eyes are like the eyelids of the morning…

"Are you ready?"

Hope nodded.

"Then try again, and this time don't fuck up. The lives of millions may depend on you. Millions, Hope. Taxpayers…"

"You must remain calm and you must remain in your home. The catastrophe cannot be escaped. Any food or water you might find outside your home will probably be poisoned. Nuclear fall-out will have made the air toxic. You cannot taste or see the effects of radioactive poisoning, and damage caused by radioactivity, both to the environment and to people, is irreparable. The roof and walls of your home will be without a doubt the best protection from the radioactivity."

Hope stopped again.

"What is it now?" Cassandra asked.

Hope felt foolish. These were just words on a page. Bombs hadn't fallen from the skies, just a single plane. Everything would be back to normal before she knew it. Before any of them knew it. Next Halloween people would be dressing like barbecued air stewardesses.

But there was something infecting her reason, something perverting her perspective. She looked at the words and could feel that gap where her distance should have been. She felt touched by all this. Wounded.

Fall-out.

"Sorry, Cass. Won't happen again."

To her credit, it didn't. She read it straight through, her voice instructive, calm, authoritative and humane.

"Further information will be added to the end of this message once it has been confirmed. This is the end of the message. It will now be repeated."

"Perfect, I love it." Cass whipped off her headphones and smiled from behind the glass. "Fancy a drink?"

She did and they went out together. Just in time for lunch.

The sun had dimmed since morning, and the snow underfoot was heavier and harder than before. The days were getting shorter.

"I didn't think they still used those civilian emergency broadcasts," Hope said.

"Well of course not, there hasn't been a nuclear war yet..."

"Asshole. I mean, I didn't think that the powers-that-be would still think that they were useful."

"I guess it's still the best way to spread the word."

"Why re-record them? I mean, I guess the advice for not melting in atomic fire hasn't changed much in fifty years has it?"

"I asked them that. Apparently they wanted a female voice. Their older version wasn't very reassuring; I think that the original broadcast actually ends with the line – *the living may envy the dead...*"

Inside the café, Cass ordered hot tea and then raised an eyebrow when Hope asked for a Bloody Mary.

"Who are you, my mother?" Hope said.

"I need you in good voice, girl, not slurring and lisping…"

"The only talking I'm doing after this is giving the pizza guy my address…"

"We haven't finished, yet. There's more to do."

"Ah, come on! I thought…"

"It's a big project, Hope…"

Hope amended the order, removing the requirement for vodka. "You know, I think it would be reassuring to know that the guy advising you in the event of a nuclear holocaust is slightly toasted: *Thank you for spending your life on Planet Earth. Please don't forget to tip your waitress on your way out…*"

After their break they trudged through the ice back to the studio. Hope imagined that the cold would have found it harder to lodge in her bones had she managed to enjoy that drink.

"Can you imagine actually tuning into our message? If the bombs do drop?"

Hope put her arm through Cassandra's. "I know, right? Somewhere there's a world where we're going through nuclear war, and we've just turned on our radio, and heard what we just recorded."

It was still daylight, but the blue sky above them was tinged with black. Hope shivered briefly, and shut the door behind her.

"Okay, what you got?"

Cass passed the next page of the script to her friend and went back into the control studio.

"Ready when you are."

Hope read through the script and shook her head.

"Really?"

"Go for it..."

"This is the State of Colorado Department of Public Safety Emergency Broadcast. This is a recording. Please listen and follow all instructions and advice. This broadcast is not live. This broadcast will be repeated.

"The Federal Emergency Management Agency and Centre for Disease Control have informed the Federal Government of the United States that the infection rate of the virus cannot be stemmed. The Government has concluded that the best strategy for this situation is to withdraw all military and medical personnel to Washington, to focus on finding treatments and preserving the central branches of government. This is necessary to continue communications with other affected countries and share learning. Be assured that all confirmed information will be shared with you immediately. No further federal personnel will be stationed outside of the capital.

"You are not being abandoned. Martial law continues to be in force across the country. Once the pandemic has been settled, federal courts will investigate cases of alleged criminality.

"It is important that you take the following steps to protect yourself and your family. Remain in your homes and avoid people as much as possible. It has been confirmed that the virus is airborne and resistant to all existing treatments. The incubation time of the virus, which is the period of time between exposure to the virus and the first sign of symptoms, is around five days. It is believed that infected can spread the virus before demonstrating symptoms, so even people who appear well may be dangerous.

"It is vital that you remember that anyone may be infected and that they may not be aware that they are infected. There are no medications available that can successfully treat a victim. Do not waste any medication in your possession on attempting to treat an infected person. Attempting to help an infected only increases the chances of further infection of others. Death as a result of the infection is swift, and you are immediately to segregate the infected by any means necessary.

"Do not keep deceased bodies within your homes. Take them outside…"

It went on. When she finally finished reading she looked up from her script into the darkness of Cassandra's studio.

"Well done, Hope."

"Is that it?"

"There's another one to your left."

Outside it would be starting to get dark.

"This is the State of Colorado Department of Public Safety Emergency Broadcast. This is a recording. Please listen and follow all instructions and advice. This broadcast is not live. This broadcast will be repeated.

"It has been confirmed that armed militias have launched concerted attacks on branches of federal government nationwide. Details are changing quickly. Please note the information in this broadcast and follow all instructions. New information will be added to the end of this broadcast as it is confirmed."

Hope put her face in her hands.

"This is ridiculous. Do I have a version of this script where the militia have taken over and are our triumphant liberators?"

Cass didn't come out of her booth. "They've worked out their main messages, Hope, they just want them ready to go out at a moment's notice."

"Doesn't the government have anything better to do with its time?"

"I think the logic is that if and when the shit hits the fan they'll have even less time to worry about this stuff. The contact I spoke with said that they got actuarial statisticians and civil defence experts corralled together to work out the most likely catastrophes that we would face without much warning and then put together some headlines."

"Great."

"Hope…"

"I said *great*.

"The identity and affiliation of the militias is not confirmed at present, but participants in this attempted coup are criminals. Any attempts by them to claim that they are acting on behalf of the United States Government or the citizenry of the United States are false. Acts of murder, attempted murder, domestic terrorism, assault, arson and mayhem have been confirmed as being carried out by these criminals. Any member of the population offering support or shelter to these criminals is themselves committing a crime. Any member of the population with knowledge about the identity or whereabouts of a criminal who does not immediately report this to the police or army is also committing a crime. Contact telephone numbers and email addresses where names and locations can be reported will be listed at the end of this broadcast.

"You must remain inside your homes. Martial law has been declared and anyone disobeying these instructions will be challenged by members of the US Army and State and Local Police. Members of the population with firearms are to lock them up. Members of the public holding or carrying firearms will be challenged by members of the US Army and State and Local Police...."

It went on.

Hope finished reading at last.

"Tell me that's it." She said.

"Do you need a break?"

"This is the way the world ends. Not with a bang, or a whimper, but with instructions."

Cass walked into the booth and rubbed Hope's shoulders. "There is some more to do, but let's stop for a bit."

Hope supposed she must have looked pretty rough, because Cass ferreted out a bottle of wine and poured them both a glass.

"Thank you."

"You're finding this tough, aren't you?"

"It is pretty morbid..."

Cass shrugged. "It is and it isn't. I think it's comforting that someone's worked out what we need to do if it all gets fucked up. There's a radio system that will be put into action. There are words that will tell us what to do. Someone has a plan."

Hope laughed. "Number One: if the bombs didn't fall in the Sixties, they aren't going to fall now. Number Two: if the bombs do fall, no one's going to be listening to their radio. They're going to be updating their Facebook profiles while they grab their ankles."

"The bombs could still drop."

"Rubbish. There's no profit in it."

Cass looked sideways at her friend. "The world won't end because someone's invested wisely. It'll end because everything always goes wrong in the end. It all gets fucked up eventually."

"You don't believe that. You've been building your own company for fifteen years."

"And one day it'll go wrong. I'll lose it."

"Cass…"

"Hope, nothing lasts. Eventually things break down, they fall apart. It's mad, literally mad, to think otherwise."

"You're thinking about David…"

"I'm always thinking about David."

"That was, what, seven years ago now…"

"You think that's the kind of lesson that you can forget? You think…"

Hope moved to face Cassandra. "I'm sorry, I wasn't being glib. I can't imagine how much it hurt when he died, how much it must still hurt…"

"But that's it, Hope. You don't have to imagine. One day it'll happen to you, too. It doesn't matter what the press said, or the police, that car accident could have happened to anyone. It was just something that was going to happen. Cars crash. Planes crash. The lights go out."

"Well…"

"Did I tell you, did I tell you that I miscarried in the accident?"

"Oh, Cass…"

They sat quietly, not moving, not looking at each other. In that windowless basement there weren't any shadows that weren't stabbed in place by the unblinking, unchanging fluorescent lights, but somehow they still seemed to creep closer to the two women.

Hope had known that Cassandra had been pregnant at the time of the accident. They hadn't been friends back then, but a friend of a friend had said something. But she had forgotten. How could she have forgotten something like that? Things fall apart. It goes wrong. Everything is changed forever. But then savaged tragedy had been sitting right next to her all the time, and she hadn't recognised it, had mistaken it for quirky cynicism. Just shit that happens to someone else.

"Let's get back to work."

"This is the State of Colorado Department of Public Safety Emergency Broadcast. This is a recording. Please listen and follow all instructions and advice. This broadcast is not live. This broadcast will be repeated…"

Hope looked up, into the studio. She could no longer see her friend's eyes, but she could feel Cass watching her. The face in the dark, waiting for it all to go wrong. The eyelids of mourning.

"…the reason for the sudden spate of sinkholes and earthquakes is unknown. Make sure that you have stored as much water as possible, as supplies may be cut off without warning. Switch off your electricity and gas supplies when not in use, to lessen the chance of a gas leak or electrical fire from ruptures to the infrastructure. Be aware that gas may have leaked into water pipes, and that water from faucets may appear to catch fire…"

Hope turned the page.

"…the insects carrying the virus are showing greater than normal signs of aggression. Many accounts describe the insects swarming, but because of their small size they may not be immediately visible. Remain indoors and keep your windows closed and sealed, ideally with tape …"

Hope turned the page.

"…the flashfloods direct water much faster than you will expect. Water will certainly flow uphill. Remain on the top floors of your homes. Share your residences with members of the public with one storey homes. The water will be poisonous – do not drink it…"

Hope turned the page.

She needed another break. Hope left the booth and went back up to the street. Stepping out into the crystal, dead cold she realised with a start that it was three in the morning. She could hear her heartbeat above the falling snow. For an undeniable moment, Hope was convinced that everyone else in the world was dead. Cass was standing behind her, suddenly.

"We have to go back to work."

"…children who have been inculcated into the covens may at first actually seem more polite and reserved than before they were recruited. You may notice that they are more helpful around the house, are less argumentative with other family members, and are less likely to use profane language. They will not make reference to their so-called religion in conversation with you, but may appear less interested in popular culture and insist upon going out after dark more often. It is important that you keep a check on household knives and restrict the amount of time they spend with younger siblings or family pets…"

"…the celebrities who have gone insane are driven by a murderous compulsion to assault any member of the public who is not themselves famous. Members of the public with a greater than average social media presence may also be affected, depending upon their individual self-esteem…"

"…the aliens are believed to be capable of disguising themselves as humans. They may have telepathic abilities that enable them to disguise themselves as people you know, and even speak in their voices or refer to shared events in your lives. Be sure never to be left on your own, or allow anyone to be on their own, as it is believed that the aliens are either parasitic beings infecting their hosts or so-called body snatchers stealing and replacing human bodies.…"

"…although the creatures can move, they are medically dead and retain nothing of their original personalities. They are no longer your friends, relatives or acquaintances, but reanimated corpses driven by a hunger for human flesh. They cannot therefore be killed by traditional means. To stop them you must destroy the brain or remove the head…"

On and on it went. Maybe the sun came up, maybe it went down again. Hope and Cass sat in their bunker, describing to some future population the face of their apocalypse. Leading survivors through the orgone labyrinth of their devastation. But in what direction?

"…your best days are behind you and your ambitions will never be met. Sleep will no longer bring you any rest and you will find yourself unable to generate any enthusiasm or agency for anything that you used to enjoy or find important. This apathy will make it increasingly difficult for anyone to hold any affection for you, and you should prepare to lose your romantic partners and the intimacy of your friends. This inability to feel or experience pleasure will lead to a deterioration of your physical health, which will decline inexorably. You will find your thoughts turning to suicide with greater and greater regularity. The belief that failure was avoidable was a poisonous thought that will cripple your ability to survive and will harm others. Accept your weaknesses and limitations…"

"…human consciousness has been cored by the new hive intelligence and it is believed that thinking in human language alerts the hive intelligence to your whereabouts. Human language is now a carrier wave for the hive intelligence and thinking in human language will cause infection by the Adversary. R'ylegg narrrrg jaddd pyswg'thrk. Y'rrrrrk w'qyufd al hrnwerrn coll'prpt…"

"…everyone is dead. No help is coming. Abandon hope. This broadcast is not live. This broadcast will be repeated."

The final page.

Across the booth, through the glass, inside the studio, no light. Hope could still feel Cassandra watching her. Hope removed her headphones and stood up from her stool. She could still hear the buzzing in her head she thought had come from the headphones. She walked over to the door into Cassandra's studio and turned the handle. It was colder than before.

The door opened and the darkness spilled out of the small room into Hope's booth.

"Cass. We've finished."

Everything was still inside the tiny, dark studio. Cassandra's laptop was dead. Hope couldn't hear her friend's breathing. Vestigial light from Hope's booth found Cass's face and reflected off her open and unresponsive eyes.

Hope reached towards her friend. The cord from Cassandra's headphones contracted, suddenly, back towards the dead laptop. It jerked Cassandra's head forwards and the light momentarily danced in her eyes.

Hope jumped back and put her hand down on her friend's console. It was sticky, slimy. She lifted her hand to her face but the stench of whatever it was on her fingers was intolerable. She stepped back, out of the studio. The cable connecting the laptop to Cassandra's head relaxed, somehow.

Something breathed, inside the dark room.

Behind Hope, the broadcast began. Her voice, spoken by something else.

"This is the State of Colorado Department of Public Safety Emergency Broadcast. This is a recording. Please listen and follow all instructions and advice. No one knows what has happened. Everyone is dead. No help is coming. Abandon hope. This broadcast is not love. This broadcast will be repeated.

"This is the State of Colorado Department of Public Safety Emergency Broadcast. This is a recording. Please listen and follow all instructions and advice. No one knows what has happened. Everyone is dead. No help is coming. Abandon hope. This broadcast is not love. This broadcast will be repeated."

"This is the State of Colorado Department of Public Safety Emergency Broadcast. This is a recording. Please listen and follow all instructions and advice. No one knows what has happened. Everyone is dead. No help is coming. Abandon hope. This broadcast is not love. This broadcast will be repeated."

Villains by Necessity
Richmond A. Clements

Robby Lancaster woke up on Monday morning. For a brief, glorious second, he was happy. Then he remembered who he was. He remembered where he was. He remembered what was in front of him that day.

School.

He pulled the quilt up over his head and rolled to face the wall. Maybe if he stayed like this it would all go away?

Who was he kidding?

There was no getting away from it. His life was shit.

Best to just get the day over with. Then he'd be one day closer to the weekend and another two days of blissful peace.

He ate breakfast in silence. He father didn't speak to him. The only meaningful contact they had was after nine p.m. when the old man was drunk enough to tell Robby just exactly what he was doing wrong. Which was almost everything.

Robby had stood up to his father once. Only once.

He had shouted, tears burning his eyes. "You've never said anything nice to me! Never gave me any encouragement!"

"You didn't deserve it," had been his father's reply.

His father never laid a hand on him. But some things hurt more than a punch to the head.

Robby pulled his coat on and snatched his bag from the table by the door.

"Bye, Dad," he said, like he always did. His father didn't answer, like he always did.

He trudged to the end of the street. Fat grey-white clouds where rolling in. Robby understood meteorology a bit. He was pretty sure that clouds like this meant there was snow on the way.

He stood by the bus stop, ignored by the other kids. They were chatting about the weekend. One of the boys was boasting about what he'd done with his girlfriend in graphic detail. It was all lies, of course. They were friends on Xbox. Robby knew he had been playing Overwatch for twenty hours straight.

The first flakes of snow started to fall as the bus pulled up to the kerb.

"All aboard! One way trip to Hell and back!" The driver made this same joke every single day. Every single time he stopped the bus to collect the next group of students. Robby hated it.

"Jesus, that joke is *really* shit. Right?"

Robby looked at the boy sitting beside him, who had just addressed him. He was taken aback. Nobody spoke to him.

The boy smiled. "Hi. I'm Ben. I'm new in town."

Robby took the offered hand and shook it. The new boy, Ben, was thin. His skin was pale as paper. His eyes were deep sunk and dark. His teeth were crooked and not quite white. He looked ill, but his grip was firm, his touch hot. Robby recognised his accent as being from London, England. Like the guy from Luther.

"Um. Hi. I'm Robby."

The boys chatted on the ten minute drive to the school. Ben had arrived in town a few days ago. This was his first day in school. They compared classes and it seemed they would have a few together. The first was English that morning.

Robby tried not to feel too hopeful. He wasn't a person who made friends. Stone would make sure of that. He always did.

"See you later, I gotta find the office. Report in, right?"

Ben headed off into the crowd of chattering teens that was filing into the school.

Most of them had their hoods pulled up against the falling snow, faces hidden.

Robby hoped that this might be a good chance to get to registration safely.

Robby slipped inside. He kept his hood pulled up and head down. He could hear Stone's loud, arrogant voice further down the corridor. Stone would say something, then as one, his acolytes would bray their laughter.

Robby kept his eyes focused on the cracked black and white tiles as he walked past. For one sweet moment he actually believed that he had made it to safety.

"Hey - Lancaster!"

He felt the familiar chill ripple up his spine. Then, despising himself for his cowardice, he sped up.

"Lancaster, you fucking *geek*," the voice yelled. Closer this time. They were following him. A hand grabbed his hood and yanked him backwards. The top of his zipper bit into his throat. The material of his coat ripped loudly. He let out a loud choking noise and staggered to the side.

Stone and his gang laughed.

"You're pathetic, you know that?"

Robby's head was still spinning. He tried to walk away. Stone was having none of it. Robby saw the bigger boy step in front of him. His blond hair fell to his shoulders. His mouth twisted into a sneer.

He swung a fist.

Robby's vision flashed brilliant white.

The force of the blow sent him stumbling sideways and into a group of girls who were chatting in front of a row of lockers. He dropped to his knees, his head ringing. His ear was searing with pain. As one, the girls turned and scowled at him in disgust. Then, again as one, their faces softened as they worked out what had happened.

"Stone, what's wrong with you? Leave him alone, why don't you?"

Stone just looked down at Robby and snorted.

"You need girls to stick up for you. You're nothing but a pussy fag, Lancaster," was his parting shot. With that he disappeared, with his laughing entourage, into the shuffle of pedestrians in the corridor.

One of the girls spoke up. "Are you okay, Rob?"

In his impotent rage and embarrassment, Robby felt the urge to throw off the offered help. But he realized that doing so would only make him look stupider. More useless.

He muttered, "Thanks."

"You know, you shouldn't let him bully you like that? You should stick up for yourself."

And just how the fuck am I supposed to do that? Robby thought.

"Yeah, kick his ass, Robby," advised a second girl in the group.

Sitting in English class that morning, Robby could feel Stone's eyes boring into the back of his neck. He didn't know why Stone hated him. He just did. Robby had done nothing. He hadn't even *known* the guy before starting this school.

Like all bullies, Stone delighted in the subtle – and not so subtle - torture of those he thought weaker than himself.

Which was pretty much everyone. And those who he thought were his intellectual superiors. Which was pretty much everyone.

From what Robby had heard, Stone's girlfriend, Shirley, was every bit as hateful towards the female pupils.

The teachers knew, of course. Other pupils had gone to them before, but what could they do? Oh sometimes they would catch him in the act. But in the act of what? Of pushing someone? Tripping someone up in the corridor? That was all they saw. They never heard the name calling. They never saw the punches or felt the hair pulling.

And besides, Stone was on the football team. That seemed to get him a free pass with almost everything.

Robby felt something hit him on the back of the head. A sharp pain. His hand instinctively went to the spot.

He could hear Stone snorting with laughter from his seat on the back row. Another sharp pain on his hand. Stone was throwing coins at him, he realised.

Robby took his hand down again. A third coin bounced off his shoulder.

"Thanks, dude."

Robby turned at the sound of the voice. It was the new guy. Ben? Yeah, that was his name. He was in the seat behind and to the left of Robby.

Ben was bending at the waist, hanging on the side of his desk with one hand and scooping the coins up with the other.

He slipped the coins into his pocket. "That's lunch sorted, right?"

He winked at Robby, who was too scared to look in Stone's direction. He could almost feel the waves of hate.

"If you're quite finished, boys?" The teacher waved a book at them. "Back to your Shakespeare, please. If it's not too much trouble."

A few minutes later, Robby chanced a quick glance at Stone. The other boy was swinging on the back legs of his chair. He sneered at Robby, mouthing the word 'asshole'.

Robby made it to lunch with no further incidents. He hurried from the class as quickly as he could. There was a bathroom just down the corridor from the classroom, but he walked past that one. He used one at the far end of the school. Stone and his crew were sure to use the one close to the classroom.

In the lunchroom, Robby sat alone as usual. Ben set a lunch tray down at the table beside him.

"Mind if I join you?" He sat down without waiting for an answer.

"So, who's that blond guy with the spare cash? He's a bit of a prick, eh?"

Robby couldn't help but smile at that. "Yeah, he is a bit."

"King Lear. Bloody heavy stuff, right?"

"King..?" Robby frowned.

"The play. English class. It was, like, ten minutes ago!"

"Oh yeah. That. Yeah, it's... it's..."

"It's fucking nuts is what it is. Who's your favourite character?"

"Favourite..." Robby tried to recall the name of *any* of the characters. "The Fool. He's pretty cool, I suppose."

"Yeah. Speaking truth to power and all that. I like Prince Edmund. The bastard son of the Duke of Gloucester!"

Ben said it like he was announcing a boxer at a fight. Robby could sort of remember that character. It was a big story with a lot of names to remember. Like Game of Thrones.

"He's the one with the revenge thing?"

"That he is, my friend, that he is." Robby gave an involuntary start. Nobody had ever called him 'friend' before. Ben was still talking.

"Yeah, fair enough, he had thin reason for revenge. But you got to admire his single-mindedness, am I right? And *yeah* in the end his plan more or less fails – sorry, spoilers! Maybe he died but he fucking got results. He got his revenge."

Ben finished up eating and stood up again.

"Yeah. Revenge, baby. There's a lot to be said for it."

Robby watched Ben as he walked away. He admired the other boy's confidence. He was jealous of it. He wished he could take revenge on the people who made his life hell.

He had chemistry class that afternoon.

Ben came in and sat beside him. Stone walked by their table on his way to the back of the class.

"Got a new boyfriend, Lancaster?"

Robby felt himself turning red, when Ben answered. "He'll never come between us, sweetheart, don't worry," the boy said, and blew Stone a kiss.

The classroom was only half full, but those that saw it laughed. Stone's face clouded in fury, but before he could respond, the teacher ordered everyone to take their seats.

"You don't have to take shit from him. You don't have to take shit from *anybody*. Not even family."

"How did you..?"

Ben smiled. It was a strange smile, Robby thought. It was both warm and glacial at the same time. He tapped the side of his nose. "I know lots of things, Robby. Lots of things. For instance, you see these two chemicals?"

He held up two vials from the rack that sat on their desk. Robby nodded. "Yeah, what about them?"

"I know that if you mixed them together and added them to, say, some drunken abusive prick's beer, chances are said abusive prick wouldn't wake up and wouldn't bother you ever again. I also know that you'd have nothing to worry about because the alcohol would mask the poison in any tests.

"For example."

Ben held the vials out to Robby. Robby looked at them, then at Ben. The other boy held his gaze. "Take them."

Ben's voice had a different tone as he spoke those two words. Something in it told Robby he couldn't refuse. He took the vials and slipped them into his pocket.

He looked around the class, but nobody had noticed. Although, as usual, Stone was staring at him, his eyes blazing with hate.

For the first time, Robby didn't turn away frightened. He held Stone's gaze. He held it until the sneer fell away and was replaced by a look of puzzlement. He smiled at the bully. Only then did he turn back.

"Something wrong, Mr Stone?" the teacher asked, spotting the frown on his face. Stone's face turned to relief at the question. It gave him a chance to get back on top. "No sir. I was just wondering if Lancaster was gay."

As usual, the class laughed. Only this time Robby didn't care.

After Chemistry class, it was business as usual for Stone. He had seemed to have forgotten his unease at being faced down by one of his victims.

"Why does he do that?" Robby asked out loud as he watched Stone trip up a younger student. He wasn't addressing the question to anyone, but Ben answered.

"He's a bully. Bullies are all cowards. He counts on people not standing up to him or fighting back. Imagine if all his victims got together and ganged up against him? He'd be royally fucked."

"They never will though…"

"Then you need to find another way to get to him. Does he have any friends? Real friends, I mean?"

"He has a girlfriend. Shirley."

"Well there you go then…"

Robby's father shouted him into the lounge. Robby was at the kitchen table doing his homework. He sighed, but did as he was told.

He stood for five minutes, listening to his father drunkenly listing the many faults he saw in his son. He took a swig from his beer after every tirade, his voice slowing and becoming more slurred as he drank.

"Stay there, I'm going for a piss…" He father grunted his way out of the chair and staggered from the room.

Robby waited until he heard the bathroom door slam shut before he moved. He ran to the kitchen and grabbed the vials from his coat.

He popped the lids from them and poured the contents into the half full beer can on the arm of his father's chair.

The old man stumbled back in and flopped into his chair. The beer can bounced into the air and started to tip to the side.

Robby gasped. His plan was about to fail.

Then, moving faster than he had ever seen, his father grabbed the can out of the air. He didn't spill a drop. He supposed his father could move fast when it was something important. Like beer.

He downed the rest of the can in a couple of loud gulps, crushed it and threw it in the trash can beside his seat. It clattered against the other cans there.

"Now, what was I saying? Oh yeah…"

His father's head slumped forward, his eyes closed and he began to snore.

"Good night, dad," Robby said. He went to bed.

His father was still on the chair next morning. One look told Robby he was dead. A streak of green vomit stuck to the vest his father was wearing. The smell of the vomit was sharp, almost overpowering.

Robby looked at the corpse. At the dead body of his father. His father who he had murdered.

Robby felt nothing.

No. That wasn't true. He felt relief. He felt… free. For the first time in his memory, he did not feel scared and oppressed in his own home.

His cell buzzed in his pocket. He pulled it out, frowning. Nobody ever called him. He didn't recognise the number. He felt a flash of panic. What if it was the cops? Could they have found out somehow?

He touched the green icon on the phone screen.

"Yeah?"

"Hey buddy!"

It was Ben. "Hi. How'd you get my number?"

"I told you. I know lots of things, Robby. So…"

"So what?"

"You know what. How did it feel?"

Robby paused a few heartbeats. "Good. It felt good."

"Sweet. See you on the bus."

It was snowing again. The bus was moving slowly. Robby had already seen a couple of minor accidents. Cars that had slid into the back of another. Their drivers where standing in the snow yelling at each other.

"There's nothing like it, right?"

"Like what?" Robby asked.

Ben waved a hand, indicating the other passengers on the bus. "Look at them. They are all so... ordinary. So small.

"They don't have the power you have. They don't understand how it feels to have been the arbiter of the ultimate decision. You know who has that power? A God, that's who. How you feel now? That's what God feels like all the time."

Robby nodded. "Do... you know the feeling? Have you..?"

"Oh many times. Many times, Robby."

Robby lowered his voice. "But God never had the practical problems I have."

"Like?"

"Like getting rid of the body."

Ben's smile was enigmatic. "That's not going to be a problem, Roddy."

"Why?"

Ben didn't speak, he just pointed out the window.

Robby couldn't quite absorb what he was seeing.

An aeroplane was falling towards the ground. It was spewing a trail of fire in its wake. Everything beneath the flightpath was blazing. The plane hit the ground.

There was a bright flash. A pillar of fire shot to the sky, curling in on itself to form a mushroom cloud. A second later the bus rocked as a loud *whoomf* sounded. The bus screeched to a halt. Everyone moved to the same side, gawking at the conflagration.

Robby could feel the heat from here.

"Looks like it hit the bridge."

"It should be fine. Aviation fuel can't melt steel beams, am I right?" Ben held his hands up as if expectant of a round of applause, but everyone was too busy staring out the window.

"On the bright side, looks like school's off today."

He nudged Robby and spoke so only he could hear. "Just as well. You got shit to do, my son."

"Aren't you going to help me?"

Robby grunted as he dragged his father onto the plastic sheet. He was tired and cold from the walk home through the snow. Ben was lying on the couch, fingers entwined behind his head.

"I'd love to, buddy. But can't I'm afraid. Them's the rules."

"Rules? What rules?"

Ben sat up. "I can suggest. I can inform. I can advise. I can nudge."

Robby stopped struggling with his father's body. Corpses were, he had discovered, awkward and difficult to move. It was called dead weight for a reason.

"Who are you? Who are you *really*?"

"Have you ever seen Dumbo?"

"The cartoon movie? With the elephant? Yeah, years ago. Why?"

"You know the little insect guy. Jiminy Cricket?"

"Yeah…"

"Well, I'm kinda the opposite of him."

Ben pointed at the body. "Talking of which. Don't worry about that right now. You're still not finished."

"What do you mean?"

"Your revenge, young Edmund. It has still not been fully realised. You know the feeling you got in ending him? You want to have that feeling again, don't you..?"

Robby did. He wanted it very much.

"What should I do?"

Ben smiled. It might have been his imagination, but Robby thought it looked a bit too wide to be natural.

"Oh I have a few ideas on that front…"

Robby didn't leave the house on Wednesday. The snowfall was noticeably heavier, and he didn't fancy heading out in it. His revenge would have to wait until another day.

Late in the evening, Robby heard a deafening thumping noise from outside. He peeked through the curtains. There was a bright orange light a few streets away. A plume of fire was unfolding into the darkening sky, bathing everything in a shining orange light.

Ben, who was still hanging around the house, joined him at the window.

"That'll be your local petrol – sorry, gas – station then. Why do you call it gas? It's a bloody liquid."

"Never really thought about it," Robby said. He wasn't paying attention to the question. He was watching the fire. It looked like it was spreading. He heard the sound of sirens getting closer. The plane crash yesterday and now this.

"What the hell is happening here?"

"What the Hell, indeed," Ben eased himself into Robby's father's chair. The body was still on the floor, but now tightly wrapped in plastic and tape. Ben cracked open a can of beer that was sitting on the coffee table beside the chair. He used the body as a foot stool.

"Do you know something? You said you know lots of things. What's happening here?"

"It's kind of hard to explain, Robby."

"Are you... are you doing this?"

"Me? Oh no. Not at all. I'm just... an interested observer."

"So you do know what's happening?"

Ben sipped from the beer and grimaced. "Jesus. How do you people drink this watered down pish? Yes. Yes, I do know what's happening. And no, I can't tell you. I'm not allowed. I'm just here to watch things unfold."

"Why?"

Ben sighed dramatically. "Because I'm bored and I need entertainment. But never mind me. Are you all set for your big day? The snow should ease off by tomorrow, it'll make it easier to move about."

"What *are* you?"

Ben waggled a finger. "Ah! Now *that* is a much better question. I think you know the answer, Robby. 'I am a man more sinned against than sinning.'"

Ben's skin rippled. His pupils grew, they swirled like ink in water until each eye was totally black. Just as quickly they returned to normal again.

"I'm your friend, Robby. That's what I am."

Robby nodded and started to get ready for tomorrow night.

Robby pulled the hood of his coat even tighter. Ben had been right, the snowfall had eased off, but it was still freezing cold.

He climbed the fence and dropped into the back garden. He walked carefully, avoiding leaving footprints in the snow whenever possible. The back door to the house was locked. That wasn't a problem. Ben had given him a key. Robby put it in the lock, and it opened with a low clunk. He slipped inside.

The kitchen was dark, but there was enough reflected light from outside for Robby to negotiate the room easily. He took off his backpack, eased out of his coat and hung it on the hook on the back of the door.

He could hear the sound of a television from the next room. The laugh track of some moronic sitcom. The person in the room was laughing along with it. Her laugh was loud, braying. He hated the sound of it instantly.

Ben was correct. This was the right thing to do.

He reached into his bag and took out a roll of duct tape and a couple of other items.

He walked quietly down the hallway to the lounge. The light from the television could be seen through a crack in the door.

Robby pushed the door open.

He knew he was safe. He knew there was only one other person in the house this week. Ben had told him.

The girl jumped with shock.

"What the fuck! How the hell did you get in here, you little freak?"

Robby smiled. "Hello to you, too, Shirley."

Later, once he had finished, Robby waited.

He looked at his handiwork and smiled. Robby moved to the window. Shirley gave a short, watery cough.

"Shhh!" he said, opening the curtains just enough to have a good view down the front path.

A minute or so later, Stone came into view. He had his collar pulled up tight. His silhouette was broken by the orange red glow of his cigarette.

As Stone walked to the front door, Robby moved across the room, hiding in a dark corner

"Shirl?" Stone said as he opened the front door.

As if in reply, Shirley gave another cough. She gurgled something that might have been a word.

The curtains were closed and the darkness in the room was so thick it was almost a physical thing. Robby could just about make out Stone's outline as he moved carefully into the room.

Shirley coughed again.

"Shirl?"

Stone reached out and flicked the light switch.

"Fuck!"

Shirley was sitting on a chair from the dining table. Her ankles and wrists were bound to the chair with duct tape. Loops of tape were wrapped around her chest, holding her upright and unmoving.

Her eye sockets were empty. There were two red holes where her eyeballs had once been. Blood ran down her cheeks like thick red tears. The eyeballs sat on the coffee table in front of her. A blood stained spoon and knife sat beside them.

Stone had still not seen Robby. His full attention was on Shirley.

She coughed again. She spat out the blood that was rolling into her mouth from her raw eye sockets.

Stone knelt beside her, putting his hand on hers. He called her name again and again. A moment or two later, she stopped breathing.

Gently, Stone let go of his girlfriend's hand. He slumped. His face was pale. Shocked. Robby almost felt a flicker of pity, but the satisfaction from the hurt he had caused his oppressor overwhelmed any negative emotion.

His gaze turned to the coffee table. Robby watched as he first lifted the knife and then the spoon.

"It's harder than it looks to sharpen the edge of a spoon."

Stone jumped at the sound of the voice.

"Lancaster? What are you doing? Help me!"

Robby ignored the request. He smiled, enjoying the desperation in the voice. It was glorious.

"What do you think of my work?" he asked.

Robby heard the sound of the siren in the distance, but getting closer.

"Huh?"

Lancaster gestured towards the dead body and spoke slowly as if to a small child. "My work, you stupid fucking prick. Her. Your dead whore. She's dead as earth."

"You..." Stone said, his mind slowly processing what he was hearing. Thinking was like wading through mud for the likes of him. "You did this?"

Lancaster smiled and held his arms out from his sides. "Yup."

Stone got to his feet. He was shaking with rage. His hands tight fists.

"You bastard…"

"Now Gods stand up for bastards," Robby said.

Stone screamed. He grabbed the knife from the table and leapt at Robby. The scream was one of pure rage. Of unthinking blind hate. He brought the knife down in a vicious motion, slashing deep into Robby's upraised arm.

Robby screamed. He felt the blade go deep. It scraped against bone.

Stone wrenched the blade free. He readied to stab again.

A voice shouted. "Freeze!"

Stone froze. There was an authority in the voice that brooked no argument.

Robby could see the figure. He managed not to smile. A uniform. A silver badge and gun.

"Drop it, son. Right. Now."

Stone looked at the Sheriff. From the Sheriff to the knife in his hand and back.

"But… but I didn't do…"

Robby clutched his arm. He was sobbing in pain. It wasn't hard to feign. The screaming ache in his arm was very real. But he still hadn't finished here.

Robby's friend smiled his cold smile again. "Something is happening here. In Hell."

"I don't know what you mean. What *is* happening here?"

Ben's eyes filled with black.

"What they are, yet I know not: but they shall be the terrors of the earth."

Angel
Matthew Cash

WELCOME TO A TOWN CALLED HELL

Jadie

The bird broke through the swollen black clouds, flashes of sheet lightning illuminated its pure white feathers. She didn't know exactly what breed of bird it was, as she was no ornithologist, but it was big and white. When its red pointed spear of a beak opened, the sound of a hundred souls in torment filled the night sky.

Something was wrong with its wing, it flapped and fluttered at a mad angle, the other beat furiously as though to make up for its destroyed partner.

It screeched with the lament of many voices and vanished into a thick rolling fog.

Jadie opened her eyes and used her middle fingers to remove the crust from the corners.

The dream had been the same for the past week, she wished whatever it was supposed to represent would just happen already. She hated that she was like her mother, abnormal. She had inherited her mother's gift of dreaming the future. Gift wasn't the right word, curse was more appropriate. This didn't feel like a gift at all. Cryptic dreams that were virtually impossible to figure out until after some random event birthed distinctive similarities.

Once, her mother had a recurring dream about two blue, white and red-striped birthday cake candles, wicks lit, with two fat bluebottle flies circling them. They hadn't been able to fathom out the meaning behind it, and only after the terrorist attack on the World Trade Centre did they compare the two burning waxen sticks to the two skyscrapers. But even then it could have meant something else entirely, it had just been her interpretation of the dream. Jadie remembered that time clearly, her mother had her fifteen minutes of fame when she showed the Press her etchings of her dreams; which were dated months before the terror attack. The way she had drawn the two burning candles with two flies circling them bore an uncanny resemblance to the disaster of September 11th, but Jadie also remembered a few months after when they found the two Baker twins, Charlie and Dixie, strung up in their stars and stripes T-shirts, hanging in the woods. Who says that her mother's premonition wasn't symbolic of their suicide?

Jadie never wrote down or recorded her dreams, she saw her ability as a curse and hoped and prayed that she wouldn't find anything coincidental in the local newspapers or news bulletins. But she knew what recurring dreams meant for her.

Jadie got out of bed and slipped into pink fluffy slippers and a matching bathrobe. She ran a hand through her hair and shuffled to the top of the stairs. *Thank god,* she thought upon seeing her mother's coat and bag had vanished from the hooks at the bottom of the stairs, her mother had gone to school already. She was surprised that she hadn't woken her, as even though she was a grown adult, whilst she stayed with her mother she insisted that they had breakfast together like they did when she lived there before. Twenty-six years old and back living with her mother wasn't the ideal situation for her to be in, but she had no other choice. Her husband Patrick had screwed her for everything she had after she had cheated on him and she barely had any savings. So it was back to the old town. Back to, for her, Hell on earth.

When she was halfway down the stairs she saw a figure appear the other side of the frosted glass of the front door. Her immediate expectation was that it would be her mother, she would have come home from school ill or something. Her mother's prophetic dreams had become more severe than ever over the last couple of weeks. Headaches, nausea and irritable moods had accompanied them as she ironically found she had trouble sleeping. She never went into details anymore about her dreams, as she feared further public attention to herself would dampen her career as a maths teacher at the local school, but she kept a sketchbook.

Jadie stopped at the base of the stairs and waited for the sound of keys in the door but it never happened. The dark figure behind the glass was joined by a shorter one and the doorbell rang. Fastening the bathrobe around herself, Jadie unlatched the door and stared wide-eyed when she saw two cops on the doorstep.

Father Sweeney

Father Sweeney gasped in agony as the red hot crucifix burnt into his flesh, wisps of smouldering skin wafting up to his nose. His yellowing teeth clenched down together with almost enough force to snap. The sound of sizzling and the smell of cooking meat filled the room as the glowing cross was brought down once again on the pasty skin of his right thigh. Father Sweeney wiped tears away so he could see the other five fresh red welts on his skin. "Enough," he pleaded with himself and lowered the cooling brand back into the embers of the fire.

His doughy white legs were covered in a multitude of scars in the shape of the cross. Years ago he had made crude cuts with knives or razor-blades and then with cigarettes. He burned them into his skin to symbolise his sin. But he had learnt that it wasn't enough, it was never enough, never. He needed to inflict more pain, to endure intense suffering. He had researched acids and chemicals but soon found out these things weren't that reliable or easy to come by, so he had chosen a more medieval approach. Six in a week. Things were obviously taking a turn for the worse. With each individual punishment that he inflicted on himself, he visualised the sinful thought or act that had merited its creation.

The first had been at the evening prayer meeting, Mr Denholm had been waffling on and on about various stomach-churning ailments he was suffering from, and whilst he sipped coffee and appeared sympathetic, he imagined pouring the boiling hot liquid from the percolator over his withered face, revelling in his screams as blisters popped like bubbles.

The second was for Katie Franks, that lovely innocent fair-haired widow, forever widening his waistbands with her culinary delights. The way she moved in her summer dresses at the Tuesday afternoon bake-out sparked the filthiest of perverted sexual fantasies to flood his mind.

Oh, how he had envisioned lifting that floral material above her waist, bending her over the banqueting table and mounting her vigorously. He would shove handfuls of the other wives' cakes into her panting mouth as he called her a filthy whore. Then he had seen himself pull out of her gaping hole and thrust his penis into the soft sponge of yet another of her prize-winning masterpieces and empty thick hot wads of his own special ingredient.

He had earned two brands of the cross for that particular subconscious act of perversion.

Four, five and six were for the car that had just sped away, for allowing himself to give into the sins of the flesh once again, for putting himself inside every hole he could find in his regular whore, Gracie. She always took twice as much money than she should as he had to buy her silence as well as her orifices.

He knew that this week he would fare even worse, his mind was becoming more and more lewd and perverted. His libido was a disgusting, ravenous, insatiable monster that was constantly forcing him to try new and more risqué things. And now that stupid teacher had killed herself, he knew the impurity of his thoughts would reach a new crescendo when her daughter finally came back to the church. It was inevitable it would happen, Miss Carter was a devout believer, was a regular, it would be what she would have wanted. Then he would be forced to see her, to see Jadie Carter again.

In a town this small, you mostly saw at least half the population in one week and her mother had confided in him months ago about her daughter's marriage break up and her eventual return to the town. She had been distraught at her daughter's way of getting out of the marriage but sympathetic as only a mother could be. Of course he had offered her support, as always and said that she should encourage Jadie to come to confessional, even though in his heart he hated the idea of it.

He didn't hate Jadie Carter, quite the opposite, he was obsessed by her. She was the reason he had started self-harming in the first place. The inner struggle he had fought whenever in her company, this child of God, he hated the power she had over him. Every movement she made whilst in his presence was watched with uncontrollable concentration, every slight glimpse of skin was mentally catalogued for future self-indulgence of the sordid kind. And she had only been fourteen then.

Whilst he had simultaneously hated the thoughts he harboured, he also had no control over them and would find himself pausing too long between passages of scripture, staying a little bit too long on her as he surveyed his congregation. The vivid dreams she inspired made him physically hurt himself even more, filthy perverse levels of sub-human depravity. He would visualise himself as some aroused, over-sexed monster, a gigantic lapping tongue enveloping her, tasting her, as he desecrated her in every way possible over and over again until he opened his colossal jaws and completely devoured her.

He knew that these thoughts and images were Satan sent and purely God's way of testing his faithfulness, but he had nearly given up the priesthood because of them. He would even ruminate her abduction and rape and possibly even murder. But he had been strong, had done the right thing by her and his congregation.

The prostitutes helped a lot, especially those that bore a slight resemblance in height and hair colour, but she never failed to have his undivided attention whenever she was near.

He had commended himself on not giving in to the desires that some of his colleagues had gotten away with for years, but it had drained everything out of him. Whilst it was sacrilegious to do so, he was happy when she turned to her later teens and shunned her mother's beliefs and the church.

Finally, he had thought, finally he would have some peace.

But now she had returned, so had the filth.

Christopher

Christopher woke up face down on his hallway carpet, his right cheek welded to the cheap pile with dried yellow vomit. He peeled his face from the rug and pushed himself to his knees. The interior of his apartment looked as if it had been trashed by some irate burglar who hadn't found anything whatsoever of value. Waking up face down on the floor covered in his own vomit, in what strangers would assume was a squat, wasn't too much of a shocking occurrence for Christopher. It was a regular thing. Too regular.

Flashes of the previous night seared across his eyelids in blinding technicolour. Alcohol. Lots of alcohol. The vision of him sitting in his boxer shorts with a concoction of numerous spirits that surprisingly didn't melt the glass, as he failed to maintain an erection over the softcore adult film, lingered the most.

That was Christopher's average Saturday night so nothing was out of the ordinary there and his housekeeping didn't ever leave much to be desired either.
The first odd thing he noticed were the white feathers everywhere, which was unusual as he had allergies to eiderdown and feathery shit so he tended to avoid that kind of thing at all costs.
The hallway looked more trashed than normal, like it had literally exploded. Everything had been upended, picture frames were askew, pot plants unearthed. This was beyond his normal level of untidiness. The lounge was in a similar state and as he stood in the centre of the room, he gazed in horror at his hi-fi system lying smashed in the fireplace.

Christopher rubbed a hand across his beard and scratched at a patch of dried sick as he surveyed the damage. *Why the hell would I have done all this?* He looked up into the mirror above the fireplace, half expecting to see crudely scrawled messages inked across his chest like the guy in that movie *Memento*. That was when he saw the big fuck-off wings. Behind him. Nothing came out of his mouth other than a slack-jawed 'whaaaa' noise.

The wings were the traditional Christian angel, white-feathered ones. When he realised he was awake and not suffering some alcohol induced hallucination, he thought he had been the target of a joke, albeit an incredibly elaborate one. Christopher studied his reflection.

He turned side on so as to get a look at how the wings were attached, but that was easier said than done with a ten foot wingspan. The last remaining item on the fireplace, a green Buddha-shaped beer bottle which he had kept for sentimental reasons from the last time he had had sex with someone real, was knocked onto the floor exploding in dusty green shards. The wings rose and fell with his rapid breathing. They didn't flap, just fluttered like leaves in a breeze, as though they were physically attached to his shoulder blades. The onset of a panic attack blossomed in his gut and chest. He closed his eyes and regulated his breathing, convincing himself that when he opened them one of two things would have happened. One, the wings would have vanished and it was purely some mind-fuck from being so wasted the night previous, or two, they would still be there and a rational explanation would be floating like a metaphysical balloon above his head.

His breathing calmed, he opened his eyes and breathed a big sigh of relief. They had gone.

He was wrong. He turned and saw that they were folded neatly down his back. He let out a cry and the wings shot out as his muscles tensed in horror. The right wingtip knocked the mirror off the wall and sent him reeling into a big, half naked, feathered heap on the floor.

Somehow, with a lot of difficulty he got to his feet. He raised a hand and touched a wing, fingering the patch where it fused with his shoulder blade.
Luckily the mirror hadn't smashed, it just lay against the electric fire at a slanted angle. Christopher relaxed and the wings folded neatly behind him, their tips brushing his naked ankles. He tugged at one and screamed almost every swear word in his vocabulary and others that weren't. It fucking hurt!

Christopher came to his first conclusion, that the things were attached.
After he had calmed, a number of thoughts crossed his mind, the predominant ones were:

What the fuck am I supposed to do? I'm not religious.

Can I fly? That could be awesome!

Will these get me laid?

The first thing he wanted to know was how to use them, and for that he would need room. He rushed into his bedroom and grabbed his biggest hoody and shoved his arms and head into it. He pulled it down over his folded wings, stuck some trousers on and got his coat. After just managing to fasten the zip on his German army parka he checked his reflection. Apart from about twenty inches of his wingtip protruding from beneath his coat he was pretty normal looking, albeit slightly hunchbacked. He pulled his hood up and left his place to search for somewhere secluded. *Let's see what these babies can do.*

    As Christopher walked from his apartment, the dregs of the previous night's hangover made him feel rough as fuck. When he opened the door to the outside world, even though the sky was dull and overcast, everything just seemed too bright. The hoody and heavy coat were making him sweat and he could feel the feathers sticking to his back. He pushed the hood back and tried his best to tame the catastrophe that he called hair.

A couple of white trash yokels passed him by and mentioned something about *Quasimodo,* which was obviously intended as an insult, what with him being very hunched in the shoulder region, but secretly he was quite impressed that they had heard about Victor Hugo's infamous, audibly-challenged bell-ringer. Then he remembered Disney did a version of *The Hunchback of Notre Dame* and wasn't so impressed.

He crossed over Main Street and shuffled through the gates to a miniscule park that ran alongside All Saints Hospital. He always found it depressing that across the road from the hospital sat All Saints Church, how morbid it must be to be terminally ill, gazing out of the window at the cemetery, knowing that you would be planted mere yards from where you died. And the fact that the two buildings, both of which welcomed people into the world and kissed them goodbye, were called All Saints, was particularly maudlin.

The park was secluded, the ideal place, he thought, to test out his new wings without drawing any attention to himself.

He was wrong.

The park was relatively empty as was usually the case for a weekday afternoon. He wandered past the lake with its multitude of ducks and geese quacking and honking at him in the vain hope that he may have some bakery produce about his person. Christopher had always liked birds but never understood their want to gather in flocks. Surely, having been given the gift of flight, it would prove to be so much easier to get your own space, some time on your own. But you rarely see a duck wandering about looking forlorn alone or a goose having some time to itself, there's usually at least another nearby. Maybe they feared solitude.

Whilst he was mentally debating the social characteristics of the feathered-kind and absent-mindedly walking along, a hissing noise brought him to a halt. He stopped and peered over his shoulder and was amazed at the sight. At least twenty Canadian geese waddled towards him, their necks straining straight up in the air, beaks stabbing skyward, with their little pink tongues like slivers of meat poking out, hissing for all their worth. Naturally he backed away from this frightful flock, or should it be a ghastly gaggle? Either way he backed off but soon noticed some more had appeared behind him.

He was surrounded.

One particularly plucky goose went for him, its beak darted forward and pinched his thigh.

"Ow, you goose-bastard!" he screamed, running at them flapping his arms and shouting.

He could feel his wings straining against his clothes, begging to be unleashed. Long black necks pecked at him from all directions as he ran through them. One caught the skin on the back of his hand and it felt like the time his brother pinched his arm in their neighbour Charlie's iron vice. He smacked one round the head and had visions of the old *Daffy Duck* cartoons, the scenes where he gets hit round the face and his orange beak would spin round to the back of his head.

Somehow he managed to fight his way through the feathered fuckers but he was majorly goosed. An old couple walking their dog stood watching the whole charade, seemingly unphased by the events, like it happened all the time. The old man puffed on a cherry red pipe, nodded and said, like it was the most normal thing ever.

"They were after your feathers!" He pointed to the wingtips that were hanging beneath coat Christopher's coat, the tips covered in mud and bird shit.
"Bit early for Halloween, ain't it?" the old woman asked Christopher.
Christopher scowled at them and muttered, "Fuck off."

After he had defended himself against the avian attackers and offended the elderly couple, he found himself a rather secluded part of the park out of view of the hospital. This part was overgrown and not often used, a gravel footpath that was hidden amongst long grass was a small glimpse to one of the old treks up to the mountains. A weathered wooden signpost and an obscured footpath were all that remained of a forgotten era.
Doing his final checks that he was alone, he took off his coat and hoodie and threw them to the ground. He felt a little exposed, the first time he had been semi-naked outdoors since the balcony incident the previous summer. He found the air pleasant on his skin, and the flakes of snow sauntering down cooled him.

Christopher took a deep breath and tried to spread his wings.

The sensation of having wings and trying to move them was alien to him. Try to imagine having four arms and two sets of shoulder blades. To start with he stretched his arms wide apart and saw that this made the wingspan do similar.

Right, he thought, simple. Obviously to engage in flight I needed to flap them, but could I just flap and go, or did I need to run or kick off like Superman? One thing that always baffled him about Superman was his arms. Why did he have to have his hands in fists with one arm straight and the other bent? Was it just to look cool, or some kind of steering aid?

The difficulty was deciding whether or not his wings could move independently from his arms as they seemed to mimic and react the same. Feeling like a prize dick, he flapped his arms up and down and pretended to fly. To his utter and complete terrified excitement his wings beat up and down and he actually felt his boots leave the ground a few inches. Frantically, he flapped as fast as he could but came down to the grass. His heart thundered in his chest. It was hard work. After a few more attempts he realised it was a lot like swimming, instead of slowly and steadily moving the water around himself, he moved the air. Whooping with childish glee, he even managed to get off the ground for at least a minute and was so high in the air that he was no longer secluded.

No matter where you go there's always some spotty, snotty-nosed annoying little red-necked kids nearby and this time was no exception. Two boys who looked like brothers, but not twins even though they wore almost identical tracksuits, stood mouths agape below him. The younger one had a BB gun slung over his shoulder.
"Motherfucker!" one of them shouted. Christopher knew not whether it was to himself or to his brother, such awful language for someone who was only about ten years old. His brother, the oldest looking of the two just drained the can he was drinking from and stared.
Christopher was flummoxed, there he was beating his arms and wings, flying. Well, hovering really, treading air, twenty feet above them.

How the hell would he explain this?
"Yo, dawg, are you an angel?" the youngest shouted up at him.
Christopher thought about this for a moment. Did he lie and say 'yes' and risk the wrath of God, for assuming he was an angel when he was an atheist and for not being honest, or tell the truth?
The boys waited patiently for an answer.
"Err… I don't know," he muttered and flapped. His arms were starting to ache, he desperately wanted to land but didn't want them pawing at his plumage.
The oldest boy stopped drinking and to his horror hurled what felt like a full can of soda at him. It struck him right on the left breast and it hurt like a bastard.

"You little shit, that fucking hurt! Who throws a can of Coke at a fucking angel?" he shouted, trying to control his flying as best he could.
The oldest one spoke, "You said you didn't know if you were an angel."
"I might be, so fuck off!" Christopher said trying to look down menacingly, rather than scared.
"Nah," said the oldest, "Angels wouldn't swear." He eyed the tattoos on Christopher's arms, "Or have tattoos."
Smug little fucker.
His little brother turned to him, "Maybe he's like one of them Dark Angels in the films."
Maybe that's what I am, thought Christopher, *an Angel of Death.*
"Nah, I know what he is," the oldest kid said knowingly. "He's the fucking fairy off of Ma's Christmas tree!" He burst into laughter and his little brother joined in.
Hang on now, Christopher thought, getting rather angry. *I'm a fucking wonder of science, a flying man, a fucking angel for all they knew and there they were being ghetto trash and taking the piss! And you don't go throwing fucking Coke cans at angels, Dark ones or Light ones!*

What happened next was a blur of confusion. Rage blinded him momentarily and the next thing he knew he had grabbed the foul-mouthed boy, much to his younger sibling's dismay. He kicked and yelled some really nasty offensive trailer shit at him and screamed for him to let him go.

Christopher didn't.

If he had have let him go, he would have turned to jam on the footpath below where his little brother would get splattered by yokel yolk. As much as this thought brought joy to Christopher's mind he knew he couldn't be that inhumane. Ahead, he spotted the whitewashed wooden spire of All Saints Church.

"You can't just leave me there!" the boy shouted as he saw where Christopher was headed. His little brother ran after them firing pellets from the BB gun, like a mini commando. Christopher soared into the air, beating his wings. He felt empowered, exhilarated. He flew up and over the sloped black roof of the church, up towards the spire. The boy's little brother got a lucky shot in and a pellet stung Christopher in the back of the head. His instinct was to grab the place where the pellet had struck and in doing so he let of the boy. Christopher tumbled and rolled around in the air as he tried his best to control his flying. The boy he dropped slid down the sloped roof and landed on the cemetery grass. Within a few seconds he was up and by his brother's side. Christopher was relieved that he hadn't been hurt, but panicked when he saw the older boy take the BB gun. He flapped his arms hard, but just like panicking whilst swimming, he started to lose propulsion.

The boy took aim with the gun.

Christopher's wings flapped about him uselessly like a spasticated pigeon.

The boy fired.

A lead pellet traveling at 180 metres per second struck Christopher in the temple and the last thing he saw before it knocked him unconscious was the tall oval stained glass window of All Saints Church.

Father Sweeney

Father Sweeney had avoided Jadie since she had been living back with her mother. If he saw so much caught a flutter of blonde hair he would turn away, avoiding every temptation that would let The Beast out of its cage. The photograph her mother had shown him of her wedding day had been bad enough. She was divine in her pristine wedding dress, perfection incarnate, he was relieved that she hadn't returned to her own town to be wed.

Even though the urges to visit her mother's house proceeding her suicide had been strong, he had been stronger and spent most of his time at home cleansing himself in the only way he thought he deserved, with the burning brand of his faith.

From home he had driven straight to All Saints Church with the intention of hiding out somewhere relatively quiet, his cell phone switched off since he heard the news of the suicide. He thought it would be the last place Jadie would go to after hearing the news. But he could not have been more wrong.

When he heard the church doors open he dived into the confession box and closed the door quietly so as not to attract the visitor of his presence.

He leant his weathered forehead against the wooden door and held his breath as footsteps approached the confession box. Call it wishful thinking, sixth sense, or what you will, but he knew it was *her*. He felt her move past him like one might do a spirit, every pore on his skin opened up, his nostrils flared to receive even the slightest of aroma of her scent. He heard the click of soles upon the stone floor and imagined the feet inside those shoes, would they be stockinged or bare? The soft flutter of material brushed the other side of the door as the visitor walked by. The door felt part of him, like she was running soft silk across his naked body. Father Sweeney did his best to control his breathing and prayed that the visitor would keep on walking. Relief flooded through him as the person continued past him and onwards to the front of the church. He heard a slight creak of the wooden pews as the visitor sat down.

Risking a glimpse, he peaked through the grille in the door and saw a blonde figure sat with her head lowered, as though in prayer. A quick sliver of her pale white neck as she adjusted her hair was enough to destroy the bindings of The Beast that Father Sweeney had kept subdued for so long. He knew it was her. *It was her*. Within seconds he was so rigid he had to drop his trousers. He pushed a fingertip against the fresh wounds he had made before coming to the church that day and scratched hard hoping that the pain would diminish his arousal, but it only furthered to increase it. Father Sweeney pushed his cheek against the grille and curled his fingers around his throbbing erection, his thumb resting on the inch-long cruciform scar that ran up its side. She was crying, sweet Jadie was weeping. Oh, how he longed to touch those tears, to bathe in them, taste them. A blinding vision of him washing in her bodily secretions as they poured from her overwhelmed him and he pumped his fist back and forth along his shaft furiously.

He needed to be shot of this devil's venom.

A noise from outside was all it took, then he caught her face, side profile as she turned towards the doors expecting someone to enter. The curved cheekbones and the small delicate nose were the same, as were the dark pinkness of her full lips. Father Sweeney was out of control, there was nothing he could do, he knew it was wrong, inside he begged, pleaded with the deity he had spent his whole life fighting devotion, to spare him from these obscene thoughts but He showed no mercy. Jadie sobbed uncontrollably and let out a low, almost orgasmic moan of help as Father Sweeney sprayed the interior of the confessional wall with spurt upon spurt of semen. It was so intense that when he heard the loud crash he thought his heart had burst inside his chest.

His bloodshot eyes widened as he saw something had crashed through the stained-glass window and landed in a heap of limbs and feathered wings in the central aisle of the church, overturning the large crucifix. It took several long drawn out seconds for him to register what he was seeing, if it wasn't for the gasp of Jadie he would have thought it hallucinatory.

An angel?

As Jadie bent down to aid the injured, what appeared to be, angel, he saw the Christ on the Cross statue stood against the altar upside down, the tattoos on the exposed torso of the male angel, the tears of blood running down his face and the fact that he resembled one of the town's more colourful drunkard characters and knew this was an abomination.

Jadie

Jadie rubbed one of the long white feathers between her thumb and forefinger marvelling at the delicacy of each individual barb. A pink, heart-patterned duvet was draped over the figure of the dark-haired man on the bed. He lay with one arm across his chest and the other resting on the pillow above his bandaged head. His wings were wrapped around him like a protective sarcophagi as he snored peacefully.

Jadie hadn't been able to stop staring at him all night, he was her miracle and possibly a sign that her mother had been right in her predictions.

She stole a glance out of her bedroom window, the flutter of snowflakes swirling about more frequently this morning. Who would have thought Armageddon would look like Christmas?

The snow reminded her of her mother, the magical look in her eyes when she caught sight of the year's first flake.

Her mother.

The police officers who had greeted her solemnly on the doorstep the previous morning were bearers of bad news. There's just something ominous about two sombre looking officers of the law on your doorstep. It had to be bad news. Two police officers hammering their fists on the door, rocking it in its hinges, meant they were coming to arrest your ass. A gentle fingertip on the doorbell's button and a gentle knuckled rap on the glass panel meant they needed to disturb you, but with some kind of compassion.

They didn't look any older than she was and they wore mournful expressions on their faces as they stood on the porch covered in a light dusting of snow.

"Mrs Jadie Troughton?" one of them had finally asked. The sound of her married name along with the underlying portentous tone made her slump down on the welcome mat before the two awkward cops. She wasn't Troughton anymore, she was a Carter. Just like her mother had changed back to her maiden name after her father had run off with his secretary, Jadie had jettisoned the names of the two men she hated more than anything in the world and chosen her mother's maiden name.

The words flitted and fluttered as finely as the snow that fell and blew through the doorway and lighted on the pink fluff of her bathrobe. "... sorry... mother... handgun... suicide... anyone... to sit with you? Anywhere you can go?"

Jadie had just stared at the police officer's mouth, the lower lip had a slight redness around the exterior, chapped from the cold air maybe. His front right tooth was chipped.

The words had sunk in somehow, as automatically as the ones that left her mouth. She was a husk, some other part of her had taken over, eager to be rid of the men, eager to have the door slammed shut so that the words could reform and replay inside her over and over again until their reality finally tore her wide open.

The angel mumbled something in his sleep and scratched at his black beard. Jadie smiled down at him and studied the grey and white hairs that ran through the wiry hair. He contradicted all of the things she thought she knew about angels. Aside from the glorious wings he appeared to be just a normal man; spots, blemishes, imperfections as any other, tattoos too for heaven's sake. But what did she know about anything really? What did anyone really know? Maybe he was a man who was sent back with some divine message? She checked his bandage hadn't leaked and wished that she could do more to help her big white bird.

Yesterday, after she had calmed down, after she had screamed and shouted and cried and kicked her legs like a child, she got up and got dressed and walked in the snow. A trip to the nearest shop to buy a bottle of vodka, back to the house to stand it on the telephone table by the front door and back out again like she was on a mission.

She hadn't known where her feet were taking her until she was almost there.

All Saints church was standing where she had last left it twelve years previous. She had been fourteen years old when she turned her back on God. She had been foolish for doing so, she realised that as she saw herself push open the wooden door and enter. Her father, the adulterer, destroying their family for some whore. She refused to go back to the church, was angry at a deity that could let such things happen. But now here she was back once again now another crisis had befallen her. Funny that it had taken her mother's death to take her back.

She walked up the central aisle, her fingers brushing the dark varnished pews that hadn't changed all her life. The church was empty. She wondered if Father Sweeney still ran the show there. She hoped not. The priest had been middle-aged and greying when she had been a frequent churchgoer. She always thought he fit the stereotypical image of a pervert priest. A meme on a social networking site sprung to mind, a split screen picture of a Muslim man in traditional garb with the words: ' When I die I will have seventy-two virgins'. The other showed The Pope with a beaming smile, his phrase read, 'I'll have seventy-two virgins before I die.'

There were never any rumours or scandals involving Father Sweeney but she had always felt uncomfortable in his presence. The way he stared a little bit too long at her and the other girls. She had never mentioned it because nobody else had and he had never done anything untoward. He just emitted a certain creepy vibe that possibly only she had picked up on.

Jadie had gazed up at the white ceiling and black beamed rafters, the church always seemed so much bigger on the inside. The focal point at the front of the church was its glorious stained glass window, a gigantic red crucifix with a whole spectrum of colours behind it and long yellow rays to look like sunlight or maybe the glory of God. She was surprised they hadn't had it removed in all this time, there had been a petition when she was little to have a new design. Sometimes when the sun was setting at a particular angle in the sky, a giant inverted red cross rode up the central aisle as though desecrating the church. Bad design in its most unfortunate form.

For a moment then she remembered asking herself why she had gone there, what was she hoping for? She had felt silly, a selfish, stubborn hypocrite. By turning her back on something that had meant so much to her, only to commit adultery and then come running back when her mother died, she had committed yet another sin. She was no better than her cheating father.

It didn't matter that her ex-husband Patrick had been an abusive drunkard. It didn't matter that he hit her. There was no excuse for what she had done. A silly stupid mistake that she hated herself for.

When she had heard voices from outside, she expected company in the empty church. Maybe if Father Sweeney showed up it would pay for her to slip into the confessional and rid herself of twelve years of filth and sin.

It had been a time of reflection for Jadie, the time she spent in the church, as the shock of her mother's suicide boiled up inside her. She didn't care who came in the church, she didn't care if anyone heard her, she didn't care if creepy Father Sweeney was still ringleader; nothing mattered.

She raised her tear-sodden face to Christ on the cross and to the red stained glass and let out two words as a long, mournful, wail. "Help me."

That was when her miracle happened.

Her sobbing stopped abruptly when she saw something large move rapidly towards the window. At first she had thought it was a large bird, as it was obviously airborne, *her big white bird*, but she heard a human cry out as the *something* smashed through the window. She stared in horror as a man wearing what she at first thought to be a cape, came crashing through the glass, collided with the wooden crucifix knocking it over, and landed in a mangled heap on the stone floor at her feet. She cried out and put her hand over her mouth when she saw that it wasn't a cape the man was wearing but wings. The way that they were joined to his back looked very realistic. He was losing consciousness and blood was seeping from a wound on his head. Instinctively she crouched down to see if he was okay and asked him his name.

The man tried to lift his head, his eyes rolled around in his head, he muttered, "Chr..." before passing out.

Jadie gasped again, He was going to say 'Christ'.

"It's a miracle!"

For the first time in as long as she could remember Jadie crossed herself and gazed down at the fallen angel in wonder.

Somehow, he had regained enough consciousness for her to stumble with him back to her mother's house, but it was like accompanying the walking dead. Blurred incomprehensible gibberish came from his mouth as he fought to stay awake. He crashed onto the floor as soon as she had opened the front door, his hand shot out grabbing the bottle of vodka and unscrewing the lid. He drank half the litre bottle in one go before passing out, and spilling the rest of the spirit onto the carpet.

Jadie stroked the angel's face and smiled in bliss as his eyelids fluttered like he was about to wake.

Then a ground shaking cacophony from outside took their breath away.

Christopher and Jadie

Christopher opened his eyes, startled at the sudden noise and instantly sat up. Head-cracking pain and dizziness made him fall back down whimpering, screwing his eyes shut tight. Everything was too bright, he risked lifting one eyelid. Everything was too pink. Where the hell was he? A face appeared in his line of vision, and as the blur cleared he noticed it was an attractive blond woman.

Chris you old dog, still got it in you, been a while since you woke up in someone else's bed, he congratulated himself, even though the only beds other than his own he had ever woken up in were hospital ones.

She looked towards the window and then back at him. She was frightened.

Oh shit, he thought, maybe I'm not supposed to be here.

Then he remembered the noise that had woken him up with a start.

"Do you know what it is?" The woman asked him gesturing towards the window.

Christopher sat up and swore when he saw his wings.

"Shit, I thought that had been a dream." He touched a hand to his bandaged head, "Ow, lord of all fuckery that hurts. What happened to me? I feel like I've been gang-raped by NWA, straight outta jellied petroleum."

Even though Jadie didn't know what he was talking about, his coarse language was giving her serious doubts as to whether his origins were as heavenly as she had previously thought.

She strained her neck gazing out of the window, trying to see over the opposite houses, for a sign as to what had made the thunderous noise. She half expected to see a mushroom cloud growing on the horizon, as the end of the world that her mother had predicted came to fruition. But there was nothing at all for her to see, so she cast her eye back to the half-naked angel sat on her bed with his head in his hands. The wings down his back rose and fell with each deep breath he took. She noticed a detail of one of his heavily tattooed arms, a thick Celtic cross that filled one shoulder and ran down almost to his elbow and the words Black Sabbath filling the crucifix.

"Are you sure you're an angel?" Jadie asked pulling her nightdress down towards her knees, suddenly aware of how much flesh she had on show.

Christopher's eyes lit on her pale white curvaceous thighs as he searched for an answer. The last thing he remembered from the previous day was flapping about swearing at a couple of squirrel-eating hillbilly kids. One thing Christopher prided himself in was his gift of blagging his way out of trouble, so he tried his best to be earnest.

"Do you remember what happened last night?"

He pointed to his head.

"I think I've suffered some kind of memory loss."

Jadie was sceptical but flushed a little when she started to recount the previous day's events.

"I was at All Saints Church mourning the loss of my mother. She killed herself yesterday morning. I was desperate, distraught. I screamed out for help, to God, maybe to anyone and you came crashing through the window and landed at my feet. I rushed to see if you were okay and saw the wings. I asked you if you were an angel, I asked you what your name was, who had sent you. You started to say Christ but passed out."

"Christopher," he said shaking his head. "I was telling you my name. My name's Christopher."

"What?" Jadie asked, a slight venomous tone in her voice.

Christopher repeated himself then asked what had happened after he had passed out.

"I helped you back here, to my mother's house, you were barely conscious, staggering as though you were drunk. You drank almost a litre of vodka and passed out again."

Christopher nodded, that last part was definitely believable. "Did anything else happen, did I say anything else, you know, angel-y?"

Jadie's cheeks reddened and she turned away.

"What? What did I do? Look if I pissed the bed or, you know, worse, then I'll buy you some new sheets or pay the dry cleaning."

"We had sex," Jadie snapped at him, he face a mixture of embarrassment and anger.

Fuck, Christopher cursed himself and took another quick glimpse at her bare thighs, *I tapped that and I don't even remember.* "Jesus."

Jadie appeared hopeful.

"How did that happen?" Christopher asked.

"The conventional way, well almost." Jadie reddened even more as the suspicion she had been well and truly duped inflated inside her like an airbag.

"You came to for a moment, it was the first time you actually spoke to me directly, and said 'I'm an angel of the lord, you've heard all about the Second Coming, well how do you think it starts?' You said I had been chosen to carry the child of God and that you must give me your seed. You're laughing."

Christopher bit the insides of his cheeks hard enough to draw blood as he held back.

"No, no I'm not," he said quickly, his voice squeaking in the way voices tend to do when one is stifling laughter.

Jadie was mortified. This man was obviously a charlatan, real wings or not, it was some elaborate hoax. "Get out of my house."

Christopher stood up. "I'm sorry, I'm sorry okay. I don't know what came over me. Maybe I was telling the truth, you never know."

Jadie fought back tears of humiliation and pointed to the door.

"Are you an angel?"

Christopher shrugged, "Look I don't know okay, I just woke up yesterday and these wings were attached to me. I don't know why the fuck they are there but they seem real. Maybe I've been, like, made into an honorary angel or something? Maybe I'm supposed to do something?"

"Get out," Jadie said pointing more furiously towards the bedroom door.

Christopher clapped his hands as an idea formed in his head.

"Aliens. Maybe it's aliens."

"Get out now," Jadie shouted angrily.

Christopher slouched towards the door and reached a hand out to open it, "You think maybe if we had sex again..."

"Get out. Get out. Get out," Jadie yelled at the top of her voice and pushed him hard towards the door.

"Ow, mind the wings. I'm going, but if you change your mind I live next to McGovern's Electricals," he said as he left the bedroom and started down the stairs. He didn't know how the hell he was going to get back to his apartment unnoticed. Jadie followed to make sure he left, her floodgates opened as she shoved him towards the front door.

As Christopher reached up to undo the latch on the door, a shadow appeared on the other side of the glass and the door crashed open towards him. A tall, fat balding priest stood menacingly in the doorway, a silver crucifix thrust before him like a loaded weapon.

"The power of Christ compels you," he spat with such ferocity that a tree-shaped web of veins bulged in the middle of his forehead.

"Yeah yeah, fuckface. Consider me compelled," Christopher muttered sarcastically before touching a fingertip to Sweeney's crucifix and making a sizzling noise with his mouth. "Your mother cleaned car windscreens in the ghetto and all that jazz." He wiggled his tongue at the priest before pushing past, casually brushing him with his wings.

Sweeney and Jadie watched open-mouthed as Christopher walked away.

Though she was still upset over her ordeal with Christopher, Jadie smiled politely at the priest she hadn't seen since she was a teenager. He was like an awkward schoolboy as he stood on the doorstep shuffling his feet, crucifix hanging limply in his hand.

"Father Sweeney, what is going on around here?"

The Priest wiped his forehead across his sleeve. He was lost for words.

He seemed smaller than she last remembered him but the uneasy feeling he sparked inside of her was still there. The way his eyes seemed to look for too long without blinking. His grey-pink sliver of a tongue wet his lips as he found something to say.

"I, um, saw what happened last night."

Jadie didn't really know what to say, so remained silent.

Father Sweeney stood up straight as he took a deep breath and tried to compose himself. "Don't be fooled by that…" he searched for a word, "…that abomination. I know that man, the last thing he is a heavenly messenger. That man is a drunkard, a blasphemous cretin and the Devil is a great deceiver."

"But the wings," Jadie began.

Father Sweeney shook his head slowly.

"Strange things are happening in this unfortunate town. I fear your mother's prediction may have been true. I believe that she may have been a modern day prophet!"

Jadie was shocked that he knew about her mother's apocalyptic prophecy, she assumed that she would have kept that from the priest.

"Father, what's wrong?"

Father Sweeney pointed down the road.

"There's been a plane crash, it's taken out the bridge. Hundreds of people are dead. Hell has finally come to Hell."

Jadie

The stomach cramps felt like someone had dropped a dumbbell onto her abdomen from a great height. She cried out and a burning geyser of vomit erupted from her gullet and splattered the duvet.

She hoped she hadn't contracted something serious.

The plane crash the day before and some kind of trouble in the woods had cut Hell off from the rest of civilisation. There was talk of radioing for outside help, but the plane crash had fucked everything up. Mobile communications were down and they were pretty much stranded. The wintery wind was threatening to whip up a blizzard and if it did these snowballs would have less than a fair chance in Hell.

She hated that the town was so cut off. The hospital would no doubt be bursting at the seams with survivors of the plane crash, if there were any.

Jadie rolled her t-shirt up and put a palm against her normally flat stomach. The skin looked stretched and distended, a slight curve outwards as though she was severely bloated. She poked a finger at it and it felt sore and hard.

She had difficulty getting to her feet and standing when she'd got there, her belly heavy. Even though she had never experienced it, pregnant was the only word she could use to explain the way her stomach felt.

She waddled through to the bathroom, one hand supporting her unnatural bulge. Inside the medicine cabinet she found a pack of pregnancy kits. It was something she had always kept in, since arriving back in Hell she had been having a little too much fun. This town tended to bring the worst out in people.

She did the thing with the urine and test strip and sat on the toilet, elbows resting on her knees, waiting for the outcome.

The indicator took an age to do anything, she breathed a sigh of relief and leant forward to stick it in the peddle bin. The strip was about to be released from her fingertips when it changed to positive.

Her instinctual reaction was denial, so she shook out another testing strip and forced out more urine.

Over the following half hour, Jadie had used up a whole packet of strips and each one of them came back positive.

She couldn't understand how. Sure, she had gotten friendly with one or two of the town's eligible bachelors since arriving back but nothing more than kissing.

Apart from the angel, a little voice reminded her. She thought it impossible, maybe the pregnancy kits were faulty. But a part of her knew that it was true. There was nothing normal about anything since her mother had taken her life. It wasn't normal for drunken louts to wake up with angel wings.

It wasn't normal for planes to fall out of the sky. It wasn't normal for wolves to roam the woods attacking campers.

She was pregnant and alone.

She was pregnant by an angel. Who knew what other rules the pregnancy might bend?

Should she go find the man she had thought was a messenger from God until the morning, or should she seek solace with the only other person who had witnessed this freak of nature, the priest who stared too much and had been mentally undressing her since she was twelve?

Father Sweeney

There hadn't been anything he could do after the plane had crash. No survivors. Father Sweeney had held a meagre service, a prayer meeting amidst the red-jewelled shards of the shattered stained glass. Half a dozen of the elderly regulars turned up, that was all, the glass grinding into fine powder beneath flat loafers and walking sticks. He had said a few words, offered prayers and sympathies to the families who had lost loved ones in the disaster, but they had been empty words, he had matters closer to home to deal with.

The Angel.

He hated that he referred to the drunkard by such a divine label but the name had stuck now. Old Buster Hancock, who ran the liquor store, had recounted an angelic figure the day previously. He said that the angel came into his store and picked up a crate of beer, at first he had been taken aback and had obviously queried the wings - the angel had insisted they were a fancy dress costume - but they looked too real to Old Buster. It was a sign of the end of times, he had said to Sweeney that afternoon, when even the angels wanted to get wasted.

The only thing Sweeney was certain of was that this, this man, was no heavenly visitor.

He knew he had done bad things in his life, maybe he had made the wrong choices all those years ago when he had joined the priesthood. But there was no turning back now and if this was the time of judgment, he knew that he must make a massive sacrifice to at least counterbalance the scales of justice where his life was concerned.

He would prevent Satan's messenger from performing whatever plan he had been raised to do.

Through Old Buster, Sweeney had found out the name of the drunk who masqueraded as an angel and where he lived.

Christopher Moore.

A bearded, foul-mouthed layabout who had repeatedly caused his neighbours grief. The Johnstons were an elderly couple who were regular customers of Buster Hancock's and were eager to spill the beans on their younger neighbour. Loud raucous music would blare from his apartment at all times of the day, he would frequently have angry outbursts where he would seemingly argue with himself and destroy anything to hand. They weren't overly religious people, choosing to worship at St. Jude's rather than his own church, but they had witnessed the young man's new deformity and were both eager to give out any information that would see him kicked out.

Father Sweeney had boldly chosen the right time to peer through Christopher's window that opened onto the communal balcony. The Hell's angel had been asleep in a tattered armchair completely naked, empty beer cans littering the filthy floor, whilst hard-core pornography played at an increased volume on the TV screen before him. All in view of the window. Tattoos snaked and swirled around his hairy body; images of skulls, serpents, fire and demons, implements of torture and blasphemous objects.

This was no angel.

Sweeney heard the sound of cursing and stepped into the shadows as someone approached the front door. It was Jadie and she looked awful. A hand over his mouth to stop him from crying out in alarm, Father Sweeney eyed the unnatural bulge that protruded over her pink tracksuit bottoms like a marbled pink watermelon. The skin so taut it appeared to be on the brink of splitting. She thumped hard on the door and screamed at the top of her voice.

"Christopher, what the fuck have you put inside me?"

Christopher

He felt the blow to his face but he was so drunk it was like being punched by a balloon. His head rolled backwards as his eyes fluttered open and a mouthful of beery drool made glass pearls in his beard. The fat pink blobs of people fucking on his telly came into focus and he felt his penis twitch once before shrivelling up inside itself. His eyes began to close again, his brain was too fussy and warm with excessive beer consumption and he really wanted to go back inside there and get comfortable.

Slap!

Ouch. That one had hurt, Christopher opened his eyes and one of the cavorting images had come out of the television and was standing in front of him. "Wake up you drunken piece of shit."

The big pink blob screamed at him and slapped the other side of his face.

Christopher smiled crookedly as his vision stayed still long enough for him to make out Jadie's face. "Hey baby, you come back for some more loving?" he said via a tongue that felt three times too big for his mouth, "I got plenty to go around." He absentmindedly pulled on his flaccid cock.

Even though her swollen belly made it hard for her to do so, Jadie bent down and as hard as she could and flicked one of Christopher's swinging testicles. He screamed out in pain and jumped to his feet, eyes wide like he was seeing her for the first time.

Black coffee. Really strong. It tasted disgusting, foul, it coated the inside of his mouth eradicating any flavours of the beer and subsequent vomit. Christopher wiped a hand across his mouth and turned from the one seater table to the armchair Jadie was now sat in, her belly covered in a network of sore-looking red stretchmarks.

"I can honestly say, that without the shadow of a doubt, I don't know what the fuck is happening around here."

Jadie poked a fingertip at her swollen stomach and winced.

"It's obvious isn't it? You've infected me, or impregnated me with something."

Christopher scratched his beard and eyed her bump suspiciously, "How do you know it's mine?"

"Are you fucking serious?"

"We only had sex a couple of days ago and I don't even remember if we did it at all. Plus, don't you think it's a bit soon?"

Jadie jumped out of the chair as though she had been given an electric shock.

"Your wings grew over night didn't they? What's to say that whatever has happened to you isn't contagious?"

Christopher was sceptical but knew that nothing about this week was following the laws of science and her belly did look very sore. He sighed and stood up, empty coffee mug in hand, a look of pride and determination on his face, the look someone who is confident and ready for anything might have.

"I'm taking you to the hospital. It's time we let the people who know more about what the fuck is going on have a look at us and see what the fuck is going on, as you and I clearly don't know what the fuck is going on. So let's go and see if they know…" He paused for breath. As speeches go it was really shit. "What's going on."

Father Sweeney heard everything, the cheap glazed windows of the apartments above the electrical shop held no secrets. He raced down the steps to his car, he knew he hadn't much time, especially if they were planning on seeking medical help. If the doctors took one look at Christopher's wings and knew they were genuine he would never be able to get near him again. He reached into the glove compartment and took out the revolver. It had never been used, well it had been used, just never fired. He had used it with Gracie, the woman he paid regularly for sex, a little bit of role play to spice things up, he had told her it wasn't loaded but it had been. He was a priest, she trusted him. He checked that the ammunition was loaded correctly even though he knew it was, switched the safety off and waited.

Christopher pushed the door open and held it for Jadie. He wore an over-sized threadbare sweater to hide most of his wings. Never too late to be the gentleman, he gestured for her to go first. As she walked out into the falling snow he heard her say the old priest's name. He locked the door, ready to face whatever Sweeney had to say when he heard Jadie yelp. Christopher turned round and gasped when he saw Sweeney standing beside a car, having pushed Jadie against the driver's door window with a gun against her temple.

"Woah dude, what the fuck man, I'm a fucking angel, don't do that shit." Christopher blurted out, instantly wishing he had left out a couple of expletives.

"Get in the car." Father Sweeney pushed the gun harder so it crinkled the pale skin on Jadie's forehead and hoped that his erection wasn't showing. He shot a look at Jadie, eyes wet from crying and fear.

"You drive?" She nodded.

Sweeney opened the door with his free hand and pushed her into the seat before climbing into the seat behind her. The gun was off her for three seconds before he had it pressed against the back of her neck, then he beckoned for Christopher to get in the car.

"Where are you taking us?" Christopher asked from the front passenger seat.

Father Sweeney scowled at him. "To church, where else?"

"Look, she needs a hospital, there's something wrong with her man. Her belly's all puffed up and shit."

Jadie was slightly taken aback by Christopher's sudden bravado but she suspected it was still the alcohol.

"She is pregnant with the spawn of the devil!" Father Sweeney spat scornfully.

Christopher sighed uneasily, "I'm not the devil. At least I don't think I am."

Father Sweeney's eyes went wide as he made out the dark pink trio of sixes on Christopher's scalp, barely visible through his short cropped hair.

"I see your mark, Beast." He poked a finger against the brand, half expecting it to burn.

"Ah shit," Christopher sighed. "I'm a metalhead, I like The Omen films, it's a tattoo I swear."

Jadie pulled the car up outside All Saints and considered making a run for it, but when she got to her feet her legs buckled under the sudden growth of her abdomen. She actually saw it change, her top split at the seams and a sharp burning sensation snaked across the manipulated skin. She cried out in pain and put a hand to her stomach. She wasn't surprised to see it covered in blood.

"Help me," she begged of the priest and the angel showing them a bloodied palm. "I think I'm splitting."

Father Sweeney and Christopher's expressions matched for the first time, before Sweeney pushed them towards the church. They were just across the threshold when

Sweeney brought the gun down heavily on Christopher's head. He went down instantly.

Sweeney locked the door behind him and frog-marched Jadie towards the front of the church. He pulled the cloth off the altar and told Jadie to lie down.

"It's okay, Jadie. I want you to trust me. I need to see what is happening with you."

Jadie shook her head in confusion.

He smiled reassuringly and placed the gun down, holding his palms up.

"I need to see what's going on. If you are giving birth to the Anti-Christ we must vanquish it immediately."

Before she could protest, an excruciating wave of pain shot across her belly as a red zigzag of skin split against the straining from within. Father Sweeney got on his knees and without hesitation yanked down her trousers.

The sight of her lying defenceless before him, her long creamy smooth legs, woke the beast within and he froze. Fire ignited in his own belly and sent rivulets of blistering lust to his loins. Everything he believed in came under question as he knelt between the legs of the object of his desire. The only thing he had one hundred percent faith in was the pleasures of flesh upon flesh. The way the wounds on her belly bled ruby ribbons over every curve, enhancing the paleness of her skin drove him insane. He ran a hand slowly up her bare legs and it was like electricity.

"Father what are you doing?" Jadie shouted through the agony.

Father Sweeney ripped her bloodied underwear off with one hand and said, "Something I should have done when you were twelve."

Jadie couldn't move, the pain was too unbearable, her stomach felt as though it was splitting open she felt the priest tear her panties off and heard him utter those disgusting evil words that confirmed her suspicions all along. He was the real evil in this church, whatever was wrong with Christopher couldn't be as bad as what this man had said and was about to do. Helpless she could only watch as the perverted old priest picked up the gun and dropped his trousers. His thighs were a battleground of scar tissue. Dozens, hundreds even, of crucifix-shaped welts and scars of all shapes and sizes covered them, running from the knees upwards and even curling around his reddened, engorged cock. A minute, freshly scabbed, cross-shaped scar opened up on the tip of his penis and wept yellow pus. Father Sweeney's eyes were filled with raw rage and unbridled animal lust.

Christopher came round in immense pain for the umpteenth time that week and was surprised to find himself in church. Events came flooding back as he crawled to a pew and got groggily to his feet. At the front of the church he saw the half-naked priest towering over Jadie, her face a macabre contortion of pain and fear. Without even thinking, Christopher shrieked out a war cry and ran as fast as he could towards the demented priest and the woman who was possibly carrying his child, or at least his mutated venereal disease.

"Cuuuuuuuuuuuuuuuuunt!"

When he leapt towards the priest, the tension in his muscles made his wings tear open his sweater as he ploughed into Sweeney, tackling him like one of the Denver Broncos.

Sweeney pulled the trigger automatically when Christopher attacked, his finger already wrapped around it. The winged man collided with him and they crashed over the altar.

Christopher barely saw the spreading pool of blood beneath the priest's head as it leaked onto the stone floor, he was back on his feet and rushing to Jadie.

Jadie lay in a bigger pool of blood, a gaping bullet hole in the middle of her pregnant belly, a dark orangey discharge like egg yolk seeping from the cavity and from her vagina mixing with the blood, like ketchup after an English breakfast. Christopher squatted to her and pushed his fingers to find a pulse in her neck, but knew she was dead. He stepped away from her and buried his face in his palms. As he brought his hands away, he noticed a fine coating of what appeared to be feathers covering their backs. He didn't have time to contemplate this new discovery as the half-dead figure of Father Sweeney hauled itself up onto the altar, gun in hand.

Christopher cried out in anger and lifted the priest into the air and flapped his wings furiously.

The angel and the half-naked priest flew up through the smashed window into the sky, snowflakes stinging their exposed skin. The priest and the angel both knew that either one of them, perhaps both, was about to die, and wanted to take the other with them.

The priest beat the angel about his bearded face with the gun, destroying his perfectly formed nose in an instant and splitting his bottom lip wide open.

The angel simply let go.

Father Sweeney fell onto the cross atop the church steeple. The cold rusted metal entered his perineum and didn't stop until it was somewhere near his throat.

Christopher the angel, the demon, Jadie's big white bird, soared higher and higher above the town called Hell until his wings tired and the remaining skin that hadn't grown fine grey eiderdown froze. His ears filled with the sound of explosions, clouds of smoke and ash surrounded him. Unconscious from exposure, his body plummeted, pirouetting like a giant dove, into the cemetery where it lay broken over a stone mausoleum.

Then, silence.

WELCOME TO A TOWN CALLED HELL

DEAD LINE
Duncan P. Bradshaw

WELCOME TO A TOWN CALLED HELL

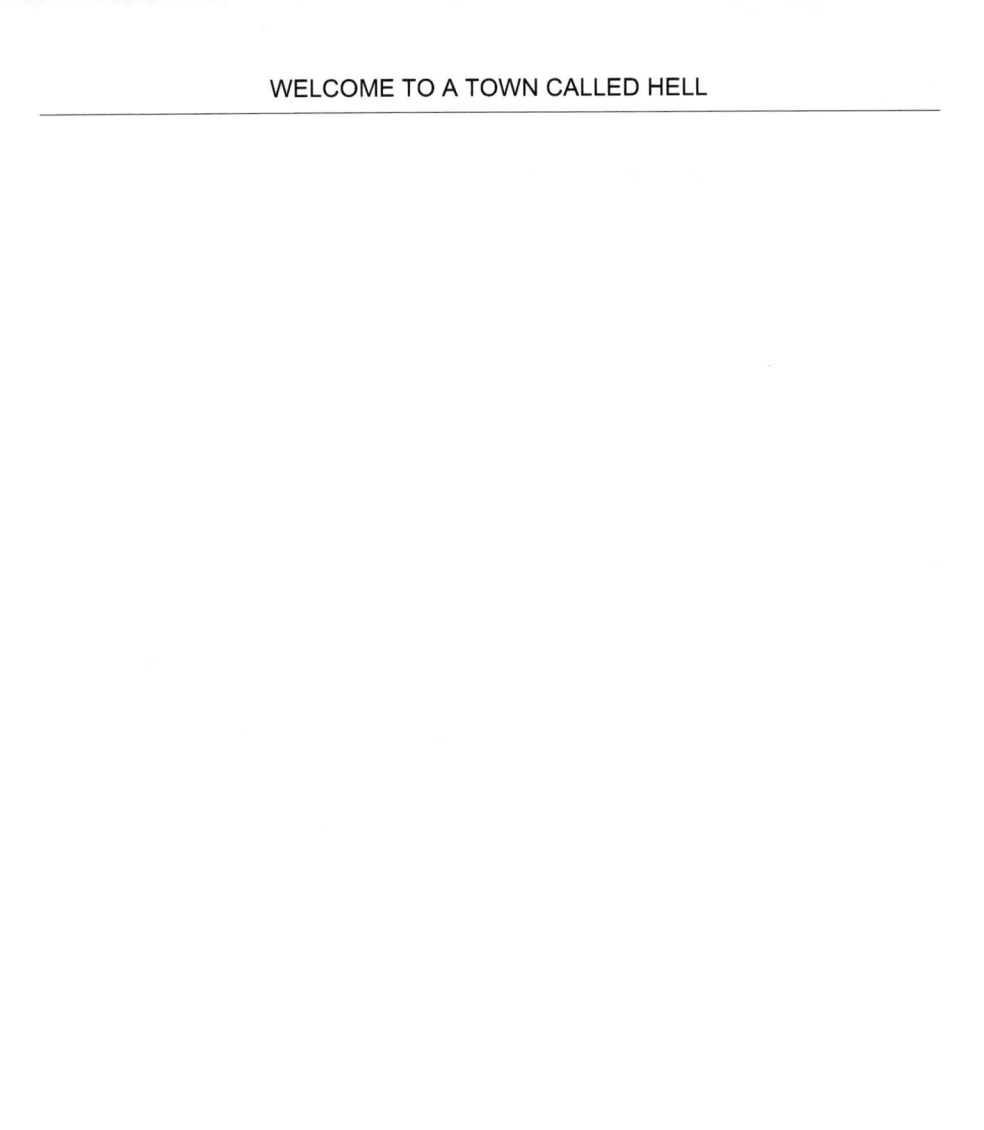

MONDAY EVENING

Joel gripped the steering wheel tighter as he leant forward and craned his neck to look up at the traffic light. Suspended from a gantry which bridged Main Street, its single illuminated eye blazed down a baleful red. The wiper arm swished again, clearing the fine layer of snow from the windscreen, before more took its place.

He shoved a hand beneath the bouquet of flowers laying on the passenger seat, trying to find the bottle of whisky he had been nursing for the last hour. His fingers curled around the pistol grip of the revolver, making his heart pound faster. Like a kick drum, he could feel the blood vessels in his skull pound against their bone prison, as if it were trying to signal to anyone listening for such a distress call.

The same rogue thought that had plagued him for the past year, flashed across his synapses again:

In three seconds, it could all be over.

He began to pull the gun out from under the flowers. *Place it under your chin.* All it would take is a slight tensing of his index finger - a barely noticeable application of pressure - and all the guilt, hurt and suffering would be splattered against the roof of his pick-up truck. His hand was now wrapped around the hilt, a finger through the guard and pressed against the trigger.

Looking back at his own reflection in the rear view mirror, he saw a single tear track down his cheek. As he went to follow through on the rogue thought, an abyssal honk, like a beached whale, rumbled from behind him. For a single moment, he wondered if it was a call from the void. A signal. But was it telling him to continue trying, or to give in and move on?

The sound blared again, lights flashed from behind him. Joel let the pistol go, it slipped beneath the arrangement of near dead lilies, and raised a hand to the mirror. The traffic light glared down at him, green light bathed the hood. Joel slipped the transmission into drive, and pulled away from the junction.

He reversed into the parking bay, and killed the engine. Duffy's was busier than he thought it would be. Perhaps the weather warnings had gotten folk all riled up.

Nothing like a good spot of panic buying to calm the soul.

Joel picked the bunch of flowers up, leaving the half empty bottle of whisky and the revolver lying on the seat. Embarrassed, he wrenched open the glove box, shoved the gun in amongst the caseless CDs, and twisted the cap off the bottle. Taking a large gulp, he felt the familiar burn trickle down into his guts. Taking one more hit to build a reservoir for his courage, he replaced the top and shoved the bottle in the compartment with the gun.

WELCOME TO A TOWN CALLED HELL

Pulling his cap down so it fit snugly, Joel got out of the truck and slammed the door. The cold hit him immediately. He pulled his jacket collar up to keep out the wind and picked a path through the snaking queue of cars, waiting to fill up at the pumps.

With the hubbub disappearing behind him, Joel got to the bottom of end of Main Street and turned left. There it was; to most a nondescript bridge, the only way out of this godforsaken town. To some, it was the gateway to freedom, to Joel it was the symbol of his life sentence, the yoke around his neck. Making sure he didn't skid on the patches of black ice on the pavement, Joel trudged towards it, the twin brake lights of vehicles disappeared into the mist which shrouded it halfway down. It was as if they had simply vanished into the ether. Gobbled up by a gigantic wraith. Consumed whole.

Reaching the point where the side of the hill fell away sharply to the River Styx below, Joel froze. It had been the same thing that befell him on every visit to this accursed place, this marker of ill will. Forcing himself to take a step forward, he made his way down the bridge walkway, every step resulting in a dull clang of boot on metal.

It didn't take long to get to his destination, marked by a change in colour of the guard rail. Where the metal railings either side were weather worn, this particular stretch was still near virginal silver. The hastily made welds like bubbles of frozen mercury.

As soon as he knelt down, he could feel the cold soak through his jeans and seep into his skin and bone. Joel rested the already wilting flowers against the metal bars, and lowered his head.

"I still can't believe you're not here. Everything seems so empty without you."

He stared at the flowers, a fine layer of snow had already covered the petals and the plastic wrapping. Joel sighed, *an offering of death to commemorate one.* Looking past the bouquet, he dared a glance into the canyon below, and the winding river, moving forever onwards. Never ceasing. Even when it iced over, the current would surge beneath the flow.

On creaking knees, Joel stood up and tipped his cap. "I miss you Lils. I thought in time it would ease up, give me a break… but I swear every single damn day is worse than the one before. But don't you fret about me. As long as there is breath in my lungs, I'll carry on. Of that you have my word."

Ducking into the biting wind, Joel turned back towards the petrol station, easily visible with its gaudily lit signs. As he started to head back, there were footsteps behind him. Squinting into the wall of fog which was laid over the bridge, a hooded figure materialised, its shape formed from tendrils of shade and mist. Joel shielded his eyes, trying to make out who else was out on this freezing cold night. Finally, when they were mere feet apart, a spark of recognition flickered in his mind. "Hey, Alan, what are you doing out here?"

Alan stomped to a sudden halt as if coming to attention, his head bowed and partially obscured within a black hoodie. Slowly, the young man looked up at Joel, as he did, the corner of his mouth pulled up, like a broken puppet.

"Hi there, Mister Rathbone. Nice night, huh?"

"I wouldn't go so far as to say it's nice…what are you doing out here?"

Moving to the railings, Alan gripped the metal with his bare hands, staring into the chasm below. "Oh, you know, just getting a look at it all. So many things which we believe will stand for ever, are actually so very impermanent, even the grand constructions of men."

Joel inched forward. "Okay… have you been drinking?"

Alan laughed, a hollow sound which seemed borne of malice than mirth, still he looked into the canyon below, bordered by ridges of frigid rock. "Oh no, I've not been drinking Mister Rathbone, just been doing some chores. Important chores."

"What the heck is so important that you need to be out in this?"

Alan turned to look at Joel, half of his face exposed, alabaster smooth features, the remainder of his face shrouded by black cloth. "I might well ask you the same thing, Mister Rathbone." The teenager shared a crooked grin as if he was in on a shared joke. "Some things have to be done, regardless of conditions. Through fire and brimstone, a man will strive to serve his master, and ensure that his tasks are done on time."

"Did… did you want a lift home? You're on Madison aren't you? I could just r-"

There was a ripping sound as Alan peeled his hands free from the guard rail, strips of skin were left in an approximation of his fingers. "No. Thank you, Mister Rathbone. My work is not done here this eve, there is much to do before I can let sleep claim me to its bosom."

"Right…I'm gonna…you know…go. Take it easy, okay? The radio said it's gonna be even worse tomorrow." Joel spun on his heels and began to march back to his car.

Alan called after him. "How right you are Mister Rathbone. Tomorrow will indeed be far graver."

TUESDAY MORNING

"You know she's got the hots for you, don't ya?" Pete asked, allowing himself a smirk as he watched his colleague squirm.

"Cut it out. She's just lonely, that's all."

Pete laughed. "You're such a dolt, that's the third time this month we've been called out to her place. Twice, she's pulled the cable out of the wall and shoved it under the carpet."

Joel turned into the diner car park and shut off the engine. "Nonsense, she lost Bobby a few years back. Kids are all moved out, she just wants some company."

"Shoot, if that's all she wanted, she could just head out to the bar, or see family, they're only upstate. Nope, if you ask me-"

"Which I ain't."

"-hey, let me finish now, if you ask me, she wants you to get her router up and running."

The pair jumped out of the pick-up truck. "I swear, you get worse every day. How much longer do I have to put up with this for?"

Pete shuffled across the gritted tarmac. "Two more months, then I'm done and dusted. Finally time for me to put my feet up and enjoy life for once."

"I'm guessing May has got a list of jobs for you already?"

"Like you wouldn't believe! I swear, that woman thinks I'm gonna remodel the entire house and garden, heck, at this rate, I may ask for my job back."

Joel slapped Pete on the back, before pulling him in. "What makes you think I'd want you back?"

"You're breaking my heart now Joel, much like the poor widow Katie Franks. You know that most people don't get that dolled up for a couple of telephone repair jockeys like us. Right?"

"Do you want me to buy your lunch, or you gonna bust my balls all day long and go hungry?"

Pete held his arm out, beckoning him towards the front doors of The Pitstop Diner.

"I won't say another word. I ain't gonna turn down free coffee and pie on account of my own observations."

Joel mock-bowed. "Why thank you old timer, now let's go and eat, I'm-"

From behind them, a loud screeching sound like a banshee riding bareback on a cruise missile, tore through the tranquil setting. Both spun around to see a blurry afterimage of what looked like a plane, before it disappeared from view. It was quickly followed by the bright lights of an explosion. The sound followed a few seconds later, out of time with the roiling clouds of soot and flame. They instinctually flinched as they saw something fly through the air towards them. It smashed into the side of a parked articulated lorry, right next to the diner. After a brief silence, Joel and Pete exchanged baffled looks, before scooting across the car park.

As they skirted round the back of the lorry, there was a clang, as metal connected with the frozen ground. Joel got there first to see the back of an airplane seat, smoke rising from the charred fabric. There was a sizzling sound as the heated up metal frame rapidly thawed out the iced up tarmac. Joel held his hand up, stopping Pete from getting closer. "Go call for help, I'll check this out."

Hearing no sound from behind him, Joel waved an arm at his colleague. "Go on now. People might need help. I'll be right behind you." The words seeped through the shock, and Pete nodded dumbly, before skating towards the diner.

Joel pulled his gloves out and put them on as he edged towards the jettisoned seat. The closer he got, the more detail he could make out. Evidently the person behind was using the tray, as it was not in the upright, locked position. A partially burned, melted, laminated set of safety instructions wafted gently from the breeze and the heat eddy created between the extremes in temperature.

With the chair on its side, Joel stood over it and recoiled at the sight that greeted him. Curled over and bent at the waist, where a smoking seatbelt still held them intact, was a body, gender unknown. Clothing hung from clumps of sodden wet skin like small ragged flags. All the hair from their head had been scoured away by fire, hands clasped the back of their skull, fused together. Sections of skin had sloughed away, revealing brown lumps of cooked meat, and pristine nodules of bone. Charred legs poked out of a pair of blacked and twisted Converse. An acrid stench of melted plastic, burned hair and flesh mixed together, forming a noxious miasma which made Joel dry retch. He knelt down by the seat, the figure taking on the appearance of having been formed from clay. Part of him wanted to help, but he knew it was way past that point.

It just felt wrong to leave them to be held hostage within the seat, moulded to its shape, bent to its form. He began to reach out with his hand, something within compelled him to do so, as if he were being guided by something primal. As his fingers reached what was left of the upper arm, there was a voice behind him. "Ladies and gentlemen, please adopt the crash position."

Joel cricked his neck to see Alan regarding the scene as if it were nothing more than an avant-garde art installation. In one of his hands, he held an empty glass jar. Summoning words, Joel spluttered. "Wh-w-what?"

"When faced with a loss of altitude, there are but two things available to the air passenger."

"Alan, wh-wh-what are you-"

"The first is the oxygen mask, though all that does is render you pliable, receptive for your impending doom."

"Can you just-"

"The second though, well, that's often the more sensible option, the choice of those who know what's coming."

"What?"

Alan dug a fingernail into the headrest and scraped off a strip of fabric and skin. Holding it to his face, he breathed it in. After a hearty sniff, he shoved it in his pocket and fixed Joel a stare. "Simple Mister Rathbone. You put your head between your legs, and kiss your ass goodbye."

With that, he winked at Joel and stood up, before heading towards the main drag. As he walked between a pair of parked cars, he hurled the empty jar behind him, which smashed, scattering shards of glass which mixed with the sparkling ice and snow.

Joel stood up. "Hey! Stop. What are you on about? What was in that jar?"

Alan kept on walking, though he cracked his head sideways. "It was home to some friends. They've gone now. Goodbye Mister Rathbone, I'll see you later." The teenager made a sharp left and carried on down the pavement, barging through crowds of people gazing at the pall of smoke rising from the horizon.

"The phones are dead," Pete shouted, making Joel jump.

"Something weird going on here, Pete."

"That's the understatement of the century, come on, we've got work to do, we best go fix the lines, else who do you think is going to get it in the neck? Here's a hint, it ain't gonna be the old timer who's outta here shortly." Pete patted Joel on the back, looked down at the vitrified body, crossed himself and headed back to the pick-up truck.

TUESDAY AFTERNOON

"Where are we going Joel?"

Eyes forward, Joel weaved between another set of hastily stopped cars, the inhabitants shielded behind their car doors, looking into the distance. He pointed to the wall of billowing ashen smoke ahead of them. "I gotta find out what happened. Any luck?"

Pete shook his head. "Nope, it's not just the landlines that are dead, got no reception on my cell or the CB either, it's like everything is-"

"Dead." The solitary word escaped its confinement, before Joel had a chance to recapture it. The two men looked at each other, before a yell outside made Joel wrench the wheel to the side, narrowly missing an SUV which had stopped on the median.

"Holy cow, look," Pete pointed off to the side.

Joel's jaw hung slack, "I was here, not even a day ago. I was parked. Just there." He pointed through the ash covered windscreen at the petrol station car park, where a smouldering aeroplane engine had parallel parked perfectly in one of the bays. The turbines still turned gently, as if trying to lift the lot to a new location.

"Don't get too close, it might not have gotten to the underground tanks yet."

Taking a wider berth on the lane, Joel picked his way past debris strewn as if they were rejects from a giant child's toy box. Coming to a halt, Joel turned the engine off, and stumbled outside in a daze.

Ahead of him, lay the bridge. Where before it had been covered in a fog, it was now bisected by smoke and small fires. Joel stumbled forward, kicking lumps of metal and rock as he went. He passed a small suitcase, ripped open. The cartoon character emblazoned on it was fixed with a huge grin which looked back up at him, its face deformed, the thumbs up it offered felt more menacing than grateful. As the lid flapped open, he saw neatly folded clothes within, held down by bungee cord and a clip. A teddy bear held fast, untouched by the heat and smoke, waiting for its owner that would never return.

Joel reached the edge of where road met bridge and stopped. The crash had sliced through the construction as if it were a martial arts demonstration. He peered through the haze at the guard rail, and saw that it had broken off at the exact spot where the state had repaired it. Miraculously, the flowers he had left the previous evening remained, encased in a thin, uneven layer of ice. Preserved, awaiting rediscovery.

He felt a hand on his shoulder, Pete's voice low and measured. "Come on, there's nothing for us here. We need to go and work out what's wrong with the line. People are depending on us now, c'mon."

Staring out at the devastation, Joel nodded and dusted his gloves. As he did so, something caught his eye within the swirling smoke and mist. A figure clothed in a white dress. His lips parted, the act seemed to usher in a gentle breeze, which pulled the phantom apart. As it dissipated, he swore he heard a tiny voice borne aloft, "Joel…" before it was stolen away by the growing sound of sirens.

"You're right Pete, there's nothing for us here."

TUESDAY NIGHT

Joel sat in his easy chair, exhausted. The changing camera angles from the football game cast random patterns of light onto the walls, silhouetting him on occasion, whilst delivering him to the shadows on others. He tenuously held onto the rim of the glass with his fingers, pinched just enough to prevent it from slipping and adding yet more liquor to the stained carpet.

The afternoon spent chasing around town - trying to see if the problem could be easily fixed – had ended an hour ago with no progress made. In the grand scheme of things, Joel considered that people could do without their phones for one night.

His mind wandered back to the petrified figure from the car park. Small details, ones he didn't even pick out at the time, were played back in high-definition. The near perfectly smooth skin, shorn of hair or imperfections, forming continents of flesh amidst a sea of blood, pus and scorched meat. Canals of exposed bone, linking the barely recognisable extremities to each other.

Finally, he raised his glass, nodded towards the myriad of unseen spectres, victims all, and toasted their memory, before sinking it in one.

Realising that tomorrow would be more of the same, he shoved the glass between the cushion and armrest of his chair and made his way to bed. Forgoing the act of disrobing, he lay on top of the sheets, staring at the ceiling. Headlights from passing cars streaked across, mixed in with the odd blue or red light from the emergency services, ferrying the dead and injured to their terminus.

His eyes began to droop, the lightshow soothing the dull ache which pervaded him. The burned body began to recede from view, replaced by the infinite blackness. Small particles, like amoeba trapped in fluid, swam across.

He felt himself falling and jolted. Panicked eyes scanned the room. Nothing but disarray and chaos, a life put on pause, waiting not for deliverance, but the end.

Better to burn out than fade away.

The thought made him smile, before the freeze frame image of the plane disappearing into the canyon made him wish he wasn't sober. Joel closed his eyes again, allowing the dark to embrace him, keep him in its thrall until daybreak.

Then the phone rang.

It was the oddest sound. Like rain on a sunny day, or ice cream in winter. He sat up and stared at the handset, barely believing it was true. The red light on top of the unit flashed, before it rang once more. How could this be? Did Pete stay out and repair the line after all? The old man was even more worn out than he was. Joel had to stir him from his slumber when he dropped him off at his home.

It rang once more. The pitch having changed, no longer one of ambivalence as to whether it was answered or not, but now demanding that he did, lest some slight was delivered to the caller. Joel rolled across the bed and sat on the edge, his feet resting in a pile of dirty clothing. He picked up the handset halfway through its next urgent reverie. "H-h-h-hello?"

From the other end, came no noise, save for a slight hissing, as if the caller were letting out air from an inner tube. Joel coughed, girded himself, and asked again, this time, more forcefully. "Hello? Who is this?"

He could make out a faint whisper, as if someone was speaking from a corner of a room, perhaps a drunkard or unwilling participant in a prank call. There was the sound of laughter, closer, more distinct, it bore the same tone as Alan's from earlier, laden with spite. Joel snapped. "Look, I don't know who the heck you are, but I'm hanging up now. Don't you be calling me back."

As he went to end the call, a woman's crackly voice wheezed. "Joel...I need you..." before the line went dead.

Reason told him it could not be true. That she was dead. Had been for a year now. But that mattered not with those four little words. It were as though they had been delivered right on cue. At his most receptive. He knew that it could not be her. But then who was it?

Though they had found her car, upside down, roof caved in and sundered on a boulder the size of a dining table, she had never been found.

"Must've been washed downstream."

"There's no way anyone could survive that fall."

"We don't need a body for a burial. It's more of a symbolic act. For you."

"It'll help with the grieving process. It'll help you move on."

But there was one voice amongst them all. The one which had lain dormant, suffocated under despair and grief. It was the one which those words now breathed new life into.

Hope.

Joel replaced the handset on the charger, having tried, with no avail to obtain the caller ID. He sat there, shivering, willing it to ring again.

What help did she need? Was she trapped somewhere? Perhaps she had survived the fall, but suffered from an indeterminate brain injury, and had achieved recall of a life once forgotten? This and a million other thoughts jostled for space, each one a seed, planted by the rebirth of hope.

Joel knew what he was going to do. He would wait. She would call again. She had to. This time though, he was ready. Whatever he had to do to save her, he would. Something, anything, had to be better than the last three hundred and sixty five days of numbed existence.

WEDNESDAY MORNING

An indistinct face appeared at the window, hands cupped, shading the eyes from the glare of the light. Fists banged on the glass, "Joel! Joel!"

Still sat on the edge of the bed, staring intently at the telephone handset, Joel stirred and looked across to his colleague. Pete lifted his hands up and he tapped his watch. Seeing that his friend was still sedentary, he disappeared from view.

Joel huffed, moved forwards so that his feet rested on the floor again. He had pins and needles running up and down his spine, his body tremored with the cold air. Drool had dried to a crust around his lips, dead skin speckled his stubble. He picked up the handset, willing to take the chance of missing the call, he dialled 911 and hit 'Call', the phone made an off kilter series of squawks, before an automated voice told him that the service was unavailable. He quickly ended the call, and rested it back on the charging cradle, the reassuring power light flickered back on. His eyes traced the power cord from the back of the unit to the wall, making sure that the light wasn't a figment of his imagination.

Nope, all good. All is ready. She's going to call now. Any minute.

"What the heck are you doing sitting there? This house is freezing."

Joel looked across to the bedroom door, where Pete stood, fresh snow peppering his shoulders like a bad case of dandruff. "Just a minute Pete, I just need a minute."

"We don't have a minute, we have to get on with our jobs, people are depending on us."

"No they're not, they don't care."

"Really? You heard what happened over at The Pitstop last night?"

Joel shook his head, still glued to the telephone.

"Something bad, that's what. Some crazy religious nut went in there, screaming about rapture and redemption. Folk are scared, we need to try and get the lines fixed so they can speak to their families, make it feel like things are getting back to normal."

"I'm fine Pete. I think I'm going to stay-"

The handset light flashed half a dozen times, then stopped, before flashing six more, then ceasing, finally ending with another series of six flashes, before reverting back to its usual state. Joel leant forwards, the display was lit up. There were two words on the digital display, 'Go Joel'. He nodded, Pete had already got the message and was heading out through the doorway. "Hang on, I'll come with you. Sorry, didn't get much sleep last night."

WEDNESDAY EVENING

"Any luck?" Pete asked.

Joel shook his head again and threw the screwdriver into the tool box. "Nope, nothing. I just don't get it. The line is still intact, sure the one across the bridge has gone, but we still have the one out west to Otisburg working. The cell tower is up, why ain't we getting a signal?"

Mopping his brow, Pete pushed his fingers deeper into his gloves, "No idea. None of this makes any sense."

"I'm gonna go and hook up, there's got to be some kind of signal."

"I tried that down in King Street, there's nothing there, just static and the automated signal."

Ignoring him, Joel was already tying the spiked soles onto his boots, he pulled the harness out from the bag and began to shimmy up the telegraph pole.

Each step made the wind find him easier. The cold wormed its way in through the minutest of chinks in his clothing. Icy tendrils wrapped around his body, lashing his aching bones. He could feel his face go numb, cheeks burned, teeth chattered like a mechanical toy. At the summit, he positioned himself behind the junction box so that his face was hidden from the Arctic wind and snow. After jimmying it open with a pry-bar, he dusted away small icicles, pulled the plug from his handset and pressed it into the port on the box.

Joel punched in the number of head office, no sooner had he finished dialling than the static squall and disembodied voice reminded him that this 'service was unavailable.' He cursed, and checked over the terminals, making sure each one was clean and not blown out. A faint voice from below said his name.

Resting in the harness, Joel leant over and looked at the ground, Pete was digging around in the back of the van. The voice said his name again. Joel looked down to the handset which was swinging from his belt. He hauled it in like an anchor rope in a storm, and held it to his head. "Hello? Hello? Lily? Is that you?"

Nothing.

"Goddammit, am I going crazy now? Is that the deal? Well, perhaps it would be easier to put a bullet in my brain if that's all I've got to look forward to."

"...oel..."

The broken word was a salve for his soul. "Lily? Please, is that you? Speak to me."

"Joel...you're there, I've been trying to...but it's...here...omething in the way...ou're going to need to..."

Joel reached into the junction box, and began to fiddle with the polarity, there was a loud popping in the handset, before the voice said. "Joel?"

"I'm here, I'm right here Lils, where are you? Is it you?"

"Joel! My love, I thought I'd never hear your voice again, it's me, it's Lily."

A tear bloomed in the corner of Joel's eye, it ran down his cheek before the cold dried it out. He rubbed his eyes with his gloves. "Where are you Lily girl?"

"I'm close Joel."

"Come to me, I'm down on-"

"I can't. Not yet. I came to warn you."

"Warn me? Of what?"

There was a silence, as if the handset was passed from one ear to the other, the same voice replied. "There are bad people in town Joel, who want to do terrible things. They want to do terrible things to me."

Joel balled his fists. "I won't let that happen, Lily, you know that, I'll protect you."

"But you didn't protect me Joel. Did you?"

Joel stuttered to a halt, before finally managing. "Wh-w-what do you mean?"

"I know it was the drink Joel, really, I do, but you shouldn't have hit me."

"I didn't mean to, I didn't know what I was doing…I just…I just…"

"What Joel? What did you just do?"

"I lost it! Okay! I lost it, I know I shouldn't have, but I did. I'm mighty sorry Lils, really, I am. Please, just tell me where you are, and I'll come and get you, we can work this out. Please."

Silence, save for the sound of Joel's breathing, before the voice said. "I want to believe you Joel, really I do, but you're going to have to prove to me that you won't do those things again."

"I will Lils, anything, you name it, I'll do it."

"You sure? Cos if not, then I'll get back in my car and drive away again. Like last time. Like last year. This time though, the bridge is out, isn't it? There's no way I'll survive the fall again."

"Please Lily…tell me what I have to do."

"I could always put you in the trunk this time Joel. We could die together. Is that what you want? I know about the gun. I know what you want to do."

"How did-"

"You're a coward Joel, but that's okay. Together, we can make you into something which is deserving of me, of another chance. Would you like that?"

Joel's body hitched up and down as he tried to stifle his sobbing. "Anything…I'd do anything."

"Good. I want you to go home, a friend will be along to help you. Okay?"

"What do you want me to do? Who's this *friend*?"

"Are you questioning me Joel? If you want, I could just go? Leave you to your nightmares?"

"NO! Please. Don't. It's fine, it just all sounds strange. I don't know what it is you want me to do."

"I want you to prove to me that you're worthy of having me. Are you Joel? Are you worthy?"

"I am, of course I am."

"Good. Now, as I said, there are bad people around in Hell tonight. I want to prove to you that you can trust me. Would you like that Joel?"

Joel nodded. "I would like that a lot Lils, this sounds all muddled right now."

"I understand. Look north, can you see Sandie's Gas? Can you see the lights? You can see the lights, can't you Joel?"

Turning, Joel scanned the horizon, until he could make out the bright lights of Hell's other gas station. "I can see 'em, bright as day."

"Good. Now. This is what happens to those who aren't worthy. Are you ready?"

"I guess, what do you-"

An explosion engulfed the gas station, killing the electric lights, replacing them with a ball of incandescent fire and fury. Clouds of lumpy smoke surged into the air, forming an acrid umbrella above the petrol station, which was now nothing more than a lake of fire and ember. Debris was hurled in a three hundred and sixty degree arc. Clumps of dust and sparks were sent up from their impact.

Still the smoke and fire rose, until it created an hourglass of conical fire, pinched into a thin waist, before being topped out with a blouse of thick black smoke. Joel felt the telegraph pole shudder as the shockwave ran through it. Below, Pete was out of the back of the van and looking out into the horizon, he shouted up, "What the heck was that?"

The voice on the phone interjected, its tone had changed, now laced with a layer of withdrawal and detachment. "Unless you want to burn with the unworthy Joel, I suggest you follow my instructions. To the letter. Now. Go home. Wait. Don't you worry none, honey. Your salvation is at hand."

WEDNESDAY NIGHT

"I still don't understand what's eating ya."

Joel could see Pete staring at him from the passenger seat, studying him as if he were a display in a museum. "Nothing, just gotta get back home tonight, feeling the effects of no sleep, that's all."

Pete rested his hand on Joel's arm, "If something is bothering you, I hope you know that you can talk to me, yeah? We've been friends for years now, especially after everything that happened, you know…with Lily."

The pick-up bucked, as Joel jerked the steering wheel. "Leave it, okay? I'm *fine*, just need to get some sleep, I'll be right as rain tomorrow, you'll see."

Joel brought the truck to a halt, and began to tap the wheel impatiently with his fingers. "Fine, I get the hint. Shutting me out didn't work then, and it ain't gonna work now. Sooner or later, you'll need to let someone in, or it'll eat you whole." Pete reached into the back, picked up his rucksack and jumped out, nodded a goodnight, then headed up the porch steps. Before he had reached the top, Joel had already put his foot down, the wheels skidding on the compacted snow, before finding purchase and growling off into the night.

The journey home had been pockmarked by sporadic gunfire and street corners marked with bins set alight, spewing smoke into the air, the heat annihilating the falling snow before it even had a chance to settle. At one point, he had to swerve the truck to miss a small, dirty dog running loose in the middle of the road.

Turning into his street, he could see his garage door had a frame of light around it. He brought the pick-up to a halt, collected his tools, and headed indoors.

"Hello?" Joel's voice echoed around the empty shell of his home. Furniture sold to subsidise funeral costs, or to keep creditors at bay. Some lay in splintered heaps in the corner of rooms, victims of random acts of drunken violence.

He walked through the kitchen, and opened the door to the garage. The usual clutter had been swept to the sides of the room, leaving the concrete floor dusty and bare. A hooded figure stood in the centre of the room, eyes fixed on the doorway. "Right on time, Mister Rathbone."

"Alan? What are you doing here? I thought-"

Alan pulled his hood back, exposing a pale face lined with liquorice black veins beneath the surface. They pulsed as something swam within the blood tributaries, looping around his cardiovascular system like kids at a water park. "It is good that you are here, are you ready?"

"I guess, what do I have to do?"

Gesturing Joel towards him, Alan pointed to the corner of the room, at something bundled under an oil spattered tarp. "I've made a start Mister Rathbone. I like you, I know what you're trying to get. So I helped you."

Joel kept his gaze fixed on Alan, who turned in time with his movements, as fluid as a record on a turntable. He reached the tarp, and looked down at it, poking out from the bottom, was a sneaker covered foot. Joel ripped the polythene sheet back, staggering backwards from the sight that greeted him.

"I caught them two doors down, sneaking through the gardens. Malice in their hearts, devilment on their mind. I admire them, of a fashion, but they will not be missed."

Lying on the ground were two men, early twenties at a guess, both had their hands and feet tied together with cable ties, each sported a purple welt on the side of their head. "Here, take this," Alan muttered, Joel spun around to see his house guest mere feet away, a lead pipe outstretched in his hand.

"Are they…are they-"

"Dead? No no no. Not yet, anyway. We need five in total Mister Rathbone, I have provided you with the first pair. Now it is up to you to get the next two, wouldn't be much of an offering if I had to do all the work now, would it?"

Joel dumbly shook his head. "I don't understand…"

Alan sighed. "You have been offered the return of your beloved wife, such things do not come cheaply. In order to take advantage of the paper thin skein between this world and the next, a sacrifice must be made. A life for a life. Though for this favour, something a little more… theatrical, is required. Now. Mister Rathbone. Time is ticking. If you do not wish to take my Master up on his generous offer, let me know. There are many others who would leap at this opportunity."

Alan pushed the metal bar forwards, Joel took it reluctantly, feeling its weight. "Good, now, I know the Johnstons next door have returned from the impromptu church service over at Saint Jude's. Render them unconscious, and return them here."

"What happens after?"

"Do not weigh yourself down with what comes next. Merely bring forth two more for the offering. Now." Alan's tone changed.

Joel opened the back door and shut it behind him.

Snow was still falling from the heavens, blanketing the wasteland which had become his back garden, and removing all detail from view. Wiping the snow from the top of the fence panel, he pulled himself up and over, landing in a frozen flower bed. There was a crunch as his boots reduced petals and stems to an icy mulch. He saw the side door, figuring that the Johnston's house was a mirror of his own, he tried the handle, and sighed with relief when it popped out of the frame and offered respite within.

Closing the door behind him with a click, he could hear a radio playing within the house. Kicking the toes of his boots against the floor to remove the snow, Joel crept towards the door which led to the kitchen and pried it open.

Inside he could see Roger, his back to him, wrists deep in the sink. Whilst the radio played a song his brain couldn't remember the words to, Roger whistled out of time to the melody. As he washed the plates from their evening meal, Joel tiptoed across the lino, pipe pulled back behind his shoulder.

This is for Lily. Nothing else.

He stood an arms-length behind Roger, they had barely exchanged more than two words since the Johnstons had moved in three years ago. His fingers unfurled from the pipe, before curling into a fist, holding the pipe easier. Just as he went to swing, Roger, halfway through whistling, turned around.

The pair stared at each other, the musical note dying from Roger's lips. Soap suds plopped from his hands onto the floor. "What are-" was all that Roger could manage, before Joel brought the pipe across, clouting him on the corner of his skull, just above the left eye.

Roger stumbled on leaden legs, before he fell, his forehead cracked into the lip of the worktop. He sank to the floor as if he had been disconnected from his power supply. Joel dropped the pipe, it clattered against the solid floor. He stood over the prone man and turned the body to face him. Joel held his hand over his mouth, trying to hold in a scream as he saw one of Roger's eyes was bulging from its socket, fixing him with a boggle eyed stare.

His neighbour looked so odd. One eye closed, a purple headband of bruising ringed the middle of his forehead, a small shard of bone sticking out through the skin, by the engorged eyeball. "Jesus, I'm sorry…" Joel pulled his gloves off and pressed his fingers against the man's neck. After frantically feeling for a sign of life, he felt Roger's heartbeat tap the end of this fingers.

Sighing, Joel sank to the floor, relieved, but also repulsed by what he had seen and done. As he sat there contemplating his next move, a keening wail screamed from behind him. Dorothy stood in the doorway her eyes wide and mad, almost matching her husband's. "What are you doing?"

Joel jumped up. "It's not what it looks like Dotty, honest… he just fell."

Dorothy pulled her hands to her chest, before looking down at the floor by her unconscious husband, she pointed. "What, onto that metal bar?"

Joel panted and looked down, by the time he returned his gaze to Dorothy, she had bolted for the front door. Setting off like an Olympic sprinter, Joel caught up just as she wrapped her fingers around the door handle. Barging into the wall with his shoulder, he grabbed hold of the back of Dorothy's head. Fingers wormed through her hair, joining the pair together as one. Using his momentum, he slammed her head against the door. She smacked into the wood, with a loud crack, blood spurted out of her nose and sprayed against the pale wood. It began to run down the gloss paint, racing towards the floor.

Joel, fingers still meshed with Dorothy's tight perm, pulled back his hand, and smashed her head against the door once more. A tooth flew out of her bloodied mouth, she fell slack in his grip as it bounced off a picture frame. As she fell to the floor, Joel kept his fingers clenched, ripping out a fistful of hair.

The garage door was kicked open, and Joel first dragged Roger in, dumping him by the now awake captives, before slinging Dorothy over his shoulder and carrying her over the threshold. He slammed the door behind him, and let the woman slip from his hold, onto the floor. Alan clapped his hands together slowly. "Well done, Mister Rathbone. Stage one is complete. Now, we need to arrange the offerings, for they must be just so."

Joel looked across to the two men, who had duct tape over their mouths. Snot and blood formed thick gloopy channels from nose to chin as the pair huffed and puffed, fighting against their bonds. Alan pulled cable ties from his pockets, and knelt down by the Johnstons, fastening them around their limbs.

"What now?" Joel asked.

"Go and get the candles from the shelf, we will need five. I have marked five points on the ground. Anoint a candle with blood from each of the offerings, and then position them on the points."

Rummaging through a dog-eared box, Joel found five white candles - usually reserved for blackouts - and walked back to the captives. In turn, he poked the bottom of the candles into their open wounds, before placing them on each point. The blood dried quick, holding the candle fast.

"Excellent, now, I take it you are aware of what a pentagram is?"

Joel nodded.

"Good, arrange each person, so that they run from point to point, there's a good fellow Mister Rathbone."

Moving the still unconscious Johnstons first - after making sure that Roger was still breathing - the other two men squirmed as he tried to move them. "If they struggle too much Mister Rathbone, please render them unto the darkness once more. They do not need to be awake for the completion of the ceremony, but they do need to be alive. So please, don't go too far. You nearly did with Mister Johnston, hmm?"

Joel raised the pipe above his head, the man shook his head desperately, allowing himself to go limp. Joel dragged the two men to their allotted positions. When they were in place, he looked down, and pulled the spare candle from his pocket. "We're one short?"

"All in good time, Mister Rathbone."

The phone on the wall rang. "Oh, a call, I wonder who that could be?"

Joel bounded over to the phone. "Lily?"

"Hello Joel."

"Lils! Thank God. What's going on here? The things I've had to do… I don't understand, what is all of this for?"

"Joel, my love, this is so we can be together. Forever. Though unfortunately, it won't be quite as you imagined."

"What do you mean? I've done everything that you asked of me, the things I've done, what you made me do, for what?"

"Joel, please, you did this for us. I'm very proud of you. I want to thank you. For allowing me to live."

"So you are coming back? For real?"

The voice on the end of the line changed, from female to male. "I am, Joel. Through your hard work and diligence, you have made it so. Alan, if you please."

The phone slipped from Joel's grip. He turned around to see Alan's leering face, half-hidden by his hood, right in front of him. He felt something connect with the side of his head, and the world went dark.

THURSDAY MORNING

Joel came to, his eyesight blurred and indistinct. As the view swum into focus, he realised he was lying on the garage floor. Beneath his head, he could feel that he was resting on something that was moving.

Alan's face appeared, eclipsing the light from the swinging lightbulb. "Good, you're awake, Mister Rathbone. My Master much prefers the offerings to be aware of the end, to see the exquisite suffering etched upon their features."

Trying to speak, he could feel that his lips were gummed together. As he tried to mouth words, he could feel his stubble being pulled. Alan laughed. "Did you truly think that you were special? That you were actually going to get your dead wife back, Mister Rathbone? No. Your situation made you a perfect candidate for my master's guidance. A pentagram has five sides, you are the final touch."

Alan patted Joel's cheek, a flash of metal glinted in his vision. "Time to get started."

The man pulled back, out of sight. Joel could hear footsteps crunch across the dusty floor. There was a sound like a plastic bag being torn, followed by a puff of air, and then a wet gurgling sound. It was repeated again, and again.

Joel turned his head sideways, and looked into the protruding eye of Roger Johnston. The lid tried to blink, but the eyeball was sticking out too far. The skin, at top and bottom, pinched the meat of the eye, making it bulge still further, before retracting. Roger's forehead was beaded with sweat.

From nowhere, a hand grabbed hold of Roger's head, turned it so it was facing skywards, then the edge of a knife was drawn across the man's throat. Arterial spray jetted into the air, it ran down Joel's cheek, before dripping onto the floor.

Alan appeared once more, he leant in close, holding the knife over Joel's head, blood ran from the edge of the curved blade and dripped onto his chin.

"Baal-Berith, from below to above, I summon thee once more, to revel in the murder of men."

Joel felt a cold thin line trace across his throat. His neck felt warm, before he took in a sudden gasp of air. It didn't quench his desire of breath, and his back arched as he tried to inhale once more. The skin tore, opening his neck up further. All he could feel was cold air, as it blew against the inside of his throat.

The need to take on oxygen subsided, and Joel spasmed once, before falling slack.

Alan stood over the pentagram of flesh, blood formed pools of various depth between stacked limbs and sagging torso. The candle flames flickered as the expanse of fluid ran out to their bases, but though they wobbled, they stood tall. Soon, the thick red ichor hit the dam of his feet, and ran around them, as he looked down at the scene of murder and sacrifice.

The blood then began to bubble, stretching out into the shape of the pentagram. It began to hiss and spit, rising up to coat the still twitching corpses which lay bound to each other. There was a sound of breaking bones, and skin being rent open. Small clawed hands reached from the marrow of bones and scratched the air, the garage filled with the smell of spoiled meat.

The bodies began to spasm and judder. Now coated in blood, the transformation continued unabated. The corporeal mulch coalesced together into a sticky ball of skin and bone. Hovering above the sigil marked out by dried blood, the mass of flesh stretched and pulled, forming into nightmarish figures of razor teeth lined mouths, goat heads with horns aflame, before settling on the visage of a man, bedecked in black robes. With arms outstretched out in cruciform, the summoned creature finally spoke. "My acolyte, you have done well."

Alan bowed forward, eyes closed. "Thank you Master, I am glad you are content with my work."

"My ascendance has been granted, and my favour curried. I will ensure that you are rewarded handsomely."

"Thank you Master. Your words honour me. Now what is your bidding?"

Baal-Berith smoothed down his robes, turning his cufflinks around so they were level and true. He knelt down by the five pointed star, the blood still tacky. Dipping a finger into it, he licked it clean.

"Mmmm, I have missed the taste. Now, I have work to do, I need to find some new playthings. It would seem that the desecration of this place is nigh. Go forth, continue to sow the seeds of fear within the cattle. I can hear more of my kin testing the veil, we must be quick, lest we miss out on all the fun."

The Lovers: Part Two
Edward Breen

WELCOME TO A TOWN CALLED HELL

Alex began to think it strange that he was still in darkness. Maybe Maria figured out that they should keep the lights in the office off so people could see him better. She's so amazing, he thought to himself. Then his thoughts strayed to why they hadn't returned. They'd been gone at least an hour. He decided to give up on the signal for now. Maybe they could try again in a while. But for now he was bored and worried about Maria.

The gym was darker than the office. With no street lamp to illuminate it, the darkness was pretty much complete. The flash light pierced it with its focused beam, which only made the dark parts of the room even blacker. Alex swung the beam left and right. His breathing quickening, his pulse pounding in his ears. The bodies were just as dead, but the smell was getting worse. He was sure some of them looked a bit different, but he shook his head and forced the thought from his mind. It must have just been the shadows.

Carefully he weaved through the gym, keeping his light low in front of his feet. Partly because he didn't want to fall over anything, partly so he wouldn't have to look at the bodies. The stairwell was clear and he made it to the reception area unscathed. The smell wasn't half as bad here. He supposed because there were less bodies and some air was getting through from the collapsed entryway. The tumbledown entrance was undisturbed. Next was the small cafe where a couple of bodies had fallen off their stools when they died, their drinks gone cold on the table. The light met with the locked emergency exit doors, they looked as immovable as ever in the cold dark.

A shuffling sound coming from the desk caused him to stop his slow sweep. His breathing got faster still and his stomach clenched. The beam of light was quivering, giving his feelings away but he could see nothing amiss. He took a tentative step toward the desk and tried to steady his hand. Then another, trying not to make too much noise. The shuffling stopped abruptly.

Alex felt sick, the flapjack he had eaten earlier being forced upward. Another step and he could almost see behind the desk. It was going to be a dead body, he knew it, crawling towards him. His foot was against the desk with the next step. The other foot came to meet it and he leaned forward as carefully as he could and saw a pair of sneakers. They were small, probably belonged to a woman. Then he saw the worst thing he could possible see: another pair of sneakers but bigger, one either side of the other two.

Randy shot upright.

"What the fuck, man? This is kind of a private moment," Randy said, gesturing to the area beneath the desk.

Maria's head rose up. She looked sheepish and flushed, but said nothing.

"You guys try the lights?"

It seemed like a stupid question in the circumstances, but Alex felt he had to say something. His failure to attract the attention of the men outside was suddenly the last thing on his mind.

"Yeah," Maria said. "They're out. Randy thinks the power was cut by the falling rocks."

"Makes sense," Alex said.

Randy and Maria got up and the three of them stood there saying nothing, nobody look at anyone else.

"It's late, I was thinking we should all sleep in the office?" Alex said, finally. "You know, for safety and it's the least cold place."

"Good idea," Maria said, a little too quickly.

All the time Randy was standing there with a huge grin on his face. Alex didn't look directly at him, he didn't want to give Randy the satisfaction.

They borrowed some clothes from the lockers and heaped them over themselves in the dark office and went to sleep.

Alex watches Maria and Randy from his meadow. They are over there, across the river in the small copse. They skip absurdly, holding hands and laughing. The river seems miles away, he could never get there if he tried, although he can see them as though they were right in front of him. Randy has pride and lust in his eyes.

Maria sees Alex. Their eyes meet. Something passes between them

Suddenly it's Alex and Maria dancing around holding hands in Alex's meadow. It's later in the day now, the sun is low, but it is still warm. The grass and flowers they kick up with their feet make an intoxicating aroma. It's perfect.

Alex sees Randy looking on. He is across the river, in the copse on his own. There's murder in his eyes.

They woke to the sound of howling. It was Wednesday morning and Alex and Maria were in each other's arms. Alex could hear Randy's snores and relaxed a bit. He tried to extricate himself from Maria's embrace without waking her or making too much noise. He put his finger to his lips when she woke suddenly. He could see the same look in her eyes that he had seen in his dream.

Luckily Randy was a heavy sleeper. They got up and Alex tried to look out the windows while Maria woke Randy. The snow had completely covered the glass, there must have been quite a blizzard in the night.

Randy snorted and jumped when Maria shook his arm. Alex thought he looked pissed and his eyes were red as if he had been crying.

"What're you looking at?" Randy said.

"Nothing," Alex said, and went back to looking at the window.

The office would have felt like a pressure cooker, if it weren't so cold. Alex could feel Randy's eyes on his back as he moped around trying to think of what to do. Maria sat in the middle of the room, half way between them, intensely studying her shoes.

Another howl made them all jump. Their eyes met. The sound seemed to be coming from inside the centre. No even closer than that, Alex was sure he felt it was coming from within himself. He could feel the vibration of it in his chest. It was accompanied by a chorus of lesser howls from the direction of the woods. Then it stopped.

"We should eat," Alex said, breaking the silence.

The scene that met them as they left the office made them stop. This time Alex was sure the bodies had moved. Each one had left a snail trail of gore in its wake. The decomposition of the corpses was impressive. There were bones showing through split skin and grey meat underneath. Faces were skeletal with shrunken sunken eyes and teeth bared in so many snarls. Alex was convinced that they were all facing the office.

"What the holy fuck?" Randy said.

Alex and Maria just gaped.

"Still hungry?" Randy grinned, shouldering past them toward the stairs.

The bodies in the foyer were in the same advanced state of decay. Nobody mentioned it this time, they just kept walking toward the cafe, trying as hard as they could not to stare at the bodies. Alex could feel the dead eyes following them.

They knew something was wrong before they even got to the cafe. It seemed as though the accelerated rate of decay didn't only affect the dead. There was a growing pool of translucent brown sludge coming from the kitchen. All of the sandwich cases were soaking wet and had only small piles of brown hummus in the bottom. The stench was like wading through a dump. Randy turned his head and vomited.

"*Still hungry?*" Alex said in a passable imitation of Randy's voice.

They opened the vending machine with Randy's keys. The packaged sugary treats seemed immune to whatever was happening. They ate candy bars and soda for breakfast and decided to have another look across the river to see if they could possibly signal for help.

They stopped in the locker room to get more clothes. It was getting colder.

"Ow," said Randy, banging his head on the locker he was halfway inside.

Another invasive howl like before made them jump.

"Did you hear that?" Alex said.

"What, the loudest howl in the world? Uh, yeah," Randy said.

"Not that. The scuffling noise after."

"Don't be an asshole," Randy said, his eyes giving the lie to his strong words.

"The bodies. I think they've moved."

"Let's just get out of here," Maria whispered.

They passed through into the pool area, where it was colder than ever. The snow was so thick that they couldn't make out the bank, never mind anyone on it they could signal.

"Hey, look at the pool," Maria said.

Alex looked into the ruddy water. He thought it looked like a chocolate slushy. Except for the bodies. And the steam.

"It's steaming," he said.

"Exactly," Maria said. Then turning to Randy. "Is there some other way of powering the heater for the pool. You know when the power goes out?"

Randy thought for a moment. "No I don't think so," he said. "We had a power cut last year, remember? We couldn't open for two days because the pool was freezing. Dad was pissed…" His voice trailed away.

"Then what's heating the pool?" Alex said.

There was something else. The bodies didn't seem to be as badly decomposed in the pool. In fact, all the bodies around the pool were pretty much as they had been the day before.

They exhausted all of their options again: checked the phones, tried their cell phones, tried to knock the snow off the outside of the office window, bashed at the emergency exit some more. By the time lunch came around they were completely fed up. Alex had taken to sitting beside the pool, huddled under a mountain off clothes, staring across at the invisible river bank in the hope of seeing someone. Maria went between him and Randy in the office talking to them and trying to come up with ideas.

The ground beneath Alex shook violently and then the sky lit up like midday for just a second. As soon as it came, the light went and it looked darker than ever. He stood up and shook off his pile of clothing. Running through the changing room he almost bumped into Maria who was running in the other direction.

"Come quick," she said.

He didn't have any time to ask what it was about before she was gone.

He followed her to the office and immediately the question became redundant. The snow was cleared from the windows and he could tell why. Sandie's Gas had exploded. There was a cloud of smoke just visible through the falling snow, but the devastation was clear. Everything around the station had been levelled and most of it was on fire. A column of black rose up into the sky above, seemingly alive. Through the smoke he seemed to think he could see the word 'die' spelled out with what remained of Sandie's signage.

"I guess we're all in the same boat now," Randy said.

Alex barely heard him. At least if he did he didn't register it immediately. The realisation happened when Maria embraced him and sobbed into his chest. Both of their homes were within the radius of that explosion. Of course it was possible that their families wouldn't be home. But were else would they be on a Wednesday evening in the middle of a snow storm?

Alex didn't cry, he was too shocked. His home was gone and entire family was probably dead. There was nothing left of them apart from burning rubble. He just held Maria. It felt colder than ever. He was vaguely aware of Randy storming out and slamming the door to the office, but it was like it was happening in another world. Somewhere far away from where he, Maria and their grief was. They watched the smoke and flames in the dwindling light as the snow started obscuring their view once again. There didn't seem to be enough of a commotion over there, like nobody cared.

Eventually the snow blocked out the horror and the orange streetlight stole in where the snow had yet to stick.

"We should sleep," Alex said.

Maria just sniffed and nodded. Then she said, "Randy."

"He's a big boy, he knows his way back. I'm sure he will be here by the time we wake up."

She nodded again and they laid out the borrowed clothing and snuggled under them.

As Alex was drifting off he felt her move toward him. She nestled into the crook of his arm and sighed. Asleep, he thought to himself, but smiled a little just the same. A shuffling scraping noise, like the one they had heard before, brought him out of his half-sleep. Maria's head snapped upright.

"What was that?" she said.

Alex didn't answer. He crept to the door and turned the key to lock it.

"What about Randy?" Maria said.

"I'll open it when he comes back," Alex said. "He'll knock."

Even under their layers of clothes he could feel her warmth and it soothed him to sleep.

Randy watches them from a distance. Alex sees him as clearly as he sees himself and Maria in their meadow. Even though he is far away he can see everything in detail.

Randy's face is black with hatred as he stands in the shadow of the trees in his little copse. The same little copse he brought Maria to. He doesn't leave, he just watches.

Alex and Maria are rolling around in the long grass. They kiss. He sees it and feels it at the same time. It is wet and warm and good. Oh so good. Their hands move at a feverish pace tearing each other's clothes off. Neither caring or thinking that they are overlooked. They make love like it's essential to their continued existence. Like a person eating their first meal in weeks.

Randy looks on, his face twisted in rage. But he doesn't move.

Embarrassed, they jump back from each other when they realise that they are naked. Maria quickly starts pulling clothes on, not caring which ones. Alex stayed still, staring but trying not to.

"I'm sorry, I…" Alex said.

"No, I'm sorry. I shouldn't have…" Maria said.

"We should probably keep this between us."

Maria said nothing.

The window was completely white again, but there was a faint glow coming from it, as though back lit by an intense celestial body. Which Alex supposed it was. This made him smile.

"Why are you smiling?" Maria said.

"Just thought of something funny," Alex said.

"Yeah, very funny," Maria said.

"What? No not that. Just something I — "

"Whatever. Where's Randy?"

Alex's heart sank, expecting to see Randy hiding beneath the mound of clothes or behind the desk.

"I don't know," he said, finally accepting Randy wasn't there. "There was no knock in the night."

"You sure? Or did you just want to keep him away?"

"Hey, I said I was sorry. I don't remember you objecting."

Maria blushed and studied her feet. "I'm sorry. I shouldn't take it out on you. It was both our fault. And I agree, by the way."

"With what?" Alex said.

"That we should keep it to ourselves," Maria said.

"We should probably go find Randy."

She got up and turned the key in the door then pressed the handle down and pushed. The door didn't budge. She fiddled with the key again and pushed.

"I can't move it," Maria said.

"Let me try."

He checked the lock and pushed as hard as he could. The door moved an inch, then stopped. It was as if there was something heavy blocking it. He pushed again and it gave a little more. The smell that flooded in made him gag.

"Shit!" Maria said through the sleeve of her jacket "What is that smell?"

"It smells like the gym did yesterday, only worse," Alex said.

They both pushed the door again as hard as they could until there was a gap wide enough for them to squeeze through. Alex was sorry he did and he was sure Maria was too. Blocking the door was a mountain of the bodies. Except they were less and less recognisable as individual bodies. It looked like they had been thrown there and had melted together against the door. There was a river of yellow liquid flowing from the mass and the whole thing seemed to be pulsating slightly. On closer inspection, Alex could see that at least half of what he was seeing was maggots.

This time he did throw up, quickly followed by Maria. It made no difference to the smell, it just made him feel worse. They trudged through the fog of stench and made it to the top of the stairs.

"Oh my God," Maria said. "What the fuck?"

"Randy?" Alex said.

"I don't think he would, he can't stand bodily fluids. When I'm on my period he makes me empty the bathroom bin out every time I use it."

Not knowing how to react to this insight into Randy and Maria's relationship, Alex carried on searching for the person he hated most in the world, hoping they would never find him.

Randy wasn't in the foyer either. The cafe was even worse than it had been before. The floor was covered in a black sticky coating and there was a carpet of feeding maggots. They decided Randy wouldn't have gone in there and went to check behind the desk. There was a door there which lead to a broom cupboard. It was where Randy had taken Maria to try the lights. No sign of Randy in either place. Alex did spy a fire axe behind some glass. He had the sudden urge to have a weapon but Maria convinced him otherwise, in case one of them got accidentally injured.

Neither of them felt much like eating, but they agreed that they should. The vending machines still had packaged foods in them, which were fairly fresh. They ate beside the tumbledown entrance where the smell was least bad. After a feast of crisps, candy and soda they decided to check the locker rooms and pool for Randy. It wasn't an appealing prospect. Both had plenty of dead people in them. But they were determined to find him. Well, Maria was. And Alex was determined to do whatever Maria wanted.

"You take the men's and I'll take the ladies," Maria said as they came to the two doors.

"Sure? Shouldn't we stay together?" Alex said.

"Aw, scared?"

"No, it's just—"

"Good, see you in the pool," Maria said before he could finish and pushed through the door into the locker room.

It smelled at least as bad as the gym, just a bit more diffuse with the bodies not having been piled up against anything. They were no less decayed, though. No less gross. There were little rivulets of the yellow liquid running into the drains in the floor. He put his sleeve to his mouth and walked quickly around the room. Glancing into the showers and toilet cubicles on his way, there was no sign of Randy.

He hurried into the pool area, unable to get out of the locker room fast enough. There was no Maria, but what he saw made him forget all about her. Snow had piled up inside the absent wall, making a long dune from one side to the other. Above the dune he could see that the weather had calmed. What shocked him, though, was the freshness of the bodies in and around the water. They weren't even any paler than they had been. The water was a little browner than before but there was no real smell now to speak of. He supposed some of that was to do with the opening where the window used to be. Even so, it was remarkably fresh.

Alex drifted toward the water in a trance. As he approached he could feel the heat from the surface. Against the cold it felt like a furnace. No wonder the snow on the other side came no closer, like a huge animal cowering from a ferocious adversary. He took another step. The heat was glorious, he felt like the cold deep in his bones was slowly melting away. He took another step and fell on his back.

Maria was standing over him looking down.

"What the hell were you doing? Going for a swim?" she said.

"I...I don't know," Alex said. "It's just so warm and..." Alex stuttered.

"Did you find Randy?" Maria said.

"No."

Maria glanced around the pool. "Eerie, isn't it?" she said.

The wind rose and fell. With each fall came sounds from outside: screaming, crying, smashing glass and sirens filled the air in turn. Alex began to feel glad they were inside and not out there. Then he remembered the smell and the corpses and wasn't so sure.

Maria suggested going back to the office and waiting for either rescue or Randy to come back. By the way she said it, Alex understood that she believed both to be unlikely, as did he. They stocked up on food from the vending machines and made their way back. Alex found some cleaning implements and gloves and they dragged as much of the mass in front of the door away as possible. It was disgusting work, but in the end they managed to get most of the bodies moved and went inside.

"What do you see in him?" Alex said, breaking an hour long silence.

"Who, Randy?" Maria said.

"Yeah," Alex said.

"I don't know, he's sweet, I guess."

"Sweet? Randy? We're talking about the same guy, right?"

"Don't be nasty, he can be sweet. I know he's a bit hard to take sometimes, but…"

"But what?"

"Nothing."

"No, tell me," Alex said.

"Well, I guess he can be a bit of a jerk sometimes and he does get angry. He has a lot of family stuff to deal with. His dad... And anyway, we've been together for, like, forever," Maria said.

"And that's a good reason for staying with him?"

"Hey, get off my back. It's none of your business anyway," Maria snapped.

"No, I guess not," Alex said. "I'm sorry."

They sat in silence again, huddled against the cold underneath a pile of steadily ripening, borrowed clothes.

Maria broke the silence this time. "No, I'm sorry, I shouldn't have shouted."

"It's okay," Alex said.

They left it at that and changed the subject. They talked about the mundane, rapidly approaching changes in their lives like college and swimming and things they were looking forward to and other things they weren't. Anything to distract themselves from the death surrounding them. They eventually talked each other into slumber as the light got low.

Alex woke from a dreamless sleep. He felt Maria shift beside him and heard the familiar scraping and shuffling from outside the door.

"What's that?" Maria whispered.

Alex couldn't see her face, but her voice said she was terrified.

He scrambled around and found the flashlight. Then he quietly unlocked the office door and turned the handle. There was no problem opening it this time. He paused when it was open enough to get his head through. It was so dark that the view with the door open was no different to the door closed. Alex clicked the little button under his thumb and it was as if a miniature sun came into existence in his hand.

The shuffling stopped as soon as the light went on. He swept the light across the gym and nothing seemed different. He saw the mounds of rot filled clothes left where he dropped them when he dragged them from the door. He turned the light off and immediately the noise recommenced. When he turned it on again the mounds had moved closer. He tested it again and again they jumped forward in the darkness. He closed and locked the door, saying nothing about it to Maria. The clock on the wall said 11:59 and as he looked the minute hand moved to straight up and it was midnight. Alex and Maria didn't speak again, they just huddled and eventually sleep took them.

It happens as before where he is watching himself and Maria in the meadow and Randy is looking on. Except it's more vivid, more intense. He can feel it more. He focuses on Randy who looks more twisted than ever. His features are bent into such an intense rage that he is barely recognisable.

Suddenly Randy charges across the river, traversing it as if it were solid ground, sword in hand. Alex isn't sure it even is Randy as he approaches the lovers. Suddenly Alex is facing down this thing that Randy has become. He fights him off and Randy flees. The lovers remain in the meadow, the grass is bloodstained from the wound in Alex's side. Randy's sword lays, crimson, a little way off.

There was a light glow from outside when Alex awoke. His side was on fire where Randy had stabbed him in his dream. His hands shot down to check for blood and he realised he was naked. Maria stirred and sat upright covering herself with the clothes. She looked at Alex with a different look in her eyes. It wasn't suspicion and wariness like before. It was softer, somehow.

They dressed, sheepishly with eyes averted and backs turned. Alex unlocked the door and pushed it. It moved, with a little resistance. Like before the bodies, or what was left of them, were pressed up against the door like a barricade. Or had they been trying to get in? The smell was no worse, but certainly no better and there was less mass. It had mostly rotted away. They stepped over the sludge and liquid that he had dislodged and walked into a cloud of fat flies.

With eyes covered and mouths closed they ran toward the stairs and down. The vending machine had very little left and it had all rotted. They picked some things up only to find that the candy bars were just like little bags of slush and the crisps were soft and rancid. Even the cans of soda had exploded under the pressure of their decomposition.

"That's it, I'm getting out of here," Alex announced and strode over to the cupboard behind the reception.

He threw open the door and smashed the glass encasing the fire axe. It was about two feet long with a large flat head and a pick at the back. He went back to the emergency door and started hammering at it with the blade side and then the pick side. He was screaming and swearing, his shoulders burned and his hands ached from the effort and vibrations of the axe hitting the solid door.

Eventually he grew tired and collapsed to the floor. The door was still standing, if scarred. There was no sign of it opening at all.

"It's okay," Maria said "Someone will come, someone has to come."

Alex just sat and stared at the door in disbelief, panting.

"What's that thing made of?" he said.

Suddenly he heard voices coming from the pool. They were arguing; a deep voice and a normal male one answering. Maria had obviously heard it too. Without speaking they got up and sprinted the pool.

It was empty. Apart from the bodies.

There were no voices, the only sound was the wind. It looked much the same as it did the day before, except the water was more opaque and the bodies more pale. As if the pool was drawing the very colour from them.

"They look more, I don't know…dead," Alex said, the words sounding stupid even to him.

"Lifeless," Maria said. "Like the life is gone from them. Before, they looked almost alive, now they don't."

"Exactly," said Alex.

Then he saw ripples on the surface of the pool. Coming from the centre and radiating out in concentric circles as if a stone had been dropped in. But there had been no stone. The water was now faintly glowing green and steaming.

Alex and Maria are running for their lives. The axe isn't in Alex's hand anymore. Instead his hand is pressed to his side where the sword punctured his skin. Blood is seeping out around his fingers. He looks back and sees the thing that was Randy running after them. He's gaining all the time. Never stopping. They run forever. Randy promising that he will never stop. That he will get the lovers in this life or the next.

The clock told Alex it was an hour earlier than he expected. Then he realised the truth.

"It's Sunday," he said.

"What?" Maria said.

"We've lost Saturday. It's Sunday already."

"Lost it?" Maria said.

She was still half asleep so he didn't press it. Then he realised he hadn't dreamed the night before. In fact the last thing he remembered was standing at the poolside with Maria. They were still clothed this morning but it was bitterly cold. Colder than it had been. Alex was sure he could see ice forming on the inside of the window. Despite this, he was sweating and he could see that Maria was too. She had a thin film of moisture on her forehead. Were they feverish? Was it that had caused him to have such a weird dream last night? There was no way to tell. It felt so real. Did that mean he was still dreaming?

"The voices," Maria said, sitting bolt upright.

Alex heard them too. They were coming from the pool.

"Let's have a look," he said.

He was wary this time. There was definitely something wrong going on in the pool. He didn't want to rush down there again. They gently pushed the door of the office. There was nothing blocking it now. The bodies were mostly soaked into the carpet. Like they had been all used up. Even the smell wasn't as bad, it was more of a cloying sweetness with a touch of the previous rot.

They crept across the gym, avoiding the puddles. There were wire reinforced portholes in the wall that allowed them to look down to the pool.

"That's Randy's voice," Maria said as they approached the windows.

"There's something wrong with it," Alex said.

They pressed their faces up against the glass and looked down at the pool. It wasn't the stagnant slush puppy it had been, it was a whirling, swirling green vortex of bodies and glass and debris. It looked like a giant blender making the most disgusting smoothie ever. The voices were louder now, but he couldn't make out what they were saying over the slushing and grinding of the whirlpool.

"It's going the wrong way," Maria said.

"What?"

"It's swirling anti-clockwise."

Now that he saw it he realised it had looked odd. Apart from the fact that it was a swimming pool filled with bodies swirling around like it was a giant food processor.

"The water level isn't going down either," Alex said. "It's not going down a drain."

From the centre of the vortex, a long black tentacle flew toward the mezzanine. It cracked like a whip and stuck in the wall between them, staying there for a long second. Then they tumbled down in a mess of dust and glass and bricks and gym machinery.

Alex's head hurt when he opened his eyes. The light was too bright and every sound was like a trumpet in his ears. He sat up and the movement induced a fit of vomiting. The world was pitching even as he sat there. He closed his eyes and waited for it to stop. The light pierced his brain afresh when he re-opened them. There was dust everywhere.

Maria was lying face down in the rubble. There was a pile of debris, topped off with a treadmill, on her legs. Blood flowed out from underneath. Alex tried to move toward her, but when he put weight on his right arm it exploded in atrocious pain. He blacked out again.

When he woke, Maria was stroking his hair. He looked at her, but she was staring at the pool, her face a mask of terror. He followed her gaze and saw what was causing it. The vortex was still swirling, but so fast now there was a hole in the centre where the centrifugal force was drawing the water away from it. Hovering over the hole was Randy, or something that might have been Randy, lit up in green from below. His hair and body were the same but his face was drawn up in a scream, mouth open but without any sound. Where his eyes used to be were two writhing tentacles and there was another wriggling out of his right nostril.

Randy's head was hanging forward and his body was completely limp. Alex saw that he wasn't actually levitating but being held up like a puppet by a thick tentacle and a number of smaller ones entering him from behind. As they looked, a thick tongue-like tip came out of Randy's mouth and he made a cracking cough. His face snapped up and looked at them, though he had no eyes.

The sound that came out of his mouth could hardly be called voice. More like something strumming Randy's vocal chords. It had notes of Randy's voice but it was infinitely harsher. It hurt Alex's ears.

"Aaah, the lovers. Welcome, welcome."

"Randy?" Maria said.

"You, my dear," said the thing that was Randy, "are a harlot and a slut."

A tentacle whipped out from behind Randy and slashed across Maria's face. It sliced clean through her cheek like a razor and she screamed in pain. A second tentacle came out and wrapped around her neck, stifling her screams.

Alex was stunned into silence. He could feel warmth bloom in his crotch.

"Nothing to say? Brother?" the thing that was Randy said.

Something stirred in Alex. Hope, or something like it, that the thing was mistaken. That it had made a mistake and it would take it all back.

"I...I'm not your brother," Alex said thickly.

"Lies."

It wasn't a shout as such. Just a louder version of the voice and it made Alex's ears bleed. In its anger, it ripped Maria from under the rubble leaving most of the skin and flesh of her leg behind. She didn't scream. Alex could see why. Her face was a dark shade of blue around bulging red eyes. The thing's tentacle was squeezing her neck so hard the blood was gathering in her head. Raising the pressure so it looked like it might explode.

Alex's thoughts went to the axe. If he could only get to it, then he could try to kill the thing.

It had destroyed the inner walls when it brought down the mezzanine. Alex could see the exit and the axe on the floor where he had flung it dejectedly after he couldn't get through the doors. He got to his feet, stumbling as he used his left arm. Then he cradled his useless right arm and ran.

The thing's tentacles whipped him, but couldn't seem to catch hold. Every blow took a lump of skin and muscle with it. Every hit should have weakened him. Every one caused him pain. But whether through adrenaline or sheer determination Alex was suddenly within five feet of the axe. He threw himself at it, diving with his left arm out to grab it.

Suddenly he entered warp speed. The axe receded into the distance as Alex flew backward.

Then, just as abruptly, he stopped.

Tentacles propped him upright and he floated beside Maria and the thing that was Randy. Her eyes were closed and the blue was gone from her face. It had regained some of its natural brown hue. The thing slashed at her face opening a gash that was a mirror image of the other side.

She awoke in agony.

This time it let her scream and sob. Though her cries were weaker now.

"You stole her from me, brother," the thing that was Randy said. "And now I will get my revenge. Too long have I chased you. Too long have you eluded me. Over the centuries people have called me terrible names: The Kraken, Cthulhu, Nephthys, but no more. No more shall I suffer in the void you have put me in. This town, this Hell has released me. Now I will have my revenge. Now I will finally punish The Lovers."

Alex realised that it was talking about the dreams. He cried out that it wasn't them. It wasn't his fault or hers. They were just kids. They didn't know, they weren't controlling it.

It held Alex and Maria up high. The thing that was Randy laughed and Alex felt a searing white pain in his head. He saw a tentacle pushing through the side of Maria's skull. Alex tried to turn his head to look away but it was no good. He watched the light fade from her eyes. In the corner of his vision he could see the writhing black of the tentacle pushing into his own temple.

It was the last thing Alex ever saw.

WELCOME TO A TOWN CALLED HELL

HELL WOMAN REPORTS NOISES COMING FROM TOILET

Lifelong Hell resident Katie Franks called the offices of The Hell Star to report strange noises coming from her drains. Widow Mrs Franks told our reporter, "I keep calling the water company out, but they aren't interested. Say everything's fine. But I know what I heard."

WELCOME TO A TOWN CALLED HELL

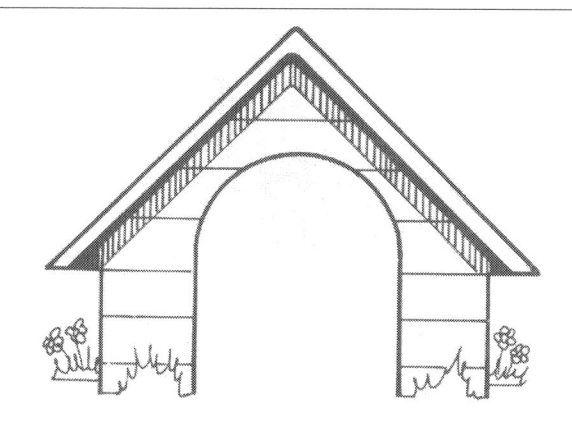

FRIEND FROM A LOW PLACE
John McNee

WELCOME TO A TOWN CALLED HELL

Myrtle Railsback was pouring her third drink of the morning when she heard a thud against the side of the house. She jumped, spilling white rum across the counter-top, then cursed herself. She should have been well-used to such sounds by now. The pounding bass from her next-door neighbour's stereo system was constant and over the past year had successfully obliterated any of her once fond feelings for the musical stylings of Garth Brooks. One more thud on top of all the rest shouldn't have startled her. Only this one had come from the wrong wall. It had come from the back of the house, the side facing onto nothing but a yard full of snow and a few acres of woodland before the mountains.

Myrtle had a little think about that as she sucked some of the spilled rum from her fingers, then decided to investigate. She walked out of the kitchen and across the hall – slippers slapping against linoleum, ice tinkling in her glass – to reach the sliding door out onto the backyard. It was cloudy with condensation. She cleared a spot with the sleeve of her bathrobe and peered out, but couldn't see anything out of place.

Another sound. Metal chain rattling against timber. Myrtle thought of the old doghouse by the fence. It had been unoccupied for some five years, since Duchess, her Anatolian shepherd, died from eating poisoned sausage meat. But her chain still dangled from a nail in the roof. Myrtle pulled open the door and stepped outside, clutching the collar of her robe against her chest, shielding her delicate parts from the cold air.

There were tracks in the snow. She spotted them as she moved along the side of the house. It looked like they started at the treeline, wove through the yard and ended at the doghouse. She couldn't tell what had caused them, but they were deep and spread out, like whatever it was had been running. Red and black stains dappled the snow between the prints. There were red and black smears on the wall of the house. Red and black liquid coated Duchess's chain.

Myrtle crept towards the doghouse, bending low to get a look at what was inside. It was too dark in there for her to make it out clearly, but she could tell something was huddled within its confines, something too big to get comfortable, the walls straining around its girth. Something that whimpered weakly from pain and cold.

"Hello?" Myrtle said, just for something to say. Whatever was in there, she already knew it wasn't human. "Hello? Are you all right in there?" She spoke to it the way she would speak to a stray dog, keeping her tone as soft and sweet as she could. "Need any help?"

The thing that leaned its heavy head out of the doghouse gave her a pained howl by way of reply, but it was no stray dog.

Myrtle's eyes widened. She straightened up, tipped the glass of rum down her throat, then went back inside for the bottle.

Sheriff Marlowe's reserve deputy, 'Lucky' Larry Teagarden, brought his pick-up to a skidding halt outside the Railsback house. He was breathless and sweating, dressed in half-scorched clothes stained by blood that wasn't his and piss that was. A long-barrelled Peacemaker-style revolver was in a custom holster on his hip. He kept his hand on it as he ran up the path and began pounding on the door.

"Myrtle," he yelled, jerking his head over his shoulder to check for signs of incoming chaos. The neighbourhood – a cul-de-sac of semi-detached, one-story homes arranged in a lazy half-circle – appeared quiet. "Myrtle! Open up!"

She did, throwing the front door wide and giving him a furious look. "Lucky, for Christ's sake, keep it down, would you? What's the matter with you?"

"What do you think?" he said, barging his way inside and slamming the door behind him. "You ain't watching the TV?"

"TV hasn't worked since that plane came down."

"The radio, then."

"I only listen to Pastor John from St Jude's. And his show don't start till noon."

"Might want to turn it on now." He started a sweep of the house, moving through the living room and kitchen, checking windows, making sure they were locked and bolted. "Things are going nuts out there. You wouldn't believe some of the shit I've seen the past couple days."

She chuckled, casting a sidelong glance at the master bedroom. "I might. But if things are as bad as all that, shouldn't you be out there lending a hand?"

"No, no, no." He shook his head. "Not me. I'm officially done. If Sheriff Marlowe needs help, he's going to have to look for it somewhere else, because I am done."

"I always said you'd be great in a crisis."

"What we need to do is get out. I'm serious. This town..."

"I haven't set foot out of this town in ten years."

"Listen to me, Myrtle! Something's happening here. Something big! Something bad! And if we don't get gone then we're gonna get got!"

"That right? And how do you fix on getting out with no road?"

"Through the mountains. There has to be some kind of trail..."

"Ain't no trail."

"Then we'll climb!"

"You'd be dead of exposure before nightfall. Talk sense, Lucky!"

Exasperated, panicking, Lucky ran both hands over his sweaty face, nearly knocking his glasses off his nose. He took a breath, then dropped both arms to his side and said, "Well, we sure as shit can't stay here. It's not secure. We need to be somewhere solid."

"I wasn't aware I was keeping you prisoner."

"You need to pack a bag. Right now."

Folding her arms, Myrtle gave him a condescending look. "Lucky, no offence, but I'm going nowhere with you."

Closing the distance between them, he placed his hands on her shoulders. "Myrtle, this is serious."

"So am I."

"I made a promise to Duke – on his deathbed – that I would keep you safe."

She rolled her eyes. "Promises made between bowling buddies are one thing. But if my Duke was here right now he'd know better than to leave this house in a crisis. He was a homesteader."

"Pack a bag," Lucky insisted, mustering as much grit into his voice as he could.

"I will not." Myrtle shrugged off his hands.

"Well, if you won't, I will," he said, turned, and moved towards the bedroom.

"Don't," she said, hurrying after him.

His hand grasped the doorknob. "I'm taking charge of this situation, Myrtle." He threw the door open. "Somebody's got..." Lucky's words died on his tongue the instant he got a look at the thing in the bed.

Stretched out across the covers, head propped up on two pillows, was a beast that he could tell at a glance had no business walking the earth. Its body looked like it had been sculpted from black bone and iron ore, lightly steaming in the warmth of the room and glistening around areas from which multiple alien orifices seeped dark, frothing slime. At the ends of its long limbs, marked by the scars of suppurating wounds, were feet and hands of twisting blade, dripping red and black oil. They hung limply over the edges of the mattress – a clue that the thing, when standing, would be a lot taller than the average man. Its head, face turned to the wall, was a cluster of intersecting horns and tendrils. Funnels in its antlers disgorged plumes of wispy grey smoke in time to the pace of its breathing, which was slow and regulated enough to imply the thing was fast asleep.

"You weren't supposed to see that," Myrtle whispered.

"What the fuck is it?" Lucky managed to choke in reply.

"Well, I'm not too sure. But if I had to take a guess at it, I'd say it's probably a demon."

Lucky's eyes roved over the creature's sprawled form, finding nothing that would stand in evidence against down, picked it up and let loose with a cry of her own. "Damn you, you Irish cocksucker!"

Maggie fired the rifle.

Myrtle fired the pistol.

And both bullets found their targets.

WELCOME TO A TOWN CALLED HELL

Suspension of Disbelief
Paul M. Feeney

Charles Naughton watched with detached horror as the severed top half of the reanimated corpse crawled toward where he lay, his back pushed up against the cold concrete wall behind. His vertebrae scraped painfully against the rough surface. Splayed out before him his ruined left leg glistened red, splinters of shocking white bone poking up through the wet, ragged mess of meat.

He looked at the empty pistol held loosely in his right hand and made a sound somewhere between a laugh and a sob; it quickly degenerated into a hacking cough. He had not even thought to save a bullet for himself. Frustrated tears slipped from his eyes and an ache twisted in his chest. To think that he had survived so much; had lived over six decades only to meet his sad, sorry end in a neglected, forgotten warehouse on the edge of a town called Hell, injured and exhausted.

The dead thing slapped one hand down on the floor and dragged its torn body closer, fingernails splitting and cracking on the bare concrete. Its other arm was nothing more than a knob of shiny bone poking through the shredded, grey flesh of its shoulder. It stared at him with unblinking eyes that were flat, milky orbs; the jaw worked ceaselessly, as if anticipating the meal it would make of his body. Trailing behind, torn strips of dry skin and guts dragged on the dusty floor, a dry whisper that echoed round the basement.

Charles thought of his wife and family – lost yesterday to these ravening monsters – and hoped there was an afterlife in which he might soon see them again. He offered up a silent prayer to a long abandoned god.

He'd always thought there was something deeply wrong with Hell; after all, who names a town after the residence of the Prince of Darkness?

Over the years he'd heard strange stories from a variety of sources, some credible, some... not so credible. He had even had a few weird experiences himself that couldn't be easily explained away, even in daylight. Yet none of these things remotely compared to the escalating series of bizarre events which seemed to have befallen the town since that goddam plane crash at the beginning of the week. Since then, Hell had been witness to a series of brutal murders, explosions and unexplained death and destruction. The skies had been filled with flying, leathery creatures and the streets had run amok with crazed wolves. Trying to escape the horrors, to make some kind of sanctuary for his family – wife, son, daughter, *their* partners their and children – and himself, they had headed to the industrial estate on the south west of town. Here Charles hoped to find somewhere abandoned where they could hole up until someone – the military, the police, the National Guard, or even the goddamn Vatican – arrived to save them. But their respite was short-lived; the series of connecting warehouses and dusty office buildings they'd taken shelter in turned out to be host to a group of – and Charles *still* couldn't wrap his head around the concept despite all the insane things they had witnessed – reanimated corpses. The few personally owned firearms they'd brought had only held these monsters off temporarily but when the bullets had run out, they had soon been overwhelmed and Charles still had no idea how he'd managed to escape with the injury his knee had sustained. This period of time was a blank for him, though not blank enough; he still recalled crawling away to the soundtrack of his family being torn to pieces by the living dead. As long as he lived, he would never forget the screams, the gurgling gasps from blood-filled lungs, the wet pops and snaps, the frenzied sound of teeth tearing through skin, flesh, and muscle. He had somehow managed to escape into another part of the complex, where he fell into an exhausted and weary sleep, still gripping onto the pistol which he had emptied into the zombie throng to no avail.

And then came to when he heard the soft, dry sibilance of this broken monster crawling toward him.

He released a choking sob and swallowed down a lump of bitterness.

Closer still, the corpse reached out its one remaining hand, eager digits trembling inches from the Charles' foot. Something rattled in its chest and he was put in mind of an old and broken clockwork toy.

It was now within reach of his foot and that rattle was getting louder and a rising buzz was building in his head and...

"...CUUUT!"

The voice rang out loud and clear, a bell trilled painfully, shockingly loud and the previously empty space was filled with people, noise and activity. Charles' head whipped back and forth in astonished confusion.

"Someone see what's wrong with that friggin' puppet. And get the old fella up."

Three people approached where he lay, and his good leg started twitching as the urge to flee flooded through him. Yet two of these people – people who, until a moment ago had not even existed in this place – paid him absolutely no concern, heading instead to the living corpse. He sucked in a breath to cry a warning to them, then realized the thing was no longer moving; and as he peered more closely, it appeared different from before, very obviously made of rubber. In addition to the ragged flesh extending from its severed torso were wires and cables snaking off into the gloom behind light stands and large cameras.

Charles' mouth gaped, confusion filling his head and making it swirl. Then a shadow crouched down beside him, causing his body to flinch, but it was only the other person who had approached. Charles squinted up into the face of a bespectacled young man and blinked, feeling lost and confused.

"Let me help you up, Mr. Naughton. The director's called a break for a half hour so they can fix the animatronic. I'll escort you back to your dressing room." The man's voice was soft and unconcerned considering there was – or had been – a moving corpse mere feet away.

Animatronic? Dressing room? What the damned hell is going on here?

Instead of asking this young fellow, Charles looked back at the zombie and found that the other two had peeled back its skin to reveal not muscle and bone, but wires and metal. It was some kind of robot or puppet. Vertigo washed through his mind.

The young man leaned closer. "Mr. Naughton? Sir? Are you okay?"

"I'm, I... I don't know. I... What is this? Where am I?"

"Sir?"

And then the memories flooded into him, like water slowly filling up a jug; his name was Charles Naughton, he was a famous actor – or had been, many years previous – best known for a plethora of horror films in the industry's heyday through the sixties and seventies; now shooting the final scene in what he hoped might be a triumphant return to the screen after a number of years in enforced retirement after the roles had started drying up. And this young man was his assistant, an eager young fellow hired by Charles' agent. In the last few weeks of filming the movie – the name of which still escaped Charles – the two had become close friends, the young fellow eager to listen to Charles' tales of the glory days, being an aspiring actor himself.

Charles gently shook his head. The sensation that the scene they had just shot was absolutely real still lingered, and though it was now fading, his mind still clung to the horror, the pain, and the awful loss of his 'family'. It felt just as if he'd woken from a particularly vivid dream; or had been immersed in an engrossing book and upon finishing, was trying to readjust to dull reality. He looked up at the young man – whose name still eluded his fickle memory – and smiled; it felt delicate and fragile on his face. "I'm sorry, I'm... I'm okay. I... I just lost myself for a moment. Caught up in the scene. I'm okay. Thank you, uh..."

"Peter, sir. Peter Trevayne." Peter offered an arm, helping Charles to his feet.

Once standing, he was just about to put weight on his left leg, then hissed a breath in anticipation of the pain before remembering it wasn't injured, it was simply a special effect. It was fake; it was all fake. Still, he tentatively allowed it to support him, half expectant that the 'injury' – which, even now, looked raw and real – would cause him to collapse and pass out in agony.

Peter led him to his dressing room, which turned out to be little bigger than a walk-in closet.

"Can I get you anything, Mr. Naughton? Tea, coffee?"

Charles turned from the small, scuffed table, where he had started flicking through a tiny scattering of good luck cards, still trying to shake off the intense feeling the scene had left him with. It had seemed so real. "Ah, yes...tea would be lovely, thank you."

Peter nodded and departed.

On top of the small table at which he, presumably, sat to have his make-up done (though most of his memory was returning, there were still short-term gaps) was a grimy mirror. Where he might have expected it to be bordered with many lights, there was only the one, solitary lamp. A vase sat on the far right of the table, half-filled with scummy water and a scattering of dying flowers, and tucked under the table was a cheap, plastic seat, one corner cracked. Behind him, the small room was further crowded out with a mobile clothes rack, laden with various costumes and clothing, none of which looked as though it were for him. Clearly, his dressing room doubled as storage space for the entire production.

He sat down on the plastic chair – which produced an ominous creak – just as Peter returned with a steaming Styrofoam cup of tea.

"Here we go, should pep you up a bit. If you don't mind me saying, you seem a little out of sorts."

"Thank you, Peter." Charles took a sip of the liquid, wincing as it scalded the tip of his tongue. He blew on the surface before setting it down. He gave Peter a small salute with the cup. "Yes, this'll do fine. Just feeling a bit dazed; the scene was especially vivid for me. I'll be fine in a moment or two."

Peter hovered just inside the doorway. "Is there anything else, sir?"

Charles considered. "Well, actually, if you wouldn't mind. I *could* do with some company. That is, if you don't have anything else to do?"

"Of course, sir. It would be my pleasure." Smiling, Peter moved further into the room, standing to the side of the dressing table.

Charles absently ran his hand over the good luck cards; there were only four. He felt sadness well up in his heart and swallowed as a painful lump lodged in his throat. "It must all seem rather pathetic to you, Peter. All of this, I mean."

Peter coughed. "Not at all, sir. It's all part of the learning process."

Charles laughed once, without humor. "'Learning process'. Ha. Yes. Indeed. Well, it's a sorry epilogue to my career. I once commanded dressing rooms three times the size of this; the table would be heaving with cards and flowers, the place would pay host to a never-ending stream of visitors and admirers, and now...well, never mind. Just the ramblings of a forgetful and forgotten old man."

He wondered how it had all slipped away from him. Once upon a time his name had been mentioned in the same company as Olivier, Burton and Guinness. Now, he barely warranted a paragraph in dissertations by film students. In his most cynical moments – which were becoming far more frequent these days – he laid most of the blame at the foot of those horror films he'd once revered. He'd thought he was making high art; they all did. Following modest successes in more artistic, 'worthy' pictures, the allure of the supernatural and horrific – a passion of his youth in the supernatural stories of James, Dickens, Onions, and Poe – had proved to be more than he could resist. And with the growing buzz following Roger Corman's successes with adaptations of Poe classics, and the rise of studios such as Hammer and Atticus, Charles had decided to throw his lot in with the likes of Price in the US, and Cushing and Lee across the pond. And at first, it had been a blast; exciting projects, great reviews, and appreciative audiences had given him – had given them all – the illusion that they were recreating the phenomenal successes of the old Universal days. But recycled ideas and increasingly derivative plots had led to diminished returns which in turn led to reduced funding and – inevitably – cheaper, trashier and more desperate films before the bubble burst, and Charles found that no one wished to hire him anymore.

And yet, here he was again, partaking of that which he thought he'd left behind years ago. But everyone had bills to pay, and he would be lying if he said he didn't miss the atmosphere, the craft.

Peter folded his arms and leaned against the side of the table. "If you don't mind me saying, sir, I think you do yourself a disservice. Even if some of those films weren't exactly the greatest, you – and other actors – still gave them your all, gave stellar performances. I've mentioned before that I'm a huge fan of yours; not just the horror movies, but all your work. You're one of the reasons I became interested in acting and film."

Scraping the chair legs on the concrete floor, Charles pushed his seat away from the table and faced Peter. "That's extremely kind of you to say, my boy, but no false modesty; some of those parts, those films, were truly awful. But still, when it was good, it was fantastic. It felt truly magical, like we were in the midst of something special, every time."

Charles felt a wash of nostalgia roll over him. Those years had been the best of his life; the parties, the money, and, of course, the films themselves. Working with some of the brightest talents in the industry, hobnobbing with genuine world-famous celebrities. Even he had been relatively well known, renowned mainly for his convincing acting method. Some wit in the press had dubbed him 'The Great Pretender', in acknowledgement of his ability to raise even the most two-dimensionally written part to levels of utmost believability, and it had caught on. What the media – and the public – had never been aware of, was just how accurate this nickname had been. It was a secret that Charles had never shared with anyone; namely, that when he fully immersed himself in a project, he had often felt that the scene he was shooting was more real than his life outside the film. It was partially why he had left the industry in the first place, and not just because the roles had been getting steadily more ludicrous. It was as if a small piece of him was chipped away with each part he played, and the longer he continued, the more his own personality, his very existence, was being slowly erased. It was a fanciful notion and one he was able to easily dismiss once he'd retired. But as soon as he'd returned to a life in front of the camera, it had come flooding back. The recent scene was a case in point; the remnants of its 'reality' still hovered around his head like the softly beating wings of tiny birds.

Charles slowly became aware that Peter had spoken. "I'm terribly sorry, Peter, what was that?"

Peter glanced at his watch. "Didn't mean to interrupt your thoughts, Mr. Naughton, but I think that's about time to get back to the set." As if on cue, the bell rang again, though here in this room, it sounded quieter, less urgent.

Charles sighed and nodded, then slowly got to his feet. "Of course. Can't keep them waiting, eh?"

It wasn't until Peter led him back to the set and the same position he had previously occupied on the 'warehouse' floor that Charles felt a low dread balloon inside. For no reason he could articulate, he suddenly did not want to lie back down on the floor, or carry on with the scene. Panic flapped at the edges of his mind. But he had no choice; what would he say? That he had a vague, unformed terror of carrying on with the scene, that he thought it might...what? Consume him utterly? It should have sounded ludicrous even to himself, if it were not for the rising buzz of fear. And yet he allowed Peter to assist him in lying down, while the film crew bustled around making last minute adjustments.

Peter stepped back into darkness and everyone else took their places, and Charles was left alone with the immobile, rubber monster staring idiotically at him with its dead, fake eyes.

And then the cameras began rolling, the set lights came up and the director called, *"ACTION!"*, and...

...Charles looked around in utter confusion, while a sound – like soft surf – on the edge of his hearing faded away in a hush. He thought he heard the echo of a whispered word, fleeing even as he tried to concentrate on it. His head felt muggy, like he'd been daydreaming in a heat wave, but whatever thoughts and images had been in his mind were now slipping away. In their place came the bright heat of pain radiating out from the very real wound in his left leg. Teeth gritted, he tipped his head back, biting down on the scream that tried to force its way out between his teeth, clenching his fist on the empty pistol.

A rough rasp from just beyond his feet brought his attention back to where he was. He looked down to see the moving corpse inching implacably closer, the fingers on its one remaining limb reaching for him, questing.

And then it was on him, clawing its way up his legs, sending bright shards of agony exploding silently through his head each time it scraped across his torn wound. He batted feebly at its head with the pistol but it paid no attention.

When it reached his abdomen, it raised its head, the jaws opening wide in creaks and snaps of dry ligaments. Charles watched in detached fascination as it lowered its mouth as delicately as a lover. Then his world exploded in pain of such intensity, he could scarcely comprehend it; it was as if an explosion had gone off destroying his hearing, a raging bloom of weighted silence.

The corpse ripped open his stomach in a frenzy of rending activity, blood and gore splashing out in gobs. It pushed its hand into the wound, tearing the skin and widening the cavity; he could feel the dead thing's limb moving inside, slipping and sliding amongst his innards, pushing and searching. His gullet rose and thin, acidic bile tinged pink with blood leaked from his mouth.

As he started choking on his own vomit, as his diaphragm was penetrated, further hampering his breathing, and as the creature slipped its thin, bony fingers around his heart, Charles felt himself begin to fade. A white fog filled his mind and the pain and pressure receded. From a great distance, he thought he heard the sound of voices, and hoped it was his family, his loved ones, his wife, come to take him to the afterlife.

And just before the zombie squeezed its fist, bursting his heart, Charles thought – or imagined – he heard the faint trill of a bell, and a voice call out a word he couldn't quite discern, all of it so far away on the very edge of his dying hearing.

WELCOME TO A TOWN CALLED HELL

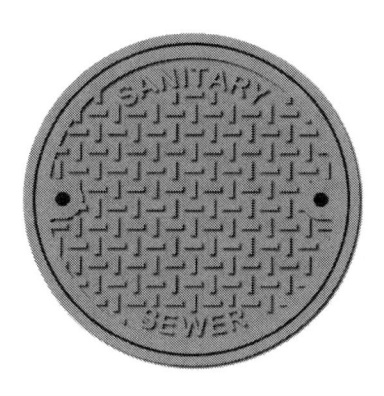

Rising: Part Two
Christopher Law

WELCOME TO A TOWN CALLED HELL

Rats were crawling on him. James knew it as soon as he woke.

He was practically naked; the explosion had torn his jeans into ragged shorts, held up by the workman's belt. The cold was numbing, eating slowly towards his bones, but he could still feel the tiny claws, skittering little razors. There was a sharper pain in his left thigh, where he had an infected cut, and then another in his right big toe. The rats had grown brave enough to try a taste for the first time.

He screamed and thrashed twice as hard when he felt one run up his face. The small, warm bodies – he had seen no more of the mutants – flew away, filling the air with squeaks and squeals. There were dull thuds and splashes as they hit the walls or fell into the water. After a few frantic minutes sweeping the area, making sure he was alone, he settled back against the wall and tried to catch his breath.

It was taking him longer every time he woke up, the time he could keep moving for growing shorter at a matching pace. It didn't hurt as much to breathe as it had a while ago, if it was hours or days didn't seem to matter, but his lungs were contracting, taking less every time he woke. He knew that by now he should be dead. Sulphur wasn't the only noxious gas in the air now, any of them able to kill him alone. If the air wasn't enough, then hunger or dehydration should have claimed him instead. The hunger was still there but it was mild, nothing urgent, and his thirst was gone. It was something he didn't have time to think about, didn't want to if he could.

Unable to completely rid himself of the feeling of rats, he found the flashlight still attached to the workman's belt. He had lost the other tools along the way without using any of them. He couldn't even be sure when he had last seen them. The flashlight batteries were running on fumes, barely strong enough to light a few inches ahead. In the dull brown light it was hard to tell his skin from the surrounding gloom, every inch of him was caked in grime.

Eventually satisfied that he had no passengers he clambered to his feet, wincing as they took his weight. He hadn't found any more tunnels with concrete or brick walkways, just the metal grid catwalks, and his feet were in a poor state. Using strips torn from his tattered jeans he had tried binding his feet but the strips hadn't lasted long, too sodden and damaged. He had considered using what was left, little more than frayed hot-pants, but couldn't bring himself to wander around down here naked.

The flashlight was useless for moving with so his progress was slow and blind, made on his hands and knees as often as not. His forearms and shins were growing as raw and bruised as his feet. Crawling would come next, if he lived long enough. There had to be a way out, if he simply kept looking. Most of the time he moved because he had to.

There was no sound except his own breathing, ragged and shallow. The rats kept still or well away when he was moving. Occasionally he heard running water but always in the distance. He tried to make his way towards it, any sense of direction better than merely groping in the dark. The echoes were deceptive and he never made it any closer. Once he'd found a wall through which he was certain he could hear it clearly, but there was no way through.

Moving by touch alone he had taken two turnings, one because the way seemed wider and the other because there was less moss and slime on the walls. The unnatural plants were something he had learned to mostly avoid, moving his hand lightly enough to recoil quickly from the sharp leaves. He couldn't avoid the other vegetation. Much of the time he was awake was wasted with coughing fits, something in the air catching in his throat. The echoes bounced into each other, rebounding into the distance.

Slumped where he ran out of energy, one place as good as another in the dark, he dreamed of the chamber, the brief hope of a way out. Instead of an explosion, his way was blocked by the rats, all the ones in his dream like the two mutants he had seen in the old tunnels. Sometimes his way was blocked by the faceless workman, others the door opened to a solid wall of rock, but the rats were the most common. Fighting them was useless and he always ran, losing his way even though in his dreams he could see.

The real rats were gathering again as he woke, dream and reality blending so seamlessly he didn't realise for a moment that he could see. The light was dim, no stronger than the first hints of dawn, but it was enough to see the silhouettes creeping closer to his legs. As his eyes adjusted he could make out the edge of the walkway and the far wall. Not far from where he lay, propped in a corner, he saw something larger clamber from the water, the light strong enough to make the sodden fur glisten.

Lurching up, ignoring the pain in his feet, James fled as fast as he could manage. Apart from the few that had reached him, who squealed and darted away, the rats watched him retreat without concern. They were finding enough down here to keep themselves plump.

It wasn't long before he had to slow down, taking the first turning he came to without caring where it led. Using the wall as support, forcing his lungs to breathe deeply without coughing, he took the next two turnings he came to equally blindly. The light had been growing steadily stronger but it wasn't until he was forced to come to a dead halt around the third corner that he noticed. The sulphur was stronger than ever and he only just repressed a choking cough before it crippled him. Rank tasting spit dribbled from the corners of his mouth as he recovered, looking around.

The light was coming from the walls, huge patches of bioluminescent mould. It was sickly green and uneven, individual patches casting their own dim shadows. Where it was strongest, near the waterline, it was bright enough to raise a sheen on the turgid water. The froth and bubbles still floated past, although the flow here was sluggish. Looking downstream he saw the patches peter out, the farthest just streaks in the dark. Upstream the growth became thicker, enough that he thought he could see a turning ahead.

Reluctant to touch the walls, he picked his way along to the turning, the sulphur finally swamped by a sicklier, sweeter smell. It took him a moment to recognise warm garbage and rotting weeds, although the damp air was as cold as ever. The mould was thick here, completely covering the walls and hanging in long clumps from the ceiling. Everything was distorted, cast into half-negative. More than a few feet away the shadows seemed to writhe and nearby there were flashes of light at the corners of his eyes. As much as the smell and lack of oxygen, the light made him nauseous, if not enough to turn back.

The way ahead was what he had become used to, a wide channel with metal paths either side. The turning had a concrete floor, free of mould. He hadn't seen a solid floor since the chamber, and before that the service tunnels he had fled through. It seemed like a memory from another life, but it was strong enough to churn his stomach. The passage he was at now could have been the one from before. There was a corner a short distance in and he couldn't see beyond.

He hobbled along as fast as he could, relieved when the corner led back into a sewer and not the tangle he remembered – maybe he'd found somewhere new and not his way back to the start. For a moment he tried to imagine how this tunnel, as large as the one he had left, fitted in – there seemed to be no other intersection. It was futile, probably even if he could see more clearly. He'd been wandering too long in the dark to have formed a mental map.

The fungus was thicker here, forming cracked bulges that distorted the light even more. Bare patches dotted the ceiling where the bulges had grown too heavy and fallen.

They floated on the scummy water, barely moving at all. Some of the fallen patches were still thriving and the empty space above was being colonised.

The walkway was made of brick, and although it still hurt to walk, the relief after the slatted metal was immense. It was enough to decide it and he set off. The tunnel began to curve, the single walkway hugging the outside edge. There were no turnings and any pipes draining in were covered by the mould.

The curve continued until he was certain he was following a circle. Every step made him more certain but he couldn't stop, not until he knew. So much had happened since then, and the mould made it impossible to tell. There was no way to be completely sure unless he carried on, kept testing where he was now against his memory. He slowed when he saw the alcove emerging from the gloom and stopped a few feet short, putting the moment off while he could. His feet refused to fully stop and he couldn't stop himself reaching the alcove and looking in.

He had gone the other direction the first time he was here. The slime had been dripping into the shaft then, not flowing freely as it was now, but there was nowhere else he could be. Holding his breath, the rotting stench intensifying over the shaft, he looked down and saw that the slime had risen halfway up. The mould stretched down to the slime and he thought the shapes floating on the surface were shadows or fallen patches. Then, as it slowly turned, he clearly saw the glistening skull of the faceless workman.

He had walked in a long and pointless circle.

He felt sick. Backing away from the shaft, clutching his head as he looked at the way he had gone before. The mould was at its thickest in that direction, the floor as coated as everywhere else. A thick layer sat on top of the water, deceptively solid. Looking the other way, his hands left his head and he clutched his stomach, starting to double up. He wanted to scream, or let himself fall head first into the water. For a moment he almost gave in to the desire, might have if a deep gurgle and potent waft of decay hadn't risen from the shaft.

By the time he made it back through the short service tunnel his breath was coming in gasps and the muscles in his legs were burning. It had taken at least an hour to complete his detour to the start; he needed to rest.

The rats were waiting for him, a patient group on the walkway.

Half-a-dozen normal ones and a single, almost bald brute with a weeping eye and open sores. They waited a moment as he lurched away, heading upstream and deeper into the mould, and then began to casually follow. Glancing back he could see them darting forward one by one, the brute following behind. They were stalking him. Or herding.

Exhausted and scared, confused by the shifting green light, he caught his own feet and fell heavily, landing half on the walkway. The air knocked from his lungs he flipped and fell face down in the water, mouth open. Icy sludge gushed in and he felt himself go completely under before hitting the bottom, covered in a layer of sticky mud that sucked and grasped like it was alive.

Gasping and retching he found the strength to pull himself up and struggle free. He took a step away from the rats and fell again, sliding down the wall as his stomach emptied – a mix of nothing but bile and the filth he'd swallowed. There was nothing to stop the rats, he was too ill and weak to move. One or two came to sniff before scuttling away. The monster kept its distance and was the first to slink away.

Too drained to care why the rats left he fell asleep quickly after the vomiting stopped, trails of it on his face.

When he woke his hands and feet were frozen numb, useless lumps as he struggled upright, sticking his hands in his armpits. His tongue was swollen and ulcers covered his gums and inner checks. It hurt to close his mouth, or to have it hanging open. He started to breathe in gulps as his mouth worked around the sources of pain, swallowing frequently as bitter, salty snot drained from his sinuses. The sides of his throat felt burned and his stomach was full of acid, sending pangs up into his heart.

The rats hadn't returned, which meant nothing without knowing how long he was out for, or why they left. Telling himself the tingling pain in his fingers was a good sign, willing his feet to move despite the knives it sent up his calves, he started walking again. With no hope of achieving more than moving from one place to another, somewhere else in the circle he'd already been, he still couldn't sit and wait. The rats had disappeared down the service tunnel so he carried on along after them.

He found the ladder to the upper chamber not long after that. Not far from the service tunnel he reached a Y shaped junction, not familiar enough to be any of the others he'd seen but still not quite new. The fungus was thinner down one branch than the other, and peering into the gloom he was sure he saw something moving in the shadows. The alcove and the ladder up were a short distance along the other branch. Remembering the other climb he realised the flashlight was no longer bashing his hip, the workman's belt was gone as well.

But at last, he'd found the way out.

Maybe not the only one left but the last he'd find. The fungus only reached a short distance up the shaft and he'd made most of the climb in darkness, realising only slowly at the top that there was a faint light coming in from outside – flickering flames and the dirty glow of streetlights reflected in the low clouds.

He had reached a storm drain opening. It wasn't a large space and despite the bad light he only took a few minutes to discover that one end went nowhere and the other was a jumble of heavy rubble as immovable as the one blocking the staircase he'd found. Thwarted at the very last he collapsed in front of the drain and waited for his first dawn since the crash, wetting his dry and cracked mouth with snow and wondering what had happened to the world whilst he was trapped.

He knew something was rising from below.

Hours later, looking up at the strip of grey sky, the air silent and still, he tried to calculate how long it had been, how many days he'd spent in the filth. His body was broken enough for weeks – emaciated and scattered with open, infected wounds. Half his toes and four fingers were black with frostbite and the soles of his feet were pulped. The rest of him was a dirty green, paling to grey as the filth slowly dried. He had tried washing some away with snow with no success, and there was not enough within reach to make more than a token effort.

He looked at the pile of rubble, imagining the short staircase up to the street underneath some collapsed building. It must have been the same explosion that blocked his first escape route.

There was a gurgle from the ladder shaft and a waft of sulphur. James closed his eyes, accepting that he was never meant to escape.

Driven up by the churning vortex deep below, the slime had been gathering for millennia deep in the mountains of Hell. Rising steadily through the cracks it filled vast cave networks sealed deeper than any mine and pushed steadily upwards, corroding paths where there were none. It consumed the insects and albino troglodytes, entire ecosystems, gaining a level of low cunning. Barely alive, far from sentient, it crudely followed the wishes of the power below.

The arrival of people, and their eagerness to dig down, drew the slime to the mines. Several times the miners had come close to digging the wrong way, breaking through into the slime. The mines all failed before one went deep enough and the slime was still there, slowly eating through the dividing rock. There was no release in the pressure from below, the vortex spinning faster all the time. Oozing back down from the mines, the slime entered the bedrock under the town of Hell itself and, in time, into the sewers.

The slime was only the leading edge of the maelstrom.

As it reached street level, dripping from faucets and bubbling in toilets as it rose, the near-frozen slime was being heated from below, long suppressed magma rising mixed with something more primal. The slime, so many long years collected, boiled on contact with the rising fire, turning to steam that exploded to the surface. The steam was corrosive, the slime's strength magnified exponentially, and James Tanner only had time for one scream before the flesh melted from his bones. A second later the slime boiled away, less explosive when unconfined but no less acidic.

Across town the scene was repeated in every sewer, backing up quickly until the toilets of Hell exploded. Manhole covers were shot into the air along the lower lying streets, fountains of violently evaporating slime shooting into the air.

Higher streets saw their drains and bathtubs eject spurting bubbles, like hissing mud volcanoes. Everywhere pipes burst from the pressure and sizzling streams ran through buildings and along the gutters.

It didn't strike everywhere at once, radiating outwards from the upper chamber. There was no warning for those caught in the first wave, just time for a scream like James before they dissolved. Around them their homes suffered the same fate, even brick and concrete left pitted and scarred. Anything organic vanished, plastics and metals left melted.

The second wave had time to wonder at the rats suddenly swarming from their toilets before meeting the same fate as the first. The third wave gave a man on King Street time to kill his only child and start to turn the gun on himself, muttering prayers as he did. His eyes melted down his cheeks and his cheeks slid away before he could pull the trigger. The gun dropped to the floor, the ammunition exploding a moment later as the remaining slime and steam was burned away and something worse began to flood Hell.

Around the edges of town the liquid fire that spilled from the sewers seemed like lava, of the slow moving, viscous kind. It tumbled slowly along, heading downhill and making the snowdrifts hiss away. That far from the centre it was hard to see that, even though the glowing, charred globs went downhill, they also veered to one side when they could.

Closer in, the fire was more like syrup, burning white hot below the blackened crust. There was nothing natural about the way it flowed, following deliberate lines that quickly formed broken spirals around the centre of Hell and the hole starting to open there. Running into buildings and bumps in the landscape that blocked the way, the edges of the syrup began to spread. The rest piled up until every obstacle was overcome or destroyed. For anyone looking down from the slopes above, the emerging pattern would have been easy to see, until the slopes erupted in rivers of fire as well and they had to run for as long as they could, screaming all the way. The seal had been broken and the mines were overflowing, with the sewers spilling destruction like vomit from a drunkard's nose.

Wide bands emerged between the spirals of fire, running withershins towards the centre. The roads, so recently covered with snow, began to melt and bubble. Car tyres burst, triggering alarms that blared until the heat melted the wires. The paint on houses caught fire, quickly followed by the window-frames, wood and plastic. Across town wooden houses flared up, just before the sap began exploding in tree trunks. Fuel tanks, cars first and then the generators, began to pop, some launching into the sky, a woman on Poe Street killed by the falling debris. A few people managed to survive long enough to run into the street, screaming as their hair caught fire and falling face down in the melting asphalt.

Outside town, the torrent of blood was gathering pace as it thundered along the course of the Styx. A vortex of fire, the long evolved cunning of the slime, passed along. It was greedy, wanted more than the river could claim. Each spiralling flow pulsed thicker, sending out linking tendrils that were twisted by the race for the centre. Ponds and rivulets began to form, until they grew large enough to merge strands. In minutes there was a single spinning disc of liquid fire, the edges ragged as pieces were flung free. At the centre, just a sinkhole when it first appeared, was an expanding black maw, raggedly circular and dominating the chaos all around. There was nothing left of the town as the vortex began to expand, the fire it fed on collapsing inside and disappearing like the town before it.

    The blood escaped Hell first, bursting from the mountains and spreading across the lowlands. The fire and darkness were close behind, chasing the blood across the world. Behind the darkness there was more blood and fire, an eternity of suffering. Every soul, living or dead, would feel it, remember every suffering and indignity without relief, feel every wound as deeply as the first.

    Welcome to Hell.

About The Authors

David Court

David Court is a frustrated Software Developer who uses writing as a means to exercise his exorcised creativity. He's the author of three increasingly heavier and thicker collections of short stories – *The Shadow Cast by the World, Forever and Ever, Armageddon* and *Scenes of Mild Peril*. His writing style has been described as "darkly cynical".

John Wagner, co-creator of Judge Dredd, once described David's writing as "Quirky and highly readable". He also told David that he didn't like his beard and that he should get rid of it, which goes to show there's no accounting for taste.

Growing up in the UK in the eighties, David's earliest influences were the books of Stephen King and Clive Barker, and the films of John Carpenter and George Romero. The first wave of Video Nasties may also have had a profound effect on his psyche.

David lives in Coventry with his wife, three cats and an ever-growing beard. David's wife once asked him if he'd write about how great she was. David replied he would, because he specialised in short fiction. Despite that, they are still happily married.

Twitter: @DavidJCourt

Facebook: https://www.facebook.com/DavidJCourt/

Amazon: https://www.amazon.co.uk/David-Court/e/B00GMCNVRE

James Jobling

James Jobling has been a fan of horror for most of his life, blaming his older brother for leaving James Herbert's fantastic novel, The Rats, lounging around the living room when he was only a child for starting his obsession. A huge fan of the horror book genre, he regards Herbert and David Moody as his writing heroes - with the latter being his inspiration for getting into writing. He is the author of National Emergency, End of the Line and The Long Road. He has also penned stories for various anthologies. He lives in Manchester, England with his world - his beautiful wife and three children. He can be contacted through Facebook and would be honoured to hear from anybody who might wish to get in touch.

Shawnee Luke

Shawnee Luke lives in the Mojave Desert, just an hour North of Los Angeles, CA. She shares her home with her husband of seventeen years, her adult son, two dogs and four cats. She also has two adult step-children. In her spare time, she enjoys reading (particularly Neil Gaiman), playing MMORPGs and writing. This is her horror debut.

Ian Bird

Ian Bird is the author of a series of decreasingly unpublishable mystery novels about unlikely things happening to implausible people in the nick of time, and when he is not aging he can be found posting stories, essays and podcasts to his website www.mrcarapace.co.uk. He is currently working on a novel called Boneditch, about a contagious catastrophe, while in turn the novel continues to work on him with a series of hammers, threats and knitting needles.

EC Robinson

Dwelling 'Up North', EC knows a thing or two about grim. Yes, this 'new to you' writer has spent the last few years as a "mature" (very grim) student (grim), undertaking not only a Bachelor's degree, but a Masters too and residing in "Great" Grimsby (also grim … so grim it's in the name!) means a whole new level of grim has been achieved.

Time spent in Louisiana (prior to, during and after hurricane Katrina), rekindled a passion for writing and the surrounding swamps were hauntingly inspirational. Currently fighting the grim in a somewhat haunted flat, EC is scribing it all on paper and working on completing a "Grimthology" of short stories.

Ryan Fleming

Born and raised in glamorous Essex in the sinking ship that is the UK, Ryan single-handedly revolutionised the independent film industry with his debut feature 'Welcome To Essex' which took 6 years to make and nose-dived into the floor upon release.

Not content with ruining movies for everyone, Ryan thought he would turn his hand to writing and his first attempt at that is what you are about to read.

Don't let his chicken-scratch nonsense put you off though: the rest of the book is written by actual authors who know what they're doing.

When he's not bigging himself up, Ryan likes to stare at people from across the street, making them uncomfortable. He also enjoys smoking cigarettes and using his legs to walk about, usually to a pub. Ryan is very tall and most women that have ever met him grow to hate him.

John McNee

John McNee is the writer of numerous strange and disturbing horror stories, published in a variety of strange and disturbing anthologies, as well as the novel 'Prince of Nightmares'.

He is also the creator of Grudgehaven and the author of 'Grudge Punk', a collection of short stories detailing the lives and deaths of its gruesome inhabitants, plus the sequel, 'Petroleum Precinct'.

He lives on the west coast of Scotland, where he is employed as a journalist. He can easily be sought out on Facebook, Goodreads, Twitter, YouTube, where he hosts the horror-themed cooking show 'A Recipe for Nightmares', and at his website, https://www.johnmcnee.com

Dion Winton-Polak

Dion Winton-Polak is an editor, an occasional writer, and a happy model for ridiculous facial hair. He started out as a reviewer and podcaster on the Geek Syndicate network, then switched tracks to develop a couple of fun small press anthologies: the oddly uplifting 'Sunny, with a Chance of Zombies' and the ambitious shared-world SF project, 'This Twisted Earth.' These days Dion spends most of his time helping authors shine with his freelance editing business, The Fine-toothed Comb. You can find out the nitty gritty over at https://www.thefinetoothed.co.uk or, if you prefer, hunt him down on social media for a friendly chat.

Em Dehaney

Em Dehaney is a mother of two, a writer of fantasy and a drinker of tea. Born in Gravesend, England, her writing is inspired by the history of her home town. She is made of tea, cake, blood and magic. By night she is editor and whip-cracker at Burdizzo Books. By day you can always find her at http://www.emdehaney.com/ or lurking about on Facebook posting pictures of witches
https://www.facebook.com/emdehaney/

Her debut short fiction collection Food Of The Gods is available now on Amazon, and her debut novel The Searcher of The Thames is due for release soon...

Edward Breen

Edward Breen is a Kent based Irish writer and student of the craft. He writes a lot when work and family allow. Novels are his favourite but he thinks short stories are neat.

Jacob Prytherch

Jacob Prytherch is an author of science fiction, horror and weird fiction. He started writing due to a love of Bradbury, Tolkien and Gaiman, and carries on writing due to restlessness. He currently lives in Birmingham with his wife and two daughters. Coffee is both his friend and his enemy. His first novel - The Binary Man, published in 2012 - has been the #1 cyberpunk bestseller on amazon.co.uk on two occasions, and his novella Carnival was credited as being one of the top five self-published Lovecraftian stories on Examiner.com.

Facebook: https://www.facebook.com/jakeprytherch

Site: http://jakeprytherch.wixsite.com/main

Justin Zimmerman

Justin Zimmerman was born on Halloween which doomed him to a lifelong obsession with all these things creepy and macabre. His stories of horror and dark fiction have appeared in numerous anthologies and he is currently finishing his first novel. He lives in New York with his wife, Melanie.

Twitter: @JDZimWriter

Amazon: https://www.amazon.com/Justin-Zimmerman/e/B01M0ACTXD

Duncan P. Bradshaw

After hitting the big time with his latest book, HOW TO PEEL ONIONS WITH YOUR TOES AND NOT CRY, Duncan P. Bradshaw took the cash from the fifteen book sales and decided to put it to use. Seeing a petrol station for sale in a small town called Hell, he figured he could make a decent living and still do his writing. What could possibly go wrong? Check out his website http://duncanpbradshaw.co.uk and marvel at his work, perhaps Like his Facebook page https://www.facebook.com/duncanpbradshaw

He knew that this was the best decision he ever made. Wait...that sounded like a low-flying plane...

Christopher Law

Christopher Law is the writer of the Chaos Tales series as well as a number of anthology appearances, including Under The Weather, Sparks and Zombies Need Love Too among others. After an unplanned quiet period to deal with family issues he is planning a return to the fray in 2019 with more anthologies and the long overdue Chaos Tales III: Infodump. He lives in Dover, England and you can find him, alongside a selection of free stories and some occasional musings at

https://evilscribbles.wordpress.com/

https://www.facebook.com/evilscribbles/

Paul M. Feeney

Paul M. Feeney began writing seriously in 2011, and a number of short story acceptances for various anthologies soon followed. To date, he has written two novellas – The Last Bus (2015) through Crowded Quarantine Publications, and Kids (2016) from Dark Minds Press. His work tends towards the dark, pulpy end of the horror spectrum (he has described his work as having a "Twilight Zone" feel), with the odd story or two that's more emotive. In addition to this, he has recently begun writing under the name Paul Michaels, aiming for more nuanced, literary territory; under this name he writes the occasional review for website, This is Horror, with the first Michaels short being published early 2019. He currently lives in the north east of England where he is beavering away on various projects, many of which will be published throughout 2019.

Richmond A. Clements

When not being Communications Coordinator at Moniack Mhor Writing Centre in the Highlands of Scotland, and not playing Red Dead 2, Richmond A. Clements writes stuff. He is the writer of the graphic novels Turning Tiger, Ketsueki, Pirates of the Lost World and The Chimera Factor. If he ever gets the final edit done, his horror novel Blow Your House Down will be published later this year.

Matthew Cash

Matthew Cash, or Matty-Bob Cash as he is known to most, was born and raised in Suffolk, which is the setting for his debut novel Pinprick. He is compiler and editor of Death By Chocolate, a chocoholic horror Anthology and the 12Days: STOCKING FILLERS Anthology. In 2016 he launched his own publishing house Burdizzo Books and took shit-hot editor and author Em Dehaney on board to keep him in shape and together they brought into existence SPARKS: an electrical horror anthology, The Reverend Burdizzo's Hymn Book, Under The Weather and Visions From the Void and he has numerous solo releases on Kindle and several collections in paperback.

Originally with Burdizzo Books, the intention was to compile charity anthologies a few times a year but his creation has grown into something so much more powerful insert mad laughter here. He is currently working on numerous projects, and his third novel FUR was launched in 2018.

With Back Road Books

With Jonathan Butcher

He has always written stories since he first learnt to write and most, although not all, tend to slip into the many layered murky depths of the Horror genre.

His influences ranged from when he first started reading to Present day are, to name but a small select few; Roald Dahl, James Herbert, Clive Barker, Stephen King, Stephen Laws, and more recently he enjoys Adam Nevill, F.R

Tallis, Michael Bray, Gary Fry, William Meikle and Iain Rob Wright (who featured Matty-Bob in his famous A-Z of Horror title M is For Matty-Bob, plus Matthew wrote his own version of events which was included as a bonus).

He is a father of two, a husband of one and a zoo keeper of numerous fur babies.

You can find him here:

www.facebook.com/pinprickbymatthewcash

https://www.amazon.co.uk/-/e/B010MQTWKK

WELCOME TO A TOWN CALLED HELL

WELCOME TO A TOWN CALLED HELL

Also From Burdizzo Books

WELCOME TO A TOWN CALLED HELL

Printed in Great Britain
by Amazon